TROPIC OF NIGHT

Michael Gruber has a PhD in marine biology from the University of Miami. He has held many jobs, virtually all of which involved writing, usually anonymously. *Tropic of Night* is his first novel. He lives in Seattle and is currently at work on another novel.

MICHAEL GRUBER

TROPIC OF NIGHT

PAN BOOKS

First published 2003 by William Morrow
an imprint of HarperCollins Publishers, New York

This edition published in Great Britain 2004 by Pan Books
an imprint of Pan Macmillan Ltd
Pan Macmillan, 20 New Wharf Road, London N1 9RR
Basingstoke and Oxford
Associated companies throughout the world
www.panmacmillan.com

ISBN 978 0 330 42684 8

Grateful acknowledgement is made for permission to reprint:

The epigraph, from *Local Knowledge* by Clifford Geertz. Copyright © 1983 Basic Books, Inc.
Reprinted by permission of Basic Books, a member of Perseus Books, L.L.C.

Excerpts from 'Jeannie C.' and 'The Flowers of Bermuda' by Stan Rogers
© Fogarty's Cove Music. Used by permission of Ariel Rogers.

Lines from 'A Lullaby' by W. H. Auden, reprinted by permission of Random House, Inc.

Excerpts from *Yoruba: Nine Centuries of African Art and Thought* by Henry J. Drewal,
John Pemberton III, and Rowland Abiodun, published by the Museum for African Art.
Used by permission of Dr Rowland Abiodun.

3 5 7 9 8 6 4

A CIP catalogue record for this book is available from
the British Library.

Typeset by Intypelibra, London
Printed and bound in the UK by
CPI Mackays, Chatham ME5 8TD

Visit www.panmacmillan.com to read more about all our books and to buy
them. You will also find features, author interviews and news of any author
events, and you can sign up for e-newsletters so that you're always first to hear
about our new releases.

For

E. W. N.

I have today become a person to be respected,
Grant me free passage!
Even if there is death on the way, let it move away
Let all evil things on my way clear off!
It is with a single stick that one scatters a thousand
    birds.
Let the path before me be safe.

Invocation to Ifa

It has, of course, often been remarked that the maintenance of religious faith is a problematic matter in any
society . . . But it is at least as true, and very much less
remarked, that maintaining faith in the reliability and
axioms of common sense is no less problematical . . .
Men plug the dikes of their most needed beliefs with
whatever mud they can find.

Clifford Geertz, *Local Knowledge*

Although this is a work of fiction, much of it is based on stories of Africa, sorcery, and Santería told to me many years ago in Miami by J. H. How much of it is true, whatever 'true' means, only she can say. Thanks, Joan.

ONE

Looking at the sleeping child, I watch myself looking at the sleeping child, placing the dyad in a cultural context, classifying the feelings I am feeling even as I feel them. This is partly the result of my training as an anthropologist and ethnographer and partly a product of wonder that I can still experience feelings other than terror. It has been a while. I assess these feelings as appropriate for female, white, American, Anglo-Saxon ethnicity, Roman Catholic (lapsed), early-twenty-first c., socioeconomic status one, working below SES.

Socioeconomic status. Having these feelings. Motherhood. Lay your sleeping head, my love, human on my faithless arm, as Auden says. *Maladie de l'anthropologie*, Marcel used to call it, a personalized version of Mannheim's paradox: the ethnographer observes the informant, at the same time observes herself observing the informant, because she, the ethnographer, is part of a culture too. Then at the same time observing herself observing herself as a member of her culture observing the informant, since the goal is complete scientific objectivity, stripping away all cultural artifacts including the one called 'scientific objectivity,' and then what do you have? Meaning itself slips from your grasp like an eyelash floating in a cup of tea. Hence the paradox.

Geertz found a theoretical solution as far as fieldwork goes, but in the heart's core? Not so easy.

It is not all that interesting to watch a child sleep, although people do it all the time. Parents do, and perhaps also Mr Auden, at least once. I am not, however, this child's mother. I am this child's mother's murderess.

The child: female, ethnicity unknown, nationality unknown, presumed American. SES probably five: rock bottom. Four years of age, though she looks younger. In Africa there were kids of eight who looked five, because of malnutrition. Plenty of food around, but the kids didn't get any. The old folks hogged all the high protein, as was their right. A cultural difference, there. Her skin is the palest red-brown, like bisque pottery. Her hair is black, thick, and quite straight, but dry and friable. She is still thin, her spine a string of staring knobs, her knees bulging out beyond the bones they articulate. I think her mother was starving her to death, although usually if they're going to starve them they do it in infancy. The bruises are gone now, but the scars remain, thin cross-hatchings on the backs of her thighs and buttocks. I expect that they were made by a wire coat hanger, an example of what Lévi-Strauss called *bricolage*: a cultural artifact used in a new and creative way. I fear brain damage, too, although so far there are no frank signs of this. She has not spoken yet, but the other day I heard her crooning to herself, in well-shaped notes. It was the first two bars of 'Maple Leaf Rag,' which is what the local ice-cream truck plays when it comes to the park. I thought that was a good sign.

My own knees are rather like hers, for I am an anorexic. My condition doesn't result from a neurotic defect in body image, like those pathetic young girls exhibited on the talk shows. I got sick in Africa and lost forty pounds and subsequently I've eaten little, for I court invisibility. This is a strategic error, I realize: to become really invisible in America, a woman must become very fat. I tried that for a while and failed; everything came up, and I worried about scarring of the esophagus. So I starve, and try to fatten the child.

In my longings, I wish to be mist, or the ripple of wind on the water, or a bird. Not a gull, a class I feel has been aesthetically overrated, no; but a little bird, a sparrow of the type God watches fall, or a swallow, like the kind we saw in Africa. We had a houseboat on the Niger, above Bamako, in Mali. From its deck we would watch them come from their nests on the soft banks and fill the sky over the river in a pattern of flitting silhouettes in the ocher dusk, and in their hundreds and dozens of hundreds they would hunt the flying insects and dip to drink sips from the oily brown surface. I would watch them for their hour, and would pray that they contained the souls of women dead in childbirth, as the Fang people are said to believe.

She blows a tiny bubble in her sleep, so babyish an action that my heart flows over with love and for an instant I am re-joined to my true self, not watching from outside, like an anthropologist, or a fugitive, which is another thing I am, and after that instant the fear flows back again like batter in a bowl from which a finger has been withdrawn. Affection, attachment, weakness, destruction, not allowed, not for me. Or remorse. I killed a human being. Did I mean to? Hard to say, it went down so quickly. Hold a knife to my throat and I'd tell the truth: the child was doomed with her, she's better off with me, I'm glad the woman's dead, God rest her soul, and I'll answer for it in heaven along with all the other stuff. Worse stuff.

Naturally, the little girl doesn't resemble me in the least, which is a problem, for people watch us and wonder who did she fuck to get *that* one? No, actually, that's unfair: most people don't see us at all, both of us are good at fading into the foliage, going gray in the shadows. We go out in the dusk, before the quick fall of the tropical night, or, as on the weekend just passing, very early. Tomorrow I will have to find a place to put her while I work. I have only a little sick time left and I need the money. She has been with me ten days. Her name is Luz.

I took her to the beach yesterday, to Matheson Hammock, very early in the day, and we paddled in the blood-warm shallows of Biscayne Bay, she holding my hand, stepping cautiously. We found a yogurt container and she filled it with various beach wrack – a cocolobo seed, a fiddler's claw, a tiny horseshoe crab – while I scanned the perimeter like a marine on point. As we waded, a car came up and rolled down the drive behind the beach. It's secluded there under the mangroves and is a favorite place for smooching and for dealing drugs. When we heard the car door open, she ran to me. Unlike me, she's afraid of strangers. I'm only afraid of people I know.

After the beach we went to the Kmart in South Miami. I bought her a pail and shovel, some cheap shorts and T-shirts, underwear and sneakers and socks. I let her choose a lunch box and some books. She chose a Bert and Ernie lunch box and a Bert and Ernie book and a Golden Book about birds. She's had some exposure to TV, clearly, although I do not own one and she seems content with that. For myself I bought a pair of polyester slacks the color of rust or of some diseased internal organ, and a sleeveless red top printed to look like patchwork and decorated with small cute animals on alternate patches. Although not quite the ugliest outfit in the store, it was at least a contender. Also, it was a size too large, and it was on sale.

The checkout lady smiled at Luz, who hid her face against my thigh.

'She's shy,' said the checkout lady.

'Yes,' I said, and reminded myself not to come through the line again when this person is on duty. Reject connection is my rule, although I now see that this will no longer be quite as feasible as it once was, when I was alone. Luz is attractive, and people will notice her and strike up conversations, and it's more memorable to coldly reject than to smear bland conversational margarine about. 'Yes, you're shy, aren't you?' I say with a coo to the girl, and to the woman, as I pay (cash, naturally), 'She's always been shy. I hope she'll grow out of it.'

'Oh, they usually do, especially a pretty little thing like that.'

Already she has forgotten us, her eyes moving automatically to the next customer.

We walked out of the frosty emporium to the sun-sizzled parking lot and into my car, a Buick Regal, in blue, from 1978. Its body is pretty well rusted out, the rocker panels having achieved the texture of autumn leaves. Both passenger windows are cracked, and the trunk doesn't lock. A yellow chenille bedspread serves as the front seat cover. On the other hand, it has the

V-8 in there and the engine, the drive train, and all the running gear are as tuned and as slick-running as it is possible for a twenty-year-old machine to be. It is the kind of car you want for pulling bank jobs and getting away: fast, reliable, anonymous. I did all the car work myself. My dad taught me. He collected and restored cars. Still does, I suppose, although I haven't been in contact with home of late. I tell myself it's for their protection.

We got into the car, and rolled out of the lot onto U.S. 1. We live in Coconut Grove, a part of the city of Miami. It's a nice place to live, if one is actually living, and if not, people there tend to leave you alone. It retains some of the louche and freewheeling atmosphere it was famous for some years ago, but if you talk to anyone who was here in the sixties and seventies, they will assure you that it's ruined. I once spoke with an old woman who said that the best time was before the war. She meant the second world one. Nobody had a dime, she said, but we knew we were living in paradise. In those days, huge flying boats used to come down from New York and land on Biscayne Bay right at Coconut Grove and the wealthy passengers would have dinner ashore. The place is still called Dinner Key and the great hangars still exist. The Grove is certainly ruined, as will be any place in America that has cheap funky housing and artists living in it and some community energy going on. The rich people want to be around that, having drained it out of their own lives in the course of making a pile, and so they move in and build great big houses and shopping malls, and create the quaint, where once there was real.

Of course, the Grove is not as ruined as it might have

been because black people live there, in their own mini-ghetto west of Grand and south of McDonald. In America, if you are willing to tolerate the sight of a black face on the street you can get a good deal on your housing and the developers will not bother you until they have chased all of them away.

We live on Hibiscus Street off Grand, in a neighborhood that clearly is scheduled for gentrification, being on the good (or white) side of Grand, but that repels the money boys still because half the houses are owned by black people who have not yet been taxed out. They are Bahamians and Dominicans and African-Americans. The rest of the inhabitants are white people who don't mind this or positively love it. Myself, I'm as indifferent to race as it is possible to be: that is, I am somewhat racist, like everyone else in my nation. There is no escape. On our street we have several run-down cinder-block apartment houses, painted pink or aqua, so there is transience and a moderate amount of crime. This is fine with me; the transience is cloaking; I have nothing to steal; I can defend my body against anything but a gun.

Our apartment is above a garage, painted brick red with white trim, like a barn. The front room has two tiny windows looking out on a dust-and-shell driveway, and the back room, where I sleep, has a big sliding glass window from which you can see a tangled hedge of cream hibiscus and pink oleander. The window is so large and the room is so small that when the window is open it is almost like sleeping outside, or in an African house.

In my bedroom is a thin mattress, resting on a door, supported by six screw-on legs, each of which stands in

a can half full of water. This is an old field-worker trick
to keep the roaches from chewing the dead skin off you
while you sleep. The child sleeps there now. I have my
string hammock, slung from hooks in the wall, low, so I
can watch her and touch her if I wish. The rest of the
furniture is junk from the garage or collected during
walks around the neighborhood: a warped pine bureau
with two out of three drawers, a chaise lounge I
restrung with thick cotton rope, a pine table, three mis-
matched wooden straight chairs, a pink fur bean bag, a
brick-and-board bookshelf. Over the table is a hanging
bulb in a Japanese paper globe. Next to the kitchen is
a tiny bathroom, with a stained claw-foot tub with
shower and the usual facilities. Its once-white walls
are scabrous with mildew. We have no air-conditioning.
A fourteen-inch Kmart fan blows garden air over us
at night. The one closet is an anal-obsessive's fantasy
of order, although I don't recall being particularly
obsessive when I was living real life. It's just that I've
spent a lot of my time in VW vans, and Land Rovers,
and tents, and hovels, and boats, and I'm very good at
storage and retrieval. Kmart sells a nice line of wire-
rack organizers and I've bought largely in their closet
department. When I moved in here, the walls were
pink-orange and the floor was covered with avocado
shag. I decided that, if I was going to die here, I didn't
want my last sensory impression to be avocado shag,
and so I ripped it up and replaced it with cheap black
vinyl tiles and I painted the walls white. The walls are
bare. When I was laying the tiles I found a corner missing out of one of the four-by-eight plywood sheets of the
floor. I made a plywood hatch for this hole, and tiled
over it, and it fits so closely that you have to yank it up

with a big glazier's suction cup. What I have to hide, I hide there.

After Kmart, we drove to the Winn-Dixie, where I now shop. I used to eat so little that it wasn't worth going to the supermarket and I'd just pick up something, yogurt, or chicken, or soup, at a convenience store. That's where I found the child, in a mini-mart on the east side of Dixie Highway, down south someplace. I forget what I was doing there, but sometimes, at night, in the summer, the sticky heat and the insect noises remind me of Africa, and I have to ride, to hear the mechanical sounds of driving and smell exhaust, the dear stench of my homeland, and feel the wind of speed on my face. At around two in the morning, I went in to get a cold drink and she was there, filthy, in ragged shorts and a torn pink T-shirt and flip-flops, standing in the aisle. She was shaking.

I said to her, 'Are you okay? Are you lost?' She didn't answer. The woman behind the counter was fussing with the frozen slush machine and had her back turned. I walked away to the drink console.

As I reached for a cup, I heard the first slap and looked around. The mother was there, a large tan woman in her twenties, with her hair in curlers under a green print scarf. She was wearing Bermudas and a tube top that barely covered her bobbling breasts. Whoever she had once been, that person was gone, or in deep hiding, and only a demon stared out of the red-rimmed eyes. The child was holding her hand to her ear, and her face was screwed up like a piece of crumpled tinfoil, but she made no sound.

'What did I tell you? Huh?' said the mother. She held a forty-ounce bottle of malt liquor in one hand.

With the other she beat the child, big roundhouse blows that knocked the little girl against a frozen-food lowboy hard enough to bounce.

'What did I tell you, you stupid little bitch? Huh? (Slap.) Huh? Did I tell you not to move? (Slap.) I told you not to move, didn't I? (Slap.) Wait'll I get you back home, I'll fix you good. (Slap.) What the fuck *you* lookin' at, bitch?'

This last was directed at me. I pulled my eyes away from the scene and left. I stood with my cold hands pressed to the warm hood of my car and took deep breaths. I thought of what the Olo say, of something that happens between an adult and a particular child, part of their weird rearing practices. But that was in Africa, I told myself. I tried hard to shut down the feeling.

I heard the door of the mini-mart slam open and the mother and her child emerged and walked toward the corner of the little building. There was a dark alley there that led to the next street, where I supposed they lived. It was a typical South Dade highway-side neighborhood, small concrete-block stucco houses, a few low apartment buildings, still looking bare and exposed after Hurricane Andrew. The woman was holding her forty-ounce beer bottles slung over her wrist in their plastic carrier bag, and was dragging the child along by the arm, twisting it cruelly, muttering to herself. The child was trying to relieve the pain by turning herself toward the woman and in the process, just as they passed into the alley, the girl got in the way of the woman's legs and she tripped. They both went down on the rough limestone gravel. The woman saved her bottles and let the girl fall on her back. Then the mother yelled out a curse and got to her feet and kicked the girl in the side. The

girl curled up into fetal position and covered her head
with her pipe-cleaner arms, whereupon I ran up to
them yelling, 'Stop that!'

The woman turned and glowered at me. 'Get the
fuck outa here, bitch! Mind your own fuckin' business.'
I moved closer and I could smell the sweat and the
alcohol boiling off her.

'Please. Let her alone,' I said, and she took two
staggering steps toward me and launched a clumsy
overhand blow at my head.

I caught her arm in *hiki-taoshi* and brought it around
behind her back, *ude-hineri*, and bent her over double
and marched her a few yards away and pressed her face
into the gravel. I had not done any serious aikido in
years but it turned out to be something you don't forget
how to do, like riding a bike. I said, 'Stay here, please,
I'm going to see if your little girl is all right.' And I rose
and walked back to where the child lay unmoving.

I suppose I was on autopilot by then, in some kind of
trance from the African thing that was happening, which
is not all that uncommon among the Olo, but still
unexpected in a South Dade mini-mart, and that is the
only excuse for what I did next. The mother did not stay
put but came after me in drunken rage, cursing, and I
whipped around and caught her left wrist and spun her
out in *jodan-aigamae-nagewaza*. In aikido dojos, subjects of this throw go easily into a forward roll to their
right and bounce up smiling; but now, in the dark alley,
the woman's 160 or so pounds were lofted at speed
through the night with the force of her own charge, and
her head struck the corner of the Dumpster parked
there with a dreadful, final sound.

Thick blood poured from an angular dent in her

head, and a dark stain was spreading along the center seam of her Bermudas. She was as still as the loaded trash bags that surrounded her. I did not check to see if she was as dead as she appeared, but went to the child and took her hand. She came willingly with me and we got in my car and rolled. As I drove, I looked back into the sickly light of the mini-mart window and saw that the proprietor was still messing with the disassembled pieces of her slush machine. She had never looked at me. I had touched nothing in the store. I asked the child what her name was, but she didn't answer. By the time we passed Dadeland, she was asleep.

I learned what her name was the next morning in the *Miami Herald*, a four-inch story on the first page of the Metro section. Mureena Davis, twenty-six, had died in an alley behind a mini-mart at 14230 Dixie Highway. The police believed that she had stumbled while drunk and struck her head, fracturing her skull and breaking her neck. Death was instantaneous. Ms Davis, a single mother, had no relatives in the area, having lately arrived from Imokalee, and lived alone in an apartment near the scene. Authorities were concerned about the woman's daughter, Luz, age four, who was seen in the mini-mart moments before the accident by Mrs Ellen Kim, the clerk on duty. A police search of the immediate area was unsuccessful. Anyone having any information about the child is urged to call . . .

No mention of a mysterious skinny white lady at the scene. And after that, nothing. Something like a million children disappear every year in this country, all but a tiny fraction either runaway teens or divorce snatches. Except where there is clear evidence of foul play, most urban police departments treat these cases with the attention they give to littering the pavement. I think we are safe for the moment. From the authorities, I mean. Not *safe* safe, no.

At the Winn-Dixie, under the maddening lights, designed to put you in a trance and make all the food look more delicious than it will taste at home ('Trance States in the Supermarket: A Commercial Application of Shamanistic Technique,' possibly a paper there for someone; not me, though), we cruise the aisles, the child perched up on the basket seat, selecting nutritious foods. I have a good understanding of nutrition actually, since a female anthropologist will necessarily have much to do with women out in the field and the women universally feed the tribe. I talk to her in a low, comforting voice, discussing the various items and how they help us grow big and strong. She seems interested, if hesitant. I doubt she has much experience with conversation, and the visit to the mini-mart that I observed the night I met her was probably a typical shopping expedition. I let her smell the fruit. I open a package of ginger snaps and offer her one, which she shyly accepts and eats, with a deliberation that is painful to watch. We buy a lot of fruit and vegetables, rice, bread, cookies, cereals, milk, butter, cheese, ice cream, red beans, peanut butter, strawberry jam, mayonnaise, eggs, and a piece of snapper I will broil tonight, perhaps with a baked potato and a salad, with ice cream for dessert. Maybe I will even keep some of it down. No meat, though, nothing so red.

She doesn't respond when I babble, nor repeat the names of the various foodstuffs I name, nor does she point and make demands as I observe the other children doing. She watches, however; her senses are alert. I tell myself she's a member of a tiny subculture of Americans, one in which the parents murder their children, usually before the age of five, and so I can't really expect her to respond as these others do, any more than I would expect an adopted Korean child to speak English right away or use a fork.

We pay for the food, $94.86, which seems like a lot, and is probably more than I used to spend on food in six months. The checkout clerk is a man and is not interested in cute little girls; a good thing to remember – avoid motherly-seeming checkers.

Back at our place, I stow away the foods, I cook, we eat. She stays with me while I prepare the meal, watching, on a chair. Since I took her, we have not been out of sight of each other. We even leave the bathroom door open. A bit like life in an African village. I cut up her fish and squoosh her potato up with butter and salt. She seems unfamiliar with any implement other than a spoon. I suspect finger foods and cereal have constituted the bulk of her diet, when she got a diet at all. I demonstrate the use of the fork, and she imitates me. She eats slowly and finishes every bit on her plate. Ice cream seems to be a revelation. She finishes a scoop, and when I ask her if she wants more, she nods solemnly.

After dinner, I wash up and I place her on a chair and show her how to dry and put the dishes on the wooden dish rack. While I wash, I sing a little song the Olo women sing when they pound karite nuts. The words are quite naughty, as might be expected in a song associated with a process that involves thrusting a long thick pestle into a deep mortar about a million times. It has an almost infinite number of verses; I suppose I learned a few hundred in my time there. I often run through them in my head at work, as I have found nothing better to pass the time during a necessary but tedious occupation. I work as a medical records clerk, a job that compares in many ways to pounding karite nuts.

The child drops a cup on the floor with a clatter. I stoop to retrieve it and I see that she has thrown her arms over her head and is cringing, bent-kneed, awaiting the blow. I approach her carefully, speaking softly. I tell her it doesn't matter, it's just a cup, the handle has broken off, but we can use it as a flowerpot. I rummage an avocado pit from the trash and suspend it by toothpicks in the cup. I let her fill the cup with water. I describe how the new avocado tree will grow, and how it will be her tree. She lets me stroke her hair and hug her, although she's stiff in my arms, like a store mannequin.

There is a scratching at the door. I open it and Jake strolls in, as if he owns the place, which in a sense he does. I put the broiling pan on the floor and he licks the fish grease out of it and then goes over to the child and licks her hands and face. She grins. This is the only situation in which she smiles, a tiny sunrise. I get out a ginger snap and give it to her. She feeds Jake. I kneel down beside the two of them and hug Jake and the child together.

Enough of that. I finish the dishes while Jake tries to teach the girl how to play. Jake is a German shepherd–golden retriever mutt, one of several miscellaneous beasts supported by my landlady, who lives with her two kids in the house of which my garage is an outbuilding. Her name is Polly Ribera. She is a fabric artist and designer. The house is a divorce settlement from Mr Ribera, who lives in L.A. and never appears. He is something in media. We are cordial, but not friends. Polly believes everyone can improve themselves, starting by listening to her advice, and she was put off when I did not welcome her attention. I pay my rent on the first of the month and fix what breaks in my apartment and am very, very quiet, so she is glad to have me as a tenant. She thinks I am a sad case, like the abandoned animals she shelters. When we happen to pass, or when I come to pay my rent, she tries to cheer me up a little, for she thinks my problem is men. That is *her* problem. She makes risqué comments, and I pretend to be flustered and she laughs and says, 'Oh, Dolores!'

Dolores Tuoey is the name I go by now. Dolores was a real person, a good Catholic girl, an American Sister of Mercy who came to Mali to do good and did good, but contracted cerebral malaria and died of it. They put her next to me in the hospital in Bamako and when they packed me up to ship me back to the States, someone grabbed her papers by mistake and stuck them in with my stuff. So when I needed to be someone else fast I became Dolores, still a good Catholic girl, no longer a nun, of course, but that explains the big blanks in the résumé, and the little problems with dress and makeup. I can talk the talk all right, having been for a long time a good Catholic girl myself. A little problem there, explaining Luz to Polly. What a good liar I am! That's why I left the order, of course, succumbed to a dark deceiver out there, and have been trying to get the child back since. It all works out, if you don't bang the box too hard and if I can phony up the paperwork. A sister of mercy indeed, Dolores.

My real name is Jane Doe.

No, not a joke. My family has little imagination and substantial pride. Like the perhaps apocryphal Mr Hogg, the Texas oil baron who named his daughters Ura and Ima, my father simply would not see that Jane Doe is the traditional name for an unidentified female corpse. The Does have a small store of female names that they recycle through the generations: Mary, Elizabeth, Jane, Clare. My paternal grandmother was Elizabeth Jane, and had four sons, and so I as the first-born daughter had to be Jane Clare, as my sister had to be Mary Elizabeth. My late sister.

I chase Jake out as night falls in the disturbing light-switch way of the tropics, disturbing to me, at least, raised as I was with the long summer twilights of the high latitudes. We amuse ourselves, Luz and I, at our table, by the light of our paper moon. She draws with Magic Markers on a big newsprint pad, complicated scribbles, densely laid on, filling the whole page. I ask her what she's drawing, but she doesn't answer. I've set up an old Underwood I got down at the Goodwill. On it, I'm carefully forging a birth certificate on a Malian form. That was in Dolores's stuff, too. A neat packet of birth certificates, and one of death certificates. She was a nurse-midwife, riding the bush circuit. I've kept them in my hidey-hole these past years, for no particular reason, and now here I am tapping out a saving fiction. Thank you again, Dolores.

I'm giving her August the tenth for her birthday, in memory of my sister. Perhaps she will grow up to be a little Leo, or maybe the stars are not fooled. In any case, she will officially be five in a couple of months. I will give her a birthday party then, and invite Polly Ribera and her kids, and any friends Luz has made at the day-care center I plan to place her in. I have reached the line where you are supposed to put in the father's name. I hesitate for a moment, thinking over the possibilities. I suppose my husband would be the logical choice. He is the right color, surely, and he would be amused by the gesture, assuming that what he has become is still capable of humor. On second thought . . . on second thought, I type in *Moussa Diara*, which is as close to John Smith as they have in Mali, and in the space marked for dwelling place of father, I type *mort*. A few more details and it is done. I fold and refold the certificate many times, to counterfeit authenticity, and then I take Dolores's envelope and shake it over the table. As I expect, a fine drift of red dust appears on the white wooden surface. I pick the dust up on my finger and rub it into the birth certificate, and now it looks like every other document in the Republic of Mali. This gives me a certain satisfaction, although the thing won't bear serious scrutiny. Still, it should be adequate to get Luz into a clinic for shots, and then into day care and school. In the *signature du médecin ou de l'accoucheuse* space I use a ballpoint pen to sign *Uluné Pa*. Uluné is certainly a doctor of sorts, and I know *he* would be amused.

I replace the forms in their envelope and put the envelope back in the box under the floor. There is other stuff in the box, manuscripts, my journals, and various implements. Cultural artifacts. A little stiffening of the belly musculature as my eye falls on them. I take out the aluminum-covered journal with the lock on it. It is also coated with the dust of Mali, and other stuff, too, and I lay it on the floor before I close the box and stamp down the tile and push the waste can over the tile. We Americans are disposed to act and there is stuff in that box that I could use against him, maybe, but my instinct says not to, or maybe I have just become a coward, or always was. Then again, perhaps I'm crazy, perhaps I'm in no danger whatsoever, he's forgotten all about me, perhaps it is just the guilt. Still, better safe than sorry, as my dad used to say.

Better to stay quiet and hidden, I think. Only a stupid monkey pulls the leopard by the tail, as the Olo say. Or as my old sensei used to say, sometimes fight, sometimes run away, sometimes do nothing. How wise these memes! In some cultures, discourse consists almost entirely of ritualized exchanges of proverbial wisdom, and an original phrasing will provoke puzzled looks and grumbling. It would be comforting to live in such a place, and not to always have to think up things to say.

We prepare for bed. I draw a lukewarm bath and we get in. I wash Luz's hair. There were nits and lice in it the first time I washed it, and I had to use a special poisonous compound, but now we are on Breck baby shampoo. I use her plastic beach bucket to pour water over her head, rinsing the suds away. She likes this; she smiles, not the hundred-watt she gives to Jake, but a softer one. 'Again,' she says. Her first word.

'Oh, you can talk,' I say, and my heart vibrates, although I don't make a big thing of it. I pour another bucket on her and she giggles. We get out of the bath and I dry her, and myself, and we don our sleeping T-shirts and go into the bedroom. She runs to the fan and switches it on.

'You turned on the fan,' I say, continuing my project of filling the air with language, as if it will do some good. She might have spent most of her short life locked down in a closet, with no one speaking to her at all, while her language faculty withered. It happens. I tuck her in under the cotton sheet and lie next to her. We look through her bird book. I say the names of all the birds and promise that we will go looking for some of them another day. Then we read the Bert and Ernie book. Bert tries to build a bookcase by himself and can't find his screwdriver and has to prop the bookcase up temporarily with a humorous collection of objects but still won't ask for Ernie's help. The bookcase falls down on Bert's head. Then Bert and Ernie build the bookcase together. Moral: cooperation is good. But the Olo would want to know the precise kin and status relationships of Bert and Ernie, and what right Ernie had to offer help and what right Bert had to refuse it when offered, and how the results of the building project were to be divided, and, of course, they would know that a screwdriver is never really missing but has been witched away because Bert did not make appropriate sacrifices when he visited the *babandolé* to consult the auguries before starting his project. So my thoughts go. It never ceases, you never get back your cultural virginity. I stay by her side as she falls asleep. My soul child, *sefuné* in the Olo tongue. Hardly a gene in common, yet I would gladly give my life for hers, and may have to someday, if he finds us, and what does evolutionary psychology make of that?

> *Mortal, guilty, but to me*
> *The entirely beautiful.*

I go back to the kitchen and sit at the table and draw little patterns in the Malian dust that speckles it. My journal draws my eye. Why have I got it out tonight? It's years since I touched it. It's got things in there I probably don't want to know, but maybe I need to know them now, because of the girl, because it's not just me anymore. Some helpful fact. An insight. There is a big water stain on the first pages, but the writing, in my own neat scientist's hand, is perfectly legible.

TWO

August 21, Sionnet, Long Island

Maybe seven months since I last took up this journal. In New York, days were much the same. No useful work, but not unhappy, exactly. Out a couple of times a week, with friends, or with W.'s friends: theater people, literary types, artists (see pages of the *New York Review of Books* for subjects, authors). At parties, always one sidling up to me, asking what he was really like, or maybe an opinion, how wonderful he was, I must be so proud. Well, I am proud.

My days blur together, but here for the anthropological record:

Residence – loft on Thomas Street in Tribeca, expensive, all the latest stuff, not ours, we are subletting from a friend of W.'s, who is off somewhere doing a film. W. does not like to be tied down to places and furnishings, and he likes that I am the same way. Birds of passage, us, nomad artists, although only he is an actual artist. Children would just tie us down. I lie abed late, stay up late, read mainly trash, or I watch TV with the sound on low. Often need a pill to put me under. I never dream.

Arising, prep. breakfast for me and W., words of greeting, some pleasantries. I do not ask him how it is going, and I make myself scarce. Unpleasant to be in the loft while he is working. Nervous vibration. I'm not his muse at all; in fact, his muse seems to dislike me.

A cab up to 62nd Street off Park, Doe Trust offices, someplace to go. Various tasks, mainly reading begging letters and reports and commenting on them for the trustees and my father; also help to run W.'s business affairs. Not a Lady Who Lunches, me. Try to keep up with the anthropological literature, I use the library at the American Museum of Natural History, and demonstrate to myself that I still have a profession. I don't go there very much, as it makes me feel sad, or, if I think about it too hard, frightened. In the late p.m., I go back downtown and find W. He is usually at the Odeon, at the same table, and there are the usual downtown types hanging out with him, being brilliant and witty, and he makes a place for me and I slide in there, and the women look little darts at me when they think I am not looking, because they would like to be married to him but are not, and I am. Chattering we all drift over to some excellent and fashionable place to eat, Bouley or Chanterelle, for example, and we always get a table because places like that always have tables for people like us, and then we go to clubs and listen to music and people press tickets and invitations on us. Jesus, I am bored even writing this. Contrast and background to the more engaging now.

But sometimes I miss the long meaningless, leisurely afternoons. Sometimes W., for example, would not be at the Odeon, but up in his room, lounging on the daybed, with some dope or an open bottle, his work finished for the day, and I would join him for whatever substance and afterward a long lazy fuck before returning again to the lush life. Now, busy busy, studying Yoruba language and culture, organizing the logistics of the expedition for Greer. W. is enormously supportive, which I confess I worried a little about, as he has never seen me in high gear

before, says it is like having an affair with a different
woman.

Later, 8/21

Omitted the real reason I stopped writing here, which is
that I discovered that W. was peeking. I never confronted
him on it, cowardice I know, and what did it matter anyway, when you get down to it, one flesh and all, and I could
have made a game of it, something to amuse us. If I were
another woman. Or I could have become angry but I don't
like what my anger does to him, and after all, with all we
have together, it's a small thing. I just include it here, for
the record. You can lie all you want in the published
papers, but keep the journals honest. M. taught me that,
and I took it seriously, although it might have been
merely one more of his ironic comments. He said I had an
underdeveloped sense of irony.

This journal is a new one, given to me by my father for
our trip, God knows where he got it, but I love it. Several
hundred unlined pages of the kind of thin all-rag paper
they used to use for Bibles, bound in boards and protected with thick aluminum covers. These can be closed
with a hasp that has a serious barrel lock on it. It will be
my African field journal.

8/24 New York

Got our visas today, Nigeria, Mali, Benin, Gambia. Others
pending. W. like a kid, showing his stamped passport off
to waiters, people on the street. I'm also assembling gear
for expedition, things people need in 3rd world. Tampons.
Vitamins. Ciprofloxin. Imodium. A pound of Xanax. Lots of

passport photos. Greer very helpful, been there lots of times. I want to call M., but can't. Why? Who am I afraid of hurting? Him? W.? Myself?

W. unhelpful as ever, this time not his fault, he's sick from shots. I am, as usual, not, which he seems to resent. People like to do things for him, however, and he has grown used to good service. I cosset him and give him materials on the Yoruba, which both of us find fascinating. He is reading the big Abrams art book, I am going through Bascom on Yoruba divination. I love them already: the artistic sensibility of quattrocento Italy melded with the religious passion of ancient Israel. Or maybe they are the closest survival into modern times of what the ancient Greeks must have been: artists in their blood and bone, warriors, close to the gods. Like the Greeks, too, they fought one another, the little kingdoms often at war, and subject to the depredations of the empires to the west and north, Fon and Hausa, and in the late eighteenth and early nineteenth centuries their chief polities collapsed and hundreds of thousands of Yoruba became prisoners in local wars and were shipped to the plantations of Cuba, Haiti, America, and Brazil, in one last and remarkably homo-geneous consignment of slaves. The survivals of African magical and religious practices in the New World – voudoun, candomblé, Santería – are all descended from the Yoruba, or secondarily from African nations influenced by the Yoruba.

This prep is very pleasant. No, more than pleasant. I am conscious of a deep happiness, something I have not felt for a long time, not, in fact, since I was a girl in the company of my father, not since our shipwreck, when every-thing went sour. And, I can confess now, I was not happy being Wife-Of. I find I need work, serious work that I'm

good at. And also, while I'm confessing, it gives me a kick
to be for once the senior member of the dyad. (I guess I was
happy with M., but that was sort of a delirium I see now, a
Gemisch of hot sex and hero worship, and which I understood at some level could not last.) Although I have to say
that in our city life W. never made much of being the main
guy. I fear that, his particular little tics aside, he is a more
decent and generous person than I am.

9/2 Sionnet Labor Day

We drove out, a miserable trip on the expressway, instead
of taking the Chris-Craft from City Island with Dad and
Mary and her boyfriend. The misery of crawling traffic I
have rationally estimated as being not as great as having
W. puking his guts over the stern, so I drove the rental with
reasonable grace, what I get for marrying a lubber. For his
part, W. felt guilty, which he is not really very good at, he
tends to get smarmy solicitous, which I can't stand. We
were a little tense therefore, but this got blown away when
we passed the Walt Whitman Mall on the road to
Huntington, and he did his usual parody, I Hear America
Shopping, line after line, biting and hilarious, and this, I
think, makes up for a lot of lost time on the water. W. loves
Whitman, and he joked once that what tipped the scales
for him asking me to marry him was when he found out
that Walt had grown up just down the road from Sionnet,
and apparently was in and out of the house all the time
with my great-great-great-great-grandfather Matthew, who
was his contemporary, and who remained a close friend all
his life. Matthew Doe backed Walt's newspaper and
received in return signed copies of all his published work
and a bunch of manuscripts. The manuscripts are in the

Library of Congress, but we kept the books, and my dad gave W. for a wedding present an 1860 Blue Copy of *Leaves of Grass*, with Walt's annotations in it, which knocked him out.

It was late afternoon before we arrived, and everyone was already out on the back terrace with drinks. My mother was there because Mary was there, because I doubt she would have changed her plans just to see me off for a year or two in Africa. Mary was her usual self, there is never anything new to say about Mary, she was fully formed at five years old. The boyfriend is new, however, and an improvement on the usual run. He is Dieter Von Schley, the photographer, very proper, blond and bony, lovely manners, a Prussian type, although he is actually from Cologne. A Catholic, too, remarkably, and not apparently a heroin addict like the last one. He and my dad are in love already, Dad has shown him the cars, amid much rolling of eyes by Mom and Mary. Dad looked unchanged, like the house. Mom unveiled the new face-lift, a Brazilian job, and I think she got taken, or maybe it is that her personality has been etched into her features so deeply that even a Brazilian surgeon can't quite re-create the lovely Lily of yore. She must be pushing sixty now, although she has forbidden birthdays for decades. She has not piled up much treasure in heaven, I'm afraid, and little flashes of fear are starting to show.

W. did his part, having turned the charm up a couple of notches, retailing New York theater and celebrity gossip, and I was doing mine, which was keeping in the background. No one asked me anything about the Yoruba. Except, I must record, that W. was talking about the new production of O'Neill's *Moon for the Misbegotten* and about the movie star, R.T., who's in it, and who everyone knows is a total queen, and Mom said, 'Ooh, I love him, he's so sexy. What part does he play?' and I, with no thought at all, said, 'He plays Miss Begotten.' Not exactly Wilde, I know, but W. cracked up anyway, and we had to explain it to Mary, and Mom frowned and gave me a stern little lecture on homophobia. W. thought that was funny, too, and made a joke out of it, another act of mercy added to his score.

Our Labor Day dinner was what it always was, the first oysters of the season and barbecued game hens; we are very traditional at Sionnet, and our big occasions invariably include oysters, upon which the family fortunes were originally founded. I do still have moments of bliss there, and this was one of them, sitting out on the north terrace, stuffed with good food and lounging in our soft and ratty wicker (the interval having arrived when Mom was drunk enough to be sentimentally nice to me and not drunk enough to start in on how I had ruined her life), and I was just reflecting that the only thing lacking was my brother's presence, when Josey walked in. I leaped up and gave him a big slightly drunken barbecue-sauce kiss and fixed him a plate. He had flown in to MacArthur–Long Island on his Learjet, and come up in a limo, a very new-money thing to do. I know he loves me, but I think he pulls stunts like that to piss off Dad.

He had going-away presents for us, too: a GPS locator for me, of spectacular complexity, and for W. a pith helmet. Which I must say, W. accepted with good enough grace. Mary gave me an Hermès scarf, something she no doubt got from a fashion shoot, but pretty all the same. Mom gave me a check, which is what she always gives me, and gave me from the age of about seven. Buy yourself something, honey. Dad gave me one of those universal tools, in a wash-leather bag. He was in heaven, of course, he lives for the moments when everyone is all together and reasonably content, and he got out the 1898 cognac and poured every one a thimbleful and made a very nice speech wishing us bon voyage, and noting that the date we were scheduled to leave, the fifth of September, was the anniversary of the first landfall of the Doe family in North America, and how proud he was of me and W. and how he hoped our journey would be as prosperous. It was a typical Dad speech, sentimental, a little embarrassing, but lovable.

After which Mary, with her unerring instinct for seizing at any moment the center of attention, spoke up and said that she and Dieter had decided to get married. Which meant Dad would get his St Patrick's wedding after all, and Mom would be able to throw the party of the year, and I would, of course, miss it, which I guess made it perfect from her point of view and Mary's.

Later, in our room, I let myself fall apart. W. comforted me, now that I think about it, rather in the way Josey used to do. And I am not comforted, although profoundly grateful as I nevertheless sink into my usual slough of self-contempt. So Mommy doesn't love me, get over it, Jane, you're a grown-up now, and so on, what a wretch you are, you have everything, everything! As my brother says, dial 1-800-BOOHOO. We are in my old room, my girlhood room, with the worn provincial furniture, my girlhood bed, too, which is a little narrow for the two of us, and when I have stopped the disgusting weepies he gives me a good one, and I make a lot of noise, more than necessary, to tell the truth, to alert the house that despite them I am happy.

I am counting the days, I am so glad to be leaving this scene, the arty city, the family drama. That's the truth, M.

THREE

Jimmy Paz knew that it was going to be a bad one when he saw Bubba Singleton puking into the gutter, supporting his huge frame on the rear bumper of his patrol car. Bubba had been doing patrol in the Central District for over a dozen years and he had had ample opportunity to learn what the heat of a South Florida summer can do to a corpse in a remarkably short time, so this had to be something more than the usual leaking, reeking, bloated, livid, maggot-squirming foulness covered in giant roaches.

Paz got out of his Impala and walked past two police cars and a crime-scene unit van to the front of the four-story concrete-block-stucco tenement. A couple of uniforms were holding the perimeter, looking uneasy, as cops always did in Overtown in the hot time, and beyond them a small crowd of the curious had gathered. Overtown is an area of Miami occupied by low-income African-Americans. If you are a tourist coming from the airport on your way to the sun and fun of Miami Beach and you mistakenly turn off the airport freeway and you realize your mistake and try to backtrack, then Overtown is the area you backtrack through. Every couple of seasons some tourist does this and comes to a bad end.

Jimmy Paz, in fact, had recently been involved in one of these unhappy events, a Japanese couple yanked from their car, the woman raped and brutalized, the man shot. He had cleared the case in twenty-four hours, in the time-honored fashion of hanging around the 'hood and asking questions and keeping his eyes open until the morons who did the thing tried to buy a set of speakers with Ishiguro Hideki's Visa card. There was even a little shoot-out, although the mope had only been wounded and nobody got on Paz's case because he, too, was black and so, under the peculiar rules of American police practice, he had a license to shoot down citizens of whatever color with only nonhysterical investigation to follow. Even more so, in his case, because he was also of Cuban extraction, which accounted for the wit of the bystanders here, shouting, 'Yo, spigger!'

Paz ignored this and kept his face neutral (a practiced skill) and made a show of checking his appearance in the car window. Paz was a stocky, muscular man of thirty-two, the color of coco matting, with a smooth round head, on which the hair had been cropped almost to the skin. His ears were small and neat and his eyes, set in lanceolate sockets, were large, intelligent, warm brown in color, but not warm at all. The roundness of his head and these eyes and the general flatness of his features gave him a feline look. This was intensified when he grinned, the bright small teeth startling against the tan of his skin.

He wore a Hugo Boss linen jacket, black Ermenegildo Zegna slacks, a short-sleeved cotton shirt in tiny black checks, and a knit navy tie, open at the neck. On his feet he wore three-hundred-dollar Lorenzo Banfi suede shoes. Paz, in other words, dressed like a cop who took bribes. But he did not take bribes. He was unmarried and undivorced and lived rent-free in a building owned by his mother. By so dressing, however, he managed to piss off both the considerable number of his MPD confreres who *did* take bribes and those who remained straight; which was the point.

Paz took a tube of Vicks VapoRub out of his jacket pocket as he entered the building and ran a bead around the interior of each nostril. This was an old cop trick designed to cover the stench of death, but it also helped with the background stink of the building. This had exterior stairways leading to narrow, open walks guarded by low concrete walls topped by a steel pipe. Painted a fecal brown, it had the architectural charm of a public lavatory, perhaps one reason why the entrance and stairs had been used as one. Paz felt, as he usually did when entering one of these dwellings, a blast of strong emotion – rage mixed with shame and pity – and waited until it subsided, when he became once again pure cop, strapped into that invulnerable persona, like a pilot in an F-18. He would have had to eat handfuls of Valium to otherwise create that much emotional armor. He enjoyed the pay and benefits, but, really, the armor was why he had become a policeman.

The patrolman at the door of the victim's apartment, a fat-faced fellow named Gomez, was slouched against the wall sniffing and clearing his throat, which suggested that he had also checked out the interior scene. The armpits of his white uniform shirt were sodden and he wiped with the back of his hand at the fine oily sweat on his forehead as Paz approached. Paz was famous in the Miami PD for not sweating. During his time in uniform, he had once chased a street robber for six blocks down Flagler Street, on a day when the asphalt had been softened to something like taffy, and grabbed the kid, and brought him in, maintaining a bone-dry face, and with the press still in his shirt. This was another thing against him from the point of view of Gomez, the first thing being his color and his features and the fact that, although possessing such a color and such features, he was yet undeniably Cuban. Paz was, technically, a mulatto, and technically, so was Gomez, but Paz was clearly on the black side of the line and Gomez was on the white, like some 98 percent of the Cubans who had fled Castro for America, and therein lay the agony of Jimmy Paz's life. He paused to pass some of it on to Gomez.

'Hey, Gomez, how you doing?' Paz asked, in Spanish.

'I'm okay, Paz,' said Gomez, responding pointedly in English.

'You don't look okay, man, you look like shit. You look like you want to puke,' said Paz.

'I said, I'm okay.'

'Hey, you want to puke over the rail, go ahead.' Paz indicated the open side of the passage. 'There's just a bunch of niggers down there. You puke on them, hell, it's just another day in Overtown.'

'Fuck you,' said Gomez in English.

Paz shrugged, said, *'No habla inglés, señor,'* and walked into the apartment. It was hot and it stank with a stink so forty-weight-crankcase-oil heavy that it seemed to drag the lungs down into the belly. The temperature had been in the nineties, cooking the carnage in the airless apartment, which would have been bad enough, but this was something else. The agents of decay and dissolution must have been helped by some elaborate butchery.

Just inside the door, Paz opened his briefcase, removed a pair of latex gloves, and put them on. He could hear noises and see strobes going off in the rear as the crime-scene crew did their work. They had already finished in here, the fingerprint powder strewn liberally about. A moment to look around, then, before he dived in.

Paz saw a small, low-ceilinged room, with walls painted a dingy yellow and the floor covered with institutional brown linoleum, worn to hairy dullness along the routes of heavy traffic. It was furnished with a blue velvet couch, relatively new, an older vinyl-covered armchair, maroon in color and cracked along the back cushion, several folding tin tables printed with a floral design, and a shiny twenty-eight-inch color TV, facing the couch and the chair. On the floor was a five-by-nine shag rug, striped to mimic a zebra's coat. Someone had spilled something brown on it – a soda or coffee. On one wall, above a worn wicker credenza painted yellow as street lines, hung a large velour cloth illustrating several Africans hunting a lion with spears. On the other wall were two African masks, mass-produced flimsy things that were on sale in local shops: a stylized face with slanted eyes and a stylized antelope. On the same wall were family portraits in cheap fake-gilt frames. A group of respectable-looking people dressed for church; a couple of school portraits of kids, smiling hopefully; two graduation pictures, one boy, one girl, clearly brother and sister; and one formal portrait of a middle-aged woman with deep-set eyes and a glossy flip to her hair. All the people in the pictures were black. The wall and the pictures were speckled with little dots of red-brown, as if someone had goosed a can of spray paint to test the nozzle. There was one brad sticking out of the wall with nothing hanging from it, and a rectangular area of clear wall with no spots, obviously a place where a picture had hung.

A crime-scene technician came into the room lugging a fat carryall, waved to Paz, and departed. A few seconds later came another CSU guy with a camera. Paz said, 'Hey, Gary, did anyone take a picture off that wall? Where the nail is?'

'Not that I saw, unless somebody snatched it before we got here.'

'Okay, I'll ask. You done in there?'

'Yeah,' he said, then paused. 'Jimmy, you'll want to catch this guy.'

'We want to catch all of them, man.'

'Uh-uh, Jimmy,' said the technician. 'I mean you'll *really* want this one.'

He left and Paz went into the bedroom. There was nothing in the tiny room but a cheap white-painted 'brass' bed, a white pine bureau, and two people, one of whom was dead and one of whom was Paz's partner. Cletis Barlow was a fiftyish white man built on Lincoln-esque lines, one of the ever fewer representatives on the Miami PD of the original population of Florida, an old-time cracker. Barlow looked like a redneck preacher, which he was, on Sundays. He had been a homicide detective for nearly thirty years, and had in common with Jimmy Paz little more than street smarts and a strong stomach.

'The M.E. been yet?' asked Paz, staring at the thing on the bed.

'Been and gone. Where were you?'

'It's my regular day off, Cletis. Monday? Yours too, I thought. I was going to my mom's. Why did we catch this thing?'

'I was hanging around and picked up the phone,' said Barlow. Paz grunted. He knew that Cletis Barlow refused point-blank to do servile labor on Sundays, so he often filled in the hours he would have been docked during what would otherwise have been his regular day off. Paz asked, 'What did the M.E. say? Who was it, by the way?'

'Echiverra. He figures she's been dead a couple of days. This is Deandra Wallace. She was supposed to go over her momma's house this morning. Her brother come by to see her when she didn't show or answer her phone. And he found her like this. They were going to go shopping. For the baby.'

'Uh-huh,' said Paz, and moved closer to the bed. The remains were those of a young woman, perhaps twenty years old, with smooth chocolate skin. She was nude, lying on her back, arms at her sides, legs extended. There was a gold bracelet on one ankle and a gold chain around her neck, with a tiny golden cross on it. Her breasts were solid, round, and swollen. Her hands were encased in the usual plastic bags, in the event that she had touched her killer in some evidentiary fashion. When murdered she had been in the most advanced state of pregnancy. The flowered sheet on which she lay was red-black with blood and there was a pool of solidified blood on the floor. Paz was careful not to step in it.

'There's no baby,' said Paz.

'No. The baby's in the sink in the kitchen. Take a look.'

Paz did. Barlow heard him say, 'Ay, mierditas! Ay, mierda! Ay, Dios mio, condenando, ay, chingada!' which, as he understood no Spanish, meant nothing to him. What Paz said when he came back was, 'My goodness, what a terrible thing!' When you worked with Cletis Barlow, you did not use the name of the Lord in vain, at least not in the official language of the state of Florida, nor utter any foul speech. Cletis would not work with anyone who did not conform to his standards, and Jimmy Paz could not afford to annoy the only detective in the homicide unit who did not actively dislike him. Paz didn't actually know how Cletis felt about him personally, although coming as he did from five generations of the most viciously racist people in the nation, one might assume that his very first choice of a partner would not have been a black Cuban. On the other hand, no one had ever heard Barlow use a racial epithet, something that made him fairly unusual in the Miami PD.

'Uh-huh, terrible,' Cletis agreed. 'You know, you read about abominations in the Bible, but Satan is usually more roundabout in his works, these days.' Cletis mentioned the name casually, as if the Prince of Darkness were a suspect now hanging out in some local pool hall.

'You think it's a ritual killing?'

'Well, let's see now. No signs of forced entry. No one heard anyone holler the night we think she died, which was Saturday, or not that we heard about yet, although we'll check some more. Then there's the body. Look at that girl. What do you see? I mean besides what they did to her.'

Paz looked. 'She looks like she's sleeping. I don't see any abrasions on her wrists or ankles . . .'

'There ain't any. I checked. And the doc said she was alive when the cutting started. So . . .' Barlow paused and waited.

'She knew the people. She let them in. They drugged her unconscious. And then they cut her. Je . . . um, gosh, what in the world did she think was going to happen to her?'

'Well, we'll just have to ask the boys who done it when we find them. Oh, yeah, another thing. What do you make of this here?'

Barlow took a plastic evidence bag out of his pocket and handed it to Paz.

It contained a pear-shaped, woody thing an inch or so across, like the thick shell of some nut or fruit, dark and shiny as a piano on the convex surface, dull and rough on the concave side, which bore a straight ridge down its center. Paz saw that two tiny holes had been drilled through either end.

'Looks kind of like a piece of a nutshell, drilled. Part of some necklace?'

They heard steps and a metallic rattle and the two guys from the morgue came in with their gurney.

'Holy fucking shit!' said the lead man when he saw what was on the bed.

'Watch your mouth, son!' said Barlow. 'Have some respect for the dead.'

The ambo man, who was relatively new on the job, was about to come back with some smart remark when he wisely took in the expression on Barlow's face and the expression on his own partner's and decided to keep his mouth shut and get on with the job.

As he watched them place the remains of Deandra Wallace into a black plastic body bag, Paz reflected, not for the first time, that humor and cheerful obscenity were what made it possible for normal people to endure daily exposure to horror. That Cletis Barlow did not so indulge demonstrated that he was not a normal person, which Paz knew already, but neither did he seem to have any trouble bearing up. Paz liked figuring people out and had found that most of them were as simple as wind-up toys. The major exceptions to this in his experience were his mother and Cletis Barlow. Another thing that kept Paz willingly at his side.

'There's another one,' said Barlow. 'A baby. In the kitchen.' The morgue guys looked startled. The younger one went into the kitchen. There was silence, and the sound of slamming cabinet doors. He came out holding a white kitchen trash bag with a dark bulge at the bottom.

'No,' said Barlow. 'Get a body bag.'

'A bod . . . for Christ's sake, it's a fu . . . it's a fetus,' said the ambo man.

'It's a child and it's the image of God,' said Barlow. 'It goes out of here in a body bag like a human being, not like some piece of garbage.'

The older ambo man said, 'Eddie, do like the man says. Go down to the bus and get another bag.'

The two detectives waited in silence until the dead were removed from the apartment. They left the bedroom. Paz pointed to the wall. 'There's a picture missing.'

Barlow looked. 'Uh-huh. And somebody went to some trouble to draw our attention to it. We'll ask the family about it.'

'We know who the father is?'

'They will,' said Barlow.

Outside the building, the crowd had dispersed somewhat, or rather had moved across the street to where a couple of television vans had parked, and its younger members were posing for the cameras. Paz and Barlow walked down the street away from this. A PI officer would supply vague semifalsehoods for the twenty seconds of coverage that Deandra Wallace's death would get on the local news that night, absent some more spectacular carnage involving whiter people.

A middle-aged, brass-haired, leathery woman in a nice grass-green cotton suit stepped out from between two parked cars and stood in their way.

'What's up, guys? I hear it's bad.' Doris Taylor had been the crime reporter for the *Miami Herald* since shortly after the invention of movable type, and she was good at it, which meant that Barlow ignored her and Paz cultivated her. Paz was a modern cop and understood publicity and what it could do for one's career, while Barlow thought that reporters and the people who read them were ghouls and unclean spirits. It was an area where the two men had agreed to disagree. Barlow stepped around Taylor without a word, as if she were a dog dropping, while Paz smiled, paused, said, 'Call me,' in a low voice, and moved on. Taylor flashed a grin at Paz, flipped a bird at Barlow's retreating back, and walked back to the murder scene to gather color.

At the next corner, Raymond Wallace, brother to the deceased, was waiting in a patrol car with a uniformed officer. Paz recognized him from the graduation picture in the apartment. He was in the backseat with his head resting against the rear deck, looking stunned. The rear door of the car was open for air, and to demonstrate that the young man was not a prisoner. Like many of the people associated with the morning's activities, he had thrown up, and his brown skin had an unhealthy gray cast to it. Barlow stuck his head in the window. 'Mr Wallace, we're going to head back to the station now so you can make your statement.' Raymond Wallace sighed and slid from the car. Paz noticed that his eyes were reddened and there was a splash of yellow puke on the toe of one of his white AJ's.

'Can I call my mother?' Wallace asked.

'You need to let us do that, sir,' said Barlow.

'Why? She gonna be worried sick if I don't call and say why I'm not back yet.'

They arrived at Paz's car. Barlow said, 'The reason is that when there's a homicide it's important that the police are the first people to tell the family about it. Sometimes we learn important things from their reaction.'

'You think my *momma* connected up with . . .'

'No, of course we don't, sir, but we have to do everything according to the book. And I'd like to say now, sir, how sorry I am about your loss.'

He meant it, too, thought Paz. He feels for these people, for all of them, the bad guys and the victims both, and yet it doesn't reduce his heart to slag and pus. Paz himself did not let himself feel anything but the coldest and most refined anger.

They traveled down Second Avenue in silence to Fifth, to the police station, a newish six-story dough-colored concrete fortification. In one of the interview rooms in the homicide unit's fifth-floor office Raymond Wallace told his story. He lived with his mother in Opa-Locka, northwest of the city, in their own house. He'd taken his mother's car to pick up his sister. They were going to go to a mall to buy baby things. Here he broke down. Barlow let him recover himself. Paz asked him about the missing picture and got a blank stare.

Barlow changed the subject to the family. There was just him and his sister. His father had been an air force sergeant, dead five years. His mother lived on the pension. He was a student at Miami-Dade. His sister had wanted to be a hairdresser and was studying for her license. The father of the baby was Julius Youghans, an older man, resident in Overtown. Youghans had a pick-up truck and did light hauling and odd jobs. No, his mother had not approved of the relationship, but only because Youghans was not a member of their church, not a churchgoing man at all.

Paz and Barlow exchanged a look. Barlow said, 'Mr Wallace, was your sister a churchgoing woman?'

'Well, we was both *raised* in the church. My momma's a amen-corner lady, you know? But, you know, you get older, sometimes you tend to drift away. I went. Dee, she didn't always make it.'

'This was from when she started going with Mr Youghans?'

'Well, yeah, but she been kicking back at it for some years now. Then she got pregnant, you know, and like, that set Momma off on her, and she didn't like coming around. I got to be like one of those UN guys going back and forth.'

'Uh-huh. Did you have any idea that your sister or her boyfriend was involved in another kind of religion?'

Wallace knotted his brows. 'What you mean, like Catholic?'

'No, sir, I mean like a cult.'

A startled expression crossed Wallace's face. 'Like that *Cuban* shit?'

'Well, anything out of the ordinary, something new she might've just got into. Or him.'

The young man thought for a moment, then shook his head. 'Not that she ever told me. Of course, since she been going with Julius, we ain't been that close. But . . . nah, I kind of doubt it. Dee's like more of a down-to-earth sort of girl. Was.' A pause here. 'There was that fortune-telling thing, if that's what you mean by something new.'

'And what was that about?'

'Oh, well, she told us, it must've been two, three weeks back, she found this fortune-teller dude, and she used to go to him for like, what d'you call 'em, readings? And anyway, he gave her a number and it hit. That's how she got that couch and TV and shit. So she was pretty pumped on him for a while.'

'Do you know this man's name or where we can get ahold of him?'

'Nah, it was some African name. Like Mandela: Mandoobu, Mandola? I can't remember. She didn't say much about him. Look, could I just *call* my mom now? I already told you everything I know, and if I don't get back to my car there ain't gonna be nothing but wheels left . . .'

The two detectives agreed with a glance and sent Raymond Wallace off with a uniform for a drive back to his car, with the cop given private instructions to take his time. Paz drove to Opa-Locka with Barlow beside him, keeping under the speed limit, as Barlow preferred, wishing he could smoke a cigar, something Barlow deplored. Paz imagined he put up with Barlow because the man was a superb detective and because Barlow's tolerance of Paz gave Paz a certain standing in a department that by and large disliked him. Kissing Barlow's ass (if that's what this was) obviated the necessity of bestowing such kissing elsewhere.

The interview with Mrs Wallace went as these things always did. The Wallaces had imagined that by staying straight, and getting married, and remaining so, and going to church, and pursuing a respectable and honorable life in the military, and moving at last to a reasonably stable lower-middle-class community they could avoid the current *Kindermord* of the black people, but no. Paz sat in his cool and watched Barlow handle the hysterics. Mrs Wallace was a hefty woman and took some handling. Peace restored, calls made, neighbor ladies flocking inward, in a ritual of comfort lamentably too well oiled, the two cops got to ask some questions. They learned that Deandra had left home after an argument, had used her survivor's benefits to pay for the apartment in 'that awful neighborhood,' had started to take courses in beauty school. The detectives learned that beauty school had not been the summit of the Wallaces' dreams for their girl, but kids today . . . what could you do? Mrs Wallace had never been in her daughter's apartment, and she confirmed her son's story of their estrangement over her affair with Julius Youghans. Julius Youghans was high on Mrs Wallace's list of suspects.

'Did he ever threaten your daughter, Mrs Wallace?' Paz asked.

'He didn't want her baby, that was for sure,' said the woman. 'Julius, he just wanted the one thing.'

By this time, Mrs Wallace was surrounded by neighbor ladies fanning her with palm fans and paper church fans, and comforting her with the homilies of their desperate, bone-hard religion. After some routine questions confirming the whereabouts of her and her son on the previous night, the detectives left their cards and departed.

Driving back south, Paz ventured, 'You starting to like Youghans?'

'Could you do that to a woman you been with? You saw the baby. Could you do that to your own flesh and blood?'

'If I was drunk, or zonked behind angel dust or crank, and if she just told me the baby wasn't mine? And I had a knife handy? Yeah, I could. Anybody could. It explains how the killer got into the apartment; the vic let him in. And the missing picture fits there, too. It was Julius's picture up there, and he snatched it off the wall when he left.'

'That wasn't the only thing he took out of there,' said Barlow pointedly.

'There's that, yeah, but if we assume he's crazed . . .'

'And your crazed jealous killer takes the time to drug his lady friend before he slits her open? And to do what looks to me like a neat little operation on that baby?' He looked at Paz sideways, out of the long white eyes. 'You're about to fall in love, you're not careful, son.'

That was the first rule of Barlow. Don't fall in love with a suspect until you know all the other girls.

'Okay, point taken,' said Paz, not at all offended. He had no problem admitting that Barlow had more experience than he did, was at present a better detective. After a brief silence, Barlow said, 'I'll be real interested in what the doc says about those cuts.'

'What do you mean?'

'Well, I seen some hogs butchered, and deer, and calves, and done it myself a time or two. I seen it done by people knew what they were doing and by people didn't have an idea in the world how to go about it, and you can tell. What I mean to say, the man that did that, what we saw up there in that apartment, knew what he was doing. He done it before.'

This last remark hung in the air like a smear of greasy smoke.

'I don't want to hear that, Cletis.'

'No, and I don't particularly care to say it, neither, but there it is. The hearing ear and the seeing eye, the Lord hath made both of them, Proverbs 20:14. We got to follow the ear and the eye wheresoever they may lead.'

'Cletis, all I'm saying, can't we just hope it's a regular domestic? Because if it's a serial, a loony, well, it's going to tie us up forever and have the politicians on our necks and the guy is probably in Pensacola anyway . . .' Paz gave up. He was conscious of the faint blips in his communication, little subvocal hiccups where, had he been speaking to a regular person, he would have inserted the verbal lubricants *fucking*, *hell*, *goddamn*. He also sensed that Barlow knew this and was enjoying it, to the extent that Barlow could ever be said to enjoy something. Barlow said, low-voiced, almost to himself, 'Who can bring a clean thing out of an unclean? No one.'

There seemed to Paz no good comeback to this, and the two men drove the rest of the way to their station in silence. There they found that Julius Youghans had a modest sheet on him, some drunk driving and two counts of receiving stolen property. Paz was ready to go out and pick him up for a conversation, but Barlow said, 'He'll keep. If he ain't run yet, he'll set. I want to go see the autopsy.'

This was fine with Paz. Barlow had taken the call and was, by rule, the primary detective on the investigation. They'll probably eliminate suicide right off, he thought, but kept the thought to himself. After Barlow retired he was going to get a partner with a sense of humor.

'You want me there?' Paz could live without autopsies.

'No, no point the two of us going up to Jackson. Why don't you find out what that nut thing is, and I'll meet you back here around five and we'll both of us go see Mr Youghans.'

Also fine. Paz went back to his car and took I-95, going south this time. He lit one of the unbanded maduro seconds he bought in bundles of fifty from a guy on Coral Way. Paz had been smoking cigars since he was fourteen, and was amused by the recently renewed fashionableness of the vice among downtown big shots. You were not supposed to smoke in police vehicles, which Paz thought was another indication of the end of civilization. Man smoked; it was what made him man, and distinguished him from the beasts.

Puffing contentedly, he turned off Dixie Highway at Douglas Road and then onto Ingraham. The roadside trees had not fully recovered from the ravages of Hurricane Andrew in '92, and Ingraham was not yet the continuous lush tunnel it had once been, but it was cooler and shadier in here than on the unforgiving sun-blasted Dixie Highway. Fairchild Tropical Gardens, his destination, is the largest tropical arboretum in the nation and a center for the study of tropical botany. It, too, had been knocked flat by Andrew but was nearly back to where it had been, a small paradise of lush growth and flowers. Paz flashed his badge at the gate guard and parked in the shadiest corner he could find. The heat of the day was building to its usual apex. Afterward, around three-thirty, when the air was nearly too thick and hot to suck into the lungs, it would be doused by the predictable thunderstorm. Now dense scent hung in the unmoving air: rot, divine perfume, clipped grass. Paz took a deep cleansing snort of this, and strolled past the fish pond and the immense banyan to the two-story gray Florida limestone building that housed the research and administration offices.

After a few false turns he found himself in the office of Dr Albert Manes, a gangling, pleasantly ugly fellow about Paz's age, tanned, spectacled, and looking very much the intrepid plant explorer in a green T-shirt and khaki shorts. He took Paz's card with interest.

'A cop, huh? Looking for dope in the garden again?' He grinned.

Paz kept his face blank. 'No, sir, this is in reference to a homicide.'

Manes's face took on a suitably chastened look. 'Wow, who got killed?' he asked, and then paled. 'Oh, shit, wait a second, you're not here because . . .' His eyes darted over to a family portrait on his desk.

'No, sir, nothing like that. We just need a little botanical advice.'

Manes took a deep breath, blew it, laughed nervously, and sat down on the edge of his desk. 'Sure, what about?'

Paz handed him the thing in its evidence bag.

Manes peered at it, holding the bag up to eye level. He sat on a steel stool, took the nutshell from its bag, examined it in a hand lens, measured it, took down a thick green volume from the shelf above him, thumbed through it for two minutes, and said, 'Here it is.'

Paz looked past his shoulder at the open book. There was a black-and-white photograph of a similar nutshell joined to its mirror image at the narrow end.

'It's *Schrebera golungensis*,' said Manes. 'The ewe's-foot tree. Also called the opele tree, although what an opele is I couldn't tell you. Did you want to know anything else besides what it is?'

'Does it grow around here?'

'Well, it probably would, everything else does. But it's native to West Africa, Nigeria down through the Congo and up to Senegal.'

'Have you got one here? In the gardens, I mean.'

'Alive and growing? I could check our database, if you'd like.'

Paz would like, and the scientist sat down in front of a large monitor and started pressing keys. Lists scrolled, windows flashed into existence and vanished.

'It doesn't look like we do. If you made me guess, I would doubt that anybody else in Miami does, either.'

Paz wrote this into his notebook. 'What do they use this tree for? I mean, they eat the fruit, or what?'

'Oh, it's not a cultivar,' said Manes. 'This grows wild in the jungle. The locals might use parts of it, but I'm not up on that kind of thing. If you have a couple of minutes, I could check on the Net.'

'Let's do it.'

Manes punched keys. The computer warbled and hissed.

'I'm in the EthnobotDB database. Uh-uh. No *S. golungensis*. There's a related *Schrebera* used in folk medicine.'

'How about to make poison?'

'Poison. Okay, that'd be the PLANTOX database. Just a second, here. I'll just check out the genus for starters. Nope, a blank. Which doesn't mean actually that much. These general databases are always a little behind the curve. You need an ethnobotanist.'

'Isn't that you?'

'No, I'm a plant systematist. I figure out which plants are related to which and also decide if something somebody collected is a new species or not. An ethnobotanist actually goes out and works with locals to see how they use plants. Drug companies hire them in platoons.'

'Got a name of one I could talk to?'

'There's Lydia Herrera, she's pretty good, at the U. I know she's around because I just saw her the other day. Your problem's going to be finding someone who knows West Africa, assuming you're interested in this particular tree.' He paused. Paz could see he was about to expire from curiosity thwarted, and was not surprised when he asked, 'So . . . what's the connection between the specimen and the murder? If I may ask . . .'

'You could, but I couldn't tell you anything. Sorry, it's procedure.'

Manes chuckled and said wryly, 'Yeah, and of course, an unusual tropical plant is connected to a murder, you can't tell, it could be a tropical botanist did it.'

'Could be,' said Paz, unsmiling. 'For the record, did you know the victim, Deandra Wallace?'

A short nervous laugh. 'No, not that I know of. Who was she?'

'Oh, just a woman, up in Overtown. Back to what you were saying, about finding someone who knew about Africa?'

Manes seemed relieved to get back to his field. 'Right. Well, most of the ethnobotanists in this part of the world are going to have experience in the American tropics – makes sense, of course, we're close and we have political and economic connections with Latin America. Most of the West African botany's been done out of France, and the East African out of Britain, for obvious reasons, the former colonial powers. I'm sorry I can't help you more.'

Paz finished writing and put away his notebook, thanked Manes, and collected his nut from the table. His opele nut. An accomplishment to know its name. Back at his car, he sat in the front seat with the door open and read through his notes. He always did this after an interview; it was another one of Barlow's rules. Make sure you got what you want before you leave the informant. In all, good news. The crime scene contained a rare nut, which was better than if the thing was growing all over South Florida. He had actually written 'rare nut.' You could say that again, he thought, and laughed. It was a shame he couldn't share it with Barlow. He used his cell phone to call the University of Miami locator, and then called Dr Herrera's office, using Manes's name but not identifying himself as a detective, making an appointment with the secretary for later in the day.

Paz drove out of Fairchild and turned north. A rare nut. He thought it would be nice to find the other half of that particular *Schrebera golungensis* shell. He had a thought and pulled out his notebook and, stopped for the light on Douglas, he made a note to ask Lydia Herrera if she knew why the thing had a little hole drilled in either end.

FOUR

It's peanut butter and jelly for lunch today in the Bert and Ernie lunch box and a banana and four Fig Newtons and orange juice in the little thermos bottle. Luz has discovered her appetite and is looking a little less peaky now, a little less like a starveling sparrow. Her hair is glossy and held by two pink plastic barrettes in the shape of bows. It reaches down to the small of her back. I've dressed her in a navy T-shirt, denim shorts, and red sneakers. If this is ever over and we survive, I'll buy her something pretty, I swear it. I'm wearing my office costume, which today is a shapeless cotton bag printed with vomit-colored picturesque ruins, a degraded Piranesi effect. My legs are bare and stuck into what we used to call health shoes, the precise color and near the shape of horse droppings. It took me a while, but I believe I have found the most unattractive hairstyle for the shape of my face, which is angular, with what my mom always called good cheekbones. I have taken much of the good out of them by choosing blue plastic harlequin eyeglasses, with lenses that tint themselves automatically in sunlight. The lenses tend also to obscure my eyes, which are pale gray-green in color. I try not to look people in the eye in any case, and I don't imagine there are many at my place of work who know what color they are. The hairdo and glasses make me look ten years older, and quite retired from the sexual sweepstakes. Which I am.

We leave the apartment, after a brief altercation about bringing her bird book to day care. They frown on personal items at day care, as it causes quarreling, a lesson we should all take from preschool and apply to our lives. Actually, I am pleased that she objects. It is a good sign, she having spent her little life so far as a terrorized punching bag. She loves that bird book, especially the section on the care and feeding of young birds. The mother bird shoves food down the gaping maw of the baby bird. She gets it. The other night I fed her with bits of cookie as we read, and it made her giggle. I'm the mother and you're the baby. Then she wanted to feed me. I let her and she said her first full sentence, in my presence at least, 'Now *I'm* the mother and *you're* the baby,' and we laughed, and I thank Saint Agnes, patroness of young girls, that the grammar engine is still intact in there under my quick kiss.

She calls me Mother, now, curiously formal, but I don't mind at all, except she says it 'Muffa,' and it sounds to me like the Olo *m'fa*, which literally means support, or pedestal, and signifies the squat wicker pedestal on which the *babandolé* places his *zanzoul*, the ritual container in which magic elements are put to blend and generate power, *ashe* as they say. Figuratively, it is the world – material reality, the web of nature, upon which God has placed the Olo, and which supports them.

We leave the bird book and go out into the typically damp south Floridian morning, thickened air hanging in quasi-visible streamers from the canary allamander, the blushing oleander, the crotons colored like plastic toys, and the gray-barked fig with its insidious brown tendrils strung with beads of moisture. We climb into the Buick and I have to run the wipers because the window is covered with dew. I crank it up, and Luz turns the radio on, always set to WTMI, classical music. I dislike drums now, I do not wish to feel the beat. They are playing some passacaglia for violin, Paganini, perhaps. I turn it down. I like Mozart, Haydn, Vivaldi. And Bach best of all, the intricate order and the illusion of rules, the ghosts of protection. Quite drumless.

It is a short hop down Hibiscus to Providence Congregational Church, which dispenses, besides an unstressful vanilla religion, the best day care in Miami. There is a long waiting list for Prov, but we jumped the list over all the Brittanys and Jasons from the good side of the Grove, because of our peculiar appearance and the sad story I spun for the director, Mrs Vance: a little African exoticism, a little heartbreaking separation, a little traumatic death, just a touch of touching impairment. A shabby white lady and her mulatto kid, striving and desperate, that was the picture. And grateful, unlike so many of the actual poor, who are so often testy and suspicious. My husband taught me a great deal about how to stimulate white guilt, and I find I can use it effectively in the service of my kid, and do. It bowled nice Mrs Vance over and she affirmatively acted.

Providence is set in perfectly trimmed grounds on Main Highway, graced by palms and banyans and bougainvillea, a set of low structures in Spanish Mission style, red tile roofing over stucco painted pink as lips. I turn Luz over to the nice Ms Lomax, her teacher, who coos a greeting tinged with that special tone people like Ms Lomax use for those not so fortunate as they.

Everyone and everything is nice at Providence. The milk of human kindness sloshes ankle-deep over its polished floors. The kids are brightly scrubbed and dressed in designer clothes, or darling faux-casual rich hippie stuff, and the mothers are all as shiny as their Mercs and Range Rovers. The nice makes me feel like a troll or a night-hag, or a *t'chona*, the river wight of the Olo, who comes at night and sits on the faces of dreamers and gives them dreams of smothering that are not only dreams. I *am* grateful; I want Luz to be surrounded by nice here and for her whole life, and yet I want to smash it, too; I want to open nice, plump Ms Lomax up like a can of beans. My husband, I know, felt like this all the time, although he managed to keep it under wraps for a good long while, until he got to Africa. Africa will do that; Carl Gustav Jung took one look and ran like a thief back to cozy Zurich.

Luz goes without a backward glance, as she has from the first day. Utter security, is it, or does she not even care, like a cat? Olo children are like that, I recall, after they have made the *sefuné* bond with their foster parents, so I suppose it's all right. Or I'm crazy, which is always around eight-to-five probable these days.

I drive back to U.S. 1 and up to I-95, which I take to the East-West freeway and then off at Twelfth Avenue. It's my only luxury, this driving to work. Parking and running the car cost nearly as much as my rent, but I don't like the metrorail, the only American equivalent of African bus travel. Now that I have a child to raise, I don't know if I can continue, although so far she's cost little more to keep than a small dog. Perhaps I can find another source of income. It can't have any sex in it, or drums, or smiling (cross out the ads that want personable, good with people) or snappy dressing. Computers? I know how to use one, and perhaps I could learn a programming language. On the other hand, so few women in that field, I wouldn't want to stand out, no. Maybe I could tell fortunes, ha-ha.

Jackson Memorial Hospital, unlovely and vast, the great public pesthouse of Miami, lifts its many mansions in Overtown, hard by the freeway, convenient for both the walking poor and their driving healers. I park in my unguarded surface lot and leave the windows open. It is cheaper than the enclosed parking palaces and I don't think anyone will bother to steal my car. I must walk two streets to the entrance to my building, however, and on the corner of Tenth is a convenience store where the homeboys hang. Hip-hop is playing loud enough to feel through my feet, but the beat is so utterly banal that it is more like the pounding of some dumb machine and it does not engage me. I try for invisibility as I go by. There are only a few boys and it's hot and no one bothers me. I have been mugged three times, which is why I carry my cash and my ID and keys in a pouch hung around my neck, a trick of travelers in the third world. My purse is plastic, yellow, $6.99 at Kmart, in case anyone wants it.

When I say 'invisible' I mean American urban invisibility, not *faila'olo*, the invisibility of the sorcerers, which I have not learned how to do. I rather suspect my husband is well up on it, though.

We work underground, in the basement of building 201, next door to the emergency room. Medical records don't require the cheering rays of the sun. Sometimes I imagine I can hear the cries of those in emergency care, but it must be only the ambulance sirens. Still, it

contributes to the impression of being confined in a
dungeon at hard labor. I pass through the swinging
doors and into the reception area, where the files are
dropped off and picked up by the ward messengers. I
nod to the clerk behind his counter, which is barely
acknowledged, and pass through to the file room where
I work. It is long and low-ceilinged and brightly lit by
tubes behind rectangles of frosted plastic. Two rows of
desks march down the center, and on either side are the
banks of motorized filing cabinets, with corridors
between them. As I enter, one of the messengers shoves
off with a cart loaded full with brightly tabbed hanging
files. 'Yo, Dolores,' he says, waving. I always get a nice
greeting from Oswaldo, as he is mentally retarded.

Several of the messengers are similarly afflicted. We
file clerks are thus the elite of the medical records
section. We are required to have total mastery of alphabetical order. Some of us, like me, work on retrieval,
while others work on putting the files back in their
proper places in the cabinets, or, to use our technical
term, 'filing' them. Lives are at stake here and well do we
know it. If we forget, Mrs Waley is there to remind us.
Mrs Waley is our supervisor, and I see her now staring
out at us from her little glassed-in office, as if she were a
tourist in an aquarium and we were the fishes.

Mrs Waley is a yellowish, freckled woman with hair
like black plastic, shiny and sculpted around her circu-
lar face. She must weigh well over 250 pounds, and I am
afraid that some of the younger staff call her the Whale.
I don't. I have the greatest respect for Mrs Waley. She's
been at Jackson for nearly twenty years and claims
never to have missed a day of work. She began before
computers, as she often remarks, and I believe she

thinks they are something of a fad. She dresses in very bright colors, purple, scarlet, primrose yellow, and today she wears a pantsuit the color of the green stripe in the flag of Mali. She wears a purplish lipstick and artificial nails, also brightly colored, and more than an inch long, like those of a mandarin. I suppose she *is* a mandarin, of sorts. She is careful never to do any physical work.

Mrs Waley does not like me overmuch. At first I thought it was because Dolores Tuoey had claimed on her phony résumé a college degree and a spell as a nun, but I heard from some of the other staff that she thought I was a management plant, a spy. Why else would someone with an education work here? I gave out that it was doctor's orders; I couldn't take any pressure. This seemed to satisfy her, and ever since she's treated me as a potentially dangerous lunatic. I hoped at first that she might relent, and move me into the harmless lunatic category, for I've given two years and four months of good service, never once forgetting the order of the alphabet or foisting a McMillan in place of a desired McMillian, a common error among the retrievers. Latterly, I've decided that she does not like me because I am a white person, the only one in her domain.

My in-basket is full of record request forms that have accumulated during the night. I sort them by service and last name. This is something of an innovation, I'm afraid. Mrs Waley instructed me during my orientation that I was to take the eldest, or bottom, request first, complete the task, and then go on to the next one. She showed me how to turn the pile of forms over so that the eldest form was (marvelously!) positioned on top. My breakthrough methodology means, however, that I can get my stack done in about a third of the time the other way requires, and so I do it, and hope that Mrs Waley doesn't catch me and make me stop. The time thus saved I devote to reading medical records, walking slowly through the narrow corridors, between the buff walls of softly shining steel. This is something so beyond the scope of Mrs Waley's imagination that she hasn't thought to specifically forbid it, although it is, of course, a state and federal crime. Reading files is much like doing anthro research. It amuses me, and passes the time.

I notice that a tape on one of the records has come loose. I leave it alone. Once I forgot myself so far as to replace some tapes myself and inspired Mrs Waley to wrath. College graduate and can't even put on tapes right. I hadn't realized the importance of the three-quarter-inch clearance between each tape strip. No one can say that I don't learn from my mistakes. I finish a cart for the medical ward and go back to my desk to get more request forms. There is a note on my desk from Mrs Waley on top of a box full of files. It says *Take these files to Billing stat.*

This is messenger's work and I am not supposed to do it, but I suspect Mrs Waley thinks I can be spared for this because of the efficiencies I generate. Mrs Waley is in something of a bind, since if everyone worked as quickly as I do, she could run the place with half the people, and such diminution of her empire would never do. So she does not compliment me but sends me out on errands; it's a creative solution.

I stuff the box under my arm and go off to Billing, which is on the ground floor. Other than menial visits, such as this one, an excursion to Billing, for a meeting, say, is a rare and valuable prize. The hearts of all medical records clerks yearn toward Billing, as the Christian's toward heaven and the Olo's toward Ifé the Golden, where the gods walked. For Billing is the heart of the hospital. Without Billing, how could the nurses care, the surgeons cut, the internists ponder, the psychiatrists push dope? They could not; people would die in the streets.

Billing is light and airy and has a carpet on the floor, unlike our green linoleum. The blessed who reside there tap on computers. Their desks are decorated with pictures of family and little furry toys and plaques with amusing sayings. We are not allowed these in medical records, since we must keep our desks clear to arrange the files. On the way back to my post, I take a small detour through the ER suite. I do this as often as I can. It adds interest to the day. Many of the people in the ER are there because of emergencies, but during the daytime the majority are there because the ER is where we have decided that poor people are to obtain medical help. They sit in colorful plastic chairs if they are older or race about if they are younger, sharing whatever viruses and bacteria they have with their socioeconomic compadres.

An elderly lady in black attracts my attention. She is prostrate and moaning softly, attended by two younger women. They are speaking to her in Spanish. I catch my breath and feel tightness in my belly. *Dulfana* is pouring out of her like smoke and I can smell it. Not smell it, exactly, but that is what it feels like, an insidious quasi-olfactory sensation. Someone has witched the old lady. I turn and quickly walk away. Early in my apprenticeship, Uluné made me eat a *kadoul*, or magical compound, a green paste that he said would enable me to sense when witches were at work. He was always feeding me stuff, or blowing stuff up my nose or rubbing it on my skin. Much of this applied biochemistry was to enable me to interpret the condition of the *fana*, the magical body. Everything alive has a *fana*. As physical bodies are to the *m'fa*, so is *fana* to the *m'doli*, the unseen world. I was sick for two days, which amused and encouraged Uluné, since by this he knew the compound was efficacious. Thereafter, to my immense surprise, I could actually pick up *dulfana*, which is the characteristic effect of sorcery upon the *fana*. Back then, I interpreted these sensations as the aftereffects of the compounds Uluné made me consume. I can no longer entertain this theory, as it's been well over four years, and I sense *dulfana* often in the streets of Miami. It is nearly as common in certain quarters as the scent of Cuban coffee.

I feel a vague shame and suppress it. I could have helped that woman, who surely won't receive what she needs from the exhausted intern who will shortly examine her, but countersorcery generates something like a tornado in the *m'doli*, and the narrow end of that tornado would point directly at me. Sex strengthens the *fana*, as does happiness and contentment, and joy and anger, which is why I'm careful not to indulge in those things now. There is the child, and my love for her, of course, which must be generating a hot little blip in the old *m'doli*, if anyone's looking, but I can't do anything about that. Everyone's *fana* is slightly different, like everyone's smell. I never learned to distinguish at a grain that fine, but Uluné could, and I expect that nowadays my husband can too. Is he actively looking for me?

My constant thought. I know he'd like to find me. He wanted us to be together, or so he said, the night before I sailed away. He wants me to watch him do his stuff.

I make my escape, find I'm trembling, and pause at the elevator to lean my forehead against the cool stainless steel of its door. Oh, the physical body, full of meat and juice, in this place regarded as merely a soup, requiring only a balancing of the ingredients and the stoppage of leaks to restore it to good order. The *m'fon*, as the Olo call this body, is the only one officially recognized by Jackson Memorial and the Western World, of which it is an atom. I want to believe in that pleasant notion: it's just a soup of proteins and water and metallic compounds, and each of these is merely a soup of electrons and other subatomics, and those in turn, merely a soup of quarks. Oh, *merely*! How I wish, wish, wish, I could get back to *merely*! The Olo have no word for merely. They never learned the trick of dividing the world into the significant and the insignificant, which is one reason why there are only about twelve hundred of them left in the world and what they know will shortly vanish from the memory of mankind.

So nobody will ever go up to the intern who is perhaps now puzzling over that old Cuban lady's symptoms and tell him his EKGs, and EEGs, and chem-sevens, and cancer panels, and sphygmomanometer readings, and tox screens are *mere objectivity*. In fact, the *m'fon* of the Cuban lady is more or less fine, except where it is destroying itself at the subtle urgings of her *fana*, which is not at all well.

I have to stop at the ladies' room because of the Cuban woman. I have a sensitive digestion nowadays, another thing that keeps me cadaverous. When I was a kid, I ate like a wolverine; it was my sister who was the delicate eater. She used to pass me stuff she didn't like at the dinner table, and sometimes we would switch plates when the parents weren't watching, and I would get to eat her dinner too. I believe Mary was an anorexic in fact, rather than in fancy, as I am. A willowy beauty, often so described, often by my mother, also thin, who I believe was disappointed in me. I was more like my father, inheriting the long heavy bones, broad shoulders, and big hands and feet of the Doe family, a reversion to the original doughty fisherfolk stock. I had at one time photos of the two of us on our boat, dressed in slickers, grinning like fools as green water comes over the gunwales. Aside from our relative sizes, it's hard to tell me from him. I guess my brother must have snapped them; he took all the family photographs, which is why there are almost no photographs of him. Yes, it would have been Josey, because I don't recall my mom ever going out in weather, or Mary. That damn boat, Mom called it, although it was *Kite*, officially.

Mary took after our mother in a number of other ways, as well. The red-gold hair. The heart-shaped face. The thins. When I was small and just learning go fish, I thought the queen of diamonds in a deck of cards was a portrait of my mother. I had a photograph of Mary, she must have been nineteen or so, when she was being a model in New York, a candid shot, not professional, and in it she has a look on her face that I don't imagine has ever been on mine, a look that says Oh, I'm so fucking terrific, don't you wish you were me and doesn't it just kill you that you're not? The eyes are void of any inner life at all. She was calling herself Mariah Do then and was extremely hot. When I was in Paris, I once saw her picture on the cover of French *Vogue*. I told no one at the museum. There was no danger of anyone commenting that I resembled her.

Her mother's girl, certainly, as I was Daddy's. Families do split that way, although around the dinner table we were cordial enough, good manners being a family value at the Does'. Josey, being the child of Mom's previous and never-to-be-mentioned marriage, did not have a horse in this race. Oddly, although he was a Mount, too, he looked rather more like us than he did like his mother or Mary. My dad tried to reach out to him, decent guy that he was, but Josey wasn't buying it. Pride, I think. He had a terror of being beholden, something he certainly didn't share with his mother, or other half sister. He wanted to be the one giving the gifts. Also, it was probably not much fun being Lily Mount Doe's *son*. He left home early, which broke my heart. In my girlish dreams it was always the three of us, out on the boat, having adventures, learning stuff. Boy stuff, naturally. My mother gave up early trying to teach me girl stuff, especially as she had such an expert and willing pupil in Mary.

I am a little shaky in the pins on the way back to my post. Mrs Waley looks meaningfully at her watch as I enter and exchanges some words with the filers. Smirks all around. It does Mrs Waley good to note the deficiencies of her one white subordinate, and I don't begrudge her that pleasure. I continue pulling files until lunchtime, which for me is one o'clock. Then I travel down dingy corridors to the cafeteria. Most of the time I go outside and find a patch of shade somewhere and eat alone, but today I am feeling too exhausted to make the trip. A spasm of nausea when the institutional food smell hits me. I pull a vanilla yogurt out of the cooler box.

I wish to be alone, but I'm spotted by two other medical recorders. Lulu waves me over to a table where she is sitting with Cleo. Dead Dolores, were she here, would be glad of company, and so I go also, doing this in her memory. They're both eating salads from the bar, where you make them up and buy them by the ounce. They are both sturdy, round-bottomed and -breasted dark women with straightened hair, looking very much alike, although I do not think they are related. Both of them are American African Non-Americans, being naturalized immigrants from the island of Barbados.

Cleo makes a comment about my yogurt and they both chuckle engagingly. Both of them have acquired along with their citizenship the American body thing and wish to keep their size under control. They know that only the thin rise in America. They're better educated than Mrs Waley, and speak a more precise English. Both are enrolled at Miami-Dade, and will get their degrees and will ride their clipped imperial accents beyond even Billing, perhaps as far as Administration itself. Mrs Waley regards them with suspicion; how can they, four shades darker than she, talk and act so white?

Lulu and Cleo feel sorry for me. Lulu is always giving me grooming tips. Dolores, child, that is not the right style for your hair, I must tell you that, no. Cleo, tell her, she should wear it pulled back, away from the face. And she has such pretty eyes, see it, girl! Dolores, you should get you some contacts, like me. They don't cost that much.

And so on, in that musical voice. I bob my head,

grin, and make excuses. I like them both and wish often that I were again myself so that we could be friends. I eat my yogurt slowly, willing my stomach to accept its bland nourishment. Cleo and Lulu are chattering about some neighborhood event. They live in the Grove, too, in the large island community there. They are always complaining about the Bahamians and Jamaicans, and explaining to each other and to me why these are both lesser breeds without the law. And, my word, the *Haitians*! I allow their talk to soothe me, like the sound of a brook, without much attention to content. Nor is it much expected. Now some remarks about their Episcopal church, their minister. I am consulted here, being a Catholic, and the arbiter of doctrine therefore. I make a mumbling reply. It has been thirteen years and seven months since my last confession. I am badly lapsed but persist in a fragment of belief. Now that I have Luz, I will probably start church again. I wish to bring her up in the faith of my father.

I'm thinking vaguely about finding a church when Lulu says, 'The police are not saying anything, but I heard from my cousin Margaret, she lives in Opa-Locka and she knows the family of that poor girl. Margaret heard that she was cut wide open down her middle and the baby was stolen away.'

'Not true!' exclaims Cleo, her eyes wide with horror. My eyes too.

'True, very true!' Lulu affirms. 'But, what you can expect, them in Overtown!'

'Terrible, them, but . . .' Here Cleo lowers her voice and looks dramatically past her shoulder, then confides, '*You* know what they want with that baby, heh? *Haitians*.'

'What?' Lulu put her hand to her mouth. 'Jesus save us! You think for human sacrifices?'

'What else for? What I think is they should have a care, the authorities, before they allow some of these people in the country. I don't say all of them by any means, but . . .' Here she stopped and I felt her stare. 'Why, my girl, what is the matter with you now? You look like you are about to be sick.'

I let my spoon fall to the table, mutter something, grab up my cheapo bag, and dash to the toilet. Out of both ends this time, top first, then the other, although I can't imagine there was much to purge, maybe old rubber bands, pieces of spleen. Another zero-calorie day for Dolores.

After, I find myself at the sink, washing, washing, mindlessly washing my hands until they are red and wrinkled. Am I developing an obsession now? That's all I need, paranoid delusions, obsessional syndrome, this is what the intern will say when he admits me to Neuropsychiatric. I wish.

Oh, Cleo, it's not Haitians, no, this is far beyond Haitians. Haiti is strictly minor league for this kind of thing: the most extreme *voudoun*, done by the most power-crazed *bokor* in that whole wretched island, is like an amateur company stumbling through *The Iceman Cometh* in Kankakee. What we have here, Cleo, in comparison, is Broadway, the ultimate source and font and center of all that, the pure neolithic technology, unadulterated by transportation and slavery, barely touched by the colonialists.

Has he found me? I recall once, when we were first in love, idly speculating on where we might live, as couples do, running through the cities, the countries, totting up the pros and cons. San Francisco? Pretty, nice climate, but everyone wanted to live there. Chicago, where we met, good school, teaching opportunities, terrible climate. New York, if you can make it there you can make it anywhere, blah, blah, and I'd said, Miami, and we both blew raspberries and laughed. Which is why I'm here, naturally. The last place we'd choose.

But now he's here and he's hungry, he's building up his *ch'andouli*, his sorcerer's power, using stuff that even Olo sorcerers don't use anymore, that no respectable Olo sorcerer will teach. But he didn't learn this from a respectable Olo sorcerer. He learned it from Durakné Den, the *dontzeh*, the abandoned, the witch of Danolo. Oh, yes, Cleo, I know just what happened to that baby. I've even seen it done, God forgive me.

I still, stupidly, think of him as he was at the beginning, the way we were together, or how I *thought* we were together. God alone knows how much of that was real. What above all blasts your confidence, makes you weak and small, poisons the past, erases the memory of joy, cripples even the possibility of joy to come? The betrayal of the deepest heart, that's what, which is always self-betrayal. No one can do you like you do yourself. The other day, when I was in Kmart with Luz, we passed the candy counter and there they had a display of caramels, a whole glass-fronted case full of caramel cubes, and I swear the color knocked me back, and out of nowhere came the memory of the color of his skin, and synesthetically, its smell. My gosh, how I loved him! And, you know, even after he changed, even after what happened in Africa, I still thought that someday we would get back together. I thought it, actually, right up to the day he murdered my sister.

FIVE

Left Paris at ten-thirty in the morning after flying all night and will arrive in Lagos at four or so. I should sleep to avoid jet lag, but am too worked up.

Fellow first-class passengers are Nigerian kleptocrats, their wives returning from shopping expeditions, plus UN or NGO types, paler than the former group, less expensive wristwatches. Also two drunk Texans, in the all bidnis, lots of all in Nigeria so they tell me. Pronounce the name of the country Nigger-rhea. In Charles de Gaulle before flight, W. away buying duty-free, made themselves at home, heard I was going to Africa for the first time, regaled me with all sorts of useful information about the country. Should've told them to fuck off, I am too polite. W. came back and I introduced him as my husband – expression on their faces worth the first-class ticket. W. said I leave you alone for ten minutes and you're practically joining the Nazi party? This is the last time I'm taking you to Africa! W. not particularly bothered by old-fashioned naked racism of the good ol' boy type, hates cryptic racism of chattering classes a lot more, his worst hate = unacknowledged skin-tone racism of African-Americans.

Later. The Mediterranean is gone and we are over land again, over Africa. Reading Yoruba cosmology. It is a lot to take in. Yoruba cosmos divided into *aye*, the tangible world, and *orun*, the world of the spirits. At top of *orun* is Olodumare, creator god, but He's really too high up there to pay attention to the small stuff. *Orun* is thickly inhabited by a variety of spirits, plus *orishas* – deities or deified ancestors. Much of their religion = communication with *orishas*, divination or spirit possession, the *orishas* come down into *aye* and speak to their devotees. Key here = two *orishas*, Eshu, gatekeeper between worlds, also cosmic trickster; and Orunmila, aka Ifa, the *orisha* of prophecy. Whole thing runs on *ashe*, kind of spiritual gasoline. Every created thing has *ashe* – rocks, trees, animals, people – *ashe* both ground of existence and power to make stuff happen and change. Social relationships determined by flow of *ashe*, also one's personal fate and achievements. (Note X-cultural, how different peoples imagine some unseen, yet controllable force underlying life: *ashe* in Yoruba, *ki* or *qi* in the Chinese culture zone, *cheg* in Siberia. Westerners don't believe?? Did we never or did we once and lost it. If so, why? Industry? Xtianity?)

Thinking of M., wonder whether I am making a mistake plunging back into fieldwork, especially fieldwork associated with sorcery. Can't recall more of my experience in Siberia = problem. Some kind of allergic reaction to food or water. Is this true?

W. just up, grumpy and hungover, lovely African flight attendant brought hot towels and orange juice and aspirin and vamped W. I will not complain to the airline, I am used to it & it makes him feel better. Watched Africa unroll beneath us, empty, blank, ocher, the desert. We flew south-southeast, the land greened up underneath us, dry savannah, wet savannah, then true rain forest. W. grinned, said de *jungle*, recited Vachel Lindsay: *then I saw the Congo creeping through the black*, etc., in overly deep Robesonian voice. Not the Congo, but the Niger basin. Poetic license. The all men glanced over suspiciously.

We're going to the Tropic of Night, I said, but he didn't hear me.

Later, Lary's Palm Court Hotel, Lagos

W. is right out, poor thing. Obviously, we landed. Usual stuff in customs and immigration, the guy looking longingly at my cameras and notebook computer; apparently it used to be quite bad here, but everyone is on good behavior since the new regime took over. Outside of baggage claim, two men from our outfit, Ajayi Okolosi, a driver, and Tunji Babangida, porter at the hotel. Ajayi said hello in English and I launched into my Yoruba greeting mode and slowly shook his hand: how are you; how is your wife; how are your children; how are your parents; is everything peaceful with you, and so on. Got big grin, language tapes work.

Outside, the usual scene at a third world airport, masses of poor people trying to grab a piece off the divine beings rich enough to fly. When they spotted Blondie, things got really insane, 'cab, miss, cab, miss,' in my ear, trying to rip the backpack off me, rescued by Tunji. The car was a venerable Land Rover, and into this I was tossed together with my gear. W. was sitting there, looking stricken. Silence in car, squeezed W.'s hand. Our welcome to Africa, sad. Up front, Tunji messed w/ old tape player wired to the dashboard, and shortly the sounds of Public Enemy, top volume, song 'Fear of a Black Planet.' Tunji checked to see how W. was enjoying this bit o' civilization. Not much, *hates* that music. Tunji adoption of rap style from U.S., interesting, wonder how widespread, analogue to same among white teens. Search for cool universal?

Clouds of gritty dust, south on an expressway of some kind. Lots of cheap motorcycles, a few big, shiny Mercedeses with smoked glass, lots of yellow buses, military vehicles in numbers. Soldiers in trucks look like children.

Left the highway at a big intersection guarded by a white-gloved cop spiffy Brit-type uniform and whistle, traffic lights not working.

Central business district of Lagos is south of here, says Ajayi, on or near Lagos Island, and that's where the tourists and the dozen or so tall towers are. We were going to Yaba, the *real* Lagos, much safer and cheaper, by the University. The streets narrower, heavily potholed, the big car lurched, I knocked against W. and laughed. He was distant and stiff, staring out the window; I wished T. would turn off that damn music.

Two of them are chattering away in Yoruba, of which I could understand hardly one word in ten. Over 300 dialects, musical language, though, talking sounds like singing a little. Streets lined w/ three- and four-story concrete block buildings, shuttered against the sun, painted white, every few streets a minareled mosque, or a church.

Passed a big street market. Ajayi steered carefully around knots of people, around stalls and stands selling food, drinks, cigarettes, raffles, clothing, shoes. The air smelled of garbage rotting, grilling meat, car exhaust, and something else, unidentifiable, high, sharp, slightly spicy, the base pong of the place. When I can no longer notice it, I will have settled in.

Lary's Palm Court Guest House is a two-story white building, hipped metal roof painted a faded red. Our team has taken over the whole place, all ten bedrooms. Lary's cooler than the street, dim, ceiling fans slowly stirring the air, worn wicker furniture, smell of cooking, peppery spices, fried meats, then as we marched to our rooms, disinfectant, wax, furniture polish. Decor amazing: in the reception area, large steel engraving of stag at bay, a litho of Jesus with children, breakfront with cheap souvenirs of English seaside, a dining room with four round tables, set with plastic-covered cloths, heavy, cheap silver and glassware, plastic flowers in vases – could be Blackpool, Brighton. Everything spotlessly clean, except for omnipresent tan dust. W. not pleased, said something about the colonial mind, complained about bath, toilet, in hall. He has not traveled much in foreign lands. I opened the shutters, found our window gives on a little courtyard, shaded by a big mango tree. There are two goats tethered there and a worn table, at which two women in bright dresses and headscarves are doing something with a mound of some vegetable. They looked up & saw me & waved, smiled & I waved back. I am going to like this place.

W. said he had a headache, took a bunch of aspirin and plopped onto the bed. I went downstairs. Mrs Bassey, proprietor, has mien of the Queen Mother, speaks perfect English in an accent like a song, every sentence ending like a query – We serve dinner at six sharp? I decided to take a walk.

Down the hot, narrow, smelly streets, music everywhere from radios and what looked like dives, dark holes stinking of beer. A wide thoroughfare, across which was Yaba Market. Every dozen or so steps a young man would approach me, asking to become my guide, or trying to sell me something or steer me to a stall. I told each, no thank

you, that would not please me, in Yoruba, which usually
got a startle, sometimes a grin, and a comment too quick
for me to catch. I found a moneychanger and traded
dollars for naira, getting a little more than twice the legal
rate. I bought a paper cone of something called *kilikili*,
because I liked the name, and it turned out to be spicy
deep-fried peanut butter, pretty good, and some gassy
local mango soda. Yaba an untouristy kind of market –
most stalls devoted to everyday stuff – plastic pans, hardware, dry goods, clothing (new and used), shoes, cheapo
electronics, music tapes. Constant pounding of music,
most of it interesting, beat driven – Yaba also a big night-
club district, lots of the musicians live here. Also market
artists, some of them better than the stuff you see in
SoHo, brilliant colors, abstracted natural forms – terrific!
In central Asia the markets are segregated by goods – here
apparently not.

Joined little crowd between a woman selling fish out of
plastic tubs of ice and a woman selling lengths of tie-dyed
adira oniku cloth, saw man squatting, bare-chested,
dressed only in khaki shorts, thought he was doing some
craft, but he was winding length of colored twine around a
dog's skull, chanting. To one side, the client – fat, elderly
man in robes and pillbox hat. Shirtless man finished
knotting up the skull, placed it on a dented tin bowl, took
a brown hen out of a straw basket. He cut the hen's throat,
let the blood spurt over the skull.

Felt faint, not the sight of blood, but confronting
sorcery after all this time. Market juju only, but still . . .
repulsion and attraction both. Rite familiar from books.
The fat guy is a moneylender or businessman. Someone
owes him money, hasn't paid. Now debtor will have
dreams of dogs chasing him every night, he'll go to a witch

doctor so he can get some sleep and witch doctor will tell him to pay his debt, if it's a just one, or if not, he can set up some counter-magic. M. used to say that immersion in a different culture was like an enema for the spirit. Could be: I feel higher than I have in months.

SIX

Professor Herrera's face registered surprise when Jimmy Paz walked into her office. Paz flashed his warmest smile and stuck his hand out and she took it with good enough grace. In Miami, when Iago Paz is announced, you don't normally expect a black man to walk in the door. Paz was used to it, expected it, had grown to appreciate its disconcerting aspects. He did his quick cop take of the office and its occupant. Fifteen by twelve maybe, neat, organized, with just enough room for a chrome-legged Formica-topped desk, with computer and monitor. A chair and visitor's chair in the same style, padded with orange plastic, a credenza in cheap institutional teak veneer, and, behind the desk, floor-to-ceiling bookshelves, crammed with books and green cardboard reprint boxes, the contents indicated with red label tape. On a shelf in the center of this array, some family pictures, knick-knacks of various kinds, a large plaster statue of Saint Francis of Assisi, brown-cowled, holding a rosary and a dove, the base wrapped around with green and gold ribbons. One small window, protected from the merciless afternoon sunlight by drawn steel venetian blinds. On the wall, diplomas: Clemson, University of Miami. A local girl, of course. Some framed photos, too, groups of people in explorer gear standing around with people wearing less clothes, lots of green foliage as background: the typical anthropology shot; also, framed antique botanical drawings of leaves, flowers, seeds, with Latin titles, something else in a frame on the credenza behind him, looked like a rosary.

The proprietor of all this was a woman in her late thirties, with blond hair, intelligent hazel eyes, reflecting a little unease now, Paz observed, which was okay from his point of view, parchment-colored skin made matte with careful makeup. She was a little heavy for her age, although not for her culture. Behind the desk, on the wooden floor-to-ceiling bookshelf, there was a picture of her with a darkly handsome, chunky man, looking younger and thinner. She'd married, had a kid, maybe – right, there was another photo, two of them, framed in silver, this next to a couple of bright leaves embedded in a block of Lucite. Not a pretty woman, but attractive in a severe way. She wore a sheer violet-colored silk shirt with a delicate stripe in it, under the beige jacket of a suit. A little formal for the professoriate, but perhaps she was teaching a class and wanted a little formality. That would be upper-class Cuban, Paz thought, the stratum from which this woman clearly sprang. Ordinarily she would have spoken with a man from his own stratum only to point out where to plant the new hibiscus or order the Lexus serviced.

But politely, of course. Politely, then, Lydia Herrera directed Paz to the visitor's chair, offered coffee (declined), asked, 'So, Mr Paz, I understand Al Manes gave you my name. I assume this is about some plant?'

'Yeah, he said you were a pretty good ethnobotanist.'

'I am.' No false modesty for Lydia. 'And you're with . . . ?'

Paz held up his ID and shield. 'Miami police,' he said, and watched her carefully plucked arcs of eyebrow rise.

'And why does the Miami police need an ethno-botanist?'

Paz took *Schrebera golungensis* in its bag from his jacket pocket and placed it before her. 'We thought you might be able to tell us what that thing is used for.'

Herrera picked it up. 'Can I take it out of the bag?'

'Be my guest.'

She examined it, replaced it, handed the bag back to Paz. 'It's part of an *opele*.'

Paz consulted his notebook. 'Yeah, that's what Dr Manes said, but what is it used for?'

'No, I mean, *opele* the thing, not opele the name of the nut. It's part of an Ifa divining chain, an *opele*, also called an *ekwele*. It's used to divine the future in Santería and other West African–derived cults. Didn't you ever see one?' The tone was slightly mocking. Of course a black Cuban ought to know everything there was to know about Santería. That's what they were *for*.

'No,' said Paz, coldly. 'Do you have one?'

She was smiling. 'As a matter of fact, I do. Over there on the credenza.' She pointed with a red-lacquered fingernail. He got up and looked. Not a rosary after all. The large black frame sat on a little stand, and in it, displayed against black velvet, like a diamond necklace, was a shiny brass chain about three feet long. Strung into the chain at widely spaced, even intervals, were eight pieces of thin tortoiseshell, gently curved. From the two terminal shells depended short cords, ending in cowries. Each tortoiseshell piece was carved into a tapering pear shape, with a ridge down the center of the concave side.

'That one's from Cuba, mid-nineteenth century,' Herrera said. 'You notice how the shell is carved?'

'Yeah, it's sort of like the nut there.'

'Right. What you just showed me is the original. The craftsman who carved that one probably never saw a real opele nut, but the memory survived. Interesting.'

'Yeah.' Paz pulled his eyes away from the frame and faced Herrera again. 'How does it work?'

'It's a machine for generating a number. You don't know *anything* about Ifa divination?'

Again the surprised, slightly mocking tone. Paz said, 'No, but perhaps you would be good enough to instruct me, Dr Herrera,' in the flattest voice he could generate. He was very close to breaking one of Barlow's rules: anybody got something you need to know about is your best friend.

Dr Herrera's smile widened. Dimples appeared on her plump cheeks. Teaching Santería to an Afro-Cuban! She would dine out on this one for months.

'All right, Detective. Ifa is the *orisha*, the demigod, of prophecy among the Yoruba and related peoples of West Africa. The *opele* is one method that the *babalawo*, the diviner, uses to consult the god. There are others, involving the number of palm nuts or cowries grasped in the hand. The purpose of both methods, as I mentioned, is to generate a number. As you can see, there are two possible ways for each of eight indicators to fall, and therefore there are sixteen basic figures that can form at each throw. The diviner marks a single line where a shell or nut has fallen concave side up, and a

double line where one has fallen concave side down.
The lines are drawn in two columns of four. In Africa the
babalawo uses a shallow box full of fine wood powder to
make the marks, but here they just use pencil and paper.
Okay, so you end up with two columns of four marks
each, single or double lines, I mean, for every throw, but
it matters which column a particular marking is in, so
you have to take account of the mirror images too. Are
you following this?'

Paz said, 'Yes, Doctor. If you include all the reverse
combinations then the total number of combinations is
sixteen times sixteen, or two hundred fifty-six. What
happens when you get the number?' Remarkable, the
nigger can do math in his head, Paz figured she was
thinking. *Guzana.* Maggot.

'Yes, well,' said Dr Herrera, deflated, 'each number
they generate relates to a particular memorized verse.
The *babalawo* recites the verse, or more commonly, he
just references it and interprets it to answer the client's
question. The information is assumed to come from the
orisha, who influences the fall of the shells. This is Ifa,
by the way.' She pointed to the statue on the bookshelf.
'In Santería, known as Orula or Orunmila. The Yoruba
slaves who brought Ifa divination to Cuba and into
Santería thought that Saint Francis's rosary looked like
an *opele* and so they made the identification. The other
santos or *orishas* in Santería have similar histories.
Eleggua, for example, is Anthony of Padua, Shango is
Saint Barbara, because . . .'

'Right, got that. What I'd like to know is if any drugs
are used in the divining ceremony, either by the diviner
or the client.'

This was abrupt, peremptory. The professor did not

like it. Not smiling now, she answered, 'You mean intoxicating drugs? Well, rum is involved, but only sacramentally.'

'Not rum. I mean narcotics, something that would cause unconsciousness, like that.'

'No, not that I've ever heard. Of course, I'm not an expert.'

'No? You sounded like one a minute ago.' It was his turn to be a little tormenting.

She glanced briefly at the diploma wall. 'I did my B.A. here at Miami. It comes with the territory – Santería, I mean. Also being a Cuban . . .'

'But you're not a participant.'

'No.'

'As an anthropologist, then, you know something about the rituals, what they do.'

'Some, but I don't practice as an anthropologist. I'm an ethnobotanist. It's a different specialty. Detective, maybe you should tell me what all this is about. The opele nut's connected with some crime?'

'It's evidence in a homicide case,' said Paz, shortly. 'Are there, let's say, sacrifices associated with this kind of divination?'

'Sacrifices? Well, many of the verses suggest sacrifices, but that usually means a tip to the diviner. Two chickens and ten dollars, that sort of thing.'

'I was thinking more of actual sacrifices. Killing things, right there, maybe before the ritual.'

'Not that I've heard of, but, as I said . . .'

'Yeah, right, you're not an expert. Who would be?'

'In Santería? Well, you have an embarrassment of riches here in Miami. On the faculty, Maria Salazar wrote the book on it.' Dr Herrera reached to the bookshelf behind her, pulled down a thick volume, and handed it to Paz. Its title was simply *Santería*. The dust jacket was red and had a picture of two red-and-yellow-painted wooden axes crossed and lying on top of an ornate covered urn. He flipped the book over. The author's photograph showed a small elderly woman with fine features, her eyes large and deeply shadowed, her hair a halo of white frizz. She was sitting on a stone bench in a garden in front of a live oak covered with epiphytes.

He inscribed the name in his notebook. 'Is she around?'

'From time to time. She's semiretired now. Works mostly out of her home. You'd have to call her. You might also want to talk to Pedro Ortiz.'

Paz wrote this name down too. 'And he is . . .'

'He's a *babalawo*,' said Dr Herrera, smiling again, into his eyes. 'He's considered the best *babalawo* in Miami.'

He returned her look and he had to concentrate on keeping his expression neutral. He knew he had a problem with Cubans of this class, and he worked at it, on his cool. Coolly, then, he asked, 'So anyway, you're not a devotee yourself? You don't believe in this . . . ?' He left the word hanging. It could have been 'crap,' or something more respectful.

'I'm a scientist. Santería uses a lot of herbs, and that's my business, to identify pharmacologically interesting folk medicines. As for the rest, the divination, the *orishas* . . . let's just say that for a certain social class it provides a relatively inexpensive form of therapy and psychological security. If a bunch of uneducated people want to believe that they can call gods down to earth and interest them in Aunt Emilia's bronchitis and Uncle Augusto's sandwich shop, then who am I to say no?' Meaning, people like you.

Paz stood and put his notebook away. 'Thank you very much, Dr Herrera,' he said. 'You've been very helpful.' He walked out, with the patronizing smile burning on his back.

Back in his car, with the A/C roaring, Paz called the university locator number and demanded, with the authority of the police, the home address and phone number of Dr Maria Salazar. The operator hesitated, he bullied, she gave in. A Coral Gables address. But he did not wish to have another interview with another upper-class Cuban lady just yet, although he did not bring this reluctance fully to mind. Instead, he imagined a more important appointment. He called Barlow, got the beeper, left a message. He sat in the car, burned gas to make cool air, watched the fountain play on Lake Osceola, watched the students stroll languorously in and out of the cafeteria, the bookstore, the immense outdoor swimming pool. There was not much evidence of heavy intellectual activity to be observed. Most of the students were dressed as for a day at the beach. A young man walked by the car, stooped over, taking tiny steps. Paz craned his neck and saw that he was following a toddler, a little golden-headed boy. The kid started toward the roadway, and the father scooped his son up in his arms, embraced him, tickled him until the child crowed with delight. Paz turned his face away, and did not feel what most normal people feel when they see paternal love. His stomach tightened and he took several deep breaths.

Paz refocused his attention, and did some light

ogling of the undergraduate girls gliding by. Suntan U. He was not a big fan of the suntan. He preferred wiry women with red hair or blond hair, milky, silky skin and pale eyes, a cliché, he well knew, but there it was. Exogamous, a word he enjoyed. Either like Mom, or not like Mom, one of his girlfriends, a sociologist, had said of male tastes in women. Paz had at the moment three girlfriends in the steady-squeeze category: that sociologist, a child psychologist, and a poet working as a library clerk. He had always had several relationships going on, never more than four, never less than two. Women drifted in and out of this skein at their will. He did not press them to stay, nor did he insist on an exclusivity he was not ready to submit to himself. He was frank with them all about this arrangement, and was rather proud of himself that he never (or almost never) lied to get laid.

His cell phone rang: Barlow. Paz learned that the autopsy was done and also that Barlow had rammed the toxicity screens through as well, which was remarkable. Barlow said, 'Yeah, I pushed them boys some. I figured it was going to be worth it.'

'Was it?'

'Un-huh, I guess so.' This was Barlow-talk for spectacular revelation.

'What?'

'Not on the line. I reckon y'all ought to get back here, though.'

Homicide is on the fifth floor of the Miami PD fortress, a small suite of modern rooms accessible via a card-eating lock. Only homicide detectives have cards.

Inside there is industrial carpeting and a bay with steel desks at which the worker bees sit, and there are private offices for the brass, the captain in charge of the unit and the shift lieutenants. No one was in the bay when Paz walked in but Barlow and the two secretaries.

Barlow nodded to Paz and pointed at a thick manila folder sitting on the corner of his desk. Barlow always had the neatest desk in the bay. It was devoid of decoration, unlike those of the other homicide cops, nor did Barlow have little yellow Post-it notes stuck all over his desk surface and lamp. Barlow kept everything in his head, said the legend, or under lock and key.

Paz went back to his own desk and read the medical examiner's report. First surprise: Deandra Wallace had not died of massive exsanguination resulting from the butchery that had been done on her. Her heart had ceased beating before blood loss would have stopped it. The baby, called Baby Boy Wallace in the report, had been withdrawn alive and operated upon shortly thereafter. The cuts on both mother and infant had been precise, with no hesitation marks observed. Tissue had been removed – here followed a short list – from the heart, liver, and spleen of the mother, and from the heart and brain of the infant. Unlike the mother, the infant had expired from its wounds. The instrument used had been extremely sharp, a short, wide, curved blade, much larger than a surgical scalpel, but smaller than a typical hunting knife. Both mother and infant had been healthy before the events under consideration. The infant was full term and – here another interesting surprise – labor had begun just before death intervened.

Next, the toxicology report. List of organs examined. Findings: negative for a whole list of recreational drugs, including alcohol and nicotine. Positive for: here followed a list of substances Paz had never heard of: tetrahydroharmaline, ibogaine, yohimbine, ouabane, 6-methoxytetrahydroharman, tetrahydra-β-carboline, 6-methoxyharmalan, plus 'several alkaloids of undetermined structure' for which the chemical formulas were given. He sighed, went over to Barlow's desk.

'Any thoughts?'

'None worth a dern until we find out more about what was in that poor girl's body. I can't hardly get to the end of some of them words, and I'm a high-school graduate. You have any luck?'

'Some,' said Paz, and related the results of his recent visits to the two scientists.

After a pause, Barlow said, 'Well. I figured all that'd be something y'all'd know about.'

'Oh, come on, Cletis! Why, because I'm *Cuban*? Where do your people come from? England, way back there, right? You know a lot about Stonehenge? We get some druid dancing around town whacking people with a flint dagger, you're gonna be all *over* his butt.'

'Y'all a lot fresher off the boat than that.'

Paz rolled his eyes. 'Look: you know my mom, right?'

'I do. A fine Christian woman.'

'Uh-huh. Not your brand of Christian, but yeah. Think about it. You think my mom would give the time of day to that kind of sh . . . cow patty? As far as she's concerned, Cuba is the Spanish language and food, period. That's how I was raised. I know as much about Santería as you know about European satanism.'

'Still. Somebody got to talk Spanish to a bunch of witch doctors . . .'

'*Santeros.*'

'See? Y'all's the expert.'

'Oh, for Pete's sake! Cut it out!'

Ordinarily, Paz did not mind this sort of teasing from Barlow. But Dr Herrera had gotten under his skin, the incurable wound prickled, or maybe it was that this case was turning in directions he did not like. The notion that he was going to be some kind of ethnic front man exploring mambo babalou-ay-yay penetrated the armor, as no amount of teasing could. Did Barlow know this? No, Paz was not going to pursue this line.

'What did the tox guy make of all this stuff?' he asked, waving the report.

'Oh, well, they had all the books out, jabbering like a bunch of monkeys. It was hard to get a straight answer out of them, or anyhow, one I could understand, being a country boy. Your ethnowhatdyacallit lady'd probably know. What I got out of it was a bunch of plant poisons. That one with the jawbreaker name's a hallucinogen, and the others are too, mostly. Plus a narcotic. She might've thought she was at the junior prom while he was cutting her.'

'What about cause of death? One of the drugs?'

'Not that they could tell,' Barlow replied, 'but like it says there, they found stuff they never seen before. Could've stopped her heart with them, or it could've been the shock, but her heart was full of blood when it turned off.'

'Well, I'll go back and show this to Herrera,' said Paz valiantly, suppressing the repugnance, 'and see if she can match these chemicals up with some plants. Meanwhile, we should go have a talk with Youghans. Maybe we'll wrap it up with him.'

Barlow gave him a sidelong look. 'What, you think a

homeboy trucker could come up with a bunch a poisons nobody ever heard of?'

'Heck, he don't have to be a pharmacologist. There's two hundred herb joints in this town. He could've just walked into one with a stack of cash and said, 'Hey, I'll take a pound of the worst knockout stuff you got.' '

'Read it again.'

'Read what?'

'That report. No drugs in the stomach contents. Found 'em in her liver and her brain and lungs. Probable route of entry lungs and skin.'

Paz cursed himself. He was usually careful with reports, and he prided himself on being the more literate member of the team. Florida education had not been up to much when Barlow finished high school, and the man had trouble with reports. On the other hand, Barlow kept a lot close to his vest, so maybe that was an act, too, like the cracker slowness.

'Oh, so he burned some stuff and she breathed it,' snapped Paz. 'What does it matter?'

'Him wearing his gas mask while he done it. And it all matters, Jimmy, every little thing.' He got up and walked toward the door. 'Let's see him and ask him how he done it. Go out into the highways and hedges and compel them to come in. Luke 13:23.'

Julius Youghans lived in a frame house on one of the better streets in Overtown. It had trees, now dripping from the recent rain, and the lawns were cut and watered and the newish large cars parked out in front, Caddys and Chryslers and giant SUVs, indicated that the people in the houses had jobs and could probably

have afforded better housing had they not been black
and dwelling in one of the most viciously segregated
and redlined housing markets in the United States. A lot
of the houses had bars on the windows. Mr Youghans's
did not. When the two cops got out of their car a dog
started to bark somewhere in the back and did not cease
barking during the time they remained. Cheaper and
better than bars, a bad dog.

Push the front doorbell. They heard it ringing in the
house. There was a late-model red Dodge Ram pickup
in the driveway, rain-speckled and steaming vapors in
the returned sunlight. The two cops exchanged a look.
Barlow pushed the bell again and Paz went down the
driveway around the side of the house. The dog was a
pit bull, white with a big black spot over one side of his
head. It was leaping up and down like a toy in a nightmare, crashing against the chain-link fence that
confined it to the backyard, spraying slaver past its
bared fangs. Paz ignored it and stood on tiptoe to look
through the window. A kitchen. Crusted dishes in the
sink, a single twelve-ounce can of malt liquor on the
table still wearing six-pack plastic rings in memory of its
vanished brothers. He went back to the front of the
house.

'Checked the back door, did you?' asked Barlow.

'No, I'd thought you'd want to do that, Cletis. You're
the one with the special gift for animals.'

' 'Fraid of a little old dog, huh?'

'Yes, I am. So. Julius must be a heavy sleeper, you
think?'

'That, or he could be in some trouble,' said Barlow,
withdrawing a set of picks wrapped in soft leather from
his breast pocket. 'Maybe fell out of bed and bust his

hip. I believe it's our Christian duty to try and help him if we can.'

The door opened on a living room, which was furnished with the sort of heavy furniture, cheaply made but expensive to buy, available in local marts. Youghans had gone for the red velvet and, his lust for velvet unslaked, had sought it as the matrix for the paintings hanging on the walls: African beauties in undress, a Zulu with spear and shield, and Jesus preaching were the themes. Some care and expense had been taken with the decoration, but the room had a neglected air. There were dust bunnies in the corners and cobwebs on the ceiling. A bottle of expensive cognac, empty, stood on a coffee table with a couple of dirty glasses. Picture: a man with some disposable income, proud, but recently distracted. The walls of the hall they entered next were hung with several examples of the same sort of wooden Africana they had found in the dead woman's apartment, of a somewhat better quality, real ebony rather than stained softwood. Kitchen to the right, two doors to the left: bathroom, a small bedroom clearly used as an office, and at the end of the hall a closed door through which issued interesting sounds: bouncing bedsprings, squeals in a high register and groans in a low one.

In a loud, stagy voice, Barlow said, 'They must be having church in there, Jimmy, that sister calling on the Lord like that. What do you think?'

'I would have to disagree with you there,' said Paz in a similar false bellow. 'I believe we're listening to the sounds of fornication.'

The sounds ceased.

'That's hard to believe,' said Barlow, and, in a good

parody of himself as a peckerwood preacher, continued, 'What kind of low, no-count, scoundrelly hound would be fornicating when the mother of his child just been murdered and is lying all cut to pieces in the morgue? Why, no self-respecting woman would truck with a man like that. A man like that would have to turn to the skankiest, drugged-outest, most disease-infested, ugliest whore in town, and serve him right. Evil man: Cursed shalt thou be in the city and cursed shalt thou be in the field. Deuteronomy 28:16.'

Within, sounds of argument, heating up. The door swung open and out popped a girl in her midteens, plump, brown, and spitting angry, wrapped in a sheet, and carrying an armful of clothes. She pushed past the two detectives, went into the bathroom, and slammed the door. They stood in the bedroom doorway.

'Who the *fuck* are you and what the fuck are you doing in my house?' yelled the man on the bed.

Youghans was a solidly built redbone man in his early forties with a wide brush mustache and thinning hair, thick gold chains at neck and wrist, and a face full of dull sensuality, upon which now bloomed a scowl of frustrated rage. He sat up on the edge of his bed, his loins covered by a scant drape of blue chenille.

After showing their badges and telling him to get dressed, they left the room, and while they waited, they looked around, so that anything in plain sight that might suggest a violation of the law might fall under their eye. They even nudged a few objects into plain sight for that purpose.

'Take a look at this, Cletis.' It had been in plain sight, leaning against a pile of magazines devoted to either sex or autos that sat on one of the side tables in the living

room. Barlow pursed his lips, but said nothing. Paz
stripped an evidence bag from a roll in his jacket
pocket and put the thing in it. He was smiling.

They got the girl's name before she slammed out.
Youghans shuffled into the kitchen some minutes later,
dressed in greasy Bermudas and a red tank top. He
grabbed and popped the tall-boy can of malt liquor,
drank half of it, belched, and said, 'You boys picked a
hell of a time to crash in here. Little bitch was polishing
my pole, man, tight as a three-dollar shoe, mmm-*mm*!
Shit, I was two minutes from getting my nut . . .' He
rubbed his crotch mournfully. 'This is about Deandra,
right? Yeah, I heard she got killed. Fucking building she
was in, I told her to move out of there, but she was the
stubbornist bitch alive, 'bout that and every other goddamn thing else.'

'When was the last time you saw her, sir?' asked
Barlow.

Youghans scratched his head. 'What is this, Monday?
Must've been Saturday night.'

'She was okay when you left her, was she?'

'Sure, running her mouth like always. I'll tell you,
because you're probably gonna hear it in the 'hood, we
did have us some words, shouting and all.'

'What did you fight about?' Paz asked.

'Oh, this hoodoo shit she was into. Hey, I got no
problem with mother Africa dah-dah-de-dah, I got my
kente cloth and all that, stuff on the walls, okay, but she
had this mojo man coming round . . .' He finished his
can in three great swallows. 'Okay, first thing, right
away, I don't appreciate that, I mean him coming round.
I mean, am I the man or ain't I? Two, that nigger messing with her head, you know what I mean? Can't eat

this, can't drink that, quit smoking, take this herb, that herb. Even told her when she could fuck. Shit! So I told her, you know, girl, get real! I told her I didn't want her to see him no more and she threw a shit fit. She said he was this great man, dah-de-dah-dah. Because he give her a number that hit and she bought the fuckin' store out. Like I didn't never give her nothing. She said he was going to make her baby this big deal, used a lot of bullshit African words . . . I lost it, you know? Dumb-ass bitch!'

'You smack her around any?' Paz asked.

'Yeah, I popped her a couple, just before I bugged out of there. Nothing heavy, and I tossed some of her hoodoo crap out the goddamn window.'

A look between the two cops. Paz said, 'Oh, yeah? Like what?'

'Some fucking statue, a little basket full of weeds and shit. Some kind of chain, with, like, big nuts strung along it. Tell the truth I was drunk. I wanted a little piece of ass and no horseshit about the great Wandingo . . .'

'That his name, this guy?' asked Barlow.

'Nah, it's something else, em, something. Mepetene, something like that. Tell you the truth I didn't pay none of that no attention.'

'You ever see him?'

'I had he would've needed a new face. But, no. And I tried, man. She told me he was gonna come one night, oh, couple weeks back, and I hung around outside her crib, maybe five, six hours, but the nigger didn't show. Then, a couple days later, she tells me, oh, he *was* there. What, the motherfucker flew in the window? Only two stairs leading up to that crib and I was watching both of them. Telling lies like that, trying to impress me, fucker can go through walls. I tell you, man, I'm sorry the little bitch dead, but, you know, you fuck with the bull, you get the horns.'

'Sir, are you trying to tell us you think this hoodoo man killed Miss Wallace?' Barlow asked.

'Well, shit! Who the fuck else want to do something like that?'

'Like what, Mr Youghans?' asked Paz gently.

'Oh, you know, slice her up like they done.'

'How did you know that, sir?' More gently still.

'Shit, her brother called me up and told me. Cursed me out, too, the lame little motherfucker. Blame me for it. Me? Shit!'

'So where were you between, say, eleven Saturday night and two Sunday morning?' asked Barlow.

In bed, was the answer, unusually as it turned out, alone but for the crotch magazines, and so they all went downtown, with Paz's heart singing tra-la-la, because this was going to be a grounder after all.

When he had Youghans in the little room, with Barlow looking on silently, Paz did the usual act, kicking chairs. You piece of shit, Youghans, you were drunk. You were pissed off. You had a fight. You admitted that. And then it went too far – you stuck her, and then you got scared, and you started thinking. You cut her up. You made it look weird, like some loony did it. And you made it all up, didn't you, the hoodoo man. And what about this?

Paz stuck it in front of Youghans's face, the thing he had found in the apartment. A framed picture of Youghans and an unpregnant Deandra Wallace in happier days, the glass covered with little brown spatters.

'You took this out of there after you killed her. You didn't want anyone to think about you, did you? That's blood, Youghans. Her blood. That you put there when you cut her open. You bastard!' He leaped across the table at Youghans and grabbed a handful of shirt, shook the man and screamed into his face. Then he allowed Barlow to pull him off, as per script, and toss him out of the interview room, with appalled commentary.

Paz got a cup of coffee and strolled back to where a one-way window gave on the room, hooked a chair with his foot, and sat down to watch Barlow work. Barlow was the best good cop in the business, and seemed particularly effective with black and Hispanic suspects. They seemed grateful that a fellow who looked and sounded like the Grand Kleagle was as calm and considerate as a social worker on quaaludes. Paz watched the action, without flipping the switch to bring sound across the thick glass. It was more restful that way and he got to concentrate on the body language. He couldn't see Barlow's face, only the hunch of his back as he leaned over the table. He could see Youghans's face, though, as it went through a series of transformations. Anger first, the brows knotted, the mouth gaping to shout, then confusion, the eyes wide and staring, the mouth slack, and then the collapse – tears, a rictus of sorrow, sobbing, and the hands brought up in shame, the head drooping. Paz looked at his watch. A little under forty minutes, not a bad time, even for Barlow.

Paz got a pad and pen from his desk and went to the interview room. Barlow met him at the door.

Paz said, 'He looks ready to write.'

'Let's leave him be for a while, Jimmy.'

'Don't you want to get the confession while he's in the mood?'

'No confession. You know he didn't do that girl.'

'What! For Christ's sake, Cletis . . . sorry. Then what the . . . what were you doing in there all this time?'

'I was helping a soul to Jesus. A man can't live the way that man's been living without its eating away at him. He really cared for that girl, you know. I just helped him to see that and see that what he was doing, the fornicating, the drinking, well, that was just a way of trying to forget what-all'd happened to her, and that maybe part of it was his fault, taking advantage of her, pulling her away from the church so she was bait for that devil.'

'Jesus *Christ*! What're you talking about? He had the damn picture with her blood on it.'

Barlow's eyes, the color of an inch of water in a tin pail, turned sharply colder.

'Jimmy, I'll thank you not to take our Lord's name in vain.'

'Sorry, but . . . I thought . . . I thought we *had* him.'

'I know you did, and I'm sorry to disappoint you, but that's not our man. You *know* that in your heart, now, don't you?'

Paz took a quick step away, kicked the baseboard hard, and cursed to himself in Spanish. Of course he did, and he knew why he'd concocted what now seemed like an absurd case against that pathetic lowlife.

He breathed deeply for a moment, facing the wall, head drooped. Then he turned around. 'Yeah, right. All right.'

Barlow strolled back to his desk and sat in his chair,

Paz trailing along after him, and then resumed as if
nothing had happened. 'But we know a couple more
things about our fella. One, he thinks he's real clever.
He went around back under Deandra's window and
picked up all his Africa things, 'cause we sure didn't find
any when we looked. He walked into that living room
with a handful of blood and sprayed it on the wall, and
then he took Youghans's picture off the wall and walked
into Youghans's place, where he knew we'd find it. A
frame.'

'So to speak. What's the other thing?'

'Oh, just something funny. He said that little thing he
was with when we showed up, she came over about
noon today. He says he was in his place all morning,
with the doors locked and that dog in the yard. Now, he
also says that picture wasn't there when he went to bed
last night and it wasn't there when he let his honey in.
And between then and when we showed up, the dog
didn't make a sound.'

'So how did the picture get there?'

Barlow gave him a long, considering look. 'Uh-hn,
that's the right question. How did it?'

'Somebody the dog knew and wouldn't bark at,' Paz
suggested.

'Possible, but not likely. Man says the dog barks at
leaves falling down from the trees. Barks at the man's
momma. Barked when the girlfriend came.'

Barlow grimaced, showing a mouthful of crooked,
yellowing, rural-bad-dental-care-type teeth. He rubbed
his face vigorously. Paz thought of a big yellow dog shaking itself.

'What, Cletis? Tell me,' Paz said when he couldn't
stand it anymore.

'When you're in the church,' said Barlow, 'when you're a churchgoing person, a believer, you believe in things you can't see. Eye hath not seen, nor ear heard, neither have entered into the heart of man, the things which God hath prepared for them that love him. Corinthians 2:9.'

Paz resisted the impulse to shove and needle. This had happened before, between them, it was part of Cletis's thing, and Paz had seen the older man crack cases in this way.

'I've seen miracles,' Barlow continued. 'I know you don't believe me, but that don't matter. I know what my eyes have seen. It was . . . two times in my life it was given to me to see glory, praise Jesus. Now, the devil can't do miracles, can he?'

Barlow was looking at him differently. It was not a rhetorical question. Paz gave it serious thought. 'Why can't he? If you believe the movies, devils can do all kinds of weird stuff. I mean, he wouldn't be much of a devil if he couldn't, like, give you money, or make you terrific looking.'

'You believe that, do you?'

'No, I don't *believe* it,' said Paz, exasperated now. 'I'm just saying, if you give me that there's a devil, then it follows that he's got magic powers. Logically.'

Barlow scratched behind his ear. 'Logically, eh? Tell me this, then: Exodus 7:10. Aaron casts his rod upon the ground and it becomes a serpent. And Pharaoh calls in his sorcerers and magicians of Egypt and they do the same thing, their rods become serpents, too. So, do you think they were the same kind of snakes?'

'I don't know, Cletis. It wasn't my case.'

Barlow ignored this. 'They were not the same, no sir!

The Lord caused Aaron's rod to become a real snake, but the magician's rods stayed plain old rods. They just made everyone think they were snakes. You see the difference?'

'Uh-huh. God makes real miracles, but the devil just tricks us.' Paz said this like a bored schoolboy in a catechism class. The payoff was not too distant.

'That's right. The devil can't do miracles, 'cause he's got no power of creation. Only the Lord has power of creation. The Lord can send an angel through walls, through the roof, anywhere he likes, but the devil's got to use the door. The only power the devil's got is what we give him, all he's got is power over whatsoever mind that is not turned to the Kingdom, which is you and me, son. And all the other poor sinners out there. The devil can twist your mind into a knot. That's who we need to look for.'

'Who? The devil? Okay, I figure our perp for around eight foot six, red complexion, wears a little beard, distinguishing marks – horns, tail, little hooves. I'll get that right out on the wires. He shouldn't be hard to spot.'

Barlow waggled a finger. 'Don't mock, Jimmy,' he said quietly. 'I know you like to, but you can't do it around this here case. It ain't good for your health.'

'What're you saying? Cut to the chase, here.'

'I'm saying look at the facts. A girl killed and cut up, and not just a girl, a girl about to have a baby. The baby's cut up too. Not just cut up in a crazy way, neither, cut up just so, in a ritual way. Two, she let whoever did it do it without fighting any, that we could see.'

'But she was drugged.'

'There was chemicals in her body, but she didn't take them through her mouth. They just got there and we don't know how, and right now we don't know what they do. For all we know, they might've made her wide awake, and she just told him to go ahead.'

'That's nuts.'

'Uh-huh. To us, but you been in the police long enough to know people do all kinds of awful stuff to themselves and other folks, stuff that seems just fine at the time. Something gets in 'em, and then later, that's just what they say. You heard it yourself about four hundred times. I don't know what got into me.'

'That's a figure of speech.'

'Yeah, but it wasn't always just a figure of speech. Not back in Bible times, it wasn't. Our Lord was always casting devils out of folks. And maybe not even now, when you come to think on it. Then we got the other fact, that this fella seems to go where he wants to, and no one sees him, not even dogs. It takes some doing to get past a dog.' He fixed Paz with his eye and said, matter-of-factly, 'I guess, when you put that together we're looking for someone with demonic powers, God help us.'

Paz goggled for a moment and then felt a flash of raw anger. There wasn't going to a be a brilliant payoff after all. With some force, he said, 'Oh, for crying out loud! Look, we have exactly one informant for all this, and he might've been half in the bag at the time when. I'll tell you what the *real* facts are. We got a perp did a killing, and he dressed it up with all kinds of African hoodoo. Is he wacko? I'll give you that. Is he some kind of spook with weird mystic powers? No, he's not. No offense, but that kind of stuff isn't real, not anymore it isn't. You want to believe it happened back in Bible times, hey, I respect your beliefs, but this is now, and we're looking for a regular guy, a regular homicidal maniac, not the spawn of Satan. Talk about something getting into people – what's got into *you*? I mean, unless you're pulling my leg . . .'

Barlow nodded calmly as Paz rapped this out, and said, 'No, I was never more serious in my life.' He sighed heavily and stood up. 'Well, we'll see, won't we? For the wisdom of this world is foolishness with God. For it is written, He taketh the wise in their own craftiness. First Corinthians 3:19.' He patted Paz absently on the arm. 'You'll want to write up your report. Just put in the facts, for now.'

SEVEN

I do not panic. I go back to Records and finish my day, alphabetical order being such a comfort in periods of tension, and it gives me time to think. Thought before action, not jumping to conclusions: aikido, anthropology, and Olo sorcery are in agreement here. I pause behind cabinet OR-OSH, get centered, and think. He's in town, or he's got a disciple in town, both possible. Who knows what he's been up to these last years? He could have hundreds, a whole cult. The important thing, does he know where I am? Not likely. New name, low profile, not doing a lot to attract his attention. I'm supposed to be dead, anyway.

The homeboys don't notice me on the way back to my car. It's after school and they are being vamped by girls who are more in tune with the times. I get into my stifling junker and think about Margaret Mead, the mother of all us girl anthropologists, and about what she would think of this. Our world is changing so fast that the kids have to figure it all out for themselves, so they reject the parents' experience as nonrelevant. A very sixties view, Margaret, and explains hippies and hip-hop but doesn't explain me. I was thirteen when she died, and never met her, but Marcel knew her quite well, thought her a nice lady, good writer, knew zip about

culture, depending as she did throughout her career on
the honesty of her informants. They all lie, darling, he
would say to me, all the informants lie. Wouldn't you?
What would you do if a person in a weird hat and the
wrong color skin accosted you on the street and asked
you, You like fuckee-fuck, eh, girlee? When you start
fuckee? Who you do it with? Old men? Boys? Other
girls? How many times? You likee orgasms? You let boy
touch-em titties? You like suck-em willie? Would you
tell this ridiculous person the truth? You would not. I
once actually peed on his foot I was laughing so hard at
one of these riffs. Marcel was not a great believer in
mere objectivity. Objectivity is the leprosy of anthropology, one of his sayings. French intellectuals are
obliged to come up with pithy, witty apothegms, and he
was no exception.

The breeze from the car window is somewhat cooler
than the waft from a hair dryer on low, but I am not
much bothered by this. People who are excessively
attached to the creature comforts would be well advised
to eschew anthro as a career. The temperature in my
car right now approximates the shade temperature
inside my *bon* in Uluné's compound at Danolo, during
nearly the whole of the dry season. My sense memories
are returning, I think. I attribute this to the child. Now,
for example, I pick up Luz in the cool shade of the
patio at Providence and I am nearly overcome by a
recollection of being held by my father, on our dock. I
must have been about Luz's age, the age when you can
still ride comfortably in an adult's arms, held easily by
one hand under your bottom. It's low tide, and I can
smell the tidal stink around us. We're at the dinghy
basin and we've just finished a ride in our tender.

My father smells of tobacco, marine varnish, and wood dust.

Luz is carrying a paper sack. When we are in the car she shows me what is in it. It's a present, she says, it's for candoos. A great lump of baked Sculpey in the shape of a candleholder, with thick flowers stuck on and all painted primrose yellow with cobalt blue splotches. Nice Ms Lomax must have pressed the butt of a candle into the soft clay because this part looks quite functional. I appreciate it lavishly. No one has given me anything for some time. We make a special trip down Grand to the rich folks' Grove to buy a candle to fit in it. We stop at the thrift shop and rummage like the poor people we are and Luz finds a tattered *Goodnight Moon*, which I gratefully buy for fifty cents.

So we dine by candlelight. I have made a big fruit salad with cottage cheese, which she seems to like, and which helps to cool me down. After dinner, she has to blow out the candle and I have to relight it many times. When I was studying aikido, sensei used to make us douse candles with our fists, to practice speed and control. The point is to compress a column of air in front of your fist and stop your knuckles dead a few millimeters short of the flame. It's harder than it looks, like everything in aikido. Or sorcery for that matter. Without thinking, to entertain Luz, I snap out my fist and find that I can still do it. More, demands Luz, and I light the wick again and then I recall how her mother died and feel a rush of grinding shame. While I am thus self-absorbed, Luz attempts the trick and slams her little fist into the candle and spills hot wax over her hand and forearm. Wails and a rush to the sink for cooling water. I bring her back into countenance with sleight-of-hand tricks. I take some quarters from a jar where I keep my spare change. I make them walk across my knuckles and I vanish them and produce them from her ears and hair and off my tongue, fingertip productions, toss vanishes, flick vanishes, French drops, and coins-through-table as a finale. I am good at this, I could amaze those even older than four. Marcel always said that legerdemain was the root of sorcery, and one of the field anthropologist's most valuable tools. It is all about attention, magic. Most of the rest of life is about attention, too.

After the tricks, we lie in my hammock together in our sleeping T-shirts and I read to her, all her books, in the order she likes them, the bird book first, then Bert and Ernie, then the new *Goodnight Moon*, a great success, three times and she's out. I had *Goodnight Moon*, too, and although I suppose my mom must have put me to bed sometimes, I can't recall being read to by anyone but my father.

Sleep won't come. There is a gibbous moon and a scent of jasmine. I rock slowly in the hammock. On its uproll the mesh overlays my view of the treetops and the cloud-scudded moonlit sky. Mesh or line, our lives, one of the great questions. I have been shaken by what happened in the office today, the old lady and the *dulfana* and the news about the slaughtered pregnant girl. Stuff is breaking loose, like rock from an eroding cliff, and poor Dolores is hanging on by her fingernails. Jane Doe is yelling from her tomb, Hey, Dolores! I'm all squashed down here, lemme out! Not yet, Jane, says Dolores. Things are still too obscure. A bird calls from the yard outside:

Whit-purr Whit-purr Whit-purr WHIT WHIT

My blood curdles, a fist presses down on my heart. It can't be, but I know very well that it could. It is the unmistakable call of a honeyguide. I have heard it a thousand times in Africa, but there are no honeyguides in South Florida. We used to say it was calling my husband; that was before we knew what the honeyguide meant, its ways, that it was a kind of sorcerers' mascot because of its magical powers, how it got men to do its work of busting up beehives, how it was never stung. How it eviscerated the nestlings of other birds with a special scalpel-like tooth on its beak.

I go through the door to the landing and listen. Ordinary twitters and creaks. Imagination. Funk. As sweat dries on my skin, I go back to the hammock. Not a honeyguide, not yet. An auditory hallucination. Speaking of which . . .

I'm thinking that it must have been just around now, a little earlier perhaps, that I first laid eyes on Marcel Vierchau. It was finals week, and I was in my Barnard room studying French and hating it, wanting to be home, out sailing, at the beach. I am quite good with languages, the speaking part at least, which put me into French lit classes over my head. This was Twentieth-Century French Prose. Colette was fine, but Sartre? Derrida? Not in balmy June. My junior year: so, fourteen years ago. I remember feeling the need to get out of the room, take a walk, get a cold one, maybe lie on the grass or join the perpetual volleyball game in front of Minor Latham for a while. The point is, I was just about to go out, I was looking for my wallet, at that very moment, that's how close I was to *not* having my life changed, when Tracy O'Neill came barging in and said,

Come on, we're going to see Marcel Vierchau. And I
said, Who's Marcel Vierchau, and she said he's the
world's greatest anthropologist, dummy, and he's
gorgeous, we're all going to go over to Low Library and
sit in the front row and masturbate. I said I wanted to
get a beer and she grinned and held out the remains of
a six-pack of Bud, sweaty-cold.

So we went, maybe five or six of us, all dorm rats,
sick of the lamp and up for something rich and strange.
Low Library rotunda is the largest venue on the
Columbia campus and they needed the seats. Maybe
three hundred people showed up, well over half passing
for maidens. We didn't get to sit in the very front, but we
had good position, well within masturbation range, as
O'Neill remarked.

The star was introduced by a dim old soul, a relic of
the Mead era named Matson, or Watson. She told us
that Vierchau was a rare piece of cheese, an ornament of
the Musée de l'Homme in Paris, French Academy, U.S.
Academy of Sciences (hon.), author of *Sorcerer's
Apprentice*, twenty-nine weeks on the *Times* bestseller
list, and on and on, lists of publications, editorships,
adding up to the hottest French anthropologist since
Lévi-Strauss (his mentor, in fact), ran the hundred in
10.1, could bench 350, and had a penis like a baguette.
O'Neill, spluttering, added these, and we were all making a small spectacle of ourselves, when the lady came
to the end of her dithyramb, and Vierchau walked out
on the stage.

Well. He really was gorgeous to the point of absolute
unfairness. I am afraid we gaped. The hair was the first
thing, a huge thick flowing mop, sunset-colored,
touched with silver on the sides, remarkable, threw a

glow out across the audience like a baby spot. Beneath this, the necessary broad brow, deep-set sea-blues behind round wire-rims, prow of a nose, icebreaker chin, and lips, as they say, red as wine. He was wearing what he almost always wore, a dark silk turtleneck, a Harris tweed jacket, and dark, beautifully cut Italian slacks.

The applause died down, he paused, smiled, wiggled his eyebrows to show that he did not take himself that seriously, thanked Watson or Matson, reminded her that she had neglected to mention his membership in the Bicycle Club of France. Titters. 'Our species,' he began, 'is approximately a hundred thousand years old.' I suppose I must have heard that speech at least fifty times, and read it too; it was the basis for an article in *Nature* in 1986. 'I must give the Speech again, Jeanne-Claire,' he would say, flourishing another invitation. He always added some new stuff, as research advanced, but basically it was the same line: his life's work. And misleading in the extreme, he always added. Only for the goyim, he used to say. So I can easily put together the themes here in my head, swinging in the moonlight.

A hundred thousand years ago, people with the same sort of brains we all have, speaking languages no less complex, lived, worked, loved, and died. Recorded history, however, begins between eight and six thousand years ago, coincident with the development of agriculture in several regions of the Old World. Before that, a great silence, some ninety thousand years of silence. And so I wonder, what were those people doing with those so excellent brains all those endless days and nights? Not working all the time. Hunter-gatherers in benign climates do not work very hard. Their tools are simply made, as are their shelters. Most hunter-gatherer tribes work fewer hours a week than Frenchmen; *far* fewer than Americans. So what do they do? This, to me, is one of the great tasks of anthropological science, to penetrate the great silence, using as our informants the tiny number of people who are still making their livings that way.

So, I ask you, what would *you* do, with your marvelous brain, all those centuries? No books, no writing, few man-made things, little pressure from the environment, no television or radio, no newspapers, only the same hundred or so people to talk to? I think you would play with the environment, *Homo ludens*, after all, and you would become intimate with it. You would invent art, to symbolize this. You would develop an intimacy with your environment so deep that we children of industrial civilization can scarcely imagine it, an intimacy deeper, perhaps, than we have with our lovers or our children, perhaps even deeper than we have with our own alienated bodies. They would be *participants* in an environment that was alive in the same way that they themselves were alive, whereas we are merely observers of an environment that is dead. All the little particles, yes? Yes. And another thing we would play with would be the most interesting thing in our environment, which is the human mind, our own minds and those of others. And with this, very slowly, centuries and centuries, remember, a technology develops. This technology is based not on the manipulation of the objective world, as our own is, but rather on the manipulation of the subjective world. Now, you may be familiar with the statement by the British scientist and science-fiction writer Arthur C. Clarke, in which he states: any sufficiently advanced technology will appear to be magic. Just so. And what I am proposing is that among traditional cultures there is a sufficiently advanced technology of which we know very little, and what little we do know of it we denigrate, yes? And for want of a better term, we call this magic.

Here he always paused, to let it sink in. The scientists in the crowd would look nervously at one another, the New Age types would beam and chortle. Yes, magic, he would say. Even the word itself connotes charlatanism, the phony, what is not to be taken seriously. From *magi*, the word the ancient Greeks contemptuously used for itinerant Persian conjurers. Today, in the West, to all sensible people, it means theatrical trickery, like this.

At this point he would take an egg out of his pocket. You have all seen this a hundred times, yes? I make the egg vanish, so. I produce it out of an empty hand, so. And out of my mouth, so. I drop it from one hand and catch it in my other hand – so – but the egg has vanished from the lower hand. You all saw it drop, but it is not where you thought it was. Ah, it is still in the hand that dropped it. But no. There is nothing in either hand. Technically, called a vanish-and-acquitment. But here is the egg again out of my ear. Technically, a production. You marvel, yes. Finally, I crack the egg on the podium and abracadabra! It turns into a pigeon which flies up to the ceiling. Do not worry, please, this pigeon is an indoor pigeon and will not make a mess.

Gasps. Screams. Vast applause.

His eyes crinkle entrancingly behind the glittering lenses. So, let us deconstruct what you have just seen. I am French, therefore I deconstruct. First, all of us bring to this phenomenon a cultural load. We do not observe it objectively; there is no such thing. And this load tells us that there is no magic. What you are observing is merely legerdemain. You cannot tell me how I did it, perhaps, you cannot explain what you saw, but you have utter confidence that the egg did not actually vanish, that the pigeon did not actually appear out of the egg. But let us take a poll, this being America: who here thinks I have actual magical powers?

Half a dozen hands shot up, waving wildly, us girls, *naturellement*, and a few of the crystal-and-patchouli crowd. Laughter, in which he joined.

I will be available for worship after the lecture, he remarked, to more chuckling. But most of you do not, and properly so, for you are all materialist empiricists. That is your culture. Of course there are people who simply believe in magic in the same way that some of you believe in a religion, but this is not what I am talking about. Again, this is a technology. It works whether you believe in it or not, just as a pistol will shoot you dead whether or not you believe that there are such things as pistols. What I just did with the egg and the pigeon was to demonstrate one element of this technology, which is the control of the consciousness of one person, or a group of persons, by another. I created an illusion, yes? One easily penetrated by the powers of science. But I am not interested in the mechanics; I am only interested in the psychic reality, the distraction itself. Among traditional peoples where the shamanic technologies are well developed, the manipulation of consciousness has advanced to a much higher degree. We have ample evidence that, for example, shamans and sorcerers can enter the dreams of sleeping people and stage-manage the dream state. Sorcerers can elicit in their subjects psychic states that are somewhere between dreaming and sleeping, so that the subject entertains elaborate illusions that seem undeniably real, a kind of induced psychosis. Sorcerers can play with some skill on the interactions between mind and body, an area in which scientific medicine is almost entirely incompetent. We speak, for example, of the placebo effect in a drug trial as junk data. We toss it out, yes? We are only interested in the drug effect, so we design the double-blind trial, no one knows what is the pharmaceutical and what is the sugar pill. The patients who get rid of the cancer or whatever with the sugar pill, we don't worry about them. They are of no interest. And when someone is sick, or in pain, and we cannot find an organic, a material cause, we dismiss it. It is *only* psychosomatic, we say. And the mental diseases . . .

Yes, those mental diseases. A scratching rustle on the roof, claws, and a grunting sound. It's happening again. I stop swinging in the hammock, my chest tightens, and my *ki* leaps up into my throat. I get out of the hammock and my knees barely support me. Deep breaths now, controlled breathing. When everything is reeling out of control, still you can control your own breathing, push the *ki* gently down where it belongs. So my sensei advised, and so I do now, and it works. The first time I was attacked by a witch, it was just like this.

More scratching and snarling and a heavy thump on the landing at the top of our steps. The child stirs in her sleep. I walk trembling to the door, wondering if I have enough *komo* in my hidden box and whether I can remember the spell. If this really is a *jinja* . . .

But upon stepping out onto the landing what I see is the fat ass of a momma raccoon waddling down my stairs, accompanied by her two kits.

I collapse on the top step, making a peculiar noise somewhere between hysterical laughter and tears. How bland and restful nature! How like Dolores not to know that there was a raccoon nesting in the neighborhood. Jane would have known.

The raccoon family vanishes into the thick foliage at the edge of the yard. There's a faint breeze, but it's blowing away from Polly Ribera's house, and so the dog Jake does not smell the raccoons and set up a holler. I don't go back to my hammock. This is unusual; Dolores does not like the night, a bed-by-ten girl ordinarily. The step I am sitting on is rough, however, and is pressing uncomfortably into my meager bottom, and so I stand and stretch and descend into the garden. I am wearing nothing but the size-large T-shirt I sleep in, a thrift-shop purchase, ragged on the bottom and washed thin as paper, bearing the logo of the Miami Marlins.

Rough grass against my feet, between my toes. I used to go barefoot in Danolo; Uluné recommended it, for drawing power from the earth. And worms too. A good deal of the sorcerer's pharmacopoeia is devoted to vermifuges. I stand in the garden and open myself to the night just a crack, arms hanging, legs apart, face up for a moonbath, so good for the complexion, as the Olo believe. Sounds, the hum of the air conditioners, distant traffic, the odd airliner. Filter those out. The tiny sigh of the breeze, creeping through the half mile of city from the bay, just strong enough to make animalish flappings in the leathery crotons, enough to stir my moronic hair-do against my ears and forehead, stir my pubic hair against the tender neglected flesh of my groin.

Oh, and there's night, there's night, when wind full of cosmic void feeds on our faces, as Rilke says, O and I wish this wind would eat my face, chew me down to the old Jane, Jane before Africa, I miss her so.

But not before Marcel, no, and that day I saw him first, golden and full of magic powers. He went on, then, to describe his theory of deep interpretation; we must be like divers he said, like Captain Cousteau, immersed in the culture, so that we comprehend its subjective reality, in our own hearts and souls. It is like literature, he said. If you ask me to tell you about Proust and I say (and here he mimicked a dry academic voice) Proust is eighteen centimeters by twelve and four centimeters thick, colored green, and consisting of five hundred and seventy-two printed pages on which the following words appear: 'the': six thousand seven hundred fifty-two times; 'of': six thousand twenty-two . . . bah! You would think me a cretin, yes? This is anthropology. They want to be objective, like physicists, so they don't ever truly *read* the book. You must read the book and let it work on your heart, and then, if you can, interpret it to your own people. And this is dangerous, as it is for scuba divers. You may *swim* like a fish, and the *fish* may think you're a fish, but don't throw away your tank and try to breathe water.

Then he told about his seven years with the Chenka in Siberia, his training as a shaman, his adventures in the spirit world. There were slides with this part.

Marcel in native dress, Marcel with various shamans, Marcel on a shaggy pony, indistinguishable from a dozen other Chenkas on shaggy ponies. Middle-distance shots, these, no faces showing. He had lived with these guys for seven years on the Siberian steppe, during which he had virtually no contact with the outer world.

I whispered to O'Neill, 'This is like Castaneda, with yurts.'

'Not like Castaneda,' she said. 'You read his book?'

I had not. 'Read it,' she said. 'It's got forty pages of footnotes. He's got reams of data, tapes, the works. It's real science; he kept his hose connected while he was doing all that. Castaneda is fiction.'

We got shushed. Marcel went into his peroration, a rant about the imbecility of objective, reductionist explanations of human consciousness. It was, he said, like a New Guinea tribesman being plonked down in New York. What would he understand? Next to nothing. He would not even be able to *see* anything but vague and alarming shapes. When Captain Cook arrived in Australia, the aborigines failed to see his frigate, although it was sitting just offshore. They had no mental compartment to put it in, so they ignored it. The city of consciousness is just as baffling to the Western mind as Manhattan to the tribesman. Do we understand pain? No. Do we understand dreams? No, nor addiction, nor mental illness, nor desperate love, nor the anger that creates war and crime. Consciousness, the one common experience of mankind, is also the last unexplored country, a challenge to the scientist, but the very métier of the sorcerer. Thank you. Thunderous applause.

My head was, as they say, in a whirl. O'Neill noticed

and asked me if anything was wrong. Nothing was wrong. I had found my Life's Vocation. I didn't say that, though; I made my face all phony-dreamy and said, 'I'm in love!' True also, but I didn't know it then. O'Neill released her famous dirty snicker.

We all giggled out of Low, like a bunch of teenies from a boy-band concert, and down Low steps. And then we all went back to the books, except me. I snuck off up the hill to the bookstore, where I bought *Sorcerer's Apprentice*, and Lévi-Strauss's *The Savage Mind*, and the text for Anthro 101; to the corner place, where I bought an Italian hero and a quart of Coke; and back to my room, where I shit-canned Sartre in French and read Vierchau and Lévi-Strauss in English, all the night through, and in the morning I bought a couple of whites from the dorm pusher and went into my French exam flying.

I should have failed but, magically (*magically!*), one selection for translation was from Colette's *Mes Apprentissages*, which I love, and knew well, and the other was from (wait for it!) *L'Apprenti du Sorcier*, and screw all of you who memorized vast uncharted realms of Foucault and Derrida.

Then I went to my adviser and got my major changed to anthropology, and later to the registrar and talked my way into a couple of already-closed summer session introductory courses, and signed up for sixteen credits in anthro and related subjects for my senior year. They wouldn't let me into the seminar that Vierchau was teaching in the fall, distinguished visiting professor, very selective, no way, that was by invitation only, but I could audit with the instructor's written permission. Which was an excuse to go see him.

Back here in the now, the moon pops out from behind her low cloud, casting into silhouette the tall coco palms in the next street, and the breeze picks up a trifle and veers north. The palm fronds set up a gentle clatter and at that moment a mockingbird starts to sing. Entrancing. I am entranced, which I have not allowed myself to be for some time. I used to be quite good at it, so said Uluné. A technical term in sorcery, of course, *ilegbo* in Olo, but among us materialistas most often only figuratively used. Tears are rolling down my cheeks now, as the creature sings its tiny heart out against the castanets of the coco palms and the low hissing of the other foliage. The American nightingale, so called, a good substitute and no hungry generations tread it down either. Oh, I don't need this, and I need it badly. For the first time since Africa it occurs to me that this life-in-death is not forever. I look up at the moon and in my trance it seems to stop moving against the clouds, the wind stops, and the clatter stops, and even the nightingale stops singing, and everything is for one long instant made of shining stone.

'Okay, thank you, I get it, I get it!' I say out loud. And the world cranks up again, moon, wind, palm, and mockingbird, all having their being, and me too. A little apotheosis in the night, hasn't happened in a long time to me, and was always rare, they don't like you to look behind the machinery of nature, uh-uh, pay no attention to the man behind the curtain. The bird stops singing and flies off, the moon slides behind a thicker cloud bank, the garden grows dark, the wind seems to drop a few knots, or maybe that's my imagination. In any case, show's over. As I climb the stairway, I notice my body feels different, and I pause and puzzle for a moment about it. Ah, yes. The Dolores slouch is missing. I am walking like Jane. This won't do, but oh, my, it's going to pinch and tickle climbing into that heavy, scratchy costume again. I was trained to stand up straight and be proud of my height and my big-boned body. *Winsoum she wase, and like a jolly colte, tall as a maste and straight as a bolte:* my husband, quoting Chaucer, of me, lovingly. Faire Alisoun, in 'The Miller's Tale.'

Where does love go when it's gone?

I am aware that my disguise is something of a libel on the actual Dolores Tuoey, S.M., who did not slouch, and whose poor taste in clothing and coiffure (if any) was masked by the modified habit she wore and her neatly cropped head. I didn't know her well, but she was a figure on the streets of Bamako and the outlying district. I model thus a product of my sick imagination: what Dolores would be like had she betrayed everything she believed in, her sisters and her church. This phantasm would, I think, be as repugnant to Dolores as it is to me.

I lie back in my hammock, and unconsciously I hook my toes into the strands of the edges on either side, opening my genitals to the tropic breezes. My hammock is a Yucatan string model, colored red, green, yellow, purple, of the larger sort called *matrimonio*, although, of course, I sleep in it alone. How to fuck in a hammock without falling out was one of the very many things taught to me by Marcel Vierchau, and I find that, what with the night, the night, and the poetry, and thinking about Marcel and my nonflaming, but nevertheless hotter than now, youth, I feel unaccustomed warmth and humidity among the nether petals. Father forgive me, it has been three years and 220 days since my last decent fuck. No, none of that, now. I am in enough trouble and I am not ready to . . .

I unhook my toes and press my legs together and roll up with sheet and pillow into the fetal crouch in which I generally sleep, and after a bit I think, not ready for what? Run, do nothing, fight. I ran already. I am more disinclined than formerly to do it again. I am presently doing nothing, but with increasing discomfort. Almost four years is a long time, a jail sentence for a fairly serious felony, although the worst of what I did is probably in the codes of neither Florida nor the state of New York. Maybe the kid makes me eligible for parole.

Which leaves fighting. The way of sorcery is often about healing, and fate, and other spiritual activities, but day in and day out it is about war, mainly skirmishes, brief firefights, I sock your guy so you blow up my guy. This goes on in Miami and New York and L.A. all the time, anyplace where *brujos*, *hougans*, *curanderos*, and *santeros* are found among the believing immigrant communities. Marcel used to point out that it was a great error to imagine that traditional technologies of power were controlled by people any less rotten in the main than those who controlled industrial technologies of power. Spiritual don't mean nice. Inuit and !Kung villages have, and always have had, murder rates in excess of those current in Miami, and most of these killings are due directly or indirectly to sorcery. There are saints and the wise among shamans, of course, but they are about as common as saints and the wise among generals, corporation presidents, and politicians.

Oh yes, fighting. Back in the day, the Melanesians living in the Solomon Islands had wars of a sort, twenty or so young guys all stoned on kava, with clubs and spears, mixing it up, maybe a busted arm or two, a rare busted head, and maybe they thought they knew what war was like, but when in 1942 the marines landed and blasted the Japanese out of the Solomons, those guys all learned something about a different kind of war, the few that survived. If my husband really is here, and I have to fight him, we will start in Miami something that stands in relation to the kind of petty crap that goes on in the Cuban and the Haitian communities as the battle of Guadalcanal stands to a Melanesian clubfest. I have to decide whether letting him kill me, or worse, is preferable to that. *Collateral casualties* is, I think, the term of art. A deeply moral question. And there's the little girl.

The Olo call it *jiladoul*, the sorcerers' war. You wonder why there are only twelve hundred Olo left. That's why. It's all a matter of technology.

And there was a time I didn't believe that either. Last thought before plunging into the grateful dark. A memory.

Marcel and I are in Paris, after our first night in his apartment on Rue Louis-David in Passy, behind the Palais de Chaillot, where the Museé de l'Homme is. Pearly dawn is peeping in. It's June again, a year after I first laid eyes on him, I'm a graduate of Barnard and I have finally let us go to bed together, and am glad I did and also glad I held off for so long. We have been at it all night, something I've never done before, not that I was at the time any kind of expert in the love arts, although he, as I have just learned, is. I am twenty-one, and it is my first serious, industrial-strength, heavy-duty, military-specification fuck. He is five years younger than my father, but I have almost stopped thinking about this. We are on his bed, sticky and exhausted, staring up at the high cream ceiling, with a flap of sheet over us, the French windows are open and that Paris scent is coming through, sharp and tickling to the nose. Marcel whispers in my ear and runs his hand down my body and places it on my sopping what I have just learned to call *le con*. I mumble about being sore, and then I feel something cool and hard and smooth inside me, and he draws out an egg. I guffaw and say gosh, I didn't think I was ovulating, and he laughs, too, and claps his hands together, crushing the egg, and out flies the pigeon. I have this stupid frozen smile on my face.

Legerdemain. Leger-my-ass! The pigeon flutters around the room and finally alights on top of a high wardrobe. We've been together all night. He is grinning at me. He's *naked.* I pull off the sheet and roll him over on his side and tear the slips off the pillows and then I get out of bed and look under it, him laughing like a lunatic, and I run out bare-assed to the little balcony outside the French windows, where sits the wicker cage in which Marcel keeps his pigeons. All four of them are sitting there on their perches, looking as stupid as I feel. I run back inside and there is no pigeon in the room at all.

EIGHT

Desmond Greer & others are back. I like him. Back story
is ghetto kid, horrible family, street-fighting man, now cool
with white academic culture. Headed for the usual, dope
& crime, one Sunday he happens to drop into the Field
Museum to get out of the cold, runs into Ndeki Mfwese,
the greatest African Africanist of his generation. Des sees
this carbon-colored guy in flowing robes & skullcap floating down the hallway & he follows him like, as he says, the
pied fucking piper. Mfwese befriends him & the rest is
history. Man knows more about Yoruba cosmology & religion than most Yorubas do, he's an initiate in the Shango
cult, adopted into the Ogunfiditimi clan. He's incredibly
sweet to me, as if he knows what happened the last time
I tried fieldwork – strange because I don't even know that.
He knows M., though . . . has he talked to him? About me?
A natural anthropologist, like M., that scuba-diver talent,
total immersion & then withdrawal. Where does it come
from? Deracination? M. a Jew, a refugee in childhood,
transplanted into French culture, family killed by the
Nazis. Des a black guy in white (mainly) profession.

W. somewhat frosty to him, and I can't figure out why.
Oedipal thing? Jealousy of Des's authentic ghetto upbringing? A little spat later in our room.

The rest of the crew reasonably pleasant. Coleman

Lyttel & Carol Washington are Des's grad students; Godwin Adepojin, Nigerian grad student, did his undergraduate work in the States at Madison, back home to do his dissertation under Des on Aripon mask dancing in the Ketu region. Godwin, unfortunately, has made himself into what seems to me a parody of hip-hop-ness, backwards ball cap, baggies, big sneaks, the boxer shorts over the belt line. Tunji worships him as a god. Music sometimes drifts through the hotel – he has a boom box in his room – and it drives W. nuts. Six thousand miles & I still have to listen to Dr Dre? A little culture war available for study without leaving the premises.

Des not pushing me, my Yoruba still crummy, also studying the dialects over in Egbado, Gelede cult center. Godwin helping me at this, because his area is in the same region, to the west, in Nigeria & the Rep. of Benin. In return I am teaching him French, as Benin (where Ketu proper is located) is Francophone. Des thinks Gelede will be a good area for me, a female-dominated witch cult, one of the few here in macho Africa.

Also working with Ola Soronmu = project major domo, semi-official liaison with the bureaucracy & our all-around fixer. Mrs Bassey has no use for him, confirms my general opinion, hints broadly that he was connected with the military government. Mrs B. says he is low, a flash man.

Ola's working w/ me on our shipment problem, cases containing laptops, tape recorders & video equipment, Honda DC generator, solar power rigs, accessories & spares. Most bought w/ Doe Foundation funds, so I have been elected to sort it out. Ola slippery as a smelt, things are complex, video equipment, the authorities don't know what you will do with it, it is political . . . short version: they claim we want to make porno films. Oh, yes, this is a big problem, Europeans come here & buy girls & little boys & make terrible movies. Lie so outrageous, I'm not sure he even believed it himself. Who wants the bribe? A Colonel Alouf Musa, who controls air shipping in & out, hence a smuggler & an extortionist. Been bribed already according to O., still refuses to part with our stuff.

Organized expedition to yell at Musa, Ola objecting. The Colonel was a busy man. The Colonel was not a small person, you understand, in the government, he had many friends, truly, Jane, seriously, this is not done, this is not at all done. All the way to the car. W. came, too, and we set out for the airport. W. & Ola are best buddies now. Ola somehow got hold of one of W.'s poetry collections, and quotes him from time to time, always the way to my man's heart. It's great that he has a pal, because I think he is more disoriented by Africa than he lets on. I don't think it was what he expected. I tried to talk to him about it the other night, when he was silent during dinner, and morose afterwards, which is not like him at all. In NY, he was always the life of the party. But he wouldn't cop to anything being wrong.

State House on Lagos Island, past the gunned-up scary teenagers in green uniforms. Ola nervous, talking rapidly, he had been here before, and got the runaround, I didn't listen to him, stupid probably, and simply barged into Colonel Musa's office. Air-conditioned, expensive furniture, raffia on the walls. I demanded to see the Colonel. The Colonel was fat & covered with medals, probably for rape above & beyond call of duty, valorous murder of helpless civilians. He was leaning back in a big leather chair, cleaning his nails with an ivory letter-opener, the complete image of not-busy. W. should put this character into a book. He said our equipment impounded subject to judicial hearing. Bullshit about making pornography — video cameras, computers — the regime was suppressing this vice.

Didn't bother to object to this absurdity, demanded to see stuff in warehouse. He refused. Light dawned, wasn't bigger bribe he wanted, bastard had ripped off the shipment, probably sold it already. I accused him of this, got yelled at, shook his fist, said I'd insulted honor of Nigerian Army, serious crime, threat of prison. I said, just try, bub. He started screaming in a language I didn't understand, prob. Hausa?, then four soldiers came in & dragged us out & tossed us onto the street. Bruises, & Ola's nice suit ripped knees & lapels. W. weird, almost jolly about it, said you sure showed him! Lawsie me, Miss Ann, she threwed a tantrum & de darky didn't do what she said. Whatever is de world coming to? Kicked him in the ankle, went back to the car, drove in silence until I saw that we were passing the main post office, stopped car, went in, called Dad.

Explained rip-off — he got upset too. Doe family gives it away but can't stand getting robbed, which made me feel that I wasn't crazy, or not crazy about this issue, & he said he'd call Hank & Uncle Bill & they'd take care of it. Famous Doe Family Emergency Red Handle, not for me personally, but principle of the thing.

Back at the truck, W. asked did I call Daddy and I said, as a matter of fact, I did. Got some more mockery. Why is he doing this?

Then back to Yaba & I went up to our room to collapse & Ola Soronmu & W. went off to get a drink. When he came back, I was pretty chilly to him, he was drunk, trying charm, like with Mom at Sionnet. Mom likes being with charming drunks, me & Dad being *no fun*. Mom not here in Lagos however & I resented it & the more he charmed the more I resented it. He tried to be masterful & sexy, said a good fuck would clear the air. Lost it then, screaming how dare he trot out that Miss Ann horseshit & how dare he imply it was *racist* to get our stuff back from a corrupt thief, representative of a regime that had murdered & tormented more black people than KKK, plus Musa stealing from locals since we were *donating* that stuff to poor starving University of Lagos.

He came back with I didn't understand, how I couldn't comprehend this country because I was locked up in white skin, I had embarrassed Ola with pushy neocolonial ways, how dare *I* impose discredited Eurocentric concepts on black men! Exactly the kind of speech W. would have put into mouth of some dashiki-wearing associate professor of black studies as parody.

Threw things then, water jug, washbasin, bedside lamp, alarm clock, a copy of *The Yoruba of Southwestern Nigeria*, by W. R. Bascom, yelling who the fuck are you & what have you done with my husband? Haven't thrown things before, so missed with most, except clock, which broke.

Flung myself onto the bed and burst into tears, *exactly* like Scarlett fucking O'Hara–type person he was making me into.

Greer came by & I let him come in. Told him the whole wretched story and he declined to give me any daddyish wise advice only asked, do you think we'll get our stuff back? & I told him that my dad was calling my uncle Bill, who was the VP of the World Bank & Hank Schorr his old sailing buddy, who was CFO of Exxon & they would probably make some calls about it. I said if we did not get it all back then neocolonialism was total bullshit & we could joint-author a paper on it. Laughed. Then he said I've seen this before, a black man, American, comes to Africa, all pumped up, he's coming home, man, precious lost Guinée. Then he finds out there's no light in the window for him. The people here see him & they don't *see* the black skin that's always defined him his whole life. They see an American, with more money than they'll ever have in their wildest dreams, just like the other Americans. But I'm *black*, the guy says, & they just look at him. Then it hits him: there ain't no *black* people in Africa. We got the Yoruba, Hausa, Ibo, Fulani, Ga, Fon, Mandinka, Dogon & Tofinu & a couple hundred others, but no black folks except maybe where there are white tribes like in S. Africa. So, hey, you want to look for roots? God bless, but don't expect to be *recognized*. Guinée's dead & gone & negritude ain't going to help you. America is your nation, heaven your destination, and tough shit. And he looked puzzled, said, It's funny, seen his plays, read his stuff, I thought if *anybody* would be hip to that, it would've been him.

He's still invisible, I said. He thought *I* would be invisible here, but I'm not.

He said, I'll go talk to him, I said thank you, he said, I honor the suffering, the history, the culture, the guts it took to survive and get over. I'm in awe. Then he pinched the skin on his arm, but this *color*? It's horseshit. He pushed a strand of my hair back behind my ear. He said, You know, they used to sell girls with hair like this to guys like me in the slave markets of Algiers.

Those were the days, I said, & we both laughed.

9/14 Lagos

This a.m. big army truck pulled up to our hotel & soldiers unloaded all our equipment. Some of it was uncrated & had obviously been used. One of the laptops had a cracked screen & 100 megabytes of hard-core porn on its disk.

Saw W. watching from inside along with Ola. I asked him if he wasn't going to help drag the stuff in off the street, but he gave me a strange look & turned away. He can't be *disappointed* that we got the stuff back?

NINE

'Doris, that's all I'm telling you, because that's all we know right now,' lied Jimmy Paz. 'You have enough for a great story, you'll win another prize. No, I don't know whether this is the work of a crazed serial killer. Okay, crazed, I'll give you crazed, serial we don't know yet. Right, go ahead and print that: police wait for him to strike again. Helplessly wait, that's better.'

Paz held the receiver a few inches from his ear and Cesar the prep cook grinned at him around a lot of gold. Paz was in the kitchen of his mother's restaurant and on the phone, as he had promised, with Doris Taylor the crime reporter. It was six-thirty, a relatively peaceful time in the kitchen, for only the tourists ate that early. Satan might be loose in Dade County, but people still had to eat, and perforce others had to cook for them. Paz, who did not believe in Satan, had left Barlow as soon as he could manage and come here.

'I understand that,' he said calmly, 'believe me, but . . . where did you hear that? Hey, if you hear stuff, you're supposed to inform the police. No, we have no evidence that it was a cult killing. No, of course it wasn't a domestic. Why don't you call it a presumed deranged individual? No, you can't quote me on that, I'm not supposed to be talking to you at all. I got to go now, Doris. Fine. Right, just keep my name out of the papers. I love you, too, Doris. Bye.'

Paz hung up and turned to face his mother, whose eye he had felt upon him for the last minute or so of this conversation. Margarita Paz had heavy eyes; sometimes Jimmy felt them upon him when he was many miles away, often when he was doing one of the very many things of which she would not approve.

'Who were you talking to, tying up my phone like that?'

'Nobody, Mami, just some business.'

'That phone's for my business, not your business. You going to work in those fancy clothes?' She looked him up and down. Cesar the prep cook had retreated to the reefer on Mrs Paz's entry.

Paz and his mother locked eyes. Hers were on a level with his own because she was wearing four-inch cork platforms on her feet. And a yellow dress, and a yellow diamond on her finger, and a comb in her black hair, elaborately done up. Real lace around the collar of the dress and a plain gold cross against the dark throat. Her uniform of every evening.

Paz had been working in the restaurant in various capacities since the age of seven, and his mother made no distinction between working a meal after school and working a meal after an eight-hour shift with the cops, except that after a shift he was even more available, since there was no homework. Paz had tried to explain the difference between after-school work and after-work work many times, but Mrs Paz was skilled at the art of not listening.

He smiled to break the stare and said, 'Okay, Mami,' which was the right answer, because she gave a *la-reine-le-veult* nod and turned away. Paz loved his mother and because of this he allowed her to believe that she was still in control of his life, Cuban fashion. But in his mother's mind, Jimmy Paz was not at all a satisfactorily controlled son. He had, for example, not finished college and gone on to a medical or law degree. He was not even a dentist! Mrs Paz did not consider law enforcement an acceptable profession for her son. Nor had he married a girl of suitable family and skin tone (pale), thus supplying her with a daughter-in-law to dominate and grandchildren to spoil. Instead, he ran around with a succession of American women, all of whom, despite their fancy educations, were little better than whores.

Paz understood that until he had an acceptable profession and a wife, his mother would continue to treat him like a schoolboy. This did not bother him much, as he had no compunction about cutting out of the restaurant when cop work called, and the restaurant work paid for, in his mind, if not in hers, a rather nice apartment.

He left the kitchen and went into the dining room. As always, this brought him a moment of delight, this contrast between the organized chaos of the kitchen and the calm of the dining room. It was high-ceilinged, decorated in shiny white, yellow, pink, and cream; the tiles underfoot were coffee-colored; the chairs and tables were of heavy rattan, painted white. The rear wall was decorated with gilt mirrors, and the two side walls bore a series of Roman arches in white plaster, through which one looked out at brightly painted representations of Guantánamo Bay. Rattan and brass fans rotated slowly and exiguously overhead, stirring the chilled, conditioned air. The room was as close as the memory and resources of Margarita Paz could come to reproducing the dining room at Tanaimo, the great tobacco *finca* where her mother had served as a cook.

Paz reflexively checked the house. Every table was occupied, most of them by pale Americanos, but there were several tables of Germans and two of Japanese. A group of crisply dressed foreign tourists waited with their tour guide on the other side of a huge saltwater fish tank. Margarita Paz was a spectacularly good cook, and her place was listed in any number of restaurant guides as worth a special trip. She trained her waiters well, they all spoke English, and Jimmy had written for the menu concise explanations of the contents and preparation of the various dishes. A tourist-friendly place, by design. Later, when the Cubans showed up, there would be larger crowds waiting for a table. In Cuban Miami they said you went to the Versailles to be seen, but to eat you went down the street. The street was Eighth Street, aka the Tamiami Trail, called Calle Ocho by nearly everyone now. (Barlow still called it the Trail.) Down the street meant this place. Every Cuban man is obliged to defend his mother's cooking as the best in the world, but in Paz's case it might have been true.

Then he went home, which was around the corner and four houses down from Calle Ocho, in a yellow stucco two-unit owned by Mrs Paz. Jimmy Paz had the top unit, and the bottom was rented out. His mother lived next door. It was more space than a single man needed, two large bedrooms, a kitchen, one and a half baths, and a living room facing the street. Paz believed that his mother let him have it so that there would be no excuse for him not putting in the hours in the kitchen and because it allowed her to keep an eye on his doings. The Cruzes, the elderly couple who inhabited the lower floor, were efficient spies, who kept Mrs Paz well informed. Paz thought it not a bad deal, having had a whole lifetime to get used to his mother's disapproval. He also was an expert nonlistener.

Paz went to his refrigerator and selected a Corona beer. There was little else in his refrigerator – a couple of bottles of Piper champagne, some limes, some mixed nuts. The freezer was loaded with cylindrical pints of fruit sherbet supporting a bottle of Finlandia vodka. Paz did not dine at home.

Beer in hand, he switched on the television and watched the local news. There had been a shoot-out and car chase down Collins Avenue on Miami Beach that afternoon, with plenty of good aerial footage. The murder of Deandra Wallace, which might otherwise have led, came a poor third (after the usual corrupt-official story) and got extra juice because of the bizarre nature of the crime and the thrill value of a possible cult killing. No interviews, just a mannequin reporter in front of Ms Wallace's dreary building, who said 'bizarrely mutilated' but did not supply the details, nor did she specify the cult involved. Paz would have liked to know that himself.

He put on a white tunic and check trousers, laced on greasy Doc Marten boots, and went back to the restaurant. There he brought a box of snapper on ice out of the reefer and began to make snapper hash, one of the place's specialties. Being the boss's son, he was not subject to the outrageous abuse that is the common lot of sous-chefs the world over, for the chef stayed out of

Paz's way and Paz stayed out of his, and all involved –
waiters and kitchen staff – got along unusually well, for
Margarita Paz believed that you could taste bad feelings
in the food and would not tolerate any prima donnas
other than herself. Among restaurant kitchens, this one
was unusual in having no actual crazy people in it. The
scullion was not even an alcoholic.

Around nine-thirty Paz took his first break. He went
out into the alley, sat on an upturned shortening barrel,
drank an iced coffee black as tar, and smoked a chico.
He felt calm and at peace, with an interesting case just
starting up, and the various tensions of the day worked
off by the meditation of simple cooking. He finished his
cigar and coffee, and thought that a woman would be
nice after work, so he went back through the kitchen
and used the pay phone outside the rest rooms to call
Beth Morgensen and ask if he could come over late. As
a readiness to entertain gentlemen arriving at midnight
was a universal quality among the girlfriends of Paz, she
said he could.

After work, he drove his battered orange Z Datsun to
her apartment on Ponce de Leon hard by the university, still dressed in his cook's outfit and carrying a cold
bottle of Korbel and a bouquet assembled from the
floral displays at the restaurant. Generous, but not
wildly so, was Paz, and the women he chose understood
this and found it endearing.

Beth Morgensen opened the door and looked at Paz
distractedly over wire-rimmed spectacles. She was a
hefty one, as tall as Paz, with a braid of cornsilk hair
thick as a python running down her back to her waist,
and the broad shoulders and narrow hips of a competi-
tive swimmer. Now she was a graduate student in

sociology, all-but-dissertation, which study was on homeless people in Dade County.

'Oh, my!' she said. 'The old flowers-and-champagne routine. Paz, you're a living fossil.' She stuck out her face and he planted a nice kiss on her pale lips. Paz liked the way she moved, loose-jointed, swaying the big body as to some inner tune. He watched her roll away into her tiny kitchen. She was wearing frayed jean cutoffs and a black T-shirt that said PUNISH ME across the front. He followed her through a living room/studio that was stacked with books and folders and so littered with sheaves of papers that the floor was scarcely visible. A desk sat in the middle of the room, similarly littered, upon which a computer glowed. In the kitchen, he watched her pop the champagne and pour out into two not-squeaky-clean juice glasses. She read the distaste on his face. 'Yeah, I know, it's a pigsty, and you're such a neat freak, and I beg your pardon, because I'm crashing on this fucking diss, and I swore before Jesus and all the saints that I would finish chapter five tonight.'

'Why did you let me come over, then?'

'Oh, well, a girl needs a little break.' She grinned, stretching the long mouth over her front teeth, the lips like pale rubber bands. They sat in two straight chairs and drank companionably.

'Want to go and hit some clubs?' he asked.

'Oh, no, not that much of a break. I thought we could finish this nice wine and have a delicious little fuck and then I'll kick your sweet ass out the door. How does that sound?'

'It sounds like you're only interested in me for my body,' putting an artificial sob into his voice.

'Yes, uh-huh, and . . . ?' She sat on his lap and undid

a few of the frogs on the front of his chef's tunic. 'Mm, what is this taste on your neck? It's terrific.'

'Deep fat, mostly, plus grilled snapper, salsa, garlic, mango, dark rum, some secret stuff.'

He let her take off the rest of his chef's clothes, including the boots, while he drank champagne. She licked him thoroughly, the entire front of his body, like a child getting all the frosting out of the bowl, and then stripped herself and straddled him, and they had a short, sharp fuck to, as she said, take the edge off. Just after this she picked up the champagne and shook the bottle with her thumb over the opening and let it shoot out, icy, over their joined groins. He chased her into her bedroom, where he gave her a good one on top of piles of books and folders, until she howled like a wolf.

She grunted and withdrew from under her buttocks a thick tome. 'Oh-ho,' she laughed, '*Nonparametric Statistics for the Social Sciences*, no wonder.' She lowered her voice an octave. 'Good study, Morgensen, but your statistics are fucked. Oh, Christ, Jimmy, I don't want you to go, but you have to.'

'That's okay, I got two more girls to see tonight.'

She rapped him on the head with the book. 'Monster! There's a full professor who's been trying to get into my pants for months, and he wanted to come over tonight and I blew him off because I thought you might call.'

'A full professor. I'm honored. Are you going to fuck him to get ahead in your chosen profession?'

'I might. Everyone else seems to be doing it. But I'm glad it was you.' She kissed his neck.

'Serendipity that I called, huh?' he said.

'No, serendipity is when you're looking for

something and you find something else that's even
better. Penicillin. Columbus too, I guess. What you
mean is synchronicity, which is when two independent
variables happen at the same time, in a pseudo-
meaningful way. Serendipity is scientific, synchronicity
isn't.'

'Why not?'

She tossed the stat book onto his belly and slipped
out of bed. 'Read the book.'

'Why should I when I have you? Where are you
going?'

'The shower, where you can join me, if you promise
not to get me started again.'

Under the lukewarm stream, he soaped her long
back, while she held her braid away from the water. He
said, 'So tell me, why isn't synchronicity scientific?'

'By definition. And, Jimmy, I want you to know that
you are the first and only man I have ever discussed
epistemology with under the shower.'

'I appreciate that,' he said. 'I know that was hard to
admit.'

'It was. In any case, science looks for causality. Event
B only occurs after Event A, or is associated with it
more than chance alone would allow. Lightning always
precedes thunder, and so we assume that lightning
causes thunder, and we look for a physical connection
between the two events, and in that case, we find it, and
science marches on. Synchronicity . . . thank you, I'll
clean that myself, if you don't mind . . . synchronicity
proposes a linkage between two events that is meaningful without being causal or related in a reproducible or
deterministic way. For instance, I have this terrible
plumbing problem and I meet a guy in a bar and we

fall in love and it turns out he's a plumber. Or me wanting to get together with you and you happen to call me from among all your hundreds of women. Pretty, but scientifically meaningless. The Jungians make a big deal of it, which is another reason for not taking it seriously.'

'It's like luck.'

'In a way. But it's supposed to be meaningful on the psychic level, too. The cosmos or the collective unconscious is trying to reach us. Horseshit, in other words.' She looked down at him and let out a yelp. 'Yikes, get that thing away from me,' she cried, and hung her washcloth on it, then turned the cold tap all the way on.

Later, driving home, Paz experienced the usual letdown, and the fetid backwash of self-contempt. He could sense that his relationship with Morgensen was approaching its conclusion. When they started talking about other, more eligible, men and the passion level went up a notch or two, as was here the case, the final kiss-off loomed not far distant. So Morgensen would get her full professor, or similar, and Paz get another bright, white lady to replace Morgensen, and so on and so on, until he was a fat sixty-year-old cop, turtle-faced with corruption and booze, paying chippies to suck him off in crime-lighted parking lots. Paz had heard about love, and believed it to be real, as he had heard about Mongolia and believed that place to be real as well. Yet while he thus believed, Paz thought that a voyage to the latter was as likely as one to the former: not very, given his record. If milk is free, why buy a cow? Paz had said this to himself and others, even to women. He said it now, waiting for a light, puffing his cigar.

Something was wrong, something was intensely disturbing, but he could not nail it down; it was like forgetting a phone number or leaving tickets home, an absence, felt but not comprehended. He ought to feel good, he told himself: an interesting and exciting day's work, a terrific piece of ass, what more could a man desire? Now came a new thought, Mr Youghans and the dead woman, and the girl he was screwing, and Barlow's contempt for the man. Which Paz shared. He wasn't like Youghans. He didn't seduce high-school girls. Only college graduates. That was a significant difference. Or was it? No, it was. A good deal, for both parties, a square deal. Like he had with his mother.

Driving, the windows open to the thick, slowly cooling air of Miami nights, Paz rolled a different sort of life around in his mind, the words *settle down* scuttling across the surface of his brain. Pick one of them and settle down. Or some other, to come. Fall in love. Move out of the free apartment, quit the restaurant. A three-bedroom ranch in Kendall. Pool and barbecue. Kids. Make friends. Invite the Barlows over.

It had no real taste, it was like water, like meringue without sugar. He would have to be a different man from the one he was now. He supposed he might become that man, but not through any act of personal will. He didn't know the way there.

In the morning, first thing, Paz called Dr Maria Salazar at home and got an answering machine that informed him, first in English, and then in a particularly limpid and refined Spanish, that Dr Salazar would be out of the country until a date three weeks in the future. Paz cursed in muddy and impure Spanish and then punched in Dr Lydia Herrera's number. Dr Herrera was busy, the secretary said, she had no room on her schedule that morning. Paz bullied, abandoning Barlow's rule. He threatened that if Dr Herrera did not see him, he would have her dragged down to police headquarters and charged with obstructing a homicide investigation, and wouldn't that screw up her busy schedule? The line went briefly dead, and then the secretary came back again and, in a stiff voice, gave Paz his appointment. Paz put on a fawn-colored Palm Beach suit and walked over to the hole-in-the-wall on Calle Ocho where he took breakfast, *café con leche* and a couple of Cuban fruit pastries. While he ate he read Doris Taylor's story in the *Herald*, which had made page 1 below the fold. Doris didn't spare the gory details, and he guessed that she had gotten to the medical examiner's staff. The police, he learned, had refused to rule out the possibility of a cult killing. It could have been worse, although he now expected that the brass would be more interested in the case than was optimal. He ripped the story out, pocketed the clip, and drove directly to the university.

Dr Herrera was dressed in mango color this morning and she frowned in a way that brought her plucked brows together like a child's drawing of a gull. The patronizing smile was missing. She stood in the doorway of her little office and radiated honest outrage.

'This is really inconvenient, Detective,' she said. 'And I resent being threatened.'

'Murder is often inconvenient, Doctor,' said Paz blandly. 'And citizens have a positive duty to help the police in an investigation.' He gestured past her. 'The sooner we start . . .'

She stalked back into her office and sat behind her desk. Paz placed before her a copy of the toxicology analysis on Wallace.

'This is a list of the chemicals we found in the victim's body. If you could, we'd like to know what plants they came from.'

She snatched up the paper, frowning. As Paz watched, her expression changed; irritation gave way to confused fascination. She spun her chair, pulled a reference volume from the shelf, paged through it, pulled down a batch of reprints, shuffled through them, read a page of one, shook her head, muttering.

'Stumped, huh?'

She stared at him, but not with hostility. 'This is remarkable. Amazing.'

'Do you know what plant that stuff comes from?' asked Paz.

'Plant? My God, there's a whole pharmacopoeia in this. The harmalines here are botanical psychedelics, monoamine oxidase inhibitors, incredibly powerful, used by shamans in both the New World and Old World tropics. In the New World they come from the *Banisteriopsis* vine, they call it *yagé* or ayahuasca; in Africa they're derived from *Leptactinia densiflora*. As to which we've got here, I'd have to look it up, but this set of indoles they have listed looks like typical contaminants from *Leptactinia* preparations. Yohimbine is from *Alchornea floribunda*, African again. Ibogaine is a powerful stimulant and psychedelic, also African, from *Tabernanthe iboga*. It's called the cocaine of Africa. It may not be purposeful here because it's a common contaminant of yohimbine preparations. It's an intoxicant and supposed aphrodisiac. Ouabain is an African arrow poison, from *Strophantus* species. It's a cardiac glyco-side.'

'A poison?'

'Yes. Extremely potent. I don't know what it's doing here. Was the woman poisoned, too? I read the story in the paper this morning. I thought it was an eviscer-ation.'

Paz decided to yield a scrap of information. 'Apparently she died before she had time to bleed to death. Her heart stopped. Could this ouabain do that?'

'No question. In Central Africa they use it to kill ele-phants.' She gestured at the tox report. 'As I said, this is remarkable. The cocktail of substances – I have no idea what the result of this combination would be.'

'We figure he wanted to knock her out, so he could, um, do his operation.'

'I don't know.' She put her finger on one of the poly-syllabic names. 'This one here is a phenanthrene.'

'What's a phenanthrene?' Paz had his notebook out and was scribbling in it.

'A narcotic. Morphine and codeine are phenan-threnes. I'd have to check, but I think it's the one derived from *Fagara zanthoxyloides*, which is widely used as a narcotic in West Africa.'

'So that would have knocked her out.'

'In the right dose, yes. But then why this other stuff? Some of them typically make the user run around hallu-cinating like crazy. But who knows what they would do in combination? And we don't know what the original dose was. What about the stomach contents?'

'Zip. She took it in through the nose or skin.'

'Hmph! That's unusual, but not unknown — snuffs and salves applied to the mucosa. Usually they ingest an infusion or eat the raw plant matter. Fascinating. And then there's this. Tetrahydra-β-carboline. What's *that* doing there?'

'What do you mean?'

'It's not a botanical. It's an alkaloid found naturally in the brain and especially in the pineal body. In her *lungs*? It's interesting because it's chemically related to ibogaine and the various *Banisteriopsis* and *Tabernanthe* alkaloids.'

'Why is that interesting?'

Dr Herrera allowed herself a sigh. 'It's fairly complicated and I don't see what forensic value it has. And, as I thought I had made clear, I'm extremely busy . . .'

'Why don't you let me be the judge of forensic value. Just give me the dummy version.'

'Fine.' She spouted rapidly and in monotone. 'Question: why should chemicals produced by plants have profound psychotropic activity in human brains? Answer: because plants have evolved to produce analogues and antagonists of alkaloids and neuroactive substances present in the brains of animals so that if animals eat them they will get sick and learn not to eat them. Opiates, for example, imitate brain endorphins and bind to the same sites, hyoscine competes with the neurotransmitter acetylcholine, the harmines and other indole derivatives are chemically similar to serotonin, which is an important neurotransmitter in brain regions associated with emotionality and perception. It's probably why they can act as hallucinogens. The fact that tetrahydra-β-carboline is related to ibogaine, et cetera, is interesting for the same reason. What it *means*, we don't know. The pineal gland's function is obscure – it seems to be some kind of endocrine gland in antagonistic relationship to the pituitary, and hence intimately connected with a whole range of physiological and psychological control functions. In fact, now that I think about it, there's another pineal hormone, adrenoglomerulotropine, that's identical to a psychotropic botanical, 6-methoxytetrahydroharman.'

Paz had more or less stopped listening. Her spiel was completely beyond him, not that he would ever admit this. The last named gobbledygook, however, was familiar. 'That was in the corpse, too, wasn't it?' he asked.

'Yes. But don't ask me what it all means, because I don't know. Nobody does. You're at the frontiers of psychopharmacology here.'

'Would Dr Salazar?'

Herrera frowned. 'Maria? Of course not. Less than I do, certainly. She's an anthropologist.'

'I don't mean the hard science. I meant the particular mix of drugs. Maybe she's seen it before.'

She shrugged. 'It's unlikely. *Santeros* don't typically use powerful psychotropics. They're more into elacampane and sarsaparilla, and botanical symbolism. Now . . . will that be all?'

Paz stashed his notebook and stood. 'Yes. You've been very helpful, Doctor, and I want to apologize for any misunderstanding with your secretary.'

A slight smile. 'You mean you wouldn't have had me locked up?'

'Only in an extremely comfortable cell. And, if the Miami PD can ever do you a favor . . .'

'Thank you. If you catch this guy, I'd love to talk with him. About plants.'

'Let's catch him first. By the way, do you happen to know when Dr Salazar will be back? I called her house and got a message . . .'

Dr Herrera looked down at her desk. 'Yes, but I can't help you there. Maria keeps her movements somewhat confidential.'

'And why is that?'

'You'd have to ask her,' said Dr Herrera, not smiling at all anymore.

Paz left, feeling he had missed something important. He didn't like being on the frontiers of science, and he did not see how the dense slug of information he had extracted from the ethnobotanist brought him any closer to the murderer, who now seemed to be not only a skilled surgeon, but a master of psychopharmacology. Ordinarily, putting an unknown suspect in a new class was a good thing. If you knew your guy was a plumber and you found he liked bass fishing, that was good. If you found out he bred beagles, even better. It was possible to interview all the bass-fishing, beagle-breeding plumbers in Dade County and ask them where they were on the night of, and there you had it. Skillful eviscerators who knew a lot about tropical pharmacology should have generated a similarly small class, but . . . where to begin looking? Hunters? Actual surgeons? Butchers? Veterinarians? With a sideline in tropical plants?

Paz stepped from the shade cast by the science building and the morning sun socked him in the face. He put on his Vuarnets and crossed Memorial Drive almost unseeing, deep in his own head. The vision: a black man slipping around a corner, climbing the stairs to Deandra Wallace's apartment. A black man because the vic was black, and that was the way it almost always went: people kill their own, plus there was Deandra's boyfriend's testimony about the African witch doctor, they had to take account of that, too. And a white fellow at night in Overtown would have registered like a comet in the minds of neighbors and passersby. An intelligent black man. He'd left no obvious clues, besides that damned nut, and they knew that Youghans's violent outburst had been responsible for it ending up under the bed. The killer had lifted the rest of the *opele*, obviously, but missed the one nut. So, not so perfect. But the attempted frame was clever, and if not for Barlow's religio-cracker intuition, Youghans would have gone down for it. So, an intelligent, educated black man. Not a homeboy. But a race man. Interested in Africa, in African ritual and culture. That's how he had hooked Deandra, who had also been an aficionado of sorts. Rebelling from the striving, conventional parents. And the African angle was looking more interesting. The plants that had produced the drugs in the victim's body were African plants. Could the guy be an actual African? He used an African-sounding name. That would be something else to check.

He was in shade again; the tower of the Richter Library loomed over him, and obeying an impulse, he entered the building. Like any autodidact, Paz knew how to use a library. He spent an hour or two in the pharmacology section, copying down chemical structures to go with the substances found in the victim and those Herrera had mentioned. He couldn't follow the neurophysiological material very well – there seemed to be an inordinate number of substances involved in producing thought, rather more than seemed necessary to Paz, given the extremely simple nature of most people's thoughts. But he read enough to recognize that Herrera had been right when she said that not much was known about the connection between the soup of chemicals and the production of mental states. Abandoning these researches, he went to seek more wisdom on the use of psychotropic botanicals by traditional shamans. His beeper went off – Barlow calling – but he ignored it and continued his pacing through the stacks. The University of Miami does not have a graduate program in anthropology, but it does have a department of Caribbean and African Studies, and a special collection in Richter to go with it. This has its own room, a typical special-collection establishment: counter with a clerk, several long blond wood tables, ceiling-high shelves all around, a few display cabinets exhibiting books and photographs.

Two dark women were working quietly at one of the long tables. They glanced up when Paz came into the quiet room and went back to what they were doing. At another table, surrounded by books and papers, sat an elderly woman writing in a notebook. The hair stood up on the back of Paz's neck as he recognized her.

He noted that her hands were ink-stained, that she used an old-fashioned fountain pen, that her white hair was thick and wiry, springing out from the sides of her head in two wedges, like pieces of angel cake. She was wearing a fawn-colored linen dress with a pointed collar and a row of closely spaced jet buttons down the front, and she had thrown a dark mohair cardigan over her shoulders against the air-conditioned chill. He stared at her; she looked up briefly and went back to her writing. He sat down opposite her and said, in Spanish, 'Dr Salazar, if you could spare me a minute or two, I very much wish to speak with you.'

Her head popped up. A peculiar series of expressions passed across her face: first surprise, then an instant of fear, then a resettling of the features into the social persona, reserved and a little wary. She said, 'Why is that, señor? And how did you know I was here?'

Her face was covered with tiny wrinkles, but the peach-colored skin still clung closely to the fine bones. A curved, bold nose, a determined chin, the eyes still bright, though sunken into their sockets and brown-shadowed beneath. She looks older than she did on the book jacket, Paz thought, and also that she must have stopped traffic in 1940s Havana. He displayed his badge and photo identification.

'I'm a homicide detective. I want to discuss certain aspects of a recent murder with you. As for how I knew you were here, I didn't. I thought you were out of the country. I came here to do some research and here you were. Synchronicity.'

'You mean serendipity, Detective,' said Dr Salazar after a considering moment. 'It would be synchronicity only if I sought you out before you knew you wanted to see me.'

TEN

Running around naked looking for the trick of it is perhaps as good a symbol of the relationship I had with Marcel Vierchau as anything else. In memory, now, he is always laughing and I am trying to find the joke, on the verge of feeling hurt. Yet it is difficult to stay angry with a man having so good a time, and he was never vindictive, or mean, or cruel. He just thought I was funny; and was I not? A large, somewhat overbred American girl, mad for sex and ethnography, desperate for approval, would have been funny to a man like Marcel, and especially amusing were my pathetic efforts to spy out his secrets. While we were together, I would actually hide myself and try to watch him, looking for the incredibly clever, spidery apparatus that enabled him to pull off his stunts. When he was out of the apartment, or the tent or the van, I made it a habit to poke through his things. Yes, embarrassing; and worse, I never found anything.

Marcel knew, and it amazed him, because his whole life was dedicated to teaching that real magic was a technology of the mind, not of smoke and mirrors. It's your Catholic prejudice against witchcraft, he'd tell me, you can't allow yourself to believe that someone you love is really a witch and so you look for wires.

We were together for seven years, continuously,

almost. Based in Paris, we traveled to every continent – city, jungle, desert, steppe. The problem with a relationship like that is that the girl gets spoiled. His friends are so much more interesting than your friends. When famous people listen to you respectfully at dinner parties, do you really want to go clubbing with twenty-somethings? You don't. They say the young woman delights in her sexual power over the older man, and that this is good for her confidence and self-esteem. Maybe so, but in exchange her real life is stolen from her, and she grows up twisted, like a pear tree espaliered against the wall of the Great Man. And what does she do when the wall crumbles? As it must.

I don't know whether thinking about Marcel and what happened in the garden last night are connected. No, I *do* know – it's *all* connected. For a long time I was spared the pangs of memory; post-traumatic shock, I suppose, or perverted will, but now things are loosening up, like the ice breaking in springtime on the Yei.

It's going to be another (*another!*) hot day today and here I am thinking about the Yei. I used to think about the Yei in Danolo, too, memories of coolness being especially precious there. I'm a northern girl. I love fog and mist, and crisp, cheek-pinching nights, and crunching through snow, and so I ask you why am I here and why have I spent much of my life in the fucking tropics? I don't suffer from the heat, as some do, though. I'm adaptable to the various extreme climates where live the sort of people anthropologists dote on: steaming jungles, baking deserts, frozen steppes.

Perhaps I could show up at Medical Records in

shorts and T-shirt, the same sort of outfit that Luz is now pulling on. She wishes to select her own clothes and dress herself. Muffa is merely to watch, and check the clock and worry about being late.

The Yei is a river in Siberia, one of those long, sluggish Arctic rivers that only ascend to literate consciousness as crossword clues. Six down: Siberian river, three letters: the mighty Mil. The winding Sem. The rushing Yei. The Chenka pass the winter on its banks, and one winter I did, too, with Marcel, so that I could harvest a doctoral dissertation out of the soil he had so brilliantly cultivated. I was twenty-seven and it had lately occurred to me that being Vierchau's beautiful assistant was not a lifetime career. I was to study woman's magic, which among the Chenka is quite different from the men's magic that Marcel knew about.

The Chenka are pastoralists related to the Yakut, and speak a similar language, but their connection with the various Yakut tribes is obscure. The other Yakut avoid them, sometimes even deny that there are any Chenka people at all. Except when they wish to learn. The Chenka operate a kind of informal, floating sorcerer's university and at any particular time you will find among them Yakuts, Buryats, Altais, Evenks, and peoples from even further off, Yukakirs, Nenets, Khants, and, once, an American, me.

Marcel discovered the Chenka in 1969 in the journal of a Soviet functionary named T. I. Berozhinski. This included an eye-witness report of how a group of Siberian nomads had walked through a cordon of OGPU troops who had come to arrest them. This occurred in daylight, and none of the secret policemen saw a thing. Berozhinski saw them, but when he told the commissar in charge, he got sent straight to the gulag, where he died. Other than this, the Chenka were unknown to history or anthropology.

Marcel was thunderstruck by the account. If Berozhinski was not bemused himself or a liar, the Chenka had witched their way through scores of the most brutal, unimaginative, and disciplined men on earth. This was no pathetic ethnic remnant like the jungle tribes he and his colleagues normally studied. He was instantly on fire to see them for himself.

Marcel arranged for a scientific study visa, went to Siberia, met the Chenka, was amazed. He went again and stayed for his seven years. The rest is now familiar from the pages of his book. The Chenka had real magic, whatever that means.

Another peg snagging the folds of the net of my life. Berozhinski begat Vierchau, and Vierchau begat Doe. Since the start of our connection, not more than days after that first marathon in bed, I had been bugging Marcel to take me to the Chenka. It was somehow never arranged. Always other commitments intervened or there was some hitch with the authorities, or they invaded Afghanistan, or something. But now at last I, too, was encamped upon the Yei, learning how to make mare's milk yogurt, kvass, and women's magic. So called. The Chenka practice a sexual egalitarianism quite remarkable among pastoral societies, which tend to be ferociously patriarchal, women being merely a sort of cattle. Among the Chenka it is otherwise, and I think it is because the women exercise substantial powers in the magical realm. The women, for example, decide who is to marry whom, and whether they will have children, and of what sex. So the Chenka and Marcel believed, and during my year with them I saw nothing to contradict it. Puniekka expressed amazement when I told her that in the lands of the *Alues*, the non-Chenka, there were such things as unwanted children, and people who wanted children and couldn't have them. She was further astounded that we did not routinely determine the sex of our babies in advance.

Puniekka was the shaman in whose yurt I lodged. This was another of the disappointments of my Siberian experience. I had imagined that Marcel and I would live together, as a team. I thought he was being hyberbolic when he said that when we got to Chenka we would hardly see each other. But it was so. Sexual segregation among the Chenka during the seasonal migration is nearly total. The men are out all day moving the herds, and the women are cooking, brewing, and making things as the carts rumble across the steppe. The men all eat together, too, in their herding camp. The women bring them their morning and evening meal, packed in clay pots. Child rearing is matrilocal: women own the yurts, carts, and all the physical apparatus of the culture, except for personal clothing, harness, and magical apparatus. The men own all the animals. Paternal care is diffuse and paternal lineage obscure. The Chenka understand the association of pregnancy with sex, but they often attribute the qualities of a child to spiritual rather than earthly parenthood.

And on top of this, Chenka shamans are celibate, or to put it more accurately, they do not engage in sex with other human beings, but only with the denizens of the spirit world. Marcel had explained this to me and it's in the book, too, but I thought . . . Jesus, you know, I can't remember what I thought.

As it turned out, I hardly saw Marcel for nine months that year, and I didn't get laid, although I did get a lot of offers from various Chenka women, several of which I accepted out of anthropological curiosity. I did not get taken on as an apprentice shaman. Marcel had warned me about that, too, but again, I failed to take it seriously. It is so hard, even for anthropologists, to take other cultures seriously.

One day, I couldn't stand it any longer and jumped on a pony and rode out to where the men were and I confronted him and demanded he spend more time with me, let me stay with the men and herd, and he took me aside and listened to me rant, his eyes getting wider, and I have to say, that was the only time he really got mad at me, although looking back I realize I must have been a colossal pain in the butt. He said, You silly woman, don't you understand who these people *are*? What they can *do*? He said, Don't you understand my status with these people? And I didn't really, because, to be fair, he hadn't exactly dwelled on it in the book, but now he told me. I'm a pet, he said, a kind of superior dog. They're teaching me a couple of tricks and it amuses them. I walk on my hind legs, I play dead, I roll over.

I didn't get it. We – we in what we are pleased to call advanced societies – don't have this experience. We've always been *ahead*, whatever that means. We could read and write, and they couldn't. We have the Maxim gun and they have not. Berozhinski's tale about the invisibility trick I took to be some kind of hallucination, probably drug-induced. The Chenka eat a lot of dope, mostly strains of fungi, hundreds of different kinds, which they grow in tubs, but also various plant and animal preparations, and I assumed that old T.I. was whacked out of his mind most of the time.

I told Marcel this. He looked at me like you look at a crazy person, pityingly. I'm sure I looked at him the same way. He walked away, and I rode back to the women's camp.

My work there was not going well, and this was perhaps a greater cause for distress than loneliness. The Chenka ladies would talk to me politely about anything *except* sorcery. You won't understand, they would say when I pressed them. Puniekka would be grinding up some foul-smelling paste. What's that for, Puniekka? You wouldn't understand. Tell me anyway. A sigh. Then, patiently, as to a child: It's a *griunat*. What is a *griunat*? Answer: when the *raaiunt teno's d'okka kiarrnkch*, we spread a *griunat* on the doorposts. I would paw desperately through my Chenka glossary, but the critical words were never there. I asked them, What did these words mean? They would explain each, using a host of other terms that I also could not connect to the world of sensation and material. Describing color to a blind man. I don't understand, I would cry, sometimes with actual tears. Yes, they would say, we *told* you that you wouldn't understand.

There is a green parrot, a flock of green parrots in the flame trees near Providence when I drop Luz off and they are shrieking like maniacs, like demons, like oh, shit, where has *this* one been hiding?

This memory. Night, in the yurt. Another little mystery: nobody in the surrounding ten thousand square miles lives in yurts, but the Chenka do. They say that Chesei-Anka gave them yurts, sheep, goats, and horses when the Chenka emerged from the sea. No Chenka to anyone's knowledge has ever seen the sea, but they know where it lies, far to the south. It was Puniekka's yurt. I slept in the place for guests on the east side. A yurt is always pitched facing south, so that the sun streaming through the smokehole makes a clocklike passage across the floor during the day. Two of Puniekka's other students were sleeping there, too, on the west wall, and the mistress herself was at the north. Spirits arrive from the north. I remember coming out of sleep, awakened by a sharp cry. The other students were wrapped in their blankets, long lumps, like logs reflecting the red glow from the dying fire in the center. Rhythmic gasps, the sound of a body moving against cloth. Another cry. I listened, fascinated. Ai! Oh! Ai! And heavy mouth-breathing, male and stertorous, like a horse. Puniekka was having a terrific fuck by the sound of it, and I was dying to know who the guy was. It had never happened before and I had been assured of the strict celibacy of all the shamans, male and female. I rolled on my side so I could make ethnographic observations. I recall feeling terrific, a warming intellectual smugness. This was something even Marcel didn't know – guys sneaked into lady shamans' tents at night. So I stared, and I could see pretty well, too: besides the glow from the fireplace, moonlight flooded down through the smokehole. She was on her back, with her knees up high. She still had her heavy woolen stockings on, but I could see her knees gleaming and moving back and forth with his thrusts. Powerful thrusts, because each one smacked the crown of her head against a large leather pillow, which creaked at the blows.

The space above her where her lover should have been was perfectly empty.

And what happens to you when you see something like that, if you're a Western materialist, is that your mind sort of splits in two. One part is thinking, Oh, how fascinating, an example of hysterical conversion in the trance state among the primitives, she's imagining a demon lover and sure enough her body is going through the motions just as if she were being violently had and she's having spectacular orgasms, too, from the sound of it and the rigid arching of her back and the shuddering, and clearly she's not manually masturbating because her hands are wrapped around the thing that isn't there. And, *How interesting*, it really does look like she has sunk deeper into the sheepskin pallet, just as if she were being pressed down by a heavy man.

As for the other part, that one's four years old and blubbering under the covers, and cold sweat is bursting forth embarrassingly all over its body. We wish to control that part, and we do, out of long practice. *Such things cannot be*. That's what we've learned to say. And having reestablished scientific objectivity, we grope among our things for a notebook and pencil and record the event, except for the personal details that are not the business of the scientific community to know, such as that the sexual field in the yurt is so intense that little ripples are running across the observer's belly and down the observer's thighs and her breath is coming in short gasps and the observer's cunt is gushing wet. There is no such thing as a 'sexual field,' for we cannot detect its elementary particles.

Finally, a series of unearthly cries, very like those of the parrots above me as I walk back to my car, a greater arching of back and flailing of limbs, something like a breathy gasp from no visible source, and relative silence. It was apparently over. I was shaking, and I became aware that Puniekka was staring at me; I could see the whites of her eyes glowing in the moonlight, sending it seemed their own light from within. She said, 'Go to sleep, Chane *Aluesfan*.' Then I was waking up and thinking, What a weird dream! I went on thinking that until, while looking through my notes a couple of days later, I found what I had written during the . . . whatever-it-was.

A hallucination, that useful word. Of course. I hallucinate, we hallucinate, Berozhinski hallucinates; yes, but when all of us hallucinate, each one of us hallucinating the same thing, then that is the hallucination we are pleased to call reality. It got worse. I once saw Puniekka turn into an owl. I once saw Ullionk, one of Puniekka's students, appear in two places at once. An old woman seen in a yurt, looking up from her pot, had a dog's head. I attributed this sort of thing to inhaling or eating the psychotropic fungal dust that was everywhere about the camp. A reasonable explanation.

I tried, like a good ethnologist of the Vierchau school, to step into their reality. Here I failed utterly, which was the last straw. My notes were a confused mess, my glossary a nonsense. My only half-useful informant was that same Ullionk, a pie-faced girl of seventeen or so, who was often to be found staring into space with her mouth drooping, or speaking animatedly to beings invisible. A schizophrenic, clearly, but well in with Puniekka and her clique. And friendly, when she wasn't being nuts.

A week or so after the night of the demon lover, I

approached Ullionk and asked her, in my paltry Yakut,
why it was that no one was paying attention to me, why
nobody would teach me anything about *teniesgu*, which
is what the Chenka call the sort of magic practiced by
women. She was amazed that I wanted to learn. I asked
her what she thought I was doing in Puniekka's yurt,
why she thought I was asking all those questions.
Because you are Vaarka's *ketzi*, she answered, with the
tone of saying something all the world knows. Vaarka
was Marcel. A *ketzi* is an animal, usually a dog, but
sometimes a sheep, in which a shaman has imprisoned
a troublesome spirit. For a moment my gape of mouth
mimicked Ullionk's in high fit. When I recovered I
asked whether Vaarka had told them this, and she said,
No, he said you were to be taught *teniesgu*, but it was
clear to everyone that this was a joke, that you were
ketzi. Why was this? Because, she explained, night after
night spirits have come to enjoy you. Surely you know
that no one can be a *fentienskin*, a shamaness, without
being enjoyed by one of the *rishen* or *rishot*. We must
have *dala* from them, and as we are women, sometimes
there is a child.

No, actually, that *had* slipped my mind, although it's
fairly clear in Marcel's book. I thought, though, that it
was figurative, that it was just a kind of dream. (*Just a
dream*, by the way, is an expression not much used
among shamans.) Yes, they came, she continued, and the
ogga within you turned them away. Puniekka told her
rish-husband to bring all his friends. Puniekka said she
would not lie with him until they had enjoyed you and
given you *dala*. But they could not come to you. And she
named here all the seducers who had tried and failed.
So at last, Puniekka gave up on you and allowed her

rishen to give her *dala*. She is not angry at you, but wishes Vaarka would put his *ketzi* in a young dog, or send it back to the other world, as it is very inconvenient having one in an *Aluesfan*, and though it was a good joke, it had stopped being funny.

I was fuming after I heard this. Marcel had said he was a kind of dog, which was fine if he wanted to believe that, but now this wacko was telling me I was less than a dog, a kind of spiritual trash can. And, rotten with pride as I was, I was mad to see Marcel and have him get me out of this insane position. I said this to Ullionk and she looked at me as if I were crazy, not very comfortable to get such a look from an actual crazy person, and reminded me that it was currently Vshenda, a long ceremonial period around the autumn equinox, in which sexual segregation was strongly enforced. I would have to wait for the end of the period, twenty days hence, when there would occur one of the regular feasts, whereat ordinary Chenkas indulged deeply in drinking, singing, dancing, and sex with other humans.

But I did not want to wait. Therefore, the next morning before dawn I took my compass, food, water, and a Russian map, and set out on a pony for the men's camp, which was about fifteen miles to the south. It was not a difficult navigational task. The steppe is flat or gently undulating, the weather was fine, dry and chilly. The sun was rising on my left hand as I set out riding, my compass clearly showing where south was. It should have been an easy three-hour jaunt toward the blue hump of the Konginskiye Gory in the distance. The direction was unmistakable, and so I was not surprised to see, some two hours later, the smoke of habitation ahead.

When I entered the enclosure, however, I found myself in the women's camp. The sun was still on my left, above the flat horizon. Jerk that I was, I whipped the pony around and, circling the camp, headed south again, a sick sweat breaking out all over me. As I rode, I kept checking the compass needle, which continued to say south, south, all the way up to the northern edge of the women's camp. Again. By that time, the sun was high in the day, and the camp was in the midst of its usual bustle. I dismounted, walked on rubber legs to Puniekka's yurt, and took to my pallet. No one spoke to me.

There I stayed, more or less, hardly eating, silent, curled up in a ball, leaking tears. I suppose I had been driven mad. I suppose I was clinically speaking a paranoid psychotic during those weeks, although I don't know whether this term is of any value in the cultural context of the Chenka. It's hard for me to reconstruct my thoughts during that time, but I know there were a lot of them, more thoughts than usually run through a human brain in a similar stretch of time, racing thoughts. Like: all the fault of Marcel Vierchau, French shit, filthy Jew, seducer, manipulator, never loved me, just wanted me as a guinea pig and a free fuck. Stupid me. Never loved me never. Fucking all the other girls, too. I wasn't the first, no. I saw his notes. I can read French. I'm not the first, no, he brought lots of girls out to Puniekka to eat up like the witch in the fairy tales, evil magician, egg in my cunt, how did he do that, how did she do that, it was pointing south, south, south all the time, they will give me a dog's head, and the *ogga* will make me into an old lady.

Marcel arrived with the other men for the feast. He

came to see me and I immediately attacked him, physically and with words, horrible stuff, and a remarkable
amount of it anti-Semitic, although I thought myself
quite free of that mental vice. Marcel had as a baby been
hidden in a Catholic orphanage during the Nazi time,
and his parents had died in the camps, so whatever was
speaking through me had a fine taste in cruelty. And the
usual lies about what an old impotent sack of shit he was
in bed, how his prick was way too small, how I'd fucked
all his graduate students, and on and on and he just sat
there looking at me, maddeningly calm until I leaped on
him, fists and nails. He cried out something. Puniekka
moved, striking like a snake, and placed both her hands
flat upon my temples. They were icy; shortly I felt the
coolness sink into my brain and I fell back upon my
pallet and into a dream.

Or something like one. I was curiously at ease,
detached but interested, like an actor in the wings,
watching the other performers, waiting for her own cue.
I remember that my vision seemed particularly acute,
the colors of the yurt's furnishing and of the dress of
Puniekka and Marcel seemed hyperreal. I want to say
jewel-like, but that's not quite it. Like food in a food ad.
The rage had quite gone, or rather I still felt it, but
abstractly, as if it didn't engage my real self.

After a long time by the clock of the sun shaft's
travel across the rugs of the yurt floor, Marcel came and
sat by me and put his arm around me and asked me how
I was, and I said I felt fine, which was perfectly true. I
remember the bright, glistening marks, like a string of
tiny garnets, where I had clawed his cheek, and I found
that interesting, too, they told a story. He helped me
gather up my gear. We left Puniekka's yurt and went

over to the tent that Marcel was renting for the festival
from some other woman. He settled me in there as if
nothing had happened.

He was gentle as he reminded me that the Chenka
do not have a psychology, as we think we do. No
neuroses, psychoses, introjects, repressions, obsessions,
phobias, or megrims. It is all a matter of spirits, independent transcendent entities who inhabit us in various
ways. One of them is the little person in the control
booth who operates our bodies and observes the world
through our sensoria, and whom we are pleased to call
our 'self.' Among the Chenka, the little person is something of a shift worker, knocking off for long periods
while others take control, sometimes several at once.
The inner life of the Chenka thus has to do with har-
monizing the relationships among the various spirits as
they pass through the control room. These beings also
have an existence in the unseen worlds, of which the
Chenka record several dozen, and a busy commuting
takes place among beings human and subhuman and
superhuman. There is a whole aesthetics involved in
this dance, which I do not have the terms to describe,
but it is the essence of Chenka existence, perilous
and ecstatic by turns. I knew this, of course, but I
had thought that it was all *imaginary*. Or symbolic. Or
merely spiritual, which is much the same thing to 99.9
percent of people in our culture. It did not occur to me
that it was about as imaginary, symbolic, and spiritual as
quantum electrodynamics.

As to why I had gone nuts, why I couldn't learn
Chenka magic: Marcel explained that the various *ogga*
lounging about my particular control room made it
impossible for me to enter into shamanic apprentice-

ship. They were in a sense wild *ogga*, who had invaded me during my childhood and adolescence, when I was angry, or sad, or envious, or wrapped in one of the other psychic states that *ogga* like to snack on. These beings could be removed or transformed. The procedure was as well known to the Chenka as an appendectomy is to an American surgeon. They would do it for me, but it had some cost. One's ego is, let us say, rectified. One dies, let us say, and is reborn, with the various resident spirits working more or less in concord. Marcel said that I was free to decide whether I wanted this done. He, naturally, had been through it during his long stay with the Chenka. In the state I was in at the moment, he allowed, I could not make a decision of such magnitude. True: it was difficult enough to decide whether I wanted to move my legs. Marcel was extremely sweet to me, especially considering how I had mauled him. He held me, and stroked my filthy hair. Time passed. Gradually I fell into something more like regular sleep.

In the morning the various *ogga* were back in charge, as yours are in charge of you – that is, I felt once again 'myself.' I now was terrified of Marcel, terrified of the Chenka, and worked hard at concealing this from myself and others. I recalled the nasty scene of the previous day, was deeply embarrassed, and took refuge in a chilly formality. Marcel did not ask me again if I wanted to have my brains scrambled in the Chenka fashion and I did not volunteer. I abandoned my efforts at penetrating Chenka shamanism. There was plenty of anthro work besides that, however, although it was a bit like doing an ethnography of a Polish village without mentioning Catholicism or the local priests. I worked all winter and by the time the ice broke on the Yei I had enough fieldwork to hack into a dissertation no more phony than most of the stuff anthro departments give Ph.D.'s for. A competent job. Even Marcel said so, not looking me in the eye.

I left the Chenka that spring as the ice on the Yei dissolved with many a groan, along with (as it turned out) the Soviet Union. By that time, I had put much of the unpleasantness behind me, and had erected the usual structure of self-justification. Marcel something of a fraud, sad to say, not the sort of man I had thought him at all, curiously cold in that French intellectual way, but helpful, of course, encouraging and helpful, and it had been quite a lark, our affair, something to dine out on for years to come. I recall saying just this in a light tone, with many an amusing anecdote, to Louis Nearing, a fellow anthropologist I dated for a couple of months in Chicago. I was in Chicago on a teaching contract, the year after Columbia gave me my doctorate. Anthro 101 and two veg. The bloom had gone off anthropology to an extent, but one must do something. Lou was a big, solid, open guy, a football player from Notre Dame, a Catholic, a year younger than me, sweet-natured and transparent as his collection of beer bottles; yes, just about as far as one could get from Marcel Vierchau. He was incredibly impressed, as were the other faculty, that I had been with Marcel for all those years, and knew all the great stars of the field, and had seen the remarkable Chenka in Siberia. In response I had developed this pathetic ironic set piece, especially to the what's-he-really-like opening. I had been well trained in this sort of dissembling at home. Getting along by not seeing or mentioning things was the prime value chez Doe.

Lou was not significant enough to be a rebound from

Marcel, and I think he knew it. I suppose I went out with him to demonstrate that I was still a regular person, that I could still have a regular life. If I had been more skillful at the lessons Mom tried to teach me, I would have married him and I'd now be living in a four-bedroom in Bloomingdale or Wheaton, teaching at the U., with a couple of kids, a retriever, and a Volvo. But I met my husband instead.

Poor Lou! I hadn't thought about Lou Nearing in years. He's gained a little weight, but that is certainly, undeniably, him walking toward me down a corridor at Jackson, me having just picked up a cart full of records at the ER. He's deep in conversation with a small brown middle-aged man dressed entirely in white, an obvious *santero*. I recall now what Lou was interested in. Medical anthropology. In another age he might have been a missionary priest, but he became a medical anthropologist.

He glances up and looks into my face as I glide by. I look back at him for an eyeblink, willing the recognition from my eyes, keeping my progress steady, not breaking into a mad run, as I wish to do. The problem is that I have forgotten my slump. Aside from the face, there is nothing so recognizable as the walking posture. I see his eyes change. The small brown man looks at me, too. His glance is bland, merely social for an instant, and then *his* eyes change.

Now I am past them, slumping for all I am worth. 'Jane?' Lou actually *introduced* me to my husband! But the next moment I am through the swinging door and then I start to run.

ELEVEN

9/16 Lagos

Things are not right. I say, it's Africa, give him time to adjust. Everyone says it. We all work hard, getting the various operations together. We lost all the ciggies, rum, much tape wrecked by being exposed to the weather, we've prob. enough, but barely. Fucking country, big, fertile, full of intelligent & creative people, large educated class, sea of oil, run into ground by criminals in power.

No, real problem's not fucking country but fucking husband. If he was *present*, all this supplies horseshit would be a joke, something to tell stories about back in NY. It's unbelievably embarrassing. He's acting like the kind of man he used to parody, the big, stupid, domineering black stud. I keep waiting for him to grin and tell me it's all an elaborate, ill-considered joke. I want to blame Ola Soronmu. It's what they call Afro-pessimism. Big on revival of African traditional politics, means male head of family gets to make all decisions, beat up on women, fuck whomever he wants, and party a lot. And traditional religion, too, white man imposed his religions, Islam and Christianity, on the black man, these represent evil as black. They say, worship like us and you will be white as us, but this is a lie. A new black god needed to rescue Africa from the whites, from neocolonialism, from corruption, from self-contempt. Will require bloodletting, all the rotten fruit must be cut off. He uses this phrase with glee, moving his arm like a man with a machete. Chop-chop. The bloodthirsty intellectual, curse of the century . . .

Night. He's not home yet, prob. out at one of the dives Ola takes him to, where can be found the *real* Africa. The others look at me with expressions varying from sympathy to satisfaction. Mrs Bassey sympathetic, invited me to church (!) w/ her tomorrow. I'm going.

9/17 Lagos

The service at St Mark's Anglican, ultra–high church. In procession everyone – priest, deacons, and altar boys (no girls here) – wearing a white gown & pointy bishop's miters. The text John 9, healing the man born blind, sermon was about miracles, priest was a skeletal man with the look of a saint in a Coptic mural. Apparently up north 163 churches had been burnt out last year by Muslim mobs. The congregations decided to hold services anyway in ruins, in rainy season. But on Sunday the sun shone. It then rained continuously for the next six days, & the sun came out again on Sunday, a pattern repeated for the next fourteen Sundays, by which time the congregations had rebuilt roofing. Muslims left them alone now. True story? Maybe. It's Africa.

The saints all blackfaced here and crude, statue of St Mark looked like a lawn jockey, w/ actual stuffed lion, decrepit, some Brit's idea of joke?

The marvelous sculptural tradition of the Yoruba has not made jump to Christian iconography, sad.

Afterwards, tea w/ Mrs B. in her private apartment at Lary's, & we let down our hair a little, cozy, her room a near-replica of one at Bournemouth & I wished I was a

Brit, and could suck the last minim of cozy out of it, am
starting to suffer from weird.

Cozy = antidote for weird? Dress for dinner in jungle, O
those Brits!

Tried to detect the signs of deracination, or phoniness
or subtle obsequiousness that Forster and Waugh have
told us is fate of the native who apes the whites, but I
couldn't find any. Mrs B. = fine Christian lady, pure
cultural choice. Real intimacy possible? I am nervous
with older women, easier with older men. No surprise
there!! Elements of shame, me being actually comforted
by this peculiar woman, in her absurd, hideous apartment,
here in heart of Africa. I almost wrote heart of darkness,
too.

Lyttel and Washington mock her behind her back, see
her as phony, a reminder of colonialism. Excused by youth,
by their American negritude? W. can't stand her, mimics
her cruelly to the others. His perfect ear.

She doesn't care for him either. Over tea and cream
buns (how can she do cream buns in Lagos? But very good
cream buns!) she broaches this. No secret in the house
that we are not getting along. What embarrassment, but I
spill, not the whole story, but all about his recent behavior
& the business with the stolen gear. I said he was
unbalanced in Africa, said I loved him, said it was my
fault.

She gave me a pitying look, said a man like that my girl
is no good, here is not in the bush you know, you don't
have no bride price paid for you, you are a Christian girl
and you have your own money. She made a gesture, a
grasping. Show him the door! Is what I would do in your
place, is what I *did* do in your place, and I didn't have
none of your wealth either, no.

Heard the whole story of Mr B., his laziness, his drinking, his cronies, his stealing from the hotel. When he started ripping off the guests, he got the boot. The fate of the strong black woman not Made in America. Strong woman, what's black to do with it? Pop sociology?

We embraced, me hard put not to blubber like a girl.

Later we had Sunday dinner. We always have some guests. Tonight's a guy named Bryan Banners and his wife, Melanie, he's an art historian, she's an anthropologist. Midwesterners both, both large and pink and blond. Banners had bought a little statue in the market. He had it with him and showed it around. It was an Ogun ax, a thin spindle of three figures, in ebony, with a triangular ax blade of iron attached to the head of the topmost. Greer looked it over and said it was a nice piece & Banners asked if it was authentic. Greer said that depended on what he meant by authentic, said it was an Ekite carving from the Kwara region, but what Banners probably meant was, 'was it old or recent?' Greer said it wasn't appropriate question to ask about African art. Age = European fetish. I could see that Banners hadn't ever thought that Europeans had fetishes & he said that he only meant did it come from a tribe with an intact tradition, or was it tourist trade? Greer said that wasn't the right question either, because you could ask also if Robert Motherwell was in an intact tradition or making stuff for the trade when he sold a painting to his New York gallery.

Greer said the reason why the Africans don't fetishize antiquity is that nothing organic lasts in Africa. Old masks and statues are routinely buried and new ones are made by clans of carvers. It's the spirit, the *ashe*, in the thing that counts, and this particular thing is full of *ashe*, so it doesn't matter if it was made a hundred years ago or last

Wednesday. There is a lot of junk, of course, you have to discriminate, as the locals do. Like in New York.

Then we got into Geertz's theories about art as a cultural system, and semiotics, and the deeper zones of modern anthro, which is home base to me, and I jumped in and we talked and talked, technical stuff, the four-color flat painting of the Abelam people of New Guinea, comparisons with Yoruba art, the unity of form and content, comparison to the Euro. Renaissance output; Moroccan poetry, its function as an indicator of social status and prestige, the relation of this to what West African griots do, praise singing in general, the Iliad, the modern epic poets of the Balkans, which way the influence traveled through these cultures, that, or an independent creation satisfying an instinctive human need, the possibility of a reliable semiotics of art.

Glanced over from time to time at W. to see how he was enjoying this, *he* was the artist here, he should be eating this up, plus I thought the discussion was better than most jabber in salons of New York, but he had a sour, bored expression on his face, and five empty lager bottles in front of him. Fact = W. can't drink. I thought, I should be like Melanie, I should go over and make nice and then I thought I was having a good time, brain was coming alive, like when I was with M., and I turned away.

The next time I looked it was because he was laughing with Soronmu, loud, and everyone stopped their conversation & waited for the other people to explain the joke. The joke was white folks trying to understand Africa, W. explained to Soronmu what an Oreo was. I looked at Greer, saw that his jovial host persona was wearing thin. He made some genial comment, inviting them to join the discussion, and W. said no, boss, us niggers'll be happier down the street, all this high-tone shit be over our heads. And the two of them staggered out, cackling.

He's still gone and it's after two. I don't know what to do now. I *know* he loves me. I *can't* be wrong about that.

TWELVE

Can we talk?' Paz asked. 'I could come back later or meet you someplace, if you're busy now.'

'Now is fine,' said Dr Salazar, 'but not here.' Something in her tone and look reminded Paz of the characteristic wariness of the fugitive, what you saw in a snitch. Dr Salazar, he thought, was on the lam.

'We could go for coffee,' he said. 'There're plenty of places on Le Jeune . . .'

'The faculty club, I think. The coffee isn't so good, but we won't be disturbed.'

Seated at a quiet table overlooking the campus lake, they passed some minutes in small talk, in Spanish, Paz consciously upgrading his diction and idiom to match hers, which was that of the prerevolutionary Havana *gratin*. After a pause, Paz asked, 'What you said before . . . who did you think was going to disturb us?'

'Oh, you know . . . unpleasant people. The last time I ate in a public restaurant, a man came up and spat into my food. I'd prefer to avoid such scenes.' Paz gave her a questioning look.

'You don't keep abreast of politics in the Cuban community? No, why should you? The politics of the Cuban community has little to do with people who look like you. I should explain, though, that I'm considered inadequate in my hatred of Fidel and his regime. I signed a petition, for example, asking that the embargo be lifted to allow the importation of medicines and baby formula. Also, I was so remiss as to tape an interview that was shown on Cuban television. It wasn't about politics, but only about my field of study; still, it was construed as being a comfort to the enemy. I was also friendly with Fidel beyond the time when it was considered appropriate, that is, when he began to seize the property of the rich.'

'You *knew* Fidel?'

'Everyone knew Fidel,' she said dismissively. 'Cuba is a small country and he never desired to hide his candle under a barrel. Also, we were at the university together.' He saw her eyes unfocus for an instant, something he had seen his mother do often, when the lost world of the Cuban past presented itself in some particularly vivid way. 'But you didn't search me out to speak of ancient history. You wish to consult me on . . . what?'

'Lydia Herrera suggested I talk to you. I went to see her because this showed up at a murder scene.' He took out the opele nut and put it on the table. She looked at it but did not pick it up. He went on, 'Besides this, the murder was . . . it looked like it might be some kind of ritual killing, and the victim's body was loaded with a bunch of exotic drugs. Narcotic and psychotropic drugs.'

'And you think it might have something to do with Santería?'

'Do you?'

'With organized Santería as it exists in the United States and Cuba? No, absolutely not. There's no tradition of drug use in Santería, aside from a few ritual swallows of rum, nor, of course, is there human sacrifice.'

'There's animal sacrifice, though,' said Paz, and got a sharp look.

'Yes, and Catholics eat their God during communion, but no one supposes that they'll depart from the symbolic to the literal and consume actual flesh and blood. You of all people should know this.'

'Why, because I'm a black Cuban? I'm sorry, but that's as wrong as assuming you're a rabid Alpha 66 supporter because you're a white Cuban.'

A bristling moment, Paz cursing himself for getting miffed at a potential information source *again*, but to his surprise, Dr Salazar smiled. 'There you have it in a nutshell, why Fidel is still in power and we are all over here. We are a waspish, disagreeable little people, are we not? I beg your pardon for my unwarranted assumption, which smacked, too, of racism.'

'No offense taken,' said Paz. 'But the fact is, my ignorance of Santería is practically total. My mother was particularly against it. She thought it was low.'

His mother. A memory flashed into his mind. He had come home from school with a slip of paper. It explained that in the fifth grade he was going to start in a remedial class. He explained to her that this was where they put the dumb kids. The mother was surprised. But you can make change, you can add up in your head, you read everything, and from an early age. Why are they doing this, in the school? It was embarrassing to say the real reason; perhaps his mother had not yet observed this element of American culture. He shrugged. He didn't answer. His mother was smarter than he thought, however. There was a *Herald* reporter who came to the restaurant. He was in love with her food, also a little with the cook. At his table one evening she stopped and told him the story. A smart boy, why do they want to put him with the *estupidos*? The reporter knew why. He knew that the school system had determined that although it could not get away with actual racial segregation, it could do the next best thing by insuring that little black and little white children would never have to sit in the same classrooms, for it was an element of the American creed that the reason They do not do well in life is that They are not very smart. A story was duly run about tracking and its discontents. Jimmy was placed in the gifted and talented track and became officially part of the Talented Tenth along with Oprah and Colin, so the Americans could go back to thinking that all was well in that area of national life.

Dr Salazar was staring at him peculiarly. Had he missed something? He said, 'Sorry, I got distracted by the past for a second there. You were saying?'

Through a faint smile she said, 'I was saying that I should have acknowledged that *any* deeply held faith can produce monstrosities. Some years ago in Matamoros, a group of men who called themselves *santeros* committed more than a dozen murders, supposedly as part of a ritual. But that had as much to do with the true religion as the Jonestown atrocity or that terrible man in Waco had to do with Christianity. So, it's entirely possible that you're dealing with someone, a madman, who's warped Santería to his own sick ends. Can you tell me something about the ritualism associated with this murder?'

Paz did, leaving out, as usual, some important

details. Dr Salazar's face became very grave, nearly stricken. She picked up the opele nut in its plastic envelope.

'This is African,' she said.

'So I understand. Does that make a difference?'

'Yes. It's quite possible that you are dealing not with a Cuban or an Afro-Cuban, but with an African, a practitioner of the original religion from which the various New World religions were derived.'

'And that original one *would* involve human sacrifice?'

'If we're talking about Africa, who knows? Certainly not me. There have been any number of cultures in which human sacrifice was accepted – the Aztecs are the most famous, but also we have Carthage, and thuggee in India, and ritual headhunting in the South Pacific, and there may be some similar cults in Africa. The Ibo certainly had some of it, by informal report. They are neighbors of the Yoruba, which is where Santería comes from. There's a published account by a former so-called juju priest in which a white man is tortured to death to help Idi Amin's career. True? Who knows? But I've never heard of it being part of the formal Yoruba religion. You said that drugs were involved? Yes? Then I would say that you are not dealing with religion, but with witchcraft.'

'What's the difference?'

The deep-set black eyes hardened surprisingly. 'Witchcraft, or sorcery, is about power, and religion is about grace. The religionist supplicates a supernatural power, and prays for spiritual benefits. The sorcerer attempts to bend occult forces to his will. The religionist prays, the sorcerer manipulates.'

'But religions make sacrifices, even human sacrifices, as you said.'

'Yes, but as part of a settled order of the universe. Santería is largely concerned with divination and the direct experience of holiness. The *santero*, the *babalawo*, the members of an *ile*, are supplicants. They believe they are taking their places in a world ordered by Olodumare and impregnated by *ashe*, a kind of spiritual energy. Devotees desire to conform themselves to this energy through honoring the ancestors, through opening themselves to direct contact with the *orishas*, the spiritual beings who are different aspects of the Godhead, or through divination. This is why Santería is identifiable as a religion. The sorcerer's world on the other hand is not ordered in this way. It is chaotic, filled with violent and often malevolent powers, which the sorcerer seeks to understand and control. Control, do you see? At least that's always been the theory.'

She stopped, her eyes drifting. Paz waited, keeping his face neutral. Then she looked at him, and it seemed to him that she read his thoughts.

'You are not a believer, are you, Detective Paz?'

'To tell the truth, I'm not.'

'Well, it's a gift, and not given to everyone, at every time. But I should refine my position to say that sorcery and religion tend to blend around the edges. Submission to the will of God has never been very common. Most of us would wish to influence him, if we could, or to know what he has in store for us. You might say that Santería itself fulfills that purpose among people who are nominally Catholic. This can blend imperceptibly into sorcery, and we then see the drugs, the curses, the love potions. *Voudoun*, as you know, which has antecedents similar to those of Santería, has gone far in this direction. I recall a line of research that suggests just that, dark doings on the fringes of the Yoruba culture. Tour de Montaille and others.'

'Excuse me?'

'A name. Charles Apollon de la Tour de Montaille was a French officer who did a good deal of ethnography in West Africa, back around the turn of the last century. He published some short articles about his discovery of a cult group of some sort who claimed to have preceded the Yoruba, who actually taught them Ifa divination. He said furthermore that this group supported a clan, I suppose, of witches with remarkable powers. I can't recall the name of the cult group, but I do recall there was a ritual involving the sacrifice of a pregnant woman. You didn't mention it, but tell me: was the fetal brain excised?'

'Yes, it was,' said Paz, and felt a chill ripple his scalp. 'So, what you're saying is this mutilation reminds you of some tribal cult ritual described in a French anthropologist's report around a hundred years ago.'

'Yes, and I wish I could remember more details, but, you know, it is nearly a hundred years since I was a student and read of it.' She laughed. 'Or so it seems. But I'll tell you something else. Much more recently there was a paper. Where was it?' She struck her temple with the heel of her hand. 'My God, I am growing dim. No, it was not a published paper. It was sent to me by a journal to referee, and I recall that it referenced Tour de Montaille. The author – oh, what was his name? I can't recall it. In any case, the author claimed to have found the same cult Tour de Montaille had studied so long ago. I tell you what – you have got me intrigued, young man.

I will do some looking for you and perhaps I can find the paper. Would that be helpful?'

'It sure would. We'd be very grateful. But in the meantime, could you give me any ideas about the man I'm looking for? I mean, are there any particular likes or dislikes he might have? Like he wears only blue and can't eat hamburgers – I mean assuming he thinks he's some kind of sorcerer in that tradition.'

'I see, yes. Well, a man, certainly, with African contacts, and he has probably spent much time in West Africa. Doesn't like to have his photograph taken, cuts his hair himself. A powerfully commanding personality, may be the head of a small group, political, let's say, or an extended family. The number sixteen is important.'

'Sixteen?'

'Yes.' She tapped the opele. 'If he uses this. The number is sacred to Ifa. Tell me, do you think you'll find this man?'

'Well, we'll do our best, but the fact is, the more time that passes after the murder, the harder it gets. Unless, God protect us, he does it again.'

'Oh, he will certainly do it again. As I recall, he has to do it four times within sixteen days. Or sixteen times in one hundred twenty-eight days. Or is that from some other ritual? I can't recall. I'll certainly have to look for that paper.'

The interview with Dr Maria Salazar was the last substantive addition to the case file on Deandra Wallace for several days. Jimmy Paz and Cletis Barlow both had their snitches and they had come up blank. No African juju man was known to any of them. No one had seen or heard anything connected to the crime. The case did not vanish from their minds, but it had receded from the foreground, replaced by more recent slaughter.

Today's corpse, the one they were on now, had been in life Sultana Davis, and had dwelled a street north of Deandra Wallace in a similar building, this one painted faded blue. Except that she was just as dead, Ms Davis's murder differed in all other respects from that of her predecessor-in-death. The chief suspect in the case was Ms Davis's estranged boyfriend, Jarell McEgan. He had gotten drunk, broken into Ms Davis's apartment the previous evening, provoked a violent argument, stabbed her twenty-one times with a steak knife, finished Ms Davis's alcohol, and made his escape in his car, or tried to, since he had merely turned on the ignition and passed out. There the police found him the next morning. He had blood on his hands, always a good clue, and on his clothes.

McEgan denied knowing anything about Ms Davis or the blood, or the origin of the bloody fingerprints on Ms Davis's bottle of vodka. He was now cuffed and snoring in the back of a patrol car. Barlow was in the apartment still, making sure of the evidence. Paz was in the front seat of his car, with the door open, scratching on his steno pad, getting a head start on the 301, the investigative report. As he did so, he reflected, with some shame, on his effort to shape the Wallace killing into the far more familiar pattern represented by this one.

Barlow came out of the building with an armful of plastic evidence bags. He stashed them in the trunk and said, 'Take a look at this.'

Paz got out of the car. Barlow pointed to the apartment house he had just left.

'That's a four-story building there.'

Paz made a show of counting floors. 'Yeah, Cletis. Four. You counted right, and here you told me you never went to college.'

'As the crackling of thorns under a pot, so is the laughter of a fool. You happen to look out the window of the vic's apartment?'

'Why?'

'The Wallace woman's place was on the second floor back. You probably can see into her kitchen pretty good from nearly the whole line of third- and fourth-floor apartments here, from the kitchens and the back bedrooms.'

'And you want me to hang around here and talk to all the residents.'

'Only those that're home. You'll want to come back this evening and speak to the people who're at work now. I'll go off and put our suspect into the system.'

'You'll write up the three-oh-one?'

'No, you will. It is good for a man that he bear the yoke in his youth. Lamentations 1:27.'

The afternoon inhabitants of the building were women on pensions or welfare, the old, the unemployed, and a few crooks. At the end of three frustrating hours, he had nearly the same nothing he had started with, except that he had been offered sex once, dope twice, and a glass of iced tea, only the last of which he had accepted, from a Mrs Meagher, sixty-eight. She lived with her two grandchildren, eight and fourteen, currently at school, their mother having recently died of the Virus, the children apparently healthy, praise Jesus, and would he like another sugar cookie? Paz confirmed that the Meagher apartment had a good view of the Wallace kitchen, but Mrs Meagher had not seen anything out that window, her eyes not being what they were. Paz said he would return when the kids were back from school. He left and continued his canvass, which yielded nothing.

He returned to his oven of a car, drove to a convenience store on Twelfth, and bought a packaged ham and cheese sandwich and a Mountain Dew soda.

Outside the store Paz observed a group of youths cutting school, dressed in costumes – hugely baggy pants worn at the level of the pubes, cutoff team sweatshirts, expensive athletic shoes worn unlaced – donned in hopes that they would be mistaken for ex-convicts, the highest status of which they could conceive. They went past him into the store to do some light shoplifting.

Paz had no particular sympathy for the youths. The previous generation of the same type had made his own life very difficult, as had (to be fair) their Cuban analogues. Whatever sympathy he might have had for the shopkeeper vanished when he started to eat: the sandwich was both stale and soggy, and tasted like clay, and the soda was warm. It was not revived even when he saw the kids running out of the store, laughing, clutching purloined bags of Fritos and M&M's. As he trashed his uneaten lunch, some lines from a poem ran through his mind:

> Those that I fight I do not hate
> Those that I guard I do not love

And this led him naturally to thoughts about the woman who had taught him the poem, and he drove away south.

Paz walked into the Coconut Grove library near Peacock Park, an elegant building made of gray wood and glass, and approached the woman behind the information desk. She was short, and slightly plump in a luscious way, with hair like polished copper wires and large round horn-rimmed glasses. Her skin was smooth, creamy, and freckled.

'Can I help you?'

'Yes,' said Paz, 'I was looking for some books with pictures of naked ladies in them and not a lot of printing.'

'I see. Well, we do have an extensive split beaver collection. It's on that low shelf right by the children's section.' She grinned at him, showing small, shiny, even teeth. Willa Shaftel was not a conventionally attractive woman – the bodice on the print sundress she was wearing was barely filled and the rest of her torso departed only slightly from the cylindrical – but she had a bright and knowing face, a big, lush mouth, remarkable blue eyes, and there was that hair. 'It's been a while, Jimmy. To what do we owe?'

'Police business. There's a big push on library-fine scofflaws.'

'Those dirty vultures, but I thought you worked for homicide.'

'I do. We've found that murderers often move on to more serious things like not returning library books or even scribbling on the pages. We want to nip it in the bud. Also, I came by to see if you wanted to go to lunch.'

'I only have a half hour,' said Shaftel.

'Take it,' said Paz.

After buying food they went to Peacock Park and sat on a bench in the shade of some casuarinas, right by the bay, watching children poke sticks in the gray mud. Paz ate from a box of conch fritters and fries, Shaftel from a little plastic salad plate and a container of yogurt.

'I was just thinking of you a while ago,' he said.

'Yes, I get that all the time. Some men can't stop obsessing about my body for a minute.'

'That too, but it was that poem.' He described the circumstances, his morning activities, a sketch of the case, his abortive lunch, and his recall of the lines.

'Oh, "Irish Airman," Yeats,' she said. '"Not law nor duty made me fight, nor public men nor cheering crowds, a lonely impulse of delight, drove to this tumult in the clouds."'

'Yeah, I like that. "A lonely impulse of delight" is good.'

'Is that why you work homicide? Clearly there's no great attachment to the public weal. As you've often said, by and large, both killers and their victims are jerks. It's not a racial chip on the shoulder . . .' She glanced sideways at him. '. . . or at least not entirely. So . . . what? Hard work, dirty work, tedious knocking on doorways . . .'

'You're going to use this in your book?' He was skilled at evading her frequent probes.

'Of course. I use everything. Not one of my relatives still speaks to me, and I've only published one novel.

But you? Well, maybe just in a short story. Or a brief lyric. I don't know you very well.'

'You don't? We know each other . . . what? A year and a half?'

'Yes, and you fall by every week or so, and take me out, and treat me like a lady, and jump on my bones afterward, and God knows it's pleasant, you're a very nice guy, and it's not like I need a velvet rope to keep all the others from rushing the door, but I probably know the checkout ladies at Winn-Dixie better than I know you.'

'Get out of here! We talk all the time.'

'About me and poetry and what to read, and what I think about writing, and my little-girl dreams. But we don't talk about you. I know you're a homicide cop and your mother owns a restaurant, and your partner is a quaint old redneck. Anecdotes, data, but the man is hidden. Wouldn't you agree?'

'All right, what do you want to know?' said Paz, nor was he able to keep the edge of challenge from his voice.

She grinned and patted his hand. 'It doesn't matter, Jimmy. It's not an interrogation.' She collected their trash and walked to a basket. When she returned she sat down on the grass in front of him cross-legged, exposing soft white thighs.

He said, 'Well, at least it'll give us something to talk about as the years slide by. You can pry out my shameful secrets.' He used his ordinary light bullshitting tone, but she smiled only faintly.

'I was going to call you,' she said. 'My grant came through the other day.'

'What, the Iowa thing? Congratulations, babe!' He

leaned forward and kissed her on the cheek. 'So, you're leaving in the fall?'

'No, as soon as I can sublet my place. Maybe a week. Anything to avoid another whole summer here.'

Paz kept his expression neutral and friendly but began to feel that stiffening of the features that follows when we separate the face from the heart. 'Well. Bye-bye, Willa. We should give you a big send-off.'

'Mm. I'd rather slink away, if you don't mind. But if you want to take me out, I'm dying to see *Race Music*. It's at the Coconut Grove Playhouse. What, you don't like it?'

Paz was not aware that his face had registered anything at all, and he said, 'I don't know. I get enough of that oh-how-our-people-have-suffered shit on the job. Picking at the scab – I mean, what good does all that do?'

'No, the guy is funny! He's not heavy, he's not portentous. It's a *musical*, for God's sake. You *like* musicals.'

'I don't like messages.'

'We went to *My Fair Lady* last month. That has a message.'

'What message?'

'People who change superficial behaviors become different people, one, and two, the old fart still can get the girl. That's why they love it on Miami Beach.'

Paz had to laugh. 'Okay, it's a date. Friday.'

'What a guy!' she crowed, and got up and sat on his lap and kissed him on the mouth. She really did have the most excellent mouth, Paz reflected, like a teacup full of hot eels.

*

Paz put in a couple of hours of routine work on this morning's shooting, which scrubbed personal musings from his surface mind. Barlow was out. He placed the folder with the completed investigation and arrest report on Barlow's pristine desk and left for the remainder of his canvass.

Traffic was building up to the afternoon rush on 95, so he took surface streets, arriving a little after four. The courtyard under the landings was now running with children back from school. He climbed the stairs. At the third-floor landing, he came upon a boy urinating in a corner. 'Don't do that!' Paz said, and the boy said, 'Shut the fuck up, motherfucker!' and continued his pee. Paz walked around the spreading puddle without further comment and rang Mrs Meagher's bell.

A chunky young girl with cornrowed hair and plastic-rimmed glasses opened the door and looked him up and down suspiciously. 'What you want?' she demanded. She wore a pink sweatshirt with some cute animals appliquéd upon it in plastic, and blue slacks. She looked younger than fourteen.

'I want to talk with you, if you're Tanzi Franklin,' Paz said.

'How you know my name?'

He showed her his badge. 'I'm the police. I know everything.' Big smile, not returned. 'Could we go inside?'

After an instant's hesitation, the girl backed away from the door and let him in.

'Where's your grandma?'

'She out, shopping or whatever. What you want to talk to me about?'

'Let's go back to your bedroom and I'll show you.'

The bedroom was a ten-foot square, walls painted powder pink, much grimed, and divided by a hanging brown plaid curtain to the right of the doorway. The girl's side of the room contained a white-painted bed, neatly made up with a yellow chintz cover, and a low dresser in battered brown wood, with a mirror over it. A poster of Ice-T hip-hopping and one of Michael Jordan leaping were taped to the walls. Paz looked through the half-window allotted the girl by the room divider. Over the low roofs of the intervening street he could see directly into Deandra Wallace's kitchen, now a dark rectangle.

'Nice view,' said Paz, pulling back and facing the girl, who stood nervously in the doorway. 'You ever look out the window? At that apartment building?'

A dull nod. He pointed out the window at the Wallace building. 'Maybe you can tell me about some of the people who live over there.'

'My friend Amy live there.' She indicated a first-floor window.

'That must be fun. You could wave to her. How about that apartment above where Amy lives and a little to the right. It's dark now. Do you know who lives there?'

'Lady got killed.'

'That's right. Did you ever look in there before she got killed?' Paz felt a little excited now, a tingle of detective instinct. Strictly speaking, the regs prohibited him from questioning a child without an adult guardian present, but he did not want to break this off just yet. This kid must spend a lot of time in this room looking out the window. It was like having real-life cable, with continuous soaps and no PG-13 ratings. She had a wary look, however, and so he asked if he could sit on her bed and wait for her grandmother to return. Would she mind sitting next to him so they could talk? She sat on the very corner of the bed, as far from him as she could.

'Tanzi, you could really be a big help to us and do yourself some good here. Did you know that the police pay money for people to help them?'

A spark of interest. 'Yeah? Like, how much?'

'Depends on what they tell us.' He pulled a clip of currency out of his pocket. 'Let's try me asking some questions and see how much you can earn. Okay, first question. Did you ever see anyone in that apartment besides the lady who lived there?'

Nodding. 'Yeah, her boyfriend.'

Paz peeled a couple of singles off the roll and dropped them on the bed. 'Very good. Now let's talk about last Saturday. Did you watch TV?'

'Uh-huh. I watched *Saturday Night Live.* 'Cause my gran went to sleep before. She don't let me watch it usually.'

'Okay, and after the show, did you look out the window, maybe wave to Amy?'

A nod, a looking-away.

'And, so, Tanzi, did you see anything that went on in that apartment?'

'He slap her.'

'Who?'

'Her boyfriend. They was running back and forth and he was throwing stuff around and out the window and she trying to stop him and he slap her in the head. And then he run out.'

Paz stripped a five from the roll and placed it on the other bills. 'And after that, what happened?'

Shrug. 'Nothing. I went to sleep.'

'Uh-huh,' Paz replied, and then, carefully, 'You went to sleep right after the other man came in, right?'

'Yeah, that's right.' Her eyes were on the pile of money.

'What did the other man look like?'

The girl took a breath, as if to answer, and then without any warning she sucked in two more whooping breaths and then collapsed on the bed, her face screwed into a knot, howling.

Paz made a feeble attempt to comfort her, but she shrank from him, curled into a ball, and continued her noise, a horrible high-pitched yowl, like a cat. He heard footsteps. The bedroom door flung open and there stood Mrs Meagher and a little boy. The woman rushed to her granddaughter, crying, 'Oh, honey, what did he do to you?'

'I didn't do anything to her,' said Paz. But she glared at him and pointed to the door. 'Get out, you! I'll tend to you later.'

He paced in the living room, wanting a smoke, a drink, baffled as to what to do next. The girl had clearly seen something, an event so terrifying that the mere mention of another man in the Wallace apartment had sent her over some psychic edge. After some minutes, the little boy came into the room and sat on a worn upholstered rocker. Paz recognized him as the landing urinator.

'How come you beat on my sister?'

'I didn't beat on your sister. Do I look like someone who beats on little girls?'

'You the *po*-lice,' said the boy, as if in explanation. 'How come she crying, then?'

'I don't know. We were just talking normal, and then I asked her a question and she went bananas.'

'What you ax her?'

'The window of you guys' room looks out on a window where a woman was murdered last weekend. I wanted to know if she saw anything.' He paused. 'Did *you* see anything?'

'I saw a ho naked.'

'That's nice. Tell me something . . . what's your name, by the way?'

'Randolph P. Franklin. Show me your piece.'

'Later. Randolph, tell me something. How come if you live right here you were pissing on the landing?'

''Cause my gran, if she be there, she make me stay in after school, and I got to hang with my homes.'

'What you got to do is do your homework and mind your granma.'

The boy shook his head in disgust. 'You so lame, man. Now can I see your piece?'

Paz flipped his jacket aside to reveal the .38 in its belt holster.

The boy said, 'Oh, man, that a *pussy* gun. You should get you a nine, man.' He adopted a crouched shooting stance and made the appropriate noises. 'That's what I'm gonna get me, a nine, a Smith or a Glock. I got a friend got a two-five.'

'You don't need friends like that,' said Paz. Mrs Meagher came in.

'How is she?' Paz asked.

'She's sleeping, no thanks to you. I got a good mind to call your boss and complain. And you a colored man, too.' The woman was only somewhat over five feet in height, but she was crackling with outrage, and formidable.

'Ma'am, I didn't do anything to your grandchild. I didn't yell at her or threaten her or touch her. In fact, all I was doing was giving her money and asking if she saw anything to do with the crime I'm investigating. And she did. I think she did see the actual killer, through that window. But as soon as I asked her to describe the man, she went into this screaming fit.'

Mrs Meagher narrowed her eyes. 'Why would she go and do that?'

'You know, ma'am, I've been asking myself the same thing, and the only thing I can come up with is that Tanzi saw something so awful that it somehow hurt her mind, so that whenever she has to think about it she goes off like she just did. And let me tell you something, Mrs Meagher. I've been a homicide detective for six years now, and this murder we're talking about was the worst thing I ever saw. I'm not talking about some hyped-up kid who shot a clerk in the 7-Eleven store. This guy's a monster. And what if he does it again?'

'Sweet Jesus!'

'Yeah. And besides that, what about Tanzi? She could be messed up for life behind this, end up in an institution.'

And more of the same, until the woman was frantic and thoroughly bamboozled. She was a confirmed watcher of the kind of daytime television in which children were indeed turned into monsters by the shock of witnessing something nasty.

Smoothly, he closed with 'So, if it's okay by you, ma'am, I'd like to arrange to have her looked at by a doctor, somebody who could talk to her and figure out what the damage was and how to fix it. No charge to you, of course; the Miami PD will take care of the whole thing.'

It was okay by her. Later, driving back to the department, Paz felt only somewhat ashamed of himself. He knew that there was no way that the PD would pay for any kind of counseling for a kid like Tanzi, even if she knew who got Hoffa. At a light, therefore, he used his cellular phone to dial a familiar number, the office of Lisa Reilly, Ph.D., child psychologist. The last remaining girlfriend.

THIRTEEN

My transmission does a little hesitation and a lurch before it pops into third gear. It's leaking fluid, too, and is the main thing that dissuades me from packing Luz and my scant trunkful of possessions in the Buick and heading out the next day toward some city picked at random. If Lou Nearing actually spotted me walking down the halls of Jackson pushing a records cart, and if he wants to come after me, say hello, talk about old times, it shouldn't take him long to find me, and then what? No, more probably he'll recall that I committed suicide. It was in all the papers. I wonder if Lou is still friendly with him. Maybe they call each other a couple of times a year. Hey, man, funny thing happened, I thought I saw Jane the other day in the hospital. And my husband would remind Lou that I was dead, but at the same time he would be thinking, triumphally, happily (if 'happy' is still a word that applies), she's alive. Because there wasn't any body, which should have made him a little suspicious in the first place. On the other hand, if I were going to kill myself, for reasons he alone knew, he would have to figure I'd do it in a way that left no body for him to find – and *use*, in the various ways he must have learned. Immolation by fire. Drowning at sea. I chose a boat explosion and drowning, being a nautical person.

Or maybe Lou's in with him. Maybe he's the disciple. Maybe he killed that woman. I can't think this way, or I'll go mad. Madder.

Unpleasant times at the office today. Mrs Waley tells me to push the records cart around again and I refuse to leave the Medical Records Office. Mrs Waley is vexed. I say that it is the job of the messengers to carry records, and she points to the section of my job description where it says other duties as assigned, and I say that is only true of duties having to do with clerkship. She says in what she imagines is an intimidating voice, are you refusing a direct order, as if we were in the marines, and I put on an air of mulish obstinacy and repeat that I am *not* going out of the office anymore. As I do so, because I am so frightened of running into Lou Nearing again, I let Crazy Jane peek out from behind my eyes for a few seconds and I see the expression on her face change. She remembers that I am a bat and envisions a scene, maybe even violence, and she backs off, muttering about a written reprimand in my personnel jacket. I will have to bear it.

Later, Lulu and Cleo grab me in the file warrens, mad to know what the fuss was about. I tell them a version of the truth, that I don't want to wander the halls because there's a man I'm avoiding, someone who's annoying me. They stare at me in amazement, and a look passes between them. A *man*? *Dolores*?

Later in the car thinking, Yes, drive to some anonymous city. Dayton. Boise. Indianapolis. Get a place to live and a meaningless job moving paper or electrons from one box to another, raise Luz, each day scratch another line on the wall, like the bearded prisoners in cartoons.

There are long shallow steps leading to the day-care center, and on one of these sits Luz in close conversation with a little blonde. She flickers a hand at me as I approach but doesn't move. Their perfect cheeks are close together, dark as bread crust, pale as milk. I have a moment of faintness. A little unstuck in time for a moment there: I was thinking of my husband's brown hand moving over my body, how happy I felt there at the beginning. Oh, it was love, true, but it was also a certain self-satisfaction, the world convulsed with the hallucination of race, and little Jane had beat it, gone beyond. I dig my nails into the palms of my hands and summon up a ghastly smile. But they are not watching me.

The blonde is Amanda, the new best friend, the subject of continuous commentary recently, a Talmud in pink sneakers. Luz has been to Amanda's house, on Trapp Avenue in the good white Grove, the earthly paradise, and desperately does she want Amanda to come to her house. I had not anticipated this, I confess. I thought she would be as I am now, a solitary, the two of us for ourselves and no one else. But no, she is now a regular little kid, the insanity of her first four years has been put out with the trash, and now she wants Barbies and My Little Pony and pals.

A thin, elegant woman gets out of a silver Audi and comes over to the girls and me. She has big sunglasses pushed up on her hair, which is beautifully cut and a few shades darker than her daughter's. She is wearing a fawn suit, and a peach silk blouse. She is something with an airline. The mister is a big-time lawyer. Julia

Pettigrew is her name. Amanda runs to her and asks if
she can go home with Luz, and Luz does the same to
me. Mrs Pettigrew looks at me kindly, the sort of patronizing look Dolores Tuoey deserves, the look saying of
course I don't mind if my precious goes in your horrible
dangerous junker and visits your half-caste kid in your
white-trash household, and I am far too liberal, and
proud of it, to ever by word or deed imply that there is
any objection to the association between our children.
And in response I sort of shuffle and begin to shake my
head negatively, so that Mrs Pettigrew rescues me, as I
knew she would, by saying, 'Girls! Why don't we go to
Cocowalk and get an ice cream!' Cries of delight, the
bribe effective, and 'I'll bring her back in a couple of
hours.'

A couple of hours, good, that will give me enough
time to pack my little box and my ugly clothes, and write
a note, please take care of my little girl, and by the time
they get there I can be in Vero Beach. The transmission
will get me to Jacksonville and then I can take a bus. I
can travel faster alone, dumb in the first place to take
the kid. The *ogga*, grasping at the controls.

Later I sit in the car in my driveway listening to it
tick. We are both troubled by transmission problems;
like my Buick, I can't get into gear. This happened after
I left Marcel, too. It is hard to leave the Chenka.
Impossible to find them if they don't want to be found,
but leaving is no simple thing either, especially in the
spring, when everything turns to bog. I went with
Marcel and a party of Chenka on their semiannual
shopping trip to Ust-Sugoy. Kmart has not come to Ust-
Sugoy yet, but you can buy salt there and tools and cloth
if you have wool to trade. Marcel put me on the weekly

boat that runs up the Kolyma River to the roadhead at
Seymchan. My eyes slid off his face, there was a repulsion there, where once there had been attraction. He
volunteered to leave his work and come with me, but I
flatly refused, I think I even got angry with him,
accused him of treating me like a child, of wanting to
continue his control. Being a good modern girl I had
reinterpreted the cosmic evisceration I had just gone
through as personal *growth*! I need my freedom – I
actually said that to him. Freedom, the one pathetic
virtue of the Americans, that and honesty. I was disappointed in him, I said, being honest. I didn't cry when
the greasy old boat pulled away, but, now that I recall it,
he did, the slow embarrassing tears running down his
face.

At Seymchan, while one waits for one's bus, one
stays at the exclusive Gulag Hilton, a two-story structure in cracked and rusty concrete, where the rooms are
little boxes without TVs, mini-bars, or windows. You get
an iron bedstead and a mattress stuffed with felt and
vermin and a twenty-watt bulb that turns off all by itself
at ten. You can get kvass at the bar, though, and pepper
vodka, which I did in some quantity. From Seymchan, it
is a two-hundred-mile bus ride through the lovely
Commie death camp district to Magadan, stopping for
the evening at romantic Myakit. There was a hotel in
Myakit, too, but it had burned down while I was in the
field, and so we all stayed the night in the bus terminal.
My fellow passengers were all Siberians and so the
temperature in the cement-block building – maybe ten
degrees of frost – did not trouble them. There was a red-
hot stove going, and a boiling samovar, and there was
ample vodka traveling around in a jolly enough manner.

I fell in with a Yakut family named Turgaliy, a man, his wife, and three children, two girls and a little boy. They had some bread, sausage, and tea, which they kindly shared with me, and I passed on a Bic lighter for Mr T., and for Mrs T. an almost-full purse spray of L'Air du Temps (oh, yes, I actually brought it along for my romantic idyll among the Chenka), and push-button ball pens for the kids. They also had a bottle of unbranded local vodka, which stood by me during much of the evening. We drank from little silver cups. I learned some doleful, droning Yakut songs and passed out singing.

And awoke in my sleeping bag, into which the Turgaliys had stuffed me, at dawn, to find myself in the middle of what appeared to be a nervous breakdown. The tiny little lady in the control room was baffled. The body refused to move. The vital levers and switches had been taken over by an *ogga*, a sad and frightened spirit, who thought that the best thing to do was to lie here in this cozy sleeping bag, zipped up over the head, until death intervened or the entropic curtain descended upon a universe grown terminally stale. I could see through my eyehole the Turgaliys moving about gathering their things. The children peered in, grinning, clicking their ballpoints like microcastanets. I heard the bus arrive, the worried pleading of the Turgaliys. They shook me, they attempted to uncocoon me, but I rolled into a ball and wept until they left. The bus pulled out, farting gaily. Silence. I had to pee. I staggered to the smelly hole provided, then back to the bag. It's just the bag I'm in, I said to myself, or rather that is what the *ogga* said to the tiny little lady, and thought it very witty, a stopper. That's just the bag I'm in, an old Fred Neil song it appears to know. I was clutching my notebook like a holy relic.

Some days passed. The daily bus pulled in and out. Someone went through my backpack, removing all valuables, then someone else removed the backpack itself. I stopped going to the hole to pee, but there was not much pee to pee anymore, since I had stopped eating and drinking.

Time went by. A shadow fell over my little blowhole. I opened my eye and there was Josiah Mount, my half brother. This was such a shock that for a moment, I regained control. I licked my cracked lips and formed the obvious 'What are you doing here?' He said, 'Don't you know that if you stay in the bus station in Myakit long enough, everyone you ever knew in your life will walk by?' Always a kidder, Josey.

Marcel, through some unknown, but probably non-sorcerous, means, had caused an e-mail message to appear in my brother's office describing my route and suggesting I might be in some serious trouble. My brother immediately chartered an airplane. He can do things like that because he made a remarkable amount of money in the telephone business; he claims to have invented the annoying dinnertime phone call asking if you want to switch your long-distance carrier.

He picked me up, stinking sleeping bag and all, and placed me in the bed of a truck parked outside. The truck roared and started. He washed my face with water from a plastic bottle and dribbled some into my mouth. Then black. Then an oatmeal sky, too bright. I was out of the sleeping bag and didn't stink anymore. I was lying flat, being carried on a stretcher by two squat Asians in brown uniform into a pale blue jet aircraft that smelled of kerosene and hot plastic. The engines made a shrill sigh. My brother's face, smiling; he stroked my hair from my eyes. A slight sticking pain. More black.

I rejoined the relatively living in a hospital room, hooked to tubes and monitors. A woman in white came into the room and said something in Japanese, another Altaic language, but one I do not speak. She took my temp and smiled and left. After a few minutes, my brother came into the room.

I get out of the Buick, enter my apartment, and replace some of the water I have sweated away with a glass of water from the tap. I get my big suction cup, wet it in the sink, and then kneel over the secret place. I pull up the tile and look down.

My brother took me north, to Yoshioda, in the hills above Sendai. It was spring then, and I could stand on the terrace behind our dojo and watch the paddies turn from black to heartbreaking green, and the slow white surf of the peach and cherry blossoms move up the mountain. Our dojo was a two-story building made of pine and cedar in the country style. My brother had built it for Mr Omura. Josey had been studying aikido for five years at a big dojo in Tokyo and had heard about Mr Omura and came to see him and stayed for a year, occupying a string bed in a cubbyhole behind the Omura noodle shop. My brother thought Mr Omura was the best aikido sensei in the world.

The rooms at Yoshioda were cedar-paneled three-mat affairs containing only a futon and a chest. It was like living in a cigar box, but very pleasant. I don't know what arrangement my brother had made with Omura-sensei, but no one bothered me or tried to make me do anything. Stroll around the grounds until you feel at home. I strolled, I looked. After a while, I picked up a broom and started to sweep the dojo. Omura-sensei and the other students would bow and smile when they saw me, and I would bow and smile back. I wore a faded blue short kimono and white drawstring pants and straw sandals.

After a while I started to help the housekeeper with her tasks. In the evenings I read over my Chenka notes and began drafting my dissertation, or as much of it as I could without access to a library. *Kinship and Property in a Siberian Nomad Tribe*. Also very restful.

One day I was wielding my broom in the dojo, and Omura-sensei called me over. Mr Omite, who was usually Mr Katanabe's partner, was out sick. Would I take *ukemi* with Mr Katanabe? Taking *ukemi* means giving the attack and receiving the throw. So I did, and so I became, by easy stages, an *aikidoka*. I fell easily, and learned to go along, in the true spirit of the art. When I did it wrong, my hands and feet were guided until I did it right. Then I became a regular, without much ceremony; I wore the *gi* and *hakama* and learned the *katas*.

There is considerable magic in aikido. The little sensei kneels on the mat and four men and a young woman cannot move him. The sensei chuckles, the students heave. It is like pushing on a fire hydrant. Also, since its founder was deep into traditional Japanese religion, there are levels of aikido that your average dojo nut does not encounter, not just the spiritual part, but concerning relations with *kami*. The spirits. Omura-sensei would

occasionally advert to these levels in his little talks, and
sometimes I thought he was looking particularly at me
when he did so, but I did not rise to the bait. No, I
learned the physical side, to move in circles, to control
with tiny pushes, to breathe properly, to feel and control
the *ki*. I learned how to decide whether to do nothing,
fight, or run away, all useful lessons. I learned enough,
as it turned out, to kill a fat, drunken woman, but not
enough to not kill her. Thus I am a failure at aikido too.
Was it only a fault in technique? No, it was some
deficiency in spirit, as Omura-sensei would have gently
said. I didn't care, I couldn't stand the torture of the girl,
I let my *ki* out of control and my passions ruled, and I
am thus doomed to mourn that unfortunate woman
every time I look into my daughter's face.

I draw out my box from the hole in the floor. It is
a twenty-two-inch cube, made of the same gauge
aluminum used in the fuselages of airliners, cornered
with steel, closed with heavy steel snaps on three sides.
It is dented and scarred and covered with the paper
scabs of ripped-off stickers. Still visible are the Air
France logo and a blue Pan Am globe. I bought it for
forty-five hundred CFA in the Petit Marché in Bamako.
At one time, it must have held a camera or other valuable equipment for a French film crew; it had a shaped
hollow made of fiberglass and foam within it, which I
had to remove. My box, my box, I never travel without
my box, as Balthazar sings in *Amahl and the Night
Visitors*. My dad made us watch the damned thing every
Christmas until we drove him off with our heathenish
jibes.

I bring the box to the kitchen table and open it. A moldy wood smell emerges, with notes of spice and dust. There is Dolores's stuff in its envelope on top. I set it aside and extract a cloth bag, like a small haversack. It is richly embroidered in gold and green thread, and the flap is hung with small cowries. I reach inside and pull out a squat covered bowl a little larger in diameter than a dinner plate, made of acacia wood. It is a divining bowl, an *opon igede*. The lid doubles as a divining tray, an *opon Ifa*, and is carved to provide a shallow concavity in the center and a raised border about two inches wide around the edge.

Stop for a minute here. My heart is beating hard, I can feel it knocking in my chest, and there is a fine cold sweat on my lips and forehead and the backs of my hands. Is there any way around this? Pocatello? Waukegan? No. I'll probably die in any case, but this path looks like the best way to save the little girl. In fact, I don't know what to do, and there's no one around to ask, except Ifa. I *hate* it, this opening to the gods, divination, throwing Ifa as they call it in West Africa; I do, I do, although I recall loving it when I thought it was just an intellectual game – figuring out the silly natives – before it was pressed home to me that it's real. My husband loved it, too, not divination, which, of course, as a witch he may not do, but the other stuff, the power. And it turns out that, for my sins, I'm very good at it. Uluné was amazed and pleased. Ifa loves me, apparently.

I lift the lid and set it aside. Inside, the bowl is divided into eight compartments radiating around a central one, which holds an embroidered yellow and green cloth bag. I remove from one of the radial compartments a squat blue glass bottle, corked. Out of it I pour a tiny mound of powdered wood from the irosun tree into the hollow of the divination tray, and spread it evenly across the smooth surface. I take up the yellow-green bag and pour its contents into my hand, seventeen shining palm nuts. I place them in the central compartment, except for one, which I place in front of the divining tray. I sprinkle a little wood dust on it, because it is the head of Eshu, and no one may look on the bare head of a king or god.

I take from their compartments a little cast bronze *irofa*, an object about the size and shape of a big fountain pen, with figures of doves on the upper end, and also a small whisk made of cow hair, and lay them on the table. Now the sixteen *ikin*, smooth, surprisingly heavy, well-grown palm nuts, with the auspicious four eyes in each of them. I hold them in my hands in front of my face and blow spit on them, which is hard because my mouth is as dry as acacia wood, and I say the prayer to wake Ifa. Then I tap on the side of the divining tray with the *irofa*, and I chant the homage prayer to Ifa, and to Eshu, and to Ogun and to Shango and the whole Yoruba pantheon, which the Olo say is really theirs, plus homages to some particular Olo spiritual entities, tapping with the rhythm I was taught, not forgetting any. Then the prayer in case I *have*, by accident, forgotten any: one word, one word alone, does not drive the diviner from home, oh, no, one word does not destroy the diviner. So we hope. I take some little time making the surface of the wood dust perfectly smooth with the cow-hair whisk.

Now I take up the sixteen palm nuts, and toss them in a continual rattling flow between my two hands, at the same time chanting the homages: to Uluné, my teacher, to my parents, to my other teachers, to the ancestors of my tribe, not hard in my case, a long succession of John, Richard, Matthew, and Peter Doe, and Mary, Elizabeth, Jane, Clare, their daughters. I remember Uluné wouldn't teach me anything until I had named my ancestors and told what I knew of their stories.

Back and forth in my hands the shining *ikin* flow, and I feel the tension building up to the instant when I shall seize a certain handful. I have not done this in a while, so it is like getting back on a horse after a bad fall, or entering the water after a near drowning, and I am trembling, the hair is standing up on the backs of my arms. I feel Somebody is in the room with me, staring at my back, I feel it itching between my shoulder blades, but I must not turn around and look. This Uluné stressed quite strongly when he taught me to divine. It is Eshu standing there, he assured me, Eshu, the guardian of the way to the unseen world, and one does not look Eshu in the face. I empty my mind of everything but my question.

Suddenly, the *orisha* moves my right hand and I clutch at the mass of *ikin*. I look down. Remaining in my left hand are two nuts. With the middle finger of my right hand I press Ifa, making a single mark on the dust of the divining tray, letting the dark wood show through. I let Ifa do this seven more times, making a single mark when there are two nuts left and a double mark when there is only one, drawing them in two vertical columns of four marks each. With the last mark the divination is over. I no longer feel anyone behind me. It is just an ordinary room again. I realize that for the past ten minutes I have been entirely oblivious to the sounds of the neighborhood, to Jake barking at cars, to Polly's daughter Shari practicing her piano next door.

I put the *ikin* back in their bag. From my box I take a notebook. This is the nontraditional part. Uluné had hundreds of verses memorized and he wanted me to learn them by heart too. I did, but I also recorded and transcribed them into this notebook. They bear some resemblance to the standard Yoruba verses, but most of them are particularly Olo in flavor. I check the figure on the divining board against the 256 possibilities. It is seven upon three, Irosun upon Iwori – Shango upon Eshu in the Ifé tradition the Olo use. I look up the verses and one pops up as the obvious answer. It says:

> *He-went-into-the-river-and-killed-the-crocodile was the one who cast Ifa for 'Is it profitable to take a caravan to the north?' Ifa says it is foolish to leave the farm before the rains. Witches are coming to carry off the eldest child. She said her strength was no match for-evil-doing. Ifa says escape by water. He said seek the son with no father. He said the woman will leave her farm and help. He said the bird with yellow feathers is of use. Four are necessary for the sacrifice: two black pigeons, two white pigeons, and thirty-two cowries.*

I copy it out onto a blank page of the notebook, tear it out, fold it, and place it to one side. Then I dab my finger in the wood powder and make a vertical line with it down my forehead. I carefully scoop up all the remaining wood powder and eat it. It is cool on the tongue, like confectioner's sugar, and tastes a little like chewing on a pencil. I put away the apparatus and stow it and the other material back in my box and then replace the box in its hide.

Just in time. I hear a car crunching on the shell drive, slam of car door, little feet on the steps. Luz and Amanda burst in, sweetly spattered with dots of ice cream. Luz wants to show Amanda her room and treasures, pathetic though they are. They go into our shared sleeping chamber. I wonder how long it will take before Luz becomes ashamed of us and the way we live. Not long, I believe, if Mrs Pettigrew has much to say about it. She has not come in. After five minutes, I go out on the landing. She is sitting in her silver car, looking up at our door and deciding whether to come up and rescue Amanda and have to interact socially with me, or to honk rudely, in either case risking a class injury. She sees me, waves weakly, I rescue her from the horror of me: turnabout is fair play. 'I'll get them,' I cry gaily. In our room, they are giggling like imps and tumbling around in my hammock and falling out of it onto Luz's mattress below, a normally forbidden game. I roust Amanda out, and then set to making our humble dinner. Spaghetti-O's, food of the gods, plus nutritious carrot sticks and cucumber slices for Luz, plus chocolate milk; for me, just the crudités and a banana. I am usually sick after having to do with the cosmic powers, but not today.

But antsy, yes, and Luz picks it up and is antsy, too. So we drive down to Dinner Key to walk on the piers, among the jangling boats, which usually relaxes both of us. Luz prances before me down the gray planking, calling out the types, which I have taught her, at about the same age as I was taught them by my father. Sloop, stinkboat, stinkboat, ketch, sloop, sloop (actually a cutter, baby, see, the mast is stepped farther back to allow the two headsails), stinkboat, yawl (because the mizzenmast is *yawl* the way back, she says), sloop, ketch, and then she stops, because it is the end of the dock and she has never seen one like this before, but I have. My heart is in my gullet. The verse pops into my mind. Escape by water. If only.

She is moored stern in, which means her charac-teristic long, sharp, graceful, pointed transom hangs halfway over the dock. She is painted a rich cerulean blue underneath, with a thin buff stripe dividing this from the deep maroon paint of the gunwales. She is gaff-rigged, of course, with two equal masts and a noble bowsprit. Her name, in gold script on the transom, is *Guitar*.

'This is a pinky schooner, dear,' I say, and she says, 'It's blue, not pink.'

'No, pinky is the name of the kind of schooner it is. Like a sharpie schooner. It has that high, pointed stern. You can use it as a boom crutch, like this one is doing, see, and it's open underneath so in a blow, the water on deck can drain away, and it shelters the helmsman from following seas. And you can pee into the ocean without getting wet.' I added, 'It's a weatherly boat.'

Yes, it is. *Kite* was a pinky schooner, nearly eighty years old when my dad bought it and fixed it up. It used to fish out of New Bedford, and you can still smell the cods of yesteryear when you go down in the hold. Or could. Her sails were tanbark canvas, heavy and stiff, but that was Dad for you, no Dacron for Dad. When we were kids, we used to spend spring break in Bermuda. The three of us kids would fly there with Mother, while Dad and one or two of his brothers would sail *Kite* down and meet us on the island. It was about his only chance to do blue-water sailing. Mother didn't approve of blue-water sailing, on the principle that he desired it, and thus it had to be stupid.

But the winter when I turned twelve and my brother was fifteen, my mother was involved in an affair even more squalid than her usual standard, and so, not out of guilt, which as far as I could tell was to her a complete stranger, but maybe attempting to recover some tactical advantage she could use later, agreed to let me and Josey crew the boat with him for the sail down. A great adventure, and it got us away from Mother, but . . . I suppose we both felt some ambivalence, especially Josey, who had reached that age where one desires that parents be perfectly anonymous and unobtrusive. Jack Doe was neither, but peculiar in the extreme. I think really, he felt he was a throwback to some earlier Doe, a crusty waterman out of a Devon gunkhole. His faith in the church remained the faith of a child, which is supposed to be a good thing, and his tastes remained the tastes of a boy: hot dogs, burgers, ice-cream sodas, tinkering with cars, messing around in small boats. Small children adored him, of course, except his own, although even I adored him for a time.

The great mystery of his life, for me at least, was why he had married my mother. I mean why he was attracted to her; he married her because she was pregnant with me, something he never mentioned and which Mom never tired of relating to me and whoever else would listen.

So we set sail, at dawn, up the Sound, the captain at the wheel, singing 'Away, Rio,' with the crew writhing in embarrassment. My brother was navigator and Sparks (even at that age he had a genius for electronics) and I was cook, steward, purser, bosun tight, midshipmanite, and crew of the captain's gig. We rounded Montauk under cold, spitting rain and set course for the southeast. At that time of year, it is normally a five-and-a-half-day run down to Bermuda, sailing into increasingly finer weather, sun, steady fifteen-knot westerly winds and a long, relaxing beam reach to the island. This year, however, instead of getting better, the weather became nastier. Josey hung by the weather radio, looking increasingly worried as he plotted the movement of a big cyclone racing down from the North Atlantic. Unlike the ocean, my father remained flat calm. We were not afraid, were we? Of a little blow?

On the fourth day it dawned red in the morning, the sailors took warning, the waves got steeper, the wind increased and backed north. By noon the sea was white all across, and we took in sail, running under double-reefed main and storm jib. By eight that evening, we were in serious trouble, the wind screaming up to a full gale. We took off everything but the storm jib. I gripped the wheel while Josey and my father rigged a chain and drogue, which is when I started to get frightened. When you rig a sea anchor it means that you are about to convert your handy sailboat into a plugged bottle, batten and tie everything down, strip to bare poles, lash yourself into your bunk, and pray that the bottle does not leak because if it does, you are fish food. The wind increased; the jib disappeared, whipped into the howling air with a crack like a shot; Dad heaved the anchor over, hustled us into our bunks, and tied us in with the auto safety belts he always carried aboard. I recall his placid smile, his reassuring voice.

The waves were by this time the size of two-story houses, which meant that every minute or so the *Kite* swooped from the roof peak of such a notional house to the ground and back up again, twisting hideously as she did so. We kids retched helplessly. Father sang 'Haul Away Me Laddie-Oh,' although the wind was so loud we could hardly hear him. I suppose that is when my girlhood faith began to drain out of me. I recall praying without cease, using every church trick I had learned, Hail Marys, Our Fathers, Glory Bes without number, the Jesus prayer. I in my girlish pride had always thought myself devout, although I suppose my devotion was a way of being with Dad and getting back a little at Mom, and didn't God know the difference, because now he refused to show. I can recall the knowledge growing in me that there was nothing there, that I was going to die, die, die, and have my face eaten by crabs, and feeling the absolute uncaring emptiness of the physical universe, that if God existed he was somewhere else than in this particular patch of wild ocean, or that if he did care, he cared in a way that would forever be beyond my understanding and useless for even a scrap of comfort. I began to despise my father for getting me into this.

It got worse as the night wore on; then we heard a horrible cracking sound, and the *Kite* seemed to leap forward and down, down, and then, incredibly, stop short, as if it had struck a stone wall. I slid forward in my straps and cracked my head painfully against the bulkhead. Then I seemed to be upside down, hanging from my bonds, looking down at the cabin ceiling, just inches from my face.

We had pitchpoled. The sea anchor had torn loose and we had shot forward, outpacing the waves, plunged our bow into the wave in front, and then, driven by the following wave, the boat had pivoted on her bow and turned over on her back. I can't remember the rest. There were crashes and rending sounds, the crackle of wood smashing, the scream of tortured metal, and a sharp acid stench. The boat was breaking up. Another heave, we were upright again, and I heard my own voice screaming in my ears. I was beyond terror now, waiting for the water. Beyond this, I have no memory.

Then it was somehow dawn, the motion of the boat was easier, a mere ten-foot corkscrew, and we all untied ourselves and went out on deck. Both masts were gone, snapped off eight feet or so from the deck. The engine had torn loose from its mounts, the prop shaft was twisted, and worst of all, the batteries were smashed. We had no power, and no way to signal or, save by celestial navigation, to find out where we were.

My father seemed delighted with this predicament. At last he was back in the seventeenth century, an era far more true to his spirit than our own. Of course, we always sailed with a complete kit of hand tools, and so, by means of the most backbreaking, hand-ripping work I have ever done, we three cleared away the wreckage, skived and fidded the main boom to the stump of the foremast to make a jury rig, resized and rerigged the foremast gaff and boom to suit a scandalized gaffsail, set up the stays and shrouds for the new mast, shot the sun to determine our location (150 miles NNW of Bermuda) and set sail. I had never seen him happier. I hated him, and grumped about my tasks, and resented that he did not see I hated him. I hated myself more, for being a coward, for deserting God, and hated God for deserting me. I looked at Josey and saw that he knew what had happened to me, and I also knew we would never talk about it to each other or to Dad. Something loved was over, the saddest thing in the world.

He was singing 'Flowers of Bermuda' over and over; and we both falsely played along with the merriment, because you would have had to have been a monster like Mom to crush that much boyish happiness, and neither of us was that bad. We even sang along on the chorus:

> He was the captain of the Nightingale
> Twenty-one days from Clyde, in coal
> He could smell the flowers of Bermuda in the gale
> When he died on the North Rock Shore.

I suppose he would have liked to sail unobtrusively into Hamilton harbor and stroll into the yacht club as if nothing much had happened. My mother, however, had raised the alarm with her characteristic shrill energy, and so, as soon as the weather cleared, the air and sea were crammed with search planes and vessels. We were picked up seventy miles out and, over my father's ferocious objections, put in tow back to the twentieth century, Hamilton, Government Dock, and my mother. She came running down the pier as we debarked from the coast guard cutter, ran up to my father, and slugged him in the mouth.

The sun sinks behind the city. We leave the lovely boat and walk back up the dock across the long shadows of the masts stretched across our path like bars. I pull a scrap of double-braided line from a waste barrel and I do some knots and string tricks for the amusement of my nondaughter, as my father used to do for me. In a few years, I will teach her to sail her first pram. Or not.

There will be no pram, *Guitar* is not *Kite*. Still, we both feel better for this, the healing power of salt water, or memory. We stroll back to the car, I make a turk's head for her, and in my head comes *And sure I could have another made*, this in my father's clear baritone, *in the boatshop down in Dover / But I would not love the keel they laid / Like the one the waves roll over / I'll go to sea no more*.

Later, getting ready for bed, Luz asks what *flaky* means and I ask her where she heard the word and she says that in the ice-cream parlor Betty Jean Stote came in with her mommy and Betty Jean Stote's mommy asked who Amanda's friend was 'and that was me, Muffa, and Amanda's mommy said who I was and she said my mommy was flaky. Is that like cornflakes?'

'Yes,' I say, and then she tells me she's going to be in a play at Providence about Noah's ark and I have to buy her a special clothes thing, but she forgot, but there is a note in her lunch box. I tell her I will look at it later. Then she says, 'Amanda and me were playing princesses. I was a Pocahontas princess and Amanda was a fairy princess, because she has golden hair. Am I adopted?'

I swallow hard. 'No, baby, you're not.' Technically the truth. I could swear to it.

'Annie Williams is adopted from Korea. Is my daddy going to come and see us?'

'I don't think so, baby.'

'Why not?'

'Because he died a long time ago.'

'He got sick and died,' she agreed. 'But we could get a new daddy.'

'That's right, we could.'

'Kids could get new daddies. Beth Weinberg has *two* new daddies. She's *so* dumb. Me and Amanda *hate* her. Kids could get new *mommies*, too, couldn't they? If their mommies get sick and die, or if they turn into witches.'

'Yes,' I say, my spine prickling, but the dreaded questions are not pressed home. She picks up the stack of books at the bedside, arranges them in order, and hands them to me. The first one is *Are You My Mother?* I read it with real feeling.

She goes out halfway through *Goodnight Moon*. Back in the kitchen I sit down at the table with my divination, and read through it several times. Uluné was a famous diviner as well as a sorcerer, an unusual combo, actually. It's a little like baseball pitchers being good hitters, not impossible, but rare. Although Uluné's clients were all believers, still they could not help but be astounded at the accuracy of his work. Typically, questioners don't tell the Ifa diviner their questions. Uluné had to select the relevant verse from a number that related to the figure cast, and as far as I could tell he always chose the right one. In the present case, doing it for myself, I knew the question, but still this was a clear bull's-eye. Okay, I won't take a caravan to the north, check. It would be foolish to leave the farm right now. Check. Witches are definitely coming to carry off the eldest child, which is me, or maybe Luz, or maybe both of us. Check. My strength is no match for his, no question, check, especially if he is really going to go ahead and do the full *okunikua*. I get up and check the Providence Church calendar by the refrigerator. I have marked the date when that woman died in Overtown. If he is going for *okunikua*, I see, he will have to do the second sacrifice and eating in the next two days, or else wait for the dark of the moon again and start over. He won't want to do that. The he is *him*. I no longer believe that it might be Lou or some other disciple. It's him. Suddenly I am weak and weeping and nauseated. I stick my head between my legs until it passes.

Perhaps I should call the police. Hello, 911? Yes, I'm calling to report a murder that's going to happen two days from now. The murderer is going to kill and eviscerate another pregnant woman. Who's the murderer? My husband. He's actually an African witch. That's right. He's doing it to accumulate power in his magical body, his *fana*. Should I spell that? Oh, if he gets it done he'll be the witchcraft equivalent of a small thermonuclear bomb. Nobody's done it in the longest time – it's against the rules. All the Olo sorcerers agreed not to do it, like the test-ban treaty. Yes, that's *O-L-O*. Am I crazy? Why, yes, as a matter of fact, I am. Thank you. Bye!

No, *focus*, Jane! No time for hysterics. I stop myself from shaking, and when I can drink tea without it sloshing out of the mug, I do so, and sit again at the table. You fear something, you adopt a host of ritual behaviors to keep it away, and when it comes you're both more frightened than you imagined you could ever be and at the same time curiously calmer. It's here, you have to deal with it. I have to stop him, and Ifa has given me the means, if I can just figure it all out.

A son with no fathers. A woman from a farm. A yellow bird. Thank you, Ifa. I have no idea what you're talking about. Allies, maybe. You have to wait for magical allies to come to you. You can keep your eyes open, of course, but you can't put an ad in the paper or treat it like a treasure hunt. Much of Olo sorcery consists of keeping your eyes open and waiting. I mean *really* open.

I can do the sacrifices tomorrow. Or . . . maybe I'm not reading this right. Does the 'four are necessary' mean I have to wait until I've contacted the son, the farm woman, and the bird, making four with me? Or does it refer to the two pairs of birds? Then what about the cowries? And the escape by water? But I have to stop him, I can't just escape. What's that about? Was it really a sign that I was impelled to go down to Dinner Key and there find a boat that could have been the sister of the boat in which I faked my suicide, the *Kite*, my father's pride and joy?

It's too much right now. Dolores is too tired to cope. Maybe it's time to lay her to rest. I would have to get another job. Work up my résumé. I can hand, reef, and steer a sailboat by compass or stars. I can ride a horse. I can shoot a pistol, a rifle, a shotgun. I can butcher a deer, a duck, a fish. I can tie flies, fix cars. I know the alphabet cold. I can speak French, and get by in Yakut, Yoruba, Bambara, and Olo. I can do ethnographic research in library and field. I can do the fifth, fourth, and third *kyu* in aikido. I can do a few tricks of legerdemain with coins and little balls. I can detect magical emanations and perform some elementary sorcerous acts. I can foretell the future. Print up five hundred copies and mail it out.

Stripped for sleep, swinging in my hammock, I think, oh, my, Jane, back in the soup again. One good thing about Miami: if my excursion with Ifa lit up the *m'doli*, it's unlikely that it stood out enough against the sort of continuous fireworks you get in this town. Eshu probably has a major substation dedicated to carrying messages to and from the Miami-Dade Standard Metropolitan Statistical Area.

And once again, I have to deal with the mystery of belief. I'm a scientist. I have a pretty good idea about what underlies the technology of sorcery, and it's perfectly explicable in standard scientific terms. But Eshu and Ifa aren't, not quite, even if you buy Roger Penrose's notion that consciousness is at least in part a quantum phenomenon and partakes of a universe in which time's arrow doesn't always point in the same direction and precognition is as ordinary as changing an electromagnetic field from positive to negative.

That Marcel! At nearly every speech, someone would stand up and say, in a confused or a hostile voice, something like, 'I don't understand, professor. Are you implying that these spirits consulted by your sorcerers are *real*?' And Marcel would say, 'Sir (or Madam), I say to you that I am a professor of anthropology, an empiricist, a materialist, a scientist, moreover a *French* scientist, the heir, if I may say so, of Descartes and Buffon, a member of the French Academy, and if you ask me if I believe in these spirits, of course I must tell you that I do not.' Here a marvelously timed pause, and then in a lower voice, *'But they're there.'* Jane would miss him like crazy, were she alive.

FOURTEEN

9/22 Lagos

The generator arrived today. NEPA, the Nigeria Electric Power Authority, or like they say here Not Enough Power Anywhere, sucks big-time & is under no real pressure to improve: big boys all have generators like us, everyone else steals it from power lines, so there is no money for capital investment. A typically African solution – simple, effective, self-destructive. W. working at last, at least typewriting noises from his room. I pray he is getting some good work done; at least something will be salvaged from this wreckage. He has his own room now.

Des away a good deal, making arrangements with his contacts, people high in clan and tribal hierarchies, finding out when ceremonies will be held, arranging for the grad students to be placed in various sites. And arranging things with the government, too. We are in bad with the government, according to him; there is often a car outside the hotel, fat guys with sunglasses and nice suits, watching. Colonel Musa would love to catch us making a pornographic film.

Talked with Des just now. David Berne is coming for sure, and he advised me to wait until I had a chance to talk with him before setting off for Ketu. I've been reading his stuff on Gelede magic and dance, and I agreed that was best. The guy is, in any case, one of the heavies in the field, and also one of the few who doesn't think M. is a total charlatan. I wonder why that's important to me at this late date; I've often called him that myself. In any case, looking forward.

9/24 Lagos

All day at the courts and jail, trying to get Tunji's brother, Ifasen, out of trouble. Ifasen is a cabdriver and apparently he ran over a goat and the cops pinched him. In Africa, if someone works for you, it is the done thing that you are thereby the patron of his or her entire extended family. I am also paying the school fees of Ajayi's two nieces. The sums are pathetically small, but it takes up so much time. W. observes this and gives me contemptuous looks. Miss Ann being kind to the darkies. I want to shake him!

9/27 Lagos

With Greer at the University here to look at the library, and introduced me to Mr Odibo, the librarian. A ramshackle place, lizards running through the books, termites eating everything. It's no wonder literacy was so long delayed in Yorubaland, and the rest of Africa. There is nothing to write on that will last more than a decade. Interesting discussion about this with Odibo, and the consequent survival of enormous feats of memory by traditional Africans, the preservation of, e.g., thousands of verses of Ifa prophecy by diviners, and of history and events by griots.

Oral culture, easy to sneer, but not when you actually observe a relatively recent shelf of books turned to powder. Odibo showed me some rarities he keeps behind steel, journals of missionaries and early British merchants and administrators. Some French material there, too, which piqued my interest. Always possible to get a paper out of crap like that, especially stuff that hasn't been translated into English.

After that, Greer took me to a man he's been working with for years, a healer named Sule Ibekwe, lives in concrete-block, tin-roofed house with a dirt yard surrounded by walls of mud-brick & rusted corrugated steel. We sat on stools in front of his house (they sat on them; I sat on the ground) and were given palm wine by a striking young woman. Greer translated. This case was interesting – a thirteen-year-old girl, Rosa, cerebral malaria, doctors had given her up. I saw her, agreed with docs, emaciated & withdrawn, goner. Ibekwe called some men in and they carried the patient out to the compound. More people filtered in from the house and the surrounding shacks, until there was a considerable crowd. Some men set up drums and began to play. It was a typical African affair – no one giving any orders, a coalescing of intent. Ibekwe explained to us etiology of Rosa's disease – it was necessary that patient be restored to harmony with her spiritual and social environment, had been upset by a curse. This was a very powerful curse, and in order to cure, Rosa would have to be placed under the tutelage of a powerful orisha. Ogun, the smith, the master of iron and war, was picked to be the one, or rather he had picked himself during a prior ceremony.

Two women, one of them the remarkable woman who had served us, pulled the girl to her feet, and the drums grew louder and more instant and a dozen or so devotees gathered into a rough dance line. The healer stood before Rosa, chanting, and anointing her with white powder and several liquids, one of them from an old Prell squeeze-bottle. He lit a clay bowl of some vegetable material, which gave off a sweet smoke. I asked Des what it was and he shushed me. Ibekwe blew smoke at the girl, and chanted some more; the dancers leaped and twirled, the drums pounded. This went on. My attention was fixed on the splendid woman. I couldn't take my eyes off her, the energy she radiated, her authority was so very intense and attractive.

Then Rosa let out a high yell and stiffened. Her eyes rolled back into her head, showing only whites, and her neck twisted stiffly to the right. The drums fell silent, the dancers froze. Ibekwe was hunched over her, chanting, his face inches from hers. She was drooling thick saliva, like a dog; one of the women holding her wiped her chin with a cloth. Then came a softer drumming. Ibekwe stopped chanting and backed away. Rosa's feet were beating rapidly on the packed earth; her head snapped back, her body bowed; she was in seizure now and the two women were having difficulty holding on to her. Other women jumped forward to help and we lost sight of her for some time. When we could observe her again, she was back on her litter, limp. The drummers and dancers wandered around, chatting, like players after a softball game in the park.

I asked Greer if the operation had been a success, he told me it was just the first stage, she'll be here for weeks, getting deeper into trance states, & letting the orisha inhabit her more deeply each time. Eventually she'll be consecrated to Ogun, like Maro. Here he pointed to the beautiful woman who'd helped hold the patient. He said she'd been brought in with encephalitis, also a Christian, also a hospital reject. She was essentially dead, and look at her now. I did and as I did she looked at me and smiled and I felt a jolt of some — I don't know, some sexual energy. Very disturbing. Greer wanted to know what was wrong, said I looked like I was about to faint. All the excitement, I said, and we hadn't eaten since breakfast and it was blazing hot. He took me back into the house, where Ibekwe was sitting on a rope bed being cared for by some of his devotees, an old woman was bathing his face with a damp rag. Greer talked with him awhile and I stood around, feeling a little awkward as you do when attending a conversation between two people with a long history between them. The healer opened his eyes & looked at me & had conversation w/ Greer, clear they were talking about me. Des said, He says he's got a busy schedule but as a favor to me he'll try to fit you in. For what? He says you're carrying a curse, Greer said. He says you're cursed in your marriage bed.

Later in the car I tried to be all clinical about it, stupidly, really. What was *really* happening in the curing ceremony, talking about hysterical conversion and oh so interesting recent speculations about the connection between mental states and the immune system and Greer said, Yeah, I know all that, and the fact is, most traditional healers are charlatans, but Ibekwe isn't, he really does it, and it's outside the science zone, and so when I write about him, I'm going to have to fudge and do all that hand waving about the fucking immune system. Fact is, we know fuck-all about the immune system and its connection to the psyche. Ibekwe thinks he's dealing on the psychic level, and we have no tools to study the psychic level because we don't think it exists. We say weak effects, uncertain effects, no causality, small N, ergo not a fact. But it *is* a fact. Ibekwe turns a lot of people away, people he says he can't help, and they mostly die, and the ones he helps get better.

Reflect later – a familiar experience, with that woman. I recall that jolt from somewhere – hair standing up on arms and neck, a tingling in the sexual parts, I thought my nipples were going to pop through my shirt. A déjà vu? I asked Greer who she was consecrated to and he said Oshun. The Yoruba Venus. Am a little frightened, also excited. Thinking of M. now, and Siberia, wishing I had more memory of what happened there, not just the events, but memory of the body.

FIFTEEN

For conventional pretty, Lisa Reilly was hard to beat, Paz thought, and she had the non-butter-melting look, too. Demure. She drove a red Saab 900 convertible, which made sense if you knew her the way Paz did. He glanced over at her from the driver's seat of his Impala. She was excited, her cheeks colored, her eyes bright. Riding in a cop car at last, helping the cops on a murder case. Reilly was a cop buff, but of a more select sort than the types that hung around cop bars. The way he met her, she had been a witness in a case. The suspect, Earl Bumpers, had been raping his two daughters for years and pounding on them, too, and he had eventually killed the older one, which brought him to the attention of Paz. The younger daughter, a nine-year-old named Cassie, was the chief witness, and Reilly had therapized away her terror and prepped her for the trial, and the guy went down for it, death, and the two of them, Paz and Reilly, had gotten a little play in the press. He had spotted her in the witness bullpen, and been attracted, the big frank china blues, the golden hair in a staid little knot at the back, the thin, tight body, and he had struck up a conversation. Later, he had spotted her in the Friday six o'clock meat market at the Taurus in the Grove with all the other single women, which surprised him. He'd moved on her in his usual respectful way, and they'd started in. Six or so months, maybe once a week. She was married but separated, no problem there.

She had a practice in the Gables, a nice paneled office, with the dolls and toys, but she dealt mainly with the eating problems of teenage girls. Getting a terrified murder witness to talk was a little out of her line, although she had done it that once and was clearly hot to do it again. Paz was stretching his authority way past the gray area, providing a private shrink for a potential witness, a minor. He had not mentioned it to Barlow, never mind his shift commander, and he was a little nervous. Excited too; both of them nervous and excited.

They were going to do it in the Meagher apartment, Paz's suggestion, a nod toward the color of legality in his mind. Just a cop who felt sorry for a scared kid, a welfare kid, too, and was bringing a personal friend by to give a little counseling. Should some constructive evidence happen to emerge, why there was nothing wrong with using it, just like you would use a piece of evidence lying in plain sight. Paz figured he could work out a plausible story if anything popped right, which was why he had not told anyone. He wanted to present this to Barlow all tied up, as a coup, as something to make up for the boner about Youghans.

Mrs Meagher offered sugary iced tea and butter cookies, the tea in tall glasses set in raffia sleeves, with a long spoon in each. They sat around in the tatty, spotless living room, in which the smell of lemon furniture polish fought bravely the base stink of the building and neighborhood. The boy was impatient and resentful of being denied either release to the streets or TV, the girl her usual silent and sullen self. The small talk did not take off. Reilly shot Paz a look: this isn't working. She changed her approach, asked to speak to the grandmother alone. They went into the kitchen. Paz could hear low talking. Randolph got up and turned on the television, a sitcom, canned laughter. Paz saw no reason to object. After ten minutes or so, Reilly came back with the grandmother. Reilly's face wore her courtroom expression of neutral goodwill. She approached the girl.

'Tanzi, your grandmother and I have been talking, and we've agreed that, if it's all right with you, I'd like to try hypnosis with you. Do you understand what that means?'

The girl nodded. Randolph said, excitedly, 'Yeah! I saw this show where the guy went into his past lives and shit.' Mrs Meagher said, 'Hush your mouth, boy!'

They shut off the television and moved a straight chair in front of the girl, and turned down the lights. Reilly sat in the straight chair and began to speak in the traditional low, insinuating tone. She had tried to do it with Paz once, but it hadn't worked. It worked with Tanzi Franklin, though – she went off like the television in less than three minutes: head sunk to her chest, eyes closed, breathing with the deep and regular pace of slumber.

'All right, Tanzi,' said Reilly. 'It's last Saturday, around eleven-thirty at night. Do you know where you are?'

'My room.' The girl's speech was slow, and muffled, as if coming through a blanket.

'Okay, I want you to look out the window of your room and tell me what you see.'

'Roofs. Windows. I was looking for Amy, but she ain't home. I see them. Theys fighting. The pregnant lady and her boyfriend. He starts in busting up stuff and she be trying to stop him. He hit her on the head. She fall down and he yell at her some more. Then he leaves. She gets up. She's crying.'

Stopped. A few words of encouragement put the needle back in the groove.

'She's trying to pick up stuff off the floor. She's on the couch. He's talking to her.'

Reilly glanced at Paz and said, immediately and carefully, to Tanzi, 'Who's talking to her, Tanzi? The boyfriend came back?'

'No,' she said. 'Not the boyfriend. Him.'

'Can you tell us what he looked like, Tanzi?' said Reilly. Paz could hear the excitement in her voice, under the professional drone.

Tanzi opened her eyes. She looked directly at Paz. Her right arm rose slowly, until the extended index finger pointed straight at him. Mrs Meagher let out a small cry.

Reilly said, 'You mean he looks like Detective Paz?'

'Yes.' The eyes shut again. The arm dropped.

'Tanzi, do you know who he is?' asked Reilly.

'Yes.'

'Who is he?'

The child's eyes opened again. Paz heard Reilly's gasp, and then the eyes looked at him, and it was not any fourteen-year-old girl who gazed out through them either. A voice far too deep and rumbling ever to have come out of the larynx of a Tanzi Franklin said, 'Me.'

It came in a long extended syllable, striking them all with the nauseating effect of an earthquake's first tremors. Mrs Meagher screamed. Tanzi rolled her eyes back in her head, twisted off the couch, and went into a

back-arching, teeth-chattering, foaming convulsion.
Randolph P. Franklin leaped from his chair and onto
Paz, tearing at his face and clothes, trying to get at Paz's
pistol. He was shouting something like 'I'll get him, I'll
get him!' Paz stood up, the boy clinging to him with his
legs, holding on with one hand and grabbing for the gun
with the other. He seemed to have an unnatural energy.
Paz himself felt blurry, as if he, too, had been somewhat
hypnotized. He saw Reilly drop down to attend to the
convulsing girl. Mrs Meagher was yelling something
that Paz couldn't make out. He had just pinned
Randolph P. Franklin's arms when something smacked
heavily against the back of his head. He looked around
and saw Mrs Meagher holding the handle of a big
saucepan in a two-handed grip, getting ready to whale
him again.

'Ma'am, please put down the pot . . .' he began. She
swung at his head, but he twisted away and this time the
pot hit his shoulder. He tripped over the writhing
Randolph and fell down. Mrs Meagher couldn't bend
over very well and so she could only pound him in a
grandmotherly way, but managed all the same to
sprinkle him with the contents of the pot.

After a while Mrs Meagher became exhausted and
dropped her weapon. She sat down on a chair, looking
gray, and cried. The boy extricated himself and
embraced his grandmother. He was crying, too. Tanzi's
convulsions had stopped. Lisa Reilly had moved her so
that she was lying flat on the couch. She was holding the
girl's hand, talking softly, but eliciting no apparent
response. Paz stood and brushed white gobbets from his
clothes. He walked over to the couch. The girl looked
destroyed; her mouth was flecked with blood and foam.

'How is she?'

'Jesus, Jimmy, I don't know,' Reilly said in a frightened whisper. 'She's breathing okay. She's not convulsing. But I'm not a doctor. I think I'm over my head here. What do we do now?'

'I don't know,' Paz whispered back. 'I think we should offer to get the kid to a hospital and then get out of here. Why don't you talk to the old lady, smooth things over?'

Reilly gave him a sharp look but did as he suggested. She spoke softly. Paz saw the old woman shake her head emphatically, her sparse hair flying. Reilly came back to him and said, 'She doesn't want any more help. Not from us. We should get out of here. I left my card, in the unlikely event . . .'

They left. Randolph P. Franklin had the last word. Glaring at Paz, he said, 'I see you around here again, nigger, I'm gonna bust a cap on your sorry black ass.'

In the car, Paz looked at Reilly and said, 'What can I say? I didn't expect that. It came out of left field.'

'Farther off than that, I think. Good Christ!' She shuddered. 'You still have some stuff in your hair.'

'Mashed potatoes,' he said, picking at himself. She brushed at him, annoyingly. 'Leave it!' he snapped, and slammed the car into gear. They drove in silence.

'Sorry. I didn't mean to snarl. I'm a little shook.'

'A *little*? Jesus! I'm jelly. Jimmy, what the hell was going on there?'

'You're asking *me*? You're the shrink.'

'No, I have a doctorate from the Barry College School of Social Work. I talk to Gables teens about their body image. I don't fucking do *exorcisms*!'

'You did great with Cassie Bumpers.'

'Oh, Cassie Bumpers! All she wanted was someone to tell her she wasn't the spawn of Satan and didn't deserve to have the devil fucked out of her by her daddy's holy prick. I can deal with frightened little kids. Back there . . . back there, that was something else entirely. I don't know *what* the hell that was. No, I *do* know, I think . . .'

'What?'

'Possession,' she said, and he looked over at her to see if she were joking, but her face was grim and pale.

'What do you mean, *possession*? Like with the head turned around backward and the green vomit?'

'Yeah, right. Go to a library sometime. There's yards of documentation on it from nearly every culture in the world, from nuns with stigmata to snake handlers in the Ozarks to Siberian shamans. I won't even mention Africa or what goes on right down the street in Miami fucking Florida. Santería. Christ, you should know more about that than I do.'

'Yeah, that's what everybody says,' said Paz sourly. 'So . . . what? The hypnosis, like, triggered this . . . thing?'

'I guess. You saw the girl. She went under like a lead sinker. Hence suggestible in the extreme. She pointed at you.' She paused and looked at him appraisingly. 'You know, it's possible that the killer really did look like you.'

'Come on.'

'Why not? Both times she freaked out it was when you were around. It's no crime. One of my brothers-in-law looks like Ted Bundy. Of course, a lot of us think he actually *is* a serial killer . . .'

'I take your point. Say more about suggestible.'

'Okay, I'm a pro, so I was very careful not to make any suggestions. That's the big confusion factor when you work with hypnosis, especially with kids. Tiffany, are you *sure* Mr Jones didn't put his hands up your panties? Didn't Mr Jones dress up as a devil and sacrifice to Satan? Oh, yes, he did, the kid agrees, and then he made me eat poo-poo. You can get people to say anything, you can implant all kinds of false memories, even without meaning to, and the subjects will swear themselves blue that the shit really happened. I know I didn't suggest anything of the kind to her, and then, when I ask her who the guy was, out comes this voice two octaves lower. Did you see her eyes?'

'Yeah, I saw.'

She shuddered. 'Jimmy,' she said, 'buy me a drink. Buy me two drinks.'

They stopped on a bar on West Flagler east of the freeway, a neon-lit, beer-smelling place with a night game from Atlanta on the TV and a mixed crowd of boat bums and genial rummies in it. They got a couple of dirty looks, but no one made any trouble and the service was fine. He ordered a Bud, she a double scotch. She inhaled it and immediately flagged the barmaid for a refill.

When he thought she was ready, he spoke. 'You said she was real suggestible. But somebody had to plant that suggestion in her head. Somebody who knew she was a potential witness.' He thought for a moment. 'That means somebody knew I was going to question her. So they grabbed her and, I don't know, hypnotized her so she would block what she saw.'

Reilly took a sip of her new drink. Her face was flushed now and her eyes were showing white around the blue iris. 'I thought you said she went nuts the first time you talked to her.'

'Yeah, but they still could have . . .' His voice trailed off.

'Right. How did they know to grab that particular kid? Unless you're proposing that a crack team of homicidal hypnotists fanned out and did everyone on that side of the building. Come to think of it, the boy and the granny weren't acting all that tightly wrapped either. Why the hell should they get homicidal all of a sudden? Maybe we're dealing with induced mass hallucination here.'

'There's such a thing?'

'Oh, yeah. Flying saucers. Thousands of people think they've been abducted by aliens. That's now, in a materialist age. In other cultures, in the past, the sky's the limit. My point . . . did I have a point? Oh, yeah, my point was that there's more to human psych than they teach in college. Your guy does ritual murders, nobody can see him coming or going, and if somebody does happen to spot him, he throws a fit on them from long distance. You don't need a nice lady social worker, baby: what you need is a fucking witch doctor.'

'You making a referral?' Trying to lighten it up a little, but she was serious.

'Yeah, for your information. Dr What's-his-face. Works at Jackson. He gave us a lecture at Barry about the dark forces rampant in Miami. Medical anthropophagist. No, that's who we're *looking* for. Anthropologist. Newman? Began with an *N*. I could think of it if I had a little more scotchie. I'll tell you one thing, darling. I'm fucking glad *I'm* not nine months pregnant.' She finished her drink and started softly to weep.

Paz took her home, which was an apartment on Fair Isle in the Grove. She opened a bottle of white wine and they finished it off. Paz had never gone to bed with Lisa Reilly without her being fairly drunk, but she was really drunk this time. She liked to get on top and pound it. He usually had bruises across his pubic bone the next day. Paz made it a point to concentrate on one woman at a time during the actual act, but now, as she pumped away, he found himself thinking of Willa Shaftel, about how plump and soft and jolly she was and how much, really, he was going to miss her. Reilly was making steam-engine noises through her teeth and moving more violently, working herself up and down and grinding, an altogether industrial sort of sex, Paz thought, and when she went off, she would flail at him with hard little fists and bony knees and elbows.

She finished and collapsed on him, drooling on his cheek. This was merely the first round, he knew. It was not mere lust. It was the kind of screwing people do in wartime, to keep away the terrors.

At work the next morning, Paz found a note from Barlow on his desk, directing him to interview room one. There he found his partner with a rummy – a sagging, middle-aged, freckle-skinned black man with bloodshot eyes. You could smell it coming off him. He seemed startled to see Paz, although Paz could not remember seeing the man before.

'Jimmy, this here's Eightball Swett,' Barlow said. 'Mr Swett got some information about our case up there in

Overtown. He seen a fella with Deandra Wallace.' Paz
sat down on a reversed chair and gave Swett the eye.
Swett looked down. His face twitched.

'Go ahead, Mr Swett,' said Barlow. 'We're all listening.'

'Was in that Gibson park,' said Swett. 'I hang there
sometimes, you know, have a couple, shoot the shit.
Anyway, last Thursday, maybe, or Friday, I seen her. She
big as a house, couldn't hardly walk, and she sat on a
bench, and there's this dude sitting with her. She talking to him and he talking to her, but real sincere, like he
trying to get into her, which was dumb, 'cause sure as
shit he already got into her, him or someone else. 'Cause
she be big as a motherfuckin' house.'

'Yes, we know that,' said Barlow. 'Could you hear
what they were talking about?'

'Nah, they's too far away. Anyway, they left together.
I ain't see them no more after that.'

'What did this man look like?' asked Barlow.

'Just a regular dude,' said Swett. Again he threw a
quick glance at Paz. 'Nothing special. Dap, though. Had
a suit on, white or tan, light color anyway, shiny shoes,
fresh shine. I used to do it, so I knows.'

'What did the man *look* like, Mr Swett?' Barlow
insisted. 'Big? Small? Light? Dark? What?'

A nervous shrug. 'You know, just a regular dude . . .
normal looking.'

Paz said, 'Mr Swett, let me ask you something. Look
at me.' Paz stood up. 'Just say it right out. Did the man
you saw have a resemblance to me?'

Swett nodded vigorously. 'Yeah, yeah, he did. I
spotted it the minute you walked in here. I said, damn,
that boy look like that other dude's brother.' He

narrowed his eyes, studying Paz. ' 'Bout the same size, same no-hair, same shade of skin. Maybe the guy was a little . . . softer, a little older, I don't know. No, something else . . . the dude was, I want to say, brighter . . .'

'You mean a lighter complexion?' asked Paz.

'No, it ain't that. Something like . . . light coming off a him, like some kind of movie star, like they look, you know? Not like real folks. What I thought, when I seen the two of them, here be a preacher and he be trying to help this sister got herself in trouble.'

They sent Swett off to work with an Identi-Kit technician, and the two detectives busied themselves for a time with other cases. The drawing came back and they looked at it together.

'You have the right to remain silent,' said Barlow.

'That's really weird,' said Paz. The likeness was the usual anti-portrait, stripped of personality, and in Paz's view, quite useless for actual identification. It showed a round-headed, high-cheeked, shaven-haired, light-skinned black man. It looked a good deal like Paz and several thousand others in Dade County.

'Yes, it is. That old boy just about jumped when y'all walked in there. I guess you can account for your whereabouts on the night of.'

'Last Saturday? Gosh, I can't recall. Oh, I know! I wrapped up my chef knives and took a long walk all by myself.'

'For the record, Jimmy. A lot of folks going to see this thing.'

'For the record, I worked at the restaurant until eleven-thirty, and spent the rest of the night with a lady named Beth Morgensen. Want her number?'

'No, but if you strike again, we may need it. Anyway,

a lucky break, Mr Swett walking in. We have a face, at least. A small reward brings in the street folks pretty good. I wonder why they call him Eightball? It looks like a long time since he was steady enough to lean over a pool table.'

'It's a drink,' said Paz. 'Olde English 800 malt liquor. The drink and people who drink it are eightball.'

'Well, well. I never knew that.'

'I never knew you played pool.'

'I don't, anymore,' said Barlow. 'But I ran some tables a time or two back when I was raising Cain. I guess you'll tell me, after a while, how come you knew our suspect looked like you before old Eightball copped to it.'

Paz felt blood rush to his face. In an instant a set of lies and evasions flashed through his mind, all dismissed as fast as they appeared.

'Someone else told me the same thing,' Paz said, and went through the sorry events of the previous night.

Barlow listened to this without reaction. When Paz was done he said, 'Son, you and your girlfriend better hope that old lady don't know any sharp lawyers.'

'I do hope. Meanwhile, we got confirmation about the physical appearance, which is good.'

'Unless he witched that, too, fixed it so anybody saw him would think he looked like the investigating officer.'

'Cletis, come on!'

'Still don't believe it?'

'What, *you* do?'

'I got to. Like I already told you, Our Lord spent a good parcel of His time driving out unclean spirits. The smartest thing Satan ever done was making folks believe he ain't real.'

There seemed nothing to say to this. Paz remained silent, waiting for Barlow to come down on him for the stupidity at Mrs Meagher's.

To Paz's relief, though, he saw that Barlow was going to let it pass, because in a lighter tone, he said, 'Now what about this medical anthropologist? We might catch us a lead there.'

'I'll get on it,' said Paz. At his desk he checked the time, then dialed Lisa Reilly's number, reaching her between her fifty-minute client hours.

'Did I do anything awful?' she asked.

'No, I wouldn't call three guys and a German shepherd *awful*. Unusual, maybe.'

'Oh, stop it! I've been walking bowlegged all morning. Was that all you?'

And more lascivious chatter. It was one of her habits, he knew, and Paz normally went along with it cheerfully enough, but today he found it wearing. There was something too bright about her tone. He decided to switch it off.

'Look, Lisa, why I called – I need the name of that anthropology guy you mentioned.'

'I'm sorry, what guy?'

'It was after that scene at Mrs Meagher's – you said I needed a medical anthropologist, and you said you heard a lecture . . .'

'Oh. Jesus, that really happened, didn't it? Are you going to check on that little girl?'

'Yeah, sure,' Paz lied, 'so, if you could look it up?'

'Right.' There was the sound of drawers opening and paper being flipped. Paz wrote down the name and phone number, and said, 'Thanks, Lisa. I'll call you later, maybe we'll get together next week sometime.'

'Yeah, about that . . . I actually was going to call you. I think maybe I'm going to get back with Alex.'

The husband. 'Oh, yeah? When did this happen?'

'Oh, we've been seeing each other more over the last couple of weeks. I guess we both decided it was time. We want to have kids.'

'That's nice. And what was last night? A farewell fuck?' He was surprised at the vehemence with which he spoke.

'No, I was going to bring it up, but after what happened and me getting a little blasted . . . and let's face it, we went into this with no promises on either side. I thought that was the deal.'

'Yeah, it was,' he said tightly. 'Well, good. What can I say? Have a nice life, Lisa.'

'Ah, Jimmy, don't be like that. We can still be friends.'

'Yeah, the pair of you can have me over sometime. It'll be great. I got to go now.'

And that was that, thought Paz, good-bye, Lisa. He called Ticketmaster and got a couple of tickets to *Race Music* for that Friday night, and then called Willa Shaftel's machine and left a message confirming the date. Then business again: a call to Jackson Memorial put him in touch with the Medical Anthropology Unit and he made an appointment with a Dr Louis Nearing.

Medical Anthropology, Paz found, was stuck in a short blind corridor in building 208, out of the way of real doctors but convenient to the ER, where nearly all of its clients arrived. Outside Nearing's office there was a corkboard nearly covered with witch-doctor cartoons cut out of magazines. He knocked, received a 'Yo!' in response, and walked in. It was a tiny place, hardly larger than a suburban bathroom, and it was the

messiest office Paz had ever seen. Nearly every horizontal surface – desk, floor, shelves, the computer monitor, and the seats of a pair of side chairs – was covered
with paper: stacks of books, some of them splayed open,
journals, clipped articles, stuffed file folders, magazines,
cardboard cartons, reprints, notebooks, and stapled
computer printouts. In the interstices and hung from
the walls and ceiling were impedimenta in startling
variety, adding to the wizard's-cave effect: cult statues,
masks, bundles of herbs and feathers, crystals, stuffed
animals and birds, colorful and folkish-looking pouches
and bags, a green-and-white Notre Dame football
helmet, and what looked like shrunken human body
parts. The occupant sat hunched over his computer key-
board, with the light from the screen giving his face an
appropriately mystic glow. He turned to Paz and
grinned, showing large tombstone teeth. 'Just let me
finish this thought. Move that shit and have a seat.'

Nearing pounded heavily on the keys. Paz couldn't
see how tall he was, but he was big, his neck thick, his
shoulders heavy, his forearms powerful and covered
with a rich golden pelt. Nearing gave a little grunt of
satisfaction, punched one last key, spun around on his
chair, and stood up, extending a meaty hand. Six four,
at least, Paz estimated, a moose. He had a wide, flat,
ingenuous face, blue eyes behind cheap plastic frames,
the lenses none too clean. He wore a plaid, short-
sleeved shirt and wrinkled chinos with a military belt.

'What can I do for you, Detective?'

Paz told him the story, the killing and its aftermath,
omitting the usual small details about the crime itself,
and editing the illegal aspects out of the Tanzi incident.
'I was wondering if you could throw some light, Doc,'

he concluded. He was not hopeful. The guy looked like he could throw light on nothing more exotic than hog production.

'Well, let's see,' said Nearing, counting elaborately on his fingers, 'we got ritual murder, cannibalism, and demonic possession, plus maybe some Ifa divination. Sounds like a typical day in the Magic City.' He had a deep, considering, midwestern voice. 'The chamber of commerce wasn't far wrong when they came up with that one. Where would you like me to start?'

'Maybe with what you do here. I'm not even sure what medical anthropology is.'

'Yeah, you and the board of this fine institution. Okay, here's the short version. A guy comes into the ER in distress. BP off the scale, severe pain in the belly, recent history of weight loss, blood in the urine, angina, shortness of breath. So they think, uh-oh, a sundae, so they order tests . . .'

'Sorry, what's a sundae?'

'A case where you got two or more potential fatal illnesses. In this case they'd figure he was hypertense, untreated, an abdominal cancer the size of a grapefruit, with kidney involvement and maybe congestive heart, too. That's what they would call the cherry.'

Paz looked blank.

'The cherry on top. Of the sundae. Hilarious intern humor.'

'Got it. Go on.'

'Anyway, the guy's hopeless, but they give him the tests anyway. And to their surprise, he passes the cancer panel, his EKG is normal, guy's got arteries like a twelve-gauge Mossberg. He's got what they call idiopathic symptomology, sick as hell but nothing wrong with him that they can find. Then they get the idea of asking the guy what *he* thinks is wrong with him, and he says a sorcerer has put the curse on him. So they call me in. I do the interview, and say the guy is Haitian, I'll call in my own *hougan* to examine the patient. He'll confirm the diagnosis: the patient is suffering under a *pwin*, a curse, sent by a *bokor*, a sorcerer. We come to some arrangement, and believe me, Medicaid doesn't want to know about this, and my *hougan* sets up a curing ceremony – that, or he finds out who the *bokor* is, and starts a countercurse, so the bad guy will lay off.'

'Does it work?'

Nearing waggled a hand and tilted his head ruefully. 'Sometimes, sometimes not. Like chemotherapy. Or surgery.'

'Right. Okay, but what I don't get is why should a Haitian or anybody who believes they're cursed come to Jackson? Why don't they just get their own witch doctor?'

Nearing looked confused. 'I'm not sure I understand the question.'

'I mean, they get sick because they believe in voodoo or whatever. Their minds control their bodies in some way. So if they believe, they should know the local what-do-you-call-'ems . . .'

'Oh, I see,' said Nearing, with a grin. 'I should have explained it better. The patients who show up at Jackson *aren't* believers. That's the *point*. You're right, in that if they were really into traditional practices they wouldn't even think about coming here. They come here because they think they're in America and Jackson Memorial is the big *hougan* where they dispense the powerful American magic. But it's not.'

'But they must believe in the voodoo at some level, or it wouldn't work.'

'That's a theory,' said Nearing, cheerfully. 'It's certainly what the NP staff subscribes to. Psychosomatic yadda-yadda-yadda, tied to primitive superstition, blah-blah and dismiss it. I'm not so sure.'

'Then what's the explanation?'

Nearing shrugged. 'The explanation is, we don't know squat about a lot of this stuff. There are drugs in some of these preparations they use, psychotropic drugs, like the ones you described in your murder victim. Okay, that's rational, that's inside the, let's say, protective circle of the scientific paradigm. We also believe that there's stuff that traditional practitioners can do that's outside that paradigm but still real. Okay, that's cool, that's how science works. We see a baffling phenomenon – radioactivity, life itself – we study the hell out of it and we figure out what shelf it goes on, fit it into the structure. Sometimes the phenomenon is so weird we have to expand the structure, what they call a paradigm shift. That's what radioactivity did to physics, and that's basically what we're doing here, studying weird phenomena and trying to find out how to fit it in.' He grinned. 'So, Detective, now you know the secrets of medical anthro. Any questions?'

'Yeah. How do you explain Tanzi Franklin and what happened up in that apartment?'

A helpless gesture. 'I can't really explain it. Not enough data. The way you tell it, as a starting hypothesis, the girl looked out her window and saw the killer. Let's say the killer saw her. He finds her, he blows some powder on her, makes her extremely suggestible. He implants a suggestion: throw a fit and do weird stuff

if anyone asks you what you saw. That'd be one explanation. It'd also be a partial explanation for why this guy
is so hard to find.'

'What do you mean?'

'There are any number of traditions in which magic
workers can render themselves invisible, and there are
hundreds of anecdotal reports of shamanic invisibility
by supposedly reputable observers. How do they do it?
One answer is drugged suggestion of the observers. The
other is the same way David Copperfield does it on TV,
by technical illusion. Thus we stay inside the paradigm.'

Paz looked at his notebook. 'You said that there could
be stuff that's outside the paradigm but still real. What's
that about?'

Nearing leaned back in his chair, with a humorous
expression on his face. 'Oh, now we come to the sticky
part.' He waved his hand, taking in the office and the
facility beyond. 'This here is a scientific establishment.
Medical anthro is tolerated as long as it plays by the
rules, and the main rule is that the poor benighted
heathens think they're hexed and that belief produces
psychosomatic symptomology. But the notion that
magic has the same reality as, say, molecular bio or the
germ theory of disease, no, we don't go there, uh-uh.
That'd be a completely *different* paradigm. To actually
find out anything about it, you'd have to immerse yourself in it, actually *become* a practitioner, and then of
course no one would take you seriously, because you
would have lost your scientific objectivity. It's a sort of
catch-22.'

Paz thought about Barlow, who was certainly operat-
ing under a different paradigm, especially in regard to
this case. Something popped into his head and he

flipped back through his notebook to his interview with Dr Salazar and found what he was looking for. 'You mean like Marcel Vierchau or Tour de Montaille.'

Nearing's ginger eyebrows shot up. 'Hey, I'm impressed. You really did some homework.'

'Is there anything in it? Vierchau, I mean.'

'You read his book? No? Here, you can borrow mine.' Nearing reached unerringly into a pile of books and brought out a hardcover. 'You can judge for yourself. In the field, it's pretty much agreed he went off the deep end. For one thing, no one's been able to find the people he said he stayed with. The Russians haven't got any records about them.'

'So, what – he made it all up?'

'Well, not entirely. Fieldwork is a tricky business. A lot of times you see what you want to see. Margaret Mead wanted to see girls growing up without sexual hang-ups and that's what she brought back from Samoa. Bateson wanted to see family dynamics causing schizophrenia, so that's what he brought back. Vierchau wanted a traditional people to have powerful magical weapons, he called it a 'technology of interiority,' and that's what he found in Siberia. What the truth is . . .'

Nearing broke off. Paz observed a dreamy look come over the man's open face. Paz asked, 'What is it?'

Nearing snapped to. 'What?'

'You were someplace else.'

Nearing gave an embarrassed laugh. 'I guess. A little private magic. No, just thinking about Vierchau . . . I knew his ex-girlfriend in grad school. Her take on him was pretty much what I've suggested. Brilliant but flaky. She was quite a girl, though. You know, I'm happily married, two kids, but a week doesn't go by without me thinking about her. She was a remarkable, remarkable woman. Not particularly gorgeous, but . . . she had something.' He laughed. 'Magic, so to speak. I mention that because it might color my, um, let's say negative opinion of Vierchau, and theories of that kind.'

'What happened to the girl?'

'She married someone else, a hot-shit poet, who *I* of course introduced her to. The guy was an old pal of mine and I was very happy for them. Broke my little heart. I got the feeling she never recovered from what happened in Siberia.'

'Which was . . . ?'

'Oh, he filled her full of shaman drugs, she had a breakdown, and apparently she kept slipping back into it. I heard she went to Africa, went crazy again.' He shook his head. 'A damn shame.' He sighed. 'Anyway, she died. Killed herself.'

Nearing turned to face him. 'Well. Anything else, Detective?'

'Human sacrifice? Cannibalism? Any ideas? Any rumors that anybody's into it around town?'

Nearing chewed his lip. 'No, although it's hard to rule anything out. As a professional anthropologist I can tell you that in our culture, those who want to eat human flesh generally keep fairly quiet about it.'

End of interview. Nearing got the usual 'Call us if you hear anything' and Paz took his book and went out into the steaming bright afternoon. He sat in his car and ran the A/C and went over his notes. Africa again. Paz didn't like the African angle at all or the magic crap. Or the Vierchau connection. He had the sense of someone playing with him, the business with his own looks, the perp seeming at least to be a ringer for Paz himself. And the incident with Tanzi, that voice, had shaken him more than he could admit, and so he filed it away with the other stuff he did not want to think about. Compartmentalization was Paz's major mental strategy. He used it now. The weird stuff was not really weird but an artifact of ignorance. When they got the guy, it would turn out that . . . what? A gang. A cult. Like those wackos down in Matamoros, but more sophisticated. With chemicals, knockout drugs, hypnosis. Inside the paradigm; that was a good new word. Inside the paradigm, weird, but essentially familiar. And something else, he couldn't quite . . .

Paz caught a flash of silver going by outside and looked up. The flash was the skin of a catering unit stuck on an old Ford pickup. It was lunchtime, and a good location, outside the hospital, for staff and visitors who might want a break from the cafeteria and were willing to brave both the heat of the day and the more subtle dangers of unsupervised food prep. Paz got out and bought a mango soda and a fruit pastry.

A memory tugged. The cab of his mother's truck, him in the front seat strapped in, he must have been very young, because as soon as he was old enough to be in school, he had been behind the counter, serving out Cubano sandwiches and making change. His mother would pick him up right at the school, with the roach-mobile. Memories of fighting about that, the shame of it. No, but that part was later, not what he was trying to pin down now. He was three or so, he was looking out the windshield and trying to grab the . . . leaning forward and reaching for . . . ? A Saint Christopher statue? That was it, a statue on the dash. The Virgin? No, it wasn't white glow-in-the-dark plastic, it was brightly painted, larger than the commercial suction-cup icons; he could see it so clearly in his mind's eye. It was painted, life-like, and he had reached for it so hard that he had heaved himself over the restraint and fallen, knocking his head against the glove compartment knob. And his mother had heard his screams and come . . .

His mother hadn't sold the truck until he was around eight. He had spent hours and hours in it, but he couldn't recall seeing that statue again. The statue on the dash was a white plastic suction-cup Virgin, bland and of no interest. But he remembered a different statue.

It came to him then, the way that a forgotten word pops into the mind, with the same sense of inarguable assurance. A statue of a man in brown monk's garb, tonsured, the face roughly painted with features, the skin pale chocolate, the mouth a drop of bright crimson, the base green and gold; from the hands clasped in prayer a wire depended, and on the wire, tiny glittering beads that trembled enticingly in the vibrations from the engine. It was a Santería figure, a *santo*, Orula, in fact, or Ifa, as he had recently learned to call him, the *santo* of prophecy. But that could not be. His mother despised all that.

Paz felt a coldness flow over the skin of his head, as when standing in the sun a cloud passes over. He looked up, but the sun was there directly overhead, unshielded, merciless.

SIXTEEN

The place is on Twenty-seventh just off the Trail, one of a line of low concrete-block stucco commercial structures selling goods to the Cubans who didn't become millionaires in Miami. They sell furniture (*compre lo bueno y páguelo luegos*), shoes (*descuentos especiales para mayoristas*), sandwiches and Cuban coffee (*comidas criollas*), fabrics (*grandes promociones, con los mas bajor precios*) and PETS. The sign that announces this last is hand-painted on a half sheet of exterior plywood, white on black. They are not running any specials in PETS, but we go in anyway, early Friday evening after work, stepping carefully around the low concrete cone placed near the doorway. The place is stifling with the heavy ammoniac smell of chickens. Luz sneezes.

'It smells bad in here,' she remarks. 'What are we buying here?'

What indeed? We are here because my transmission joint is up the street and I had spotted this place the last time I was by. There are dozens of them in the region we are now in, known to its inhabitants as Souwesera. They do not sell cute puppies or kitties or tropical fish, but only pigeons, chickens, and an occasional goat. All the animals are either pure white or dead black. The *orishas* are extremely particular about what they eat; they dislike complex color schemes.

I say to her, 'I just have some business to do here. It won't take long.'

'Who's those?' Luz asks, pointing to the brightly painted plaster statues.

Three of them are lined up on the dusty shelf below the street window. In the center, the largest, nearly four feet tall, shows a dark woman of serene face, in a yellow dress, crowned with gold, holding a crowned child, and worshiped by three kneeling fishermen: Caridad del Cobré, the Virgin of Charity, patroness of Cuba. Flanking her on the left is another dark woman in a blue and white dress, standing on roiling waves, holding a fan shell. On the right is an old man, bearded, in rags, leaning on a crutch. I point to Caridad. 'This is the Virgin Mary, and you know who this is?'

'Baby Jesus.'

'Right. This lady is Saint Regla. She watches out for people who go out on the ocean, and also for mommies.'

'Does she watch out for you?'

'I hope so.' I privately doubt that great Yemaya will watch over my fruitless womb. And I don't go to sea anymore.

'And this is Saint Lazarus,' I say, 'he helps you if you're sick.'

'He looks sad.'

'Well, yes, there are so many sick people, aren't there?'

Heavy steps, the chickens flutter noisily. A short, stocky woman comes in from the back of the shop. She is dressed in a yellow print cotton dress, her face is the

color of an old saddle, and it has the gloss and the fine
creases of worn leather, too. Her hair is dark and frizzy,
and she could be any age from fifty to seventy-five. She
is smoking a Virginia Slim, and looks at me and Luz with
a blank look, out of deep-set eyes whose whites are pale
yellow. In my clunky Spanish I say, 'Señora, please, I
would like to arrange for an *ebo*.'

The woman's eyes go narrow. She is still trying to put
together the white-trash lady in the ugly brown dress
and the pretty little black girl into some familiar social
category. She asks, 'You are *omo-orisha*?'

She wants to know if I am a child of the spirits, a
devotee of Santería. Something like that, I answer. She
wants to know who my *babalawo* is. I tell her I haven't
got one, and she frowns. Makes sense. This is a neighborhood shop; 90 percent of her business must come
from one or two local *iles*. She doesn't much care for
strangers wandering in and trying to order sacrifices.
Why don't they use their own PETS? She asks, 'Who
threw Ifa for you, then?' and I answer, 'I threw Ifa by
myself, for myself.'

A little gaping here, a show of missing teeth, of gold
ones glimmering. Female *babalawos* are extremely rare,
white female ones virtually unknown. I watch her trying
to make up her mind. Suddenly she is nervous. She
senses *brujisma*, I can tell. She says, 'Wait, please,' and
stumps back past the chickens and the goats. Luz is
inspecting the place like the bold gringa kid she has
miraculously become. I have to make a leaping stride to
keep her from stepping on the concrete cone placed next
to the doorway. It looks like a parking-lot button, and she
likes to balance on parking-lot buttons in the Winn-
Dixie lot. This is not a parking-lot button, however, but

Eleggua-Eshu, guardian of portals, not to be trodden upon.

I turn around then, and *of course*, there is the small brown man dressed in white who was walking near the ER with Lou Nearing. I have Luz by the hand and the impulse to run is nearly overwhelming, but then I think, no. Ifa has set his hook in me, and is dragging me upward, to the true light or the ax, and clearly, this is a part of it.

The man is looking at me curiously, standing in the doorway to the back room. The old woman is behind him, in the shadows, peeking out from behind his shoulder. He is dressed in a white Cuban shirt and white trousers and he has a faded khaki baseball hat on his head. He steps forward and stands behind the dusty glass-topped counter of the shop, near the old iron far-from-digital cash register, as if he is about to take my order. He looks about fifty, a smooth, round pale brown face, no mustache, unlined, or nearly so. His eyes, shadowed by the bill of his cap, look enormous, like a lemur's, all pupil.

In soft Spanish, he asks, 'Can I help you in any way, señora?'

I get my breathing under control. 'I want to arrange *ebó*. Two black and two white pigeons, and thirty-two cowries.'

He says, 'If you come to the *ile*, I would be happy to help you.'

'I can't come to the *ile*.'

He shrugs. 'Well, then I can't help you.' Suddenly his face splits into a grin, showing swathes of pink gum and two golden teeth. In barely accented English, he adds,

'It's like the motor vehicle department. You have to be there. You can't send anyone else.'

I feel myself smiling, too, remembering Uluné. He was always cracking up at little things. Delight seems to be a by-product of screwing around with the unseen world. Marcel, also. Unless you're a witch.

I say, in English, now, with gratitude, because my Spanish is not quite up to this, 'Then I guess I'll have to buy the birds and do it myself.'

Shrug again. 'You have to do it just right, or the *orisha* can't eat. You really don't want to offer the food and then snatch it away.'

'I understand that,' I say, 'but I don't think I should appear at an *ile*.'

'As you said. What was the verse Ifa gave you, if I may ask?'

Of course I have it now by heart, so I recite it for him.

He says, 'I'm not familiar with that verse. Where did you learn it?'

'In Africa.'

'Africa. I'm envious. I always wanted to study with a Yoruba *babalawo*.'

Suddenly I realize what's missing. This guy should stink of *dulfana* and he doesn't. That peculiar vibration behind the sinuses, or whatever it is, isn't there. This means that he's either a fraud and doesn't work any real magic at all, or he knows how to mask. It is unlikely that he's a fraud, which means that he is a very serious player. Becoming invisible in the *m'fa* is hard enough; becoming invisible in the *m'doli* is apparently a lot harder. Uluné could do it, of course, or he would hardly have survived, but I did not expect to find the skill in Miami.

I say, 'It wasn't a Yoruba. I studied with the Olo.'

An inquiring look. Which is good. It would be bad if he knew about the Olo. What are you doing? screams the *ogga* in the control room. Why are you talking to this guy? Why aren't you heading for Paducah, Moline, Provo? I ignore her; pulled by the hook, tied to the line. I explain, 'The Olo claim they taught the Yoruba about the *orishas* long ago. In Ifé the Golden. They claim that the *orishas* were originally Olo, human people who became gods. They claim that in their ceremonies, the *orishas* come, but not mounted on people. They come themselves.'

'I see. Tell me, señora, do you believe this?'

'I don't know what I believe anymore. I've seen things in Africa that are very hard to explain except by believing this. Those wiser than I am might explain them in some other way.'

He nods, gently takes my hand. He says, 'Señora, you really should come to the *ile*. The way to escape this *brujo* is not by hiding or running anymore but by honoring the *santos* and obeying them. Then you will find your allies, and then you will find freedom and peace.'

A wave of stark terror. My *ki* is up in my throat. 'You know about . . . um?' I croak out.

'Oh, yes. He is here and he is looking very hard for you. Who is he?'

'My husband. His name is DeWitt Moore.' I have not spoken my husband's name in some years now, and have worked hard to keep it out of even my thoughts. And now there it is, vomited out into the dusty air of PETS.

No recognition, although it is a reasonably famous

name in some circles. The *santero* takes a receipt from a pad on the counter, scratches at it with a Bic, and hands it to me. Pedro Ortiz, it says, with an address nearby in Sowesera.

I put the slip of paper into my bag. Ortiz is beaming at Luz now. He reaches out over the counter and caresses her cheek. She doesn't pull away as she does with most other people. Maybe I'll trust this man. He likes children, and my husband did not. He thought the insects did a better job, locking their offspring up in cocoons until they were adults. Stupid, really, to trust, says the *ogga*, and serves up images of Hitler patting the cheeks of the boy soldiers, of Saddam and the little hostages before the Gulf War.

'You should come to the *ile*,' Ortiz says. 'We should discuss things. This is a bad thing that's happening. Bad for you, bad for Santería.'

'How much do you know?'

'Very little, really. Rumors, feelings, a great disturbance in the currents of *ashe*, warnings from the *orishas*. Is it his child?'

'No.'

I converse with Ortiz, about Yoruba, about Africa, avoiding the details of my Olo vacation, making no commitments. I don't tell him about the *okunikua*, so that there are still, to my knowledge, only two people in North America who know what it is. He suspects that I am holding something back, I see it swimming in his black eyes. These fixed on me, boring in, he says, 'You know, the simple people think that we, I mean we *santeros*, have power over the *santos*, but we both know that isn't true. We have learned to open ourselves, that's all. The truth is, we are in their hands.' Here he clenches both of his hands into fists. 'It's frightening to be in the hands of the *santos*, isn't it? We love to think we're in control. But we do it because we know they love us and they know we love them. Even Shango, who's so terrible when he comes. They are of God in the end, a path to God.'

I am nodding like one of those cheap dolls that people install over the backseats of their cars. I can't stop myself. My face feels stiff. Do I have a phony smile on? He says, 'But you know, there are other kinds of spirits in the *orun* besides *orishas*. The simple make the mistake of thinking that everything spiritual is good. But you know what I'm talking about, don't you?'

'*Ajogun*,' I say.

His eyes close briefly and his lips move. 'Yes, them. The *orishas* help the *ashe* flow and fill our hearts with peace. But the *ajogun* eat it. Greedy things, the *ajogun*. I hope you have never yourself . . .'

'No, never. But he has.'

'Of course. But he's not just a *brujo*, is he?'

'No. I don't know what he is. Something no one has seen in a long time, not even in Africa. I should go. I didn't want to involve anyone in . . .'

He reaches out and gently grasps my hand. 'We are people of the *santos*, so of course we are involved already. Listen to me, señora. Pay attention to what the *orisha* says. That's the only thing now. Pay attention! Come to the *ile*!'

But I can't think of anything just now save escaping. It is hot and humid in PETS and I can feel sweat trickling down my sides. It's hard to breathe the thick ammoniac air. In a second I will be fainting, or falling at his feet crying, 'Save me!'

Luz skips back and asks if she can have a baby chick. I am about to say no when the *santero* says a few words I don't quite catch to the woman. She goes out and returns a minute or so later with a paper bag punched with holes and the top stapled shut. Luz and I peer into the holes. She is delighted.

A yellow bird.

Outside again, in the waning heat of the day, the afternoon's rainstorm turned back into humidity, Luz announces that she is hungry, and so we go next door to the Cuban coffee place for a couple of flat fruit pastries and a chocolate milk, and I have a *café con leche*. I am in a dilemma. I must make the sacrifice, I must find my allies, but in order to do that, it seems I will have to go to a Santería ritual, and if I do that, I will light up the *m'doli* like a fireball and he will know I am alive, for sure. Uluné could tell when someone he knew died, even if it was far away, and perhaps my husband has learned that trick too. Maybe all this running and hiding has been completely useless. Maybe he just hasn't gotten around to me yet, and was waiting until chance brought him here to Miami. I sense large forces, thunderheads closing in, huge and hard like millstones. I will be ground to powder, unless Ifa is right, and I get the right allies. Magical allies, a concept unknown to mere objectivity. When you venture into the unseen world, the allies weave a circle of protection around you, a kind of sorcerous space shuttle. They don't have to do anything, or even to know that they're allies. This chicken probably doesn't have the faintest idea that Ifa has picked her to guard my white ass. But you have to trust Ifa, and you have to pick them right. Not a trivial task.

'I'm going to call my chicken Peeper,' says Luz. 'That's her name.'

Some Proustian circuit closes in my head once again – the strong flavor of coffee, the heat, the peeping of the chick, a line from Ellison: 'A hibernation is a covert preparation for a more overt action.' That's from *Invisible Man*, and I reflect, not for the first time, that what I have been doing these last few years is a lot like what the anonymous protagonist of Ellison's book did after his experiences on the front lines of our race wars.

In my mind, I'm in Chicago again, on the back veranda of Lou Nearing's apartment, the top floor of a gigantic Victorian on the South Side, Fiftieth or Fifty-first, off Michigan, near the university. It was summer, hot in the afternoon, a white sky overhead, and I was looking down into the backyard, an overgrown tangle of ailanthus and honeysuckle and bindweed, with birds cheeping, and I was holding a drink, Kahlúa and cream on ice, which was my drink that summer. Lou always threw a big party on July Fourth, which was what this was. I was not, I recall, much of a party person myself at that time – this was a couple of years after my return from Siberia. I preferred to stand back and observe, sucking on drinks until oblivion approached and I could slip into an acceptably louche persona. Then I would go fairly wild, which is how I got together with Lou at another party, at which, if memory serves (and it does not), I removed my underpants during the dancing and threw them up upon a lighting fixture. He was taken in; he thought I was a fun person like him.

Which was why I was standing alone on the veranda, getting my bag on, when Lou came out and said, 'Hey

Janey, there you are! I want you to meet someone. Jane, DeWitt Moore; Witt, meet Jane Doe.'

The usual widening of the eyes at the name. My eyes must have widened, too, as he extended his hand. There was a definite tingle. The first thing that hit me was his skin, not the butterscotch color of it, but the texture, which was smooth as ivory, like a child's skin. Lickable skin; it looked like it would actually dissolve sweetly on your tongue. He was a fine-boned, medium-size man, only a hair taller than I was, dressed in a blue-striped button-down shirt, with the sleeves rolled above the elbow, chinos, and the same kind of Sperry deck shoes I had on. He was holding a large plastic cup with a Bears logo on it. Our eyes met; his were hazel, intelligent, sardonic, wary, amused, which was exactly the look I was then practicing myself with my green ones. So we had a little something, even before either of us was aware of it. A little too long on the handshake, that was another danger sign. Lou was talking away, supplying background, his canned version of my adventures, and his connection with Witt.

'Old Witt and I went to school together.'

'At Notre Dame?'

'Yeah,' said Witt, 'on the football team. We were both linebackers.'

Lou laughed. 'No, in high school, in Morristown.'

'That's right. Lou used his mighty thews to protect me from the racists.'

I looked inquiringly at Lou, but at that moment, a huge chocolate-colored woman strode out on the deck. She was wearing a scarlet and pink print muumuu and a sparkly pink turban and was carrying the kind of box people used to carry 45 records in. She dragged Lou off into the apartment, promising serious Motown.

I drained my drink. Witt made no move to leave, just looked at me, smiling, making me nervous. I said, 'That's interesting. Was racism much of a problem in Morristown? I mean what was it, white gangs . . . ?'

'Yes, everyone assumes that, but these particular racists were black guys. They thought I was being too white. There's a certain stratum of black society that responds to uppity niggers in about the same way as your basic Alabama ax-handle cracker does. Or did, since we've officially solved our racial problems here in America.'

I ignored the theatrical bitterness. 'That must have been extremely painful.'

'Extremely. But enough of me. Lou talks about you all the time. Apparently, you've had some wild adventures. Central Asia. Maurice Vierchau . . .'

'Marcel.'

'Right. What's he like? Lou says the latest on him in the profession is a few sandwiches short of a picnic. A plausible charlatan.'

'Read his book.' My usual line. 'Decide for yourself.'

'I was hoping for the scoop. Secrets of primitive rites.'

'Well, you won't get them from me,' I said coolly. 'Marcel is . . . an unusual man, but I can't practice his kind of anthropology myself. I prefer a little more distance from the subject. What's your subject, Witt?'

'Me? I'm in hibernation,' he said, and that's when I got the Ellison line. We talked about Ellison awhile, and we agreed that it was one of the half-dozen best books of the century. I pressed him a little about what he did.

'I'm a poet. A promising *black* poet, as the expression has it.'

I was getting irritated with this. 'What sort of black poet are you? Very black? Langston Hughes raisin-in-the-sun black? Or black like Maya Angelou, passionate songster of the unforgivable sins inflicted on your people? Or are you a black poet like Aleksandr Pushkin?'

He held up his hands in front of his face, in a mock cringe. 'Wow, what a blast! I guess I have to take my identity politics elsewhere.'

'You do. And I need another drink.'

We talked until the sun sank over the western city, and the trees in the yard turned into silhouettes and disappeared, with the party swirling around us, and the air cooling and then thickening sweetly with the smoke from many barbecues. We talked a bit about anthro, not much, because he didn't know anything about the field and because my work bored me then, smothered by my lies, and a lot about poetry, which he knew deeply and I a little. He recited some of his for me, shyly, including the one from his first book, that got into all the anthologies later, that starts, *There is a plantation in my brain, broad wet acres under the arching skull.* The book was *Tropic of Night*, and it had won some kind of poetry award, and five hundred whole dollars for him to spend any way he wanted.

'It must have been pretty good to win a prize like that,' I said.

He checked me out to see if I was putting in the needle, but I wasn't. He was needling himself pretty well without my help. So we talked about *Tropic of Night*. That was the steamy zone where the white folks stuck all their nasty shadows, the zone of projection on the Others. Who were mainly Negroes in America, but other weirdos, like Catholics and Jews, would do, too. The great thing about black people, though, he said, is that they were so conveniently identifiable. Every time we look in a mirror, all that shit is reinforced, he said, and so that's where we live, at least part of the time, every day: permanent denizens of the Tropic of Night. I asked him if he really believed that, and he laughed, and said he didn't know. A lot of people did, and he liked to inhabit different kinds of mentalities. He liked to play with roles and masks. But what did he *really* believe, then, I asked in my crudely earnest way, but he let the question slide away with a shrug. Did I ever get an answer to that one?

He said he had written a sort of opera, which I thought remarkable, and I wanted to hear all about it. That turned out to be *Race Music*, which made him famous later, a wonder boy at what was it? Twenty-six or twenty-seven. I was actually the first white person to see *Race Music*, in a basement he had rented from a church out on Garfield. When it opened later at the Victory Gardens there was practically a riot. Makes Spike Lee look like Aunt Jemima, that was in one review. And afterward the same in New York.

But that first night we were being careful. Witt was always careful about relationships, and I was . . . burned doesn't quite encompass my emotional state. Cratered? Incinerated? The *oggas* were in charge, at any rate. So we didn't actually touch the first night, although our hormones were flowing thick enough to bead up on the skin surfaces. When it got dark, the whole party wandered down to the shore and watched the fireworks.

I was *with* Lou, but Witt was sitting on the other side of me on the grass, radiating on the microwave band hot enough to brown meat. In a moment when we were alone, he asked me where I lived and I pointed to it, a big fancy apartment house by the lake shore.

'You must be rich.'

'Stinking.'

'You want to invest in my play?' he asked.

We drive back to our house and I make dinner and afterward we play. I do sleight-of-hand tricks for Luz. She fools around with her chicken, which I am having a hard time thinking of as a magical ally. Later, I stand on a kitchen chair and heave myself up into the crawl space via the plywood-covered hole set into the kitchen ceiling, and have a look around, eyeballing dimensions. I do some rough figuring.

What am I thinking? Making a bedroom for Luz so she will be able to hold her head high in day care? Something to do while we wait for Armageddon. No, it feels right.

It will be a bitch to build, a cramped, oven-hot workspace, and I will have to enlarge the access hole to drag standard-size plywood and drywall sheets in there, but love will find a way, I suppose.

When Luz is in bed, I walk across to Polly Ribera's house. The family – Polly herself, Jasper, who is twelve, and Shari, who is fourteen – are watching TV. Polly waves me in and I sit. It is a Steven Seagal movie, and the hero is knocking over the bad guys like duckpins, using aikido moves. I could comment on his technique, but instead I tell her my plan. I want to build a bedroom for Luz in the crawl space of the garage. The roof peak is a good seven feet high and there is enough room for a kid, and also there are louvered windows set into the gable on either side for ventilation. I would do all the work myself: insulation, drywall, paint and plaster, flooring, wiring, if she will take care of the materials and the tool rental. I give her the rough estimate I have cooked up and she agrees it's a good deal for her. She says jokingly that she won't raise my rent when it's done.

So, the next day, Saturday, I drive Luz over to Trapp Avenue, to the Pettigrews' lovely home, and drop her for a day, fortunately prearranged, of exotic pleasures. Yes, I *am* taking advantage, but it is so easy to play on the guilt of people like Mrs P. and I try to keep the contempt and resentment out of my heart. Such people flocked to my husband's plays in great numbers to delight in seeing themselves abused on the stage.

We did actually get married, which for people of our age and class and intellectual pretensions was unusual. *He* asked me, too; even more unusual. Now that I look back, I must resist the impulse to put a malign light on everything that occurred between us. I could, for example, say that he asked me to marry him to see whether a cloud passed across my eyes, whether I was worried about what my parents might think. I *was* worried about what my parents might think, but it was the religion, not the race, something that never would have occurred to him. I had drifted considerably from the church, but my father had looked forward to giving me away in Saint Patrick's, in the presence of a thousand or so Doe family and friends. Witt was not merely not-Catholic, but an aggressive atheist. He would not be married in a church, nor speak with a priest, nor make any commitments as to children's education, not that he had any intention of having children. Nobody takes that shit seriously anymore. As he often remarked. The only thing that really mattered to him, I suppose, was his writing. And race, as it turned out.

And the hatred. I thought in the beginning that I could cure him of that if I just loved him enough, that we could somehow build a magic circle within which we could have real life, not life strained through the mangle of racism. I have to think he truly loved me then, and the love was doubly precious because it was obvious that I was the only thing he actually loved. While it is the case that some of the African-American men who go with white women take out upon those women the suffering imposed by the famous Four Hundred Years Of, Witt never did, not in New York, anyway.

We only had one fight before Africa. He had told me from the outset that he was an orphan, that his parents were dead, that he had been raised by an elderly aunt and uncle, also deceased. (Faithful Lou Nearing, who knew the truth, never said a word.) I can't imagine how he thought he would get away with it after he became notorious. Shortly after *Race Music* opened in New York and created pandemonium among the great and the good of both races, an enterprising reporter for the *Voice* located the two people who had raised DeWitt Moore from infancy. The man was a professor of English at a New Jersey community college and the woman worked for a state social welfare agency in Trenton. Both of them were impeccably liberal, both were terribly hurt that their son had not contacted them in over seven years, and both of them were white as Senator Bilbo.

The reporter called me for a comment just before the story broke. I no-commented him, slammed down the phone, stormed into the big room at the end of our loft where he worked. I confronted him, spitting with rage. Is it true? He admitted it. Made a joke. How could you! How could you lie to me. *Me!* I was so mad I kicked him in the shin. His eyes got wide, his teeth bared in a grimace of rage, he swung a clumsy slap at my face. I caught the blow in *ude-hineri* and tossed him across the room. Then I walked out. I stayed in the Plaza under a fake name for a week, watching television. The talking heads made the most of it, anatomizing the self-hating black male, comparing him to the self-hating Jew, blaming it on the Four Hundred Years, on the collapse of the black family, on the great and perhaps excessive power of the black family, on liberal mollycoddling, on ineradicable racism, on affirmative action, on lack of affirmative action, and on drugs, because it emerged, too, that Witt had managed to locate his birth mother some years back, a burnt-out junkie whore in Newark, lately deceased.

So I went back. He was pathetically glad to see me when I came into the loft. He looked like he hadn't washed, shaved, or eaten since the thing broke. He apologized, I apologized, we talked, we turned off the phone and ordered in, and had an extraordinary amount of sexual intercourse for something like ten days.

I haven't thought of all this in years, but now I am, as I drag heavy pieces of drywall and plywood up the ladder to the loft, which becomes hot enough to make pizza in as the day wears on. By three, I have the floor in and the insulation tacked up between the rafters, and with my rented recip saw I have cut the hole for the exhaust fan. I eat lunch in the mango shade of the yard, and wonder why I am doing this crude and wearisome task. As homage to my dad? Could be. The thing about being rich is that you never ever have to move an object from one place on the earth's surface to another, unless you are playing a game. My father thought this corrupting, and so he, and later I, spent many hours doing sweaty, abrasive, back-straining work on old cars and on boats. I built my first boat, an eight-foot lapstrake tender, when I was eleven. My mother and sister in contrast never, as the phrase has it, lifted a finger. Nor did my husband, another interesting contrast. This is truly odd because sorcery is a physical thing, and clearly he learned to do that very well, the collecting, the mixing, the stirring, the boiling. The cutting.

While I am eating, Jasper comes by and asks if he can help. He is a strong, stocky kid with a big mass of dark curls and a bright and humorous eye, and I am glad to have him, because I need someone to hold the other end of the drywall panels as I tack them up to the rafters with the nail gun. By the time the sun goes down, I have the ceiling and the walls done, and the exhaust fan fitted into place. Polly Ribera comes by and takes a look and praises clever Dolores, who feels pretty good herself, having let old Jane out of the cage for a little stretch.

I take a cool shower, put on fresh clothes, eat some mangos with cottage cheese and feed Luz's chicken some bran flakes. I knock together a little box for it out of scrap wood and hardware cloth. Then I sleep, dreamlessly as usual. The Olo regard dreamlessness as a very serious malady, on the same order as aphasia or paralysis. You really still dream, Uluné explained to me, but some curse or malign entity is blocking the vital messages from coming through. I dreamed vividly all the time I was in Africa, and at breakfast each morning, I would share these with Uluné and he would share his with me. Some were not so pleasant, as I am starting to recall. Did you ever have a nightmare in which you 'awakened' into yet another nightmare? And couldn't move? And thought it would never stop? The witch dreams of the Olo are to that sort of thing as the aircraft carrier *Chester A. Nimitz* is to Uluné's twelve-foot log pirogue.

The next morning, I awake early, with unfamiliar hunger pangs. Jane is getting rambunctious, obviously. I make myself a batch of French toast and eat it with maple syrup and jam, a pot of coffee, a whole Hayden mango at the picnic table in the backyard, serenaded by the birds. I used to like honey on French toast, back before Africa, but now the idea of honey makes me a little faint. I examine the birds and listen to them carefully. There don't seem to be any honeyguides among them. Then I go out and pick up Polly's *Herald* from the front yard where the paper boy has dropped it. I glance at the headline. I rip it out of its plastic wrapper and read the story. Then I drop it on the ground, stagger into the bushes, and throw up my breakfast.

SEVENTEEN

10/2 Lagos

Dave Berne is here. Originally a Brit, famous womanizer, not with me, tho, been at Stanford for ages. He said M. had told him all about me, and sent his love, and said we would get along. Been here many times, speaks all the languages, is completely at ease. As we drove from the airport, he regaled us with a story (in mixed English and Yoruba) about a grad student of his who couldn't get the Yoruba language tonalities right. No one would talk to him after he asked, very politely, when the next circumcision ceremony was to take place. Berne asked him exactly what he had said and the kid repeated it & what he'd actually said was, 'Please, I require to have intercourse with three billy goats.' Tunji laughing so hard he could hardly steer.

Back at the Palm Court, Berne insisted on running off to Yaba Market for a big street lunch and so we all did, plus W. Berne found a horrible-looking little stand that he said sold the best *akara* in Lagos & we all sat around on rickety stools and ate the fried pastry, dipping it in blazing chili sauce, and washing it down with beer & it was very good, too. Someone tried to sell him an old Gelede mask, D.B. instantly identified it as fake, explained why, brilliant rap on aesthetics and symbology of the western Yoruba, grad students in awe. I thought it was pretty good myself, but my awe is all dried up, now, M. used to do shit like that all the time. Greer slipped into the background, grinning tho, I think he finds it a relief not always to have to be the big kahuna. W. not in awe at all, shooting D.B. daggerlike looks.

Good discussion at dinner, talked about origins – where do religious ideas arise, can you trace a myth back to some primal source and say, oh, here marks the spot where that particular belief entered the consciousness of a people? Greer talked about Mami Wata, a Ewe cult he's been studying for years, where we know the origins with some precision, since it dates from the coming of Europeans to the West African coast. From POV of Africans, these people appeared in floating islands that arose out of the sea. Their skins were the color of drowned corpses. They possessed tools and weapons of a kind and power never before seen on earth, clearly of magical origin. They worshiped carved figures, like real people do, & placed them in front of their floating islands. The Ewe adapted existing water spirits into a new cult, giving it a name in pidgin – Mother Water, or Mami Wata – & began to worship the figureheads of trading vessels. Mami Wata wants you to be rich like the white man, is the message. Her devotees dress in white and smear their faces with chalk or flour, and dance around figures painted bright pink, which still bear the expression of benign stupidity found on the original carved figureheads.

W. is eating this up, asking questions, and scratching away on a pad – his area of expertise, the weird way in which the races ape one another. Knew he was getting it all wrong – nothing to do with race, everything to do with money – but was so happy to see him animated again that I didn't butt in.

Greer talked about Yoruba origins, said the old bards of

the kings of Oyo claimed the Yoruba came from Mecca, but that's obvious fabrication based on prestige of Islam. That Y. not entirely autochthonous seems beyond doubt, most probably they came from the east, in waves during the early first millennium A.D. His best guess is that they came from Meroë, a kingdom in upper Egypt that flourished between the second and fourth centuries.

A little discussion of Afrocentrism here, the name of Meroë always sparks that, Meroë having conquered Egypt proper at one point, a rare example of black folks getting over on the other kind and thus to be cherished. Then a giant leap to: Egypt equals black, Egypt founded Western civ. thus white civilization another rip-off from the good guys. Demolished (I thought a bit unkindly) by Berne; he's got a quick fuse in the presence of nonsense. He said this obsession with Egypt and Nilotic ethnic types has been a disaster in West Africa, and was invented by white colonialists in the first place, so that they could rule by favoring people who looked like them – light skins, thin lips and noses. The Tutsi in Rwanda, the Hausa in Nigeria, and it was disgusting to see Africans falling for it. You got a world-class culture right here in Yoruba and you despise it because it doesn't have MTV and chrome trim. W. did a long angry rant about how the white man would never respect the black man until the black man had real power, power to hurt the white man. What Africa needed was a black Hitler!

Stunned silence. Greer stepped in, asked Berne to talk about the Olo.

Odd tale. A crazy Frenchman back in the 19th C. found a small group in isolated district in Fr. Equatorial who claimed to be from Ifé, but Ifé before the Yoruba got there. The Yoruba pantheon, they claimed, were *them*. They had godlike powers back then, in the golden age, now they've fallen on hard times. Tour de Montaille, his name was. Don't recall hearing it before, said so — Berne explained he had discovered the original journals, but was unable to verify the existence of Olo, so assumed either the Frenchie made it all up, or they were extinguished or dispersed in the past century. Wrote a brief piece in *J. African Hist.*, probably in library here. I said I would check it out. He said read the Fr. journals, too, they're here also, if the termites haven't got them.

Actually, a jolly evening, the best in a while. W. did not go out carousing with Ola and his pals as usual. Instead, later, a polite knock on my door. I succumbed. After, I wanted to talk, about us, about the craziness, about how he was *feeling*, for God's sake, but he fell asleep, is sleeping now as I write this. I can't sleep. It will have to be Xanax again. Still, maybe the worst is over.

10/4 Ado-Joga

Here in this little village west of Lagos, Berne setting me up w/ Adedayo, Gelede mask carver, most gorgeous woodcarving tradition in Yoruba art. Interesting: Gelede artists are men, but tradition pays homage to the spiritual power of elderly women, called *awon iya wa*, 'our mothers.' Not common in Africa, needless to say. Or anywhere else. Feminist in me finds it terribly exciting. These women have such power that they have to be entertained, cosseted, praised, and placated, lest they turn into witches, and bring destruction down on communities. Result = Gelede masked dance ritual. Unlike other Yoruba dance rituals, which address the forces of the spirit world, Gelede concerned mainly with this world, as personified in the terrible old women. The dances speak to social and spiritual issues affecting daily life, like art in Europe in Greece, in Middle Ages.

Mr Adedayo very old, dignified, aristocratic, works in a tiny yard in front of his atelier, sitting on the ground with his back against a fig tree. Berne asked him if I could video him at work, A. gave me funny look, said he 'didn't think you could take pictures of that,' meaning the spiritual work. Taped mere physical work, however, for hours, strange, a *numen* coming off him and off the mask he was working on, hard to describe. A sense of groundedness in culture, in the earth, in the flow of *ashe*?

He was using a tool that made a tiny triangular dent in the wood and he was making a pattern with it on the side of the mask, just hundreds of tiny three-cornered dents, in lines and swirls, and I could not pull my eyes away. Night fell. A woman came out with a lantern. Both Berne and I gasped and then laughed. It was like being in church used to be like. Compare artists' studios in SoHo, they don't have this there.

Mentioned this later to Berne, he called it the unspoken and secret rewards of anthro, far more significant than the plaudits of our peers, why we put up with the sulky camels and the insects. Said, surely *he* taught you that, meaning M., who actually did teach me that, or tried; he lived for it, and I have been trying to forget it, because it's a drug for us poor etiolated, alienated, mechanical corpse-colored people, and I think I have a tendency to OD. Changed subject just then, because I knew if conversation went on in this vein, he would press me on what happened in Chenka, which I can't talk about.

10/5 Lagos

Reading the paper on Tour de Montaille. I took our little Canon down to the library this afternoon, and copied Berne's paper and the original French journal. Interesting stuff – the Olo or Oleau, 'real magic' again? It would be like discovering a tribe in Iran or Russia who still had the oral version of Homer as a living, bardic experience. TdM. was vague about the location but somewhere north of the Baoulé in present Mali. (??ethnographic traces, artifacts?) Interesting tradition of infant sacrifice, too. Not uncommon in recent Nigeria, but typically a mere ritual murder, a burial with the chief, or you knock a kid on the head in hard times, avert some curse, or the old Ibo habit of burying twins alive in jars. According to these journals this is not the same thing – this is somehow *using* the body of the neonate, ritual cannibalism, or drugs. M. would say drugs – using the mother-child system as a chemical retort? To produce what? If I didn't have the Gelede project set up already, I'd take a shot at going up to Mali and poking around.

W. not at dinner, no one seems to know where he's off to. Asked Soronmu, but got a shifty answer. He's with some of the *loki*, local hard boys, getting color (so to speak) for his work.

10/6 Fucking Lagos

Total disaster. Can't write now. The idiot!

EIGHTEEN

Where are you going?' Mrs Paz asked as he headed for the door.

'I'm going out, Mami,' he answered. 'I'm going to do some shopping, and get my car washed and cleaned up, and then I'm going to clean my place. Then I might go over to the pool and swim. Or I might do nothing.'

'What do you mean, nothing?' Giving him the stone face.

'Nothing means nothing. See, Mami, this is what we call in English *a day off*. I'm taking *a day off* today, and I plan on taking *a day off* tomorrow, too. It's the *weekend*. I only get one weekend in every four off and I'm going to take it easy.'

'I need you here tomorrow,' she said, not amused.

'You may need me, but you won't have me. I realize you don't think the police do work, but we do, and so I'm taking what we Americans call *a break*.'

'You know, son of mine, you're not too big that I can't slap your face if you talk to me like that. What about tonight?'

'I'm going out,' Paz said.

'Who with?'

'With a young woman. I will buy her a meal, not here, and take her to the theater, and afterward I expect to take her home and have as much sexual intercourse as I can manage.'

She threw a good one at his ear, but he was ready for it and rocked back so that her fist sailed past his face, and then he made his escape out the back door of the kitchen. She stood in the door and yelled imprecations at him as he trotted down the alley. As always after these incidents, he resolved to quit working for her and move out of the rent-free apartment. The place was booming; she had more money than God and could easily afford to hire any chef in the city. These resolves never bore fruit, however, other than a dull depression that blighted a day he had anticipated for weeks. He did not do the errands he had planned, nor did he go to the pool. Instead, after showering, he sat in his shorts in his apartment with the shades pulled down and watched sports on television and drank Coronas until they were all gone, and then fell into a doze. As he slipped off he remembered the dashboard statue. He had meant to ask his mother about it but hadn't, and probably wouldn't now. Not that she would tell him the straight story anyway. Lies and secrets chez Paz, that was the rule. Why he had become a dick, he thought, and slept.

Willa lived in a tiny apartment on McDonald, from one window of which, when the wind was just in the right quarter to move the leaves of a royal palm, one could see a patch of bay the size of a paperback novel. She was ready, and looked as well as Willa ever looked in clothes: a loose knit top with a roll collar, made of some rough and sparkly dark purple yarn, and wide white trousers in a silky material. Her springy hair was piled high up on top, compressed, but still allowing delicious little red coils to protrude against her white neck. Paz planted a soft kiss beneath one of these. Out they went.

He took her to a ferny joint on Commodore Plaza, the kind with incompetent (hi, my name is Melanie) young women waiting table and a menu of dishes that were healthy, generally pastel in color, and pale in taste. He did not care for this sort of food, but she liked it, and she knew he didn't, and was grateful. They walked holding hands down Main to the Coconut Grove Playhouse and took their seats.

After a few disorienting minutes, Paz to his surprise found himself enjoying the show. It was really a series of satirical sketches, loosely tied together by the story of Simple, a black kid who wanders Candide-like across America in search of the authentic black experience. When playing black people, the cast members put on 'black' masks and costumes, right onstage, and sometimes they also layered 'white' masks and costumes on top of the black ones. The actors exchanged masks and costumes and shifted around on the minstrel-style set, and their skill was such that after a while it was hard to tell the actual race of the performer. You saw only the masks, which was the main point.

'This is un-fucking-believable,' said Paz to Willa during the intermission. 'I'm glad you talked me into it.'

'Yeah, it's terrific. You notice people checking us out, we being the only interracial couple in the place.'

'What interracial? I'm Cuban,' said Paz, and she laughed. 'Who is this guy? Moore, the writer?'

'Oh, DeWitt Moore — he was quite the enfant terrible a couple years back. He had a couple of smashes, including this one here, and since then he's been keeping a low profile, reviews and poetry mostly. He's got a lot of enemies.'

'I can see why. This thing's an equal-opportunity fuck-you.'

'Indeed. He's supposed to be here tonight, by the way.'

'Yeah?' Paz looked around the crowded lobby. 'Where?'

'Onstage. He likes to show up and take one of the chorus parts, like Alfred Hitchcock. In New York, people who hated him used to buy tickets on the off chance that he'd take a bow after and they could pelt him with refuse. That man is staring at you.'

'Where?'

'Don't look. Middle-aged white guy in a turtleneck. Arty type. Now he's telling his date. She's staring, too. Are you more famous than you've let on?'

'No, probably someone I arrested,' said Paz, turning to look the arty gent in the eye. The man nodded at him familiarly. Paz had no idea who he was.

'What's that buzzing noise?' Willa asked.

'Shit! It's my damn beeper.' Paz pulled it out of his pocket and studied its tiny screen, his brows twisted. 'Some asshole probably misplaced a time sheet or something. Wait here, I'll go call.'

But when Paz called on his cell phone, the operator patched him through to a radio car, and after a minute or so he found himself talking to Cletis Barlow.

'Jimmy, you got a pen? You need to get out here right now.'

'What? I'm in the middle of a date. I'm at the theater. What the heck is so important?'

'He done it again. Cuban woman. In Cocoplum.'

'Oh . . . *fuck*!' cried Paz, with his thumb over the phone mike. Cocoplum was a wealthy bayside development south of the Grove, favored by the Cuban upper crust. If the bastard wanted the absolute maximum in police attention he had made a good choice of victim.

'You still there, Jimmy?'

'Yeah. Look, are we sure it's the same guy?'

'It's a carbon copy of Deandra Wallace,' said Barlow. 'No break-in. No struggle. The same cuts, the baby done the same. Bet you a bag of silver dollars they find the same drugs in her. Man came home and found his wife and baby like that? Jesus wept! Take down the address.'

Paz did. When he got back to Willa, they were flashing the lights and the lobby was draining of people.

'What?' she asked, seeing his face.

'That guy killed another pregnant woman. I got to go. You can watch the rest of this, if you want, or I can drive you home, but I'll probably be tied up all night. If you want to stay, I can give you cab fare . . .'

'No, I want to come with you.'

Paz looked up at the ceiling, registering extreme disbelief. 'Come on, babes, it's police business. I can't take a *date* to a murder scene.'

'I won't be at a murder scene. I'll stay on the good side of the yellow tape like the rest of the gawkers. Please, Jimmy – it's our last night and I'll never see you again until I'm a famous writer and I come to the Miami Book Fair and you come up to the table to get an autograph . . .'

Paz sighed dramatically. 'It'll be hours and hours. What in hell will you *do*?'

'I'll absorb atmosphere. I'll have conversations. I'm a writer. *Puh-leeeeze* . . . ?'

So they drove down together, Paz having made her swear on the ghost of William Butler Yeats that she would keep out of trouble. In a little while they were at the crime scene, a more impressive showing than the one that had attended the death of Deandra Wallace. There were more than a dozen official cars in the cul-de-sac, radio cars and the big Ford sedans used by the brass, besides an ambulance, a crime-scene-unit van, a generator truck supplying power to the floodlights that illuminated what was clearly the victim's home. This was a large, two-story, Spanish-style affair, with a tile roof and two wings, one of which enclosed a four-car garage, all set amid lavish plantings and irrigated lawns backing on Biscayne Bay. It looked like a stage set under the lights.

Paz parked a good distance away, reminded Willa to stay put, and walked toward the house, shoving his badge wallet onto his breast pocket to display the shield. There were little knots of neighbors at the head of the cul-de-sac, as well as three TV vans setting up to broadcast live, all under the supervision of a couple of uniforms. The neighbors looked stunned and worried. Good, thought Paz, unkindly, as he went by. He stopped by the crime-scene truck and picked up a steno pad, a set of plastic booties, and a pair of rubber gloves.

The suits were out in numbers in front of the house, among whom Paz spotted his homicide shift lieutenant, Romeo Posada, and the homicide unit commander, Captain Arnie Mendés. He did not care for either of them, but Mendés at least had a set of brains. He nodded to both of them as he stepped into the house and took in the scene. An oval entrance hall, high-ceilinged with a gilt chandelier hanging on chains, a tile floor, white, gold-flecked, underfoot, straight ahead a formal stairway, doors to the left and right. A crime-scene tech was dusting the French windows in the huge living room to the right. Paz asked him where the scene was. The guy pointed upward. 'The master bedroom, hang a left at the head of the stairs. You want to bring a vomit bag, Jimmy. Fucker did a number on the poor bitch. You figure it's the same guy from Overtown?'

'We'll have to see,' said Paz, and headed up the stair-case. The master bedroom was the size of a helipad, and done in shades of yellow – drapes, shag rug, the trim on the king-size four-poster. A cheerful color, which made the prevailing color of the bed and its occupant a particularly obscene contrast. Barlow was staring at the dead woman, motionless, his head down. A couple of CSU cops wandered around taking strobe photos and vacuuming every surface.

Paz stood next to his partner and studied the woman's face. The eyes were slightly open, but other-wise she looked like she was sleeping. Early twenties, Paz estimated, tanned body, thick blond hair in a shag cut, a little plump in the cheeks, but nice even features.

'Where's the baby?' Paz asked after several heavy swallows that tasted unpleasantly of semidigested grilled pompano with mango confit.

'Bathroom,' said Barlow.

Paz took a look in the adjoining bathroom, which was huge also, and brightly lit, yellow like the bedroom, and equipped with a shower stall, a Jacuzzi bath, two sinks, and a vanity table of the type used by movie stars, with the lightbulbs all around the mirror. The little gray corpse was lying half on this table and half in the sink, with its severed umbilicus hanging down like an appliance cord. There was a CSU man in the shower stall, clanking tools.

Paz pulled his eyes away from the never-born baby. 'Anything good?'

'I'll know when I get the trap up,' the CSU guy said. 'He used the shower after, we know that. There's blood marks behind the grab bar. Maybe we'll get some hairs.' More clanking, a muffled curse. 'We found one thing, near the baby. I gave it to Cletis already.'

'What?'

'Probably nothing. Looks like a sliver of black plastic or glass. Doesn't match anything I could see in the room.'

Paz went back to the bedroom. Barlow had not moved.

'So what do you think, Cletis?'

'Yea, they sacrificed their sons and their daughters unto devils.'

'Besides that, Cletis. Do we have anything?'

'Well, she's fresher than Deandra. Look, the blood's just about done setting up. He couldn't have finished more than half an hour before Vargas got home. He says he was at a Marlins game with some clients, which I guess we'll check out just to dot the i's. This here's his wife, Teresa, age twenty-four. There's a housekeeper, too, who you need to talk to. Her English ain't that hot. Amelia Ferrer, we're keeping her in her room downstairs. You also need to talk to the people in the other two houses on this strip, maybe they saw or heard something.'

'Obviously Amelia didn't or she would've called the cops.'

'You'll find out. Let me handle the scene and you go talk the language to these people.'

'What about this piece of glass CSU found?'

Barlow took an evidence bag from his pocket and held it up to the light. In it was a fragment a little larger than a fingernail clipping, and with nearly the same crescent shape.

'That's not as good as a rare nut, is it?'

Barlow said nothing and put the bag back in his pocket. Paz said, 'Well, I got to admit you called it right. We're deep in it now. The bosses are all over this already. Did Posada or Mendés have anything to say?'

'Oh, yeah. The department called the Feebs already. Guy's flying down from Quantico, the expert on serial killers. It's butt-covering time. Meeting Monday morning in the chief's office.'

'Mendés's?'

'No, *the* chief. Of police. Horton. This is going to be high-level right down the line. The big boys'll be looking over our shoulders from inside of our suit jackets from now on. You better go talk to them people now.'

Barlow returned to his silent contemplation of the eviscerated Teresa, or maybe he was praying for guidance. Paz went out of the death-stinking room, down the stairs to the maid's room near the kitchen, and found the housekeeper, a stocky, thirtyish woman a shade or two darker than Paz, wearing a tan uniform and apron. A policewoman was keeping an eye on her. Amelia Ferrer had been crying and dabbed at her reddened eyes with a wad of paper towel while he conducted the interview. She had last seen her employer alive at just before eight that evening. Mrs Vargas had been watching television in her bedroom and Mrs Ferrer had gone up as she usually did to see if anything was wanted before she herself settled down to watch her favorite program (*Wheel of Fortune*) in her own room. She had not left her room until she heard Mr Vargas's horrified shriek at shortly after ten, while *E.R.* was playing. Yes, her door had been slightly ajar, as always. Yes, she had heard Mr Vargas enter the house. No, she had not heard anyone else come in, but she recalled dozing off for a few minutes. No, the elaborate alarm system had not been turned on; they did not turn it on, usually, until the family was ready for bed.

Mr Vargas was in his living room, with a stiff drink. He wanted someone to blame, and it was Paz. After some shouting and raving, which Paz did not allow to affect him, he took Vargas through his day, in English. He'd worked the morning (he was in real estate, office in Coral Gables) and then gone out for a spin in the boat (a big Bayliner, docked behind the house). Then he'd had supper with his wife (here he broke down briefly) and picked up a trio of heavy investors at the Biltmore in the Gables and driven them up to Joe Robbie Stadium for the game, using his firm's skybox. He wouldn't have gone off with his wife just about to have a baby had it not been a major deal. He had called her on his cell phone during the seventh-inning stretch, about eight-fifty. She had been fine. The game was over at nine-twenty, he had dropped his clients at their hotel, making excuses when they invited him for drinks. He had hurried home, arriving just past ten, and found . . . Another breakdown.

Now there was a bustle outside the living room, voices raised. It was the family, the famous Cuban

family – Vargas's father, mother, two sisters, their
husbands, the victim's father. By the book, Paz should
have isolated all these people and interviewed them
separately, but it was so hideously clear that this thing
wasn't a domestic that he let them come in for a shriek-
ing-and-comfort-fest with Alex Vargas. He did not, however, avoid a dirty look from the victim's father, and an
angry spurt of Spanish to his son-in-law – 'That's the
detective? What, we don't pay enough taxes, they stick
you with a nigger?'

Paz went out through the rear of the house, through
the French doors that led to a broad terrace, which
included a long lit-up pool and a little palm-thatched
bar. He stood and breathed salt-scented air until his gut
stopped roiling. He didn't really blame the *gusanos*, who
were hopeless; he blamed himself for still, *still*, after all
these years, letting it get to him.

He walked off the terrace out onto the dock, and
determined that no one was lurking in the Bayliner, nor
had the murderer left any obvious clues on it. Beyond
the boat there was nothing but the dark bay and beyond
that the lights of Key Biscayne. There were cops all
around the place kneeling, squatting, looking for evidence. Paz did not think they would find much.

He checked out the other two houses on the cul-de-
sac. One was closed up for the summer. The other was
occupied by a frightened family who had seen and
heard nothing. No cars, no boats. They would have
heard. They asked Paz what had happened, and Paz told
them they were investigating a homicide. Paz agreed
with them that it was awful for something like this to
happen in a neighborhood as nice as this one.

As Paz arrived back at the Vargas house, he was

buttonholed by Arnie Mendés. The homicide chief was
a burly man, of the size and shape characteristic of football tackles, with a broad, humorous, fleshy face
decorated by a brush mustache and sideburns. Mendés
was not a Cuban at all, but a third-generation Spaniard,
who barely spoke the language. His people had come
over from Segovia in 1894 to roll cigars. His name, however, had clinched him the job.

'Solve it yet, Jimmy?'

'Yes, sir. We're pretty sure it was a mentally retarded
itinerant Negro person. I'm just about to drive along
under the expressway and pick him up out of his
refrigerator carton. I'm sure he'll confess.'

'It may come to that,' said Mendés, laughing. 'Do
you have any idea who these people are?' He gestured
broadly to the house and grounds.

'Rich Cubans?'

'You could say that. The husband's daddy is Ignacio
Vargas. Owns the Southeast Company. You've seen their
ads?'

'Developers.'

'Gigantic fucking developers, hence dear friends of
every politician in the state. The dead girl's father is
Hector Guzman, the founder and president of Hemi-
sphere Bank, which is that great big black glass thing on
Brickell. What they call a dynastic marriage, and the
little heir to it all is lying in that fucking yellow bathroom with his head sliced open. As of this moment, the
total detective resources of the Miami PD are on this
case and will remain on it until it goes down, or we give
up hope of putting it down, in which case all of us will
be looking for employment. So what do you have for
me?'

'Boss, we just got here. We haven't got an autopsy yet, we haven't looked at the crime-scene stuff . . .'

'I mean is it what it looks like?'

Paz paused. Of course the man would've already spoken with Cletis. So Paz said, 'What it *looks* like, subject to revision, is a ritual murder similar in all obvious respects to the murder of Deandra Wallace and her unborn baby. That means a ritual serial killer, and this guy is very smart, very sneaky, and he seems to move around without anyone seeing him.'

'A black, I understand. I mean seriously.'

'There are some indications, Chief.'

'Perfect. The icing on the cake. Cletis tell you we're bringing the Bureau in?'

'Yes, sir.' In a perfectly flat tone.

'Yeah, you're as enthusiastic as I am, but the boss and the mayor want them in on it. As far as I'm concerned, they can advise, but you and Cletis are the point guys on this business. I want you to understand you have my total support. You can absolutely count on me.'

'I appreciate that, sir.'

'Right. Up to the point where you fuck up or it becomes politically inconvenient to support you, in which case you're both shit-canned.'

Paz couldn't help smiling. 'Please, sir, I don't need a pep talk. Give it to me straight.'

Mendés smiled, too, but Paz knew he was serious. A bright man, and honest according to his lights, but ambitious as Lucifer. He leaned forward a little, placing his head a little closer to Paz's face. 'Okay, you said *ritual* killings. Did you mean something like a psychotic ritual or a ritual from some actual cult?'

'Unclear, at the moment. There's some kind of

African connection, with African fortune-telling, in the Wallace case. And I've got people checking to see whether the situation, the pregnant woman, the cuts, the parts taken from the corpses, the drugs involved, are connected to anything in the anthropological record. I was just going to get with the family and ask them if the vic had any interest in that stuff.'

'Yeah, well, why don't you let Cletis handle that end of things,' said the homicide chief.

'Any particular reason for that?' asked Paz, an edge in his voice. 'My interview technique not quite polished enough?'

'Oh, fuck it, man!' the chief snapped. 'The whole fucking department knows you have a beef with upper-class Cubanos. You just let the preacher talk with the family, and you find something else useful to do. Supervise the goddamn canvass. This guy must've got here somehow, and every one of these fucking piles has a guard dog and a proximity alarm. People must have heard something. Oh, and Jimmy? You're both off all other unrelated cases, off the chart entirely. And you'll both report directly to me on this one, from now on, until further notice.'

'What about Lieutenant Posada?'

'You let me worry about Posada. We'll need a high-level liaison with the Bureau, and that ought to be right up Romeo's alley.'

'Yes, sir,' said Paz, and walked off to find the patrol sergeant in charge of the local canvass.

So the hours passed. Paz kept busy, interviewing cops, interviewing neighbors who had told the cops he interviewed that they might have seen something, talking to the crime-scene guys, in hopes of picking up something obvious, some lead besides a tiny piece of fractured black glass. The results were thin. Two people walking dogs on Cocoplum Boulevard had seen a man go by on a bike at about the right time, but the guy was white, with blond hair. Nobody closer to the murder scene had seen this person. The crime-scene techs had picked up some grains of soil off the rug near the French windows leading to the terrace and there was an indentation from a bike tire in the dirt under one of the big palms that lined the driveway. Hooray, a clue. The CSU people took a plaster impression.

At about midnight, Paz decided to pass on some of the misery and called Manny Echiverra at home, told him what had happened, and suggested that it would be a smart career move for him to get down to the morgue and autopsy Mrs Vargas, forgetting about normal procedure and schedules or any other bureaucrap, because he was the pathologist who had done the work on Deandra and did he want someone to maybe miss a significant similarity? And blame it on him?

He had just folded away the cell phone when a familiar voice said, 'I hope you're not avoiding me.' He turned to see Doris Taylor standing there in her famous grass-green pantsuit.

'Can't talk to you now,' he said, covertly looking around to see if anyone was observing them together. 'Also, you need to get behind the barrier with the other press.'

'Oh, I'm moving along, like the cops are always telling us to do. I just wanted to let you know there's a young woman sitting in your car. A real interesting young woman. I didn't realize you had such good taste. Me and Willa, why, we just talked and talked. In fact, I might even do a piece on the after-hours life of Miami's hardworking dicks, how they bring their girlfriends to crime scenes so as not to lose a minute . . .'

Paz grabbed the woman's arm and backed into the dense shadow of a ficus tree. 'What do you want, Doris?'

'Everything. This is the biggest murder in a decade. I hear it's bloody. Is it the same guy?'

'Looks like it.'

'Any clues about who it is?'

'Not as yet. It's early days.'

'It's a black man, though. The same as with Wallace?'

'We don't know that. We have no ID, no witnesses . . .'

'Oh, please! White boys don't kill black girls in Overtown in the middle of the night and then just stroll away. It's the same guy here, so he's black. What did the murder scene look like?'

He told her, and answered all her avid questions, omitting and changing some small details, as always. He left her full of sucked blood, a happy woman.

They buttoned the place up at about one, the crime-scene lights packed away, the cop cars gone, and the press vans, the corpse now down at the morgue, the rest of the extended family still in the house, unbuttoned and wailing loudly enough for the noise to reach Paz where he stood with his partner on the street.

'He come on a bike, huh?' Cletis ventured.

'He could've,' said Paz. 'He sure didn't come by car. If he came by bike, then according to our witnesses he turned himself white, which should be right up this guy's alley. Or maybe he walked on water. And someone let him in there, like before. Any luck with the family?'

'Some. The sister-in-laws say the victim was talking to someone about a lucky charm thing for her baby, but they didn't know much more than that. I got a bunch of stuff I took out of the victim's room, address books, handbags. I'll study it some and see if there's any good for us there.' He pulled a plastic bag out of his pocket. 'Whyn't y'all take this glass splinter, seeing as how you're in with the boys at the U. See what it is, what it come off of.'

Paz put it away. They spoke briefly about arrangements for the morrow. Barlow was heading for the morgue, where he would observe the autopsy and generate zeal among the toxicologists. Paz walked back to his car, where he found Willa dozing. He got in and drove off. She awoke, stretched.

'Well, was it as exciting as you dreamed?' he asked sourly.

'Yes,' she replied, 'it was like watching an anthill poked with a stick. And I had a real interesting conversation with Doris Taylor. She told me all about your exploits.'

'I bet she did. But because she spotted my car and you, and you spilled your guts, instead of, for example, saying you were a witness, she now has me by the balls. She'll pump me dry on this goddamn case.'

Willa looked genuinely remorseful. 'Gosh, Jimmy, I'm sorry. She seemed so friendly, and like she really liked you.' She paused and slid closer. 'Would it make it up a little if *I* got you by the balls and pumped you dry?'

'To an extent,' said Paz.

An hour later, upon her hard futon, this had been

accomplished, and they were back at it again, she on top, he solidly engulfed, she not moving very much, her little breasts occasionally brushing his face, and chatting away as she generally did during the second act. This feature of Willa Shaftel's sex life was not actually one he would have ordered off a menu, but he had grown used to it. Every so often, she would pause and utter a pleasant small cry, and shudder, her face and chest would flush, her eyes would roll back in her head, and there would be a delightful spasm in the moist flesh that gripped him, and then she would take up where she left off.

'Gosh, that was a lovely one,' she said huskily after one of these caesuras, 'and I can hardly bear it that this is our penultimate fuck.'

'Penultimate?'

'Unless you're not staying over. I was planning on a lazy one tomorrow morn, plus the usual shower encounter.'

'I have a gigantic day tomorrow. A serial killer who whacked someone important is about the worst thing that can happen to a police force, and I'm in the bull's-eye. Sorry.'

'The ultimate, then. This will have to last you all the lonely nights, or all the lonely twenty minutes before you find someone superior to me in every way, with even more gigantic tits, if your imagination can encompass that. Unless you contrive to visit Iowa City. Do you think you ever might?'

'Every weekend.'

A chortle. 'Yeah, we could meet in the airport Marriott. Ah, Jimmy, you know even though I've realized these many months that you were fucking everything above room temperature, I guess in my little girl's heart I still wished that you'd say, "Willa, love of my life, you're the best pony in the stable, so stay, stay, stay and be my tender bride, and spawn delightful Judeo-Afro-Cubano babies, each with your blazing intelligence and my preternatural beauty." Like in the movies.'

Paz said, 'Would you, if I did?'

She stopped her slow grinding and looked him in the face. 'Oh, wait a minute, I have to consider this. Here's a good-looking man, a body from heaven, luscious skin, smart, good steady job, sensitive but not a wuss, a penis of adequate size and function . . .'

'Adequate?'

'A great kisser, at both ends, too, a lover who, while slowing down a bit with approaching middle age, can still fuck one's brains out, a great dresser, polite, decent, generous to a point, not anything of a pig. A catch, you would say, and so I ask myself, why is there hanging over his head a forty-foot state highway sign with yellow flashers that reads 'Heartbreak Ahead! Do Not Get Serious!'? Why is that, Jimmy? No quick answers? I'll leave you to consider it while I work up another one, and I believe I'll ask you to join me here.'

And that was Willa gone, he thought, as he strode with shaky steps to his car. After they finished she had been almost businesslike, not willing to chat at length, not cold exactly, but anxious to close out a chapter. She'd kissed him quickly after he was dressed and very nearly hustled him out the door. He thought about her forty-foot highway sign. His sign. Yes, he knew about that. It was part of what he considered his honesty, almost his honor. He knew that guys lied to get laid, cops joked about it in cop bars after work, but Paz had a horror of false pretenses.

As he got in his car he experienced a pang of remorse so powerful that his breath choked for an instant. He thought for a moment of going back. This was it, something he needed, a grenade to blast him out of that pleasant long, slow slide. But Paz had a good imagination and brought it into play to rescue him, as it had so many times before, from living real life in the moment. Okay, sure, Willa was cute, smart, a terrific piece of ass, but she was a little plump, even at twenty-six, and in a decade or so she might look like a fireplug. And she had a mouth on her, too, that might get boring after a few years. He thought of Willa getting together with his mother. His mother would hate anyone he got close to, that was a given, and he considered this as a revenge fantasy for a moment. It would be amusing, at least. But maybe Willa would *love* his mother. Willa claimed to be able to talk to anyone. She might get in good with Margarita and then he'd have the two of them running his life. And it would pinch the money, too, he'd have to get his own place and support her, poets didn't bring in the cash, that was for sure, and they'd fight about money, and then the sex would fade, and who the hell needed it? So the *ogga* slyly chatted, and soothed, and stifled all real feelings, and Jimmy Paz drove off into the night, himself again.

NINETEEN

I work like an animal all Sunday, or as my husband was fond of saying when I used to ask him how the writing went that day, *like a nigger*. It was okay for him to use this vile expression, he explained to me at length, and many times, because for his race the N-word was communal, warm, palsy. I never believed this, and I always felt a slight repugnance on the many occasions when he used it. Jews don't warmly call one another kikes, I believe.

He and his ways are ever in my thoughts now, since this last murder. Two down, he has two to go for the *okunikua*. In Olo, an *ikua* is a song, a bird song, or a lullaby, and the same word is used, as in our language, for a sorcerous work, an enchantment. *Okun* means four. *Owo*, *aga*, *iko*, *okun*, *olai* . . . as I was taught to count by poor Tourma in Uluné's compound. But in the low tone *ikua* means a gift. Or a sacrifice. *Okunikua* is thus the four song or the fourfold sacrifice.

Four is an important number in Olo affairs, and he must murder four women within sixteen days to complete the ritual. What he will be able to do when he has finished is something no one knows, not even Uluné. No Olo has done *okunikua* since some time before the turn of the last century. I recall the first time I actually read about it, in Tour de Montaille's work, in Lagos. He regarded it as a relic of the bad old days before French civilization arrived. The Olo witch who did it, whose name the Olo never mention, was annoyed by French civilization, and wished to make it go away, which in time, of course, it did. Uluné and his fellow tribal patriarchs considered that the two World Wars, the Great Depression, and the consequent reduction of the proud colonial powers to quaint little postcard nations were a direct result of this guy's *okunikua*. They approved the result but, as moral people, thought the means excessive. Western historiography does not agree, since it is much more logical and scientific to assume that millions of fairly rational, marvelously educated, prosperous people went crazy and ripped the heart out of their own civilization.

I must suppose that he is waiting to complete the four sacrifices before paying me a visit. But one can only be frightened so much, and I am at this point nearly beyond fear. Numb. I take some tiny comfort in the realization that it can't be much longer now. Meanwhile, I find that the kind of hard, precise, physical work I am doing keeps actual paralysis away during whatever meantime remains. I prime the walls and ceiling of Luz's room, and while this is drying, I install the patent ladder. It is spring-loaded and has its own trapdoor. A cord with a red knob hangs down and when you pull it the trapdoor falls and the ladder slides smoothly down into place with a pleasant *sproing*. A slight lift of the lowest step, and it sucks itself out of sight. I work it several times when I am done, for the pleasure of seeing something elegant, simple, and functional, much like the sort of gear one sees in boats. Then I install the exhaust fan in its hole, switch it on, and apply the top coat of semigloss to the walls (dove) and ceiling (eggshell). More downtime for drying, during which I drive over to the unpainted-furniture store on Twenty-seventh Avenue and buy, with some of my transmission money, a little bed frame, a four-drawer chest, a night table, a toy chest, and a wooden lamp base jigsawed to represent a crescent moon on a ball. A Cuban discounter sells me a mattress, and I drive away with it stacked on top, like the Joads, and don't I wish I were driving to California too. Back at the garage, I assemble these and paint them with quick-drying enamel.

I am just finishing gluing down the last of the gray carpet squares when Luz tromps into the kitchen. She has experienced wonders – the Monkey Jungle, *The Little Mermaid* and *Pocahontas* on video, Burger King with the playground adjoining, a sleepover with five other girls, junk food without stint. Thank you, Mrs Pettigrew. I say I have a surprise for her, and show her the red knob hanging down and ask her to pull it. She does. The expression on her face as the ladder slides down is worth the fifteen gallons of sweat. Magic. She ascends, I follow.

'It's very stinky in here.'

'That's the glue. It'll go away soon. Do you like it?'

'Uh-huh. Do I have to sleep here all by myself?'

'If you want. I have some furniture, too. Do you want to see it?'

She does, and we go down to the garage to check it out.

'Amanda has flowers on her dresser,' she says.

'I have some flowers, too, and when the paint is dry, you can put them on just where you want them.' I show her the decals I've bought and she wants to put them on right now and we have a little spat about that. She's cranky then, and hyper because of all the stimulation and the strange foods, and I'm cross with her, at which point she crumples utterly and I feel like a monster. I'm afraid I am going to spoil her, and when I think this, I laugh inwardly, since it is at present unlikely that either of us will live long enough for spoiling to occur. Spoil away, then, Jane!

After she's been calmed and cosseted extravagantly, I show her Peeper in its new cage, and we play with it, and plan the furnishings of the chicken house. Then Jasper comes by and asks if I want to have pizza with his family and our across-the-street neighbor, Dawn Slotsky, and her four-year-old, Eleanor. Luz answers for both of us, such a schmoozer she has become, and I tie a head scarf over my filthy hair, and wash my face and hands, and over we go.

We are eating on the concrete terrace behind the big house. Dawn is already there, with her child, a chubby, grubby, cherubic red-blonde in a pink dress. She and Luz immediately march off to follow Jasper, who is running around the backyard with a jar, accompanied by Jake the dog, searching for a kind of beetle that has two bright luminous spots on its back. We adults go up and look at the new room, and I shyly accept their applause. We all go sit in tatty plastic loungers with our beers (except Dawn) and I ask Dawn how she is feeling, a suitable question, I think, for someone as grossly pregnant as she is. Dawn is a second-generation Grove hippie, and no one has ever seen her in anything but cutoffs and a spaghetti-strapped top, even now, although she has elastics and aprons to conceal her great belly. Until I got

Luz, we had not exchanged a word, although she always had a friendly smile. With a child, I have become a significant person on the street.

She says she can't wait for it to be over, and she'll never, ever get pregnant again, two is enough, and Polly agrees, and they look at me and I modestly turn my eyes down, and I can see them thinking, Oh, looking like that she's lucky to have the one. I don't mind this too much. Then Shari Ribera comes out with a bunch of plates and cups and utensils, and stays to chat. The subject of the Mad Abortionist comes up, which is what the papers have tastefully chosen to call my husband, and we all shudder, especially, of course, Dawn, whose significant other is a roadie, often away from home, as now. She has window bars and a large and barky mutt dog. I ache to tell her that these will do no good at all, but what, after all, could I say?

We talk about guns, then, not very knowledgeably, although I myself know a good deal about guns of all kinds, but I don't contribute. Dawn asserts she could never kill anyone, and Polly scoffs and says she would have no trouble dispatching that guy, and she has a short list of some others, and then, catching her daughter's eye, says, 'Not your father, sugar. I would shoot him in the leg, though,' and we all laugh. Mr Ribera is of Dominican extraction, and both his children have the unearthly beauty that sometimes occurs when the best qualities of the contributory races combine to form a perfect genetic soufflé. At fourteen Shari is being hit on by everyone in pants, and is especially subjected to the sort of courtship favored by young colored gangsters in passing cars. Jasper is in middle school, and is learning, as my husband famously did, not only of the regular cracker bigotry, which the white Cubans happily share, but also of the ferocious and socially invisible racism practiced by those of darker hue than him. Jasper does well in school, which makes it worse. Or, did well. Polly is now talking about his attitude changing, hoping he will not be a problem teen. Oh, he will, Polly. *There's not a moment's mercy from the brain poison leaching from my skin, no, not in my whole nation*, as my husband once put it in a poem.

So we talk, and the pizza is delivered, and I have half a Stroh's and a slice, and hope I will keep it down. After a really lovely evening, very like actual life, with Luz bathed and put down in her old bed, I drag out my box. I have to look things up. Uluné taught me some countermagic in Danolo, all part of the basic course, and I secretly wrote the procedures down. I have a lot of the botanicals in there, too, although I haven't let myself think about them in a while. Perhaps I was afraid of provoking the spirits, not that I believe in spirits, or perhaps it was that nothing of note happened to me until quite recently, when I found Luz. I put it to one side, and also put aside my divining bag, and the sad if handy manila portfolio that contains Dolores's life. Next below there is a waxed cardboard box, fuzzy with wear. It's filled to the brim with corked bottles, cans sealed with gaffer's tape, and dozens of small envelopes, similarly sealed, all neatly labeled in black ink in a familiar hand, my own.

It's all chemicals, of course, as dull as that. No eldritch horrors from beyond time, no special demonic gifts, just chemistry, but not chemistry 101, and not Du Pont or Upjohn chemistry. What would you rather play with given the choice and a hundred thousand years?

Would you rather dick around with stone tools, clay pots, baskets, and skins, or master the most sophisticated neuropharmacological synthesizer in the world? It's all *homo ludens*. Man at play. Or so Marcel used to say, that old materialist. I walk my own sophisticated neuropharmacological synthesizer over to the sink and get it a drink of water. I wasn't keeping a personal journal when I was with Marcel, which I rather regret. I have to reconstruct his arguments from my battered memory. You, my angel, he used to say, are a series of transient electrochemical states – perceptions, feelings, memories: very fast, very subtle, chemical states, and the amounts of chemicals required to modify these states are typically tiny, and they work in combinations of which we have no idea. Modern psychopharmacology, these tranquilizers, this Prozac the Americans are so fond of – this is the savage hitting the fine Swiss watch with a flint hammer to make it work again. In contrast, we have the sorcerer. He has tens of thousands of chemical species available to him in plant tissue, not to mention commensal bacteria and fungi and viruses that can live in and modify the human body, not to mention mutagens that can actually change the DNA in the human brain, and he has for his laboratory bench, himself, or his victims or allies, and he has time, all the time in the world.

But, says the angel, okay, they can drug themselves, have trances, visions galore, and they can drug their subjects, or victims, with or without their knowledge, but what about all the weird stuff, affecting people at a distance, influencing dreams, cursing, being invisible . . .

No, no, you haven't understood, my sparrow. Their

bodies are *changed*. They can make psychotropic chemicals to order, even chemicals affecting a single person. They make them in their own bodies, and expel them through the breath or the pores. The melanocytes all over the skin surface are deeply connected to the limbic system and the pineal body and they can produce exohormones, which, entering the bloodstream of the target through any number of routes, proceed to the brain, where they have the most profound mental and emotional effects. Interesting, *hein*? The same bodies that control skin pigmentation? An irony, no? Yet here is the essence of what we call sorcery. The sparrow has questions. How come science hasn't detected these exohormones? Well, science has; am I not a scientist? But what you mean, my artichoke, is 'detected chemically.' And the answer is that science is not looking. Science looks largely for what it expects to find, and it does not expect to find any real effects in the claims of sorcerers. Also, science is good at searching for what can be controlled in a laboratory setting, and what can be repeated, so that a certain cause always associates with the same effect. But this is not the case with sorcery, which is an art.

All this was before I met the Chenka, so my questions were like those of a person from a culture that had no music: how can mere ordered sounds affect the emotions? Preposterous! How could a great musician talk to such a person? Looking back now, I see how incredibly patient Marcel was with me, and I blush to recall it, blushing being a good example of psychophysiological effects. And others: did you ever, while sitting in a public place, get the feeling that someone was staring at you, and you looked up and sure enough there was?

One of Marcel's favorites. What do you think that is, mental rays? Beams from the eye? And love. We say, 'it's chemistry,' but it really *is* chemistry. How little we know, how much to discover, what chemical forces flow, from lover to lover. Yes, indeed.

Marcel's chemical theory 'explained,' if that is the word, much of the anecdotal material about shamanism and sorcery that anthropologists had gathered over the years. He thought that all these were the scattered remains of a very, very old technology. What do witches do, in stories? Two things: they make brews and they cast spells. Brews, of course, are obviously the traditional use of biologicals, and spells are, despite common belief, not silly callings to demons or spirits, but mnemonics. At least, originally. Chenka sorcerers, Marcel claimed, typically had fifty to seventy-five thousand recipes and procedures in memory. And, of course, there is the rub. If you multiply your body's powers through technology as our culture has done for the last four centuries you are much better off in a material sense than if you only amplify the subjective ones. This is why Sioux shamans no longer rule on the Great Plains, and why, throughout the world, preindustrial peoples are happy to trade fifty-thousand-year-old traditions for cigarettes, whiskey, steel knives, and plastic jugs.

Except for the Chenka, who were a special case. Why did their tradition survive intact? Marcel didn't know, but he used to grin and say, moving his hands as a conjurer, 'the mysteries of the normal curve!' When you get out three or four or five standard deviations from the mean you find some weird stuff. Genius. Golden ages. Giants and dwarves. Two-headed babies.

And the Chenka. It's a good nonexplanation. We thought the Chenka were unique, until I discovered the Olo.

Enough musing. I page through my notebooks until I find what I'm looking for, a *kadoul*, a ticket to the magic kingdom. I take *kwa*-leaf, a West African member of the *Boraginceae* rich in pyrrolizidine alkaloids, mash it with some powders, use a cereal bowl and the handle of a screwdriver as a mortar and pestle to grind the stuff that needs grinding, add a little of my own spit and piss and some water, and put it on the stove to boil down. I say the necessary words, in Olo. The spell, the witch's brew. It smells dank and rank as it boils. When it has cooked to sludge, I affix a dish towel to a bowl with a rubber band and strain it through, getting about a quarter of a cup of a strong-smelling greenish-brown liquid. I add to this some brown powder, some red powder, some of my blood. The liquid turns a sludgy black and seems to shrink in volume, which is what it's supposed to do. My artillery. I pour it into an old jam jar. It will keep indefinitely. A good thing, too, because I realize I am not up to changing my interior chemistry just yet, for there are two problems. First, after the drug, and during the time I am under its influence, I will not be fit for anything else but sorcery: not working for Mrs Waley, not driving a car in accordance with the highway code, not caring for Luz. A sorcerer needs a support team when he or she travels in the *m'doli*, like an astronaut does on a space mission, and I have none as yet. It was not something I contemplated Dolores ever needing. The second reason is that once I take the stuff, I will be out in *m'doli*, and my husband will no longer be in any doubt as to my continued earthly existence. A dilemma. I tell myself I am awaiting allies and I go up on a chair and push the jar to the back of the top shelf in my food cupboard. And a third reason: I am scared shitless.

While I am considering protective measures, I decide I may as well take care of the *m'fa*, too. In the very bottom of my box is a triangular package wrapped in rubberized fabric and gaffer tape. It is my Red Nine. I unwrap it and pick it up. A handful. It weighs, if I recall, two and three-quarter pounds unloaded, and this one has ten rounds in it. My dad kept it on the *Kite*, and I stole it back when I stole the *Kite*. I put it on the high shelf next to the *kadoul*. Maybe I can shoot him if he comes in his body. Could I shoot him? I never killed anyone but me on purpose. In any case, I know it will shoot me, so it will serve in the last extremity, if I find myself literally falling under his spell. Odd, how those common dead metaphors spring horribly to life. Entranced. Enchanted. Bewitched.

Now everything goes back into the box, except the journal, which I continue to read. I wish to reacquaint myself with Jane. The period of Jane's life between Chenka and Olo was an album of self-delusion, with good examples of all the major types – professional, social, romantic . . . no, I am being too hard on her. She was a tough girl. It's not easy losing your first big romantic thing and your sense of the underlying reality of the cosmos at one and the same time.

This gets me thinking again about Dad (for I have gone to see that boat, *Guitar*, several times, down at Dinner Key). I wonder, is that kind of person still around, will we ever have people like that again? He always said it was his generation, that peculiar lost one that was born during the Second World War. He used to tote up the things that his generation was last at. Last to experience segregation of the races, last to come to sexual maturity before women's lib and the Pill, last to believe that the United States was invariably the good guy, last to defer without much question to teachers and elders in general, last to get the full load of dead white male culture force-fed into their brains and souls, last to grow up before TV became the ruling power. If Catholic, last to get raised in the pre-Vatican II shut-up-and-do-what-we-say, superstitious, devotional American church. The last to start screwing before *Roe v. Wade*, and hence and finally, the last to think it mandatory to marry the girl you got pregnant. Thus me.

I was like him, or tried to be, perhaps to be less like my mother, who was thoroughly modern, although only five years younger than he. As she often told me, she went to him to get money for an abortion and he said, before she could ask, let's get married, and she did. She imagined a life rather like that of the Kennedys, and tried to have one to the extent that she could. Dad stayed home with us kids while she did so. I will give her this, that she made it home for the major holidays, and here they all are, dutifully recorded in short entries about home visits. A dull story, even to the author, who seems to be the sort who will end up wearing a plain brown dress and a bun, with a ring of keys at her waist, standing in the doorway of the big house saying, 'I am afraid my father cannot be disturbed.'

Until Witt. That was a surprise, and registered as one in the journal. I am addicted to genius, so Jane wrote back then. If true, I believe I am in recovery now. We did not end up in bed on the night we met, I am happy to say; Witt had that much care for his old pal Lou, but he called me the next day and invited me to that rehearsal and I was a goner. It seems that I actually believed at the time that someone who could ring the changes on race hysteria and hypocrisy the way he could would be fairly immune to racial insanity. Such immunity is not impossible, I must believe. Needless to say, in both Chicago and New York we were acquainted with any number of interracial couples. They were not even unusual in the arty circles we hung out in. Maybe they were writhing secretly, but I saw no evidence of this. Some people, I believe, are just happy to be alive and successful. I thought we would be like them. As I read this, I see I had not a clue. And maybe he didn't, either. This is what I like to think, even now, that it was Africa that changed him, the witch stuff. He would not be the first decent man to succumb to the temptations of power. And there is a part of me, of course, that says it was all my fault. *What did I do?*

Money was fine. We had, both of us, more than enough, and, as everyone knows, rich people are happy. He was never interested in mine, or where it came from, and only seemed to notice it when I was being stingy, when he would poke fun. He was generous with his own, although his refinement of taste kept him from being too hideously nouveau. The excesses I noticed I blamed on his status as an artist. Everyone knew artists were nuts. We had a coterie of hangers-on, but not an embarrassingly large one. He was decent to the people who started out with him in Chicago, too, which I thought was a good sign.

Sex was fine. We were hot for each other from the

start and stayed hot. I think he was a little surprised at me, since I look like a gawky, boyish, convent-school product, and I guess he was looking forward to stripping off my Catholic *pudence*. This had, of course, been quite stripped off already by a lover of encyclopedic technical scope and virtuosity. Was he as 'good' as Marcel? What's good? The Jane Clare Doe Gold Medal for Most Spine-Cracking Orgasms in a Standard Time Period remains in Marcel's possession, but while I was kid-crazy about Marcel, I was in love with Witt, and that made a difference. I thought it was for life, if you want to know, and so I laid everything I'd been taught by Marcel at Witt's feet, or penis, the love secrets of exotic civilizations and tribal peoples. So, all in all, one could ask for nothing better. I mean, what is there besides sex and money? Could I have predicted what happened? Are there signs in the journals that even now I can't see? He always tried to make me happy. He had a gift for it, for delight. Once on my birthday he hadn't said anything about it and I thought he'd forgotten and when we got back to the loft the whole place was full of flowers, I mean thousands and thousands of flowers. He once hired a whole choir to sing to me out in the street under the window of our loft. Once he picked me up at the museum and put me in a cab and I thought we were just going home but we drove to Kennedy, where we boarded the Concorde and flew to London. He liked making me happy.

Okay, that's only money, but he gave me his attention, too. When he wasn't working, which was a lot of the time, he had no other interests. Not like Marcel, who kind of squeezed me into his famous man's life. He listened, hours and hours of listening, like I was some kind of oracle. Not something I had much experience of, to say the least. A perfect husband, right?

Yes, there was that little detail of his parentage. There are entries here covering the great unveiling, our fight, the happy reunion. I come across as understanding itself. My wounded hero! What a sucker I am for the wounded hero, especially the genius wounded hero. Marcel hiding from the Nazis, Witt hiding from White America, my father hiding from my mother.

I visited his parents once, without telling him. Stan and Cynthia Moore, of Morristown, New Jersey. I called them and asked if I could come by, and they said I could, so one Sunday in late spring I drove out. There I found more or less what I expected: a suburban split-level on a mapled street, the newish VW van in the driveway, bearing an Amnesty decal on the rear window and a sticker on the bumper opposing some state referendum (VOTE NO ON 171!), a hoop attached to the garage. (Witt playing b-ball? A strange notion. He could barely ride a bike.) And the Moores themselves, decent, middle-aged, liberal people, givers to Greenpeace and the ACLU, Democratic voters, Unitarian churchgoers (she a lapsed Jew), sadly infertile, former peaceniks, marchers for civil rights, wracked, confused, failed by the gods of niceness and decency.

Their house was casually furnished with an ex-hippie-gone-straight miscellany, blocky Ikea and Door Store stuff, steel-framed posters and original art on the walls, Rya rugs, hand-thrown pottery, not very tidy. The living room, where they sat me on a brown corduroy sofa, was filled with books that looked read; on one wall a huge stereo loomed, flanked by a wall of LPs and CDs. I used my best anthro techniques on them, I fear, me who was trained in childhood not to ask impertinent questions. They were, fortunately, the sort of American couple who had been through so many group sessions of one kind or another that they had dumped any pretensions to privacy. They were desperate for intimate news of their son.

So I learned that back when the Moores found that one of Cindy's several abortions had screwed up her pipes, they decided to adopt, and decided also that they would not be one of the selfish racist bourgeois who demanded a white kid, but would specifically look for a child of one of the oppressed minorities. Then the great carnival wheel of fate revolved, Ifa cast his hook and line, and out popped the ten-week-old abandoned child of a woman who had staggered into Bellevue Hospital in New York, dropped a boy baby, and slipped out a day later, having left a phony address. They named him Malcolm (after you-know-who) DeWitt (after Mr Moore's recently deceased dad). He was a doll. This I have transcribed verbatim from Mrs Moore's lips. A doll, and from the first week, sharp as a tack, as Stan Moore noted. The Moores raised him according to the latest liberal nostrums – lots of mobiles, lots of attention, pickup on demand, no sugars, Mozart in the nursery, Montessori preschool. And they had tried to give him an interracial upbringing. The Moores had plenty of African-American friends, and friends who had adopted kids of other races. Their church was full of them – little Koreans, little Chinese, little Cherokees, little mulattoes of all shades – the Moores made it sound like the anteroom to Utopia. And it might have been. God bless all their liberal souls – they were all of them nice people.

I saw the album, smiling baby Witt (or Malcolm, as he was then called), grinning toddler Witt, gap-toothed Witt on a carnival ride, the family at Disneyland, a Halloween picture, the smile for elementary school graduation, and then the photos petered out, and became darker, no more smiling poses; instead, candid snaps of the morose or snarling adolescent.

They thought it was a phase. Kids are like that. They themselves were handfuls back in the sixties. They had met, in fact, in jail, after a demonstration in Madison, where they were both at school. The Movement; they both still pronounced it as if capitalized. So they didn't worry too much, although they were hurt. He didn't love them? Impossible. *They loved him!*

I probed the wound. He had gone to Chicago on a full scholarship. His grades and SATs were excellent. She still knew them all by heart. They thought he was going to be prelaw. They had no idea he was writing poetry. He didn't come home for Christmas the first year, nor for spring break, nor for the summer; he had a job. They said they'd fly out; they wanted to see him, meet his friends, see where he lived. No, he was very busy. Too busy for Mom and Dad?

They found out what he was busy at that summer, when the Chicago cops called. He'd been arrested in a crack house, charged with possession. They were there the next day.

I knew about this part. Witt had woven it into his life tale of coming up rough in the ghetto. He'd never been a user or a dealer, just hangin' with the homies, and the Man had jumped them. This was true. He *had* just been hangin' with the homies, to whom he'd lied just like he'd lied to everyone else. Naturally, the Moores were on his side, they knew all about the racist pigs, but it turned out he didn't want them on his side. There was a horrible scene in the lawyer's office, where they went after bailing him out of Cook County jail. He blamed them for his not having a real identity, for depriving him of his black soul, for using him as a convenient tool to assuage their stinking honky guilt. He wished he'd been raised by his junkie whore mother in the community, at least he'd be *something*. He might be a black junkie killer, but that was better than being a white nigger. And so forth. The charges were dismissed and they left. It was like leaving a morgue after they'd made you identify your kid on a slab, Cindy said. Why? Why? We did the best we could. I didn't know why either. I did the best I could, too.

He never came home again, never contacted them, refused calls, returned letters. He got a job in the library to support himself. For five years, nothing. And then *Race Music* opened and eventually came to New York. And, with not a little trepidation, they'd gone to see it on Broadway. And they'd seen the much-remarked-on scene in the second act, the scarifying, vicious lampoon of the white liberal couple who adopt a black baby. They'd left at the intermission. She'd cried for a week afterward.

I thought I could fix it up. I always think I can fix things up. I said good-bye to Stan and Cindy on an up note, therefore, saying I'd keep in touch, intending to lay it out for Witt when the time was right: Look this is crazy, you're not a kid anymore, they're your parents, they raised you, they're decent people, this is wrong.

But the right time did not immediately appear. He was working; he actually never stopped working, not

even in the summers, when we went out to Sionnet.
There was a little apartment over the boathouse there
that our dockman used to have when we had a dockman,
and we converted it into a studio for him. Oddly
enough, my family got on pretty well with him. My
father, of course, likes everyone and dwells in that zone
in which social status is so absolutely secure that one
can treat all beings with perfect, thoughtless equality. To
Dad, there is the Doe family and there is everyone else
– the Roosevelts, the Kennedys, the guy who comes by
in a pickup to collect the trash. And Witt can be charming, too, which helps.

My mother likes lovely people and the famous, and
she was both surprised and delighted that clunky old
Jane got a lovely, famous one, and his race simply added
a little panache to the mix, something else besides her
affairs with which to shock the girls at the club. Mary,
my sister, or Mariah, as she called herself then, immediately put a heavy make on him, which he deflected
amusingly, thus winning my heart even more than it was
already won – the only human male on the planet
besides my stepbrother who preferred me to her.
Mariah, although lovely as the dawn, is a couple of steps
slow in the flashing wit department. Witt would say
absolutely outrageous things to her in my presence that
would go right past her, that wouldn't even dent the
famous smile. You have to give her game, though. She
never stopped trying, even after she outdid her big
sister by announcing she was pregnant. Something I
was not, and not likely to be, given my husband's attitude. *She* got married in Saint Pat's.

My brother was there that time, too. And now I'm
reminded, reading along, that Josey never much cared

for Witt, nothing he ever said, but there was a stiffness there. I thought it was because my dad liked him, and so Josey had to not like him. Witt never said anything about it. Few entries for that summer, actually. I guess I was happy. Fortunate are those whose annals are brief. I remember him waving from his window when we took the boat out. He never came with us. He got seasick on a floating dock. I thought he was happy, too, a member of *our* family at least. He had a knack of fitting in, although if you believed his writing you would have thought here's a guy who would never fit in anywhere. Maybe that was his invisible part, adapting the local coloration. He pronounced *Sionnet* SIGH-nit, instead of sigh-ON-et, like the tourists, and Montauk with the accent on the second syllable, like an old Long Islander, and exhibited the proper contempt for the south shore.

Was the real Witt lurking beneath the surface then? Was the camouflage that of a leopard lying in wait? There's nothing here to suggest it in these pages, not the slightest suspicion. As it turned out, that was the last summer we were all together. After it ended, Witt and I went on our trip.

Suddenly I don't want to read anymore. I'd rather not read the Africa stuff just now. I put the thing into a cupboard and go out on the landing. The sky is low and wet and there is lightning to the west over the Glades. I am thinking about our first night in Africa, when we got to Lagos, and how fast it all collapsed. A week and the whole thing was gone, or so it now seems, all the flowers and singing and the making me happy, all eaten up. No, not a leopard inside. A certain weakness, a hollow place in Witt, that his nice parents couldn't reach and, as it turned out, I couldn't either. But something did, in Africa.

TWENTY

10/24 Lagos

Can't believe this happened, even as I write it down words seem unreal, as if writing down in a dream journal something that didn't really happen. Seem compelled to, tho, habit of keeping a record of everything that happens, discipline of fieldwork. This actually happened, I was there.

Evening of the fifth, the day I got back from the field, W. came in late, pounded on my door, yelling, should have told him to get lost, but polite me, ashamed, not wanting to wake the whole house. W. a mess, stank of beer, smoke & something stinky sweet, like cheap deodorizer. Talking grandiose, not like him at all: he was imbibing the true spirit of Guineé, African night, the music, alive as never before, etc. I told him he was full of it, said it was parroted horseshit, Soronmu's negritude line, besides it was late, I was tired, & he stank. He said that I was the one parroting the hegemonic line, bloodless, overintellectualized yawp of the dying white civilization, & that I knew he was right, which was why I had attached myself to him, sucking his black energy to keep myself inflated the way American culture sucked energy out of blacks & turned it into money. So he jumped on me and I got raped.

Thinking now, why didn't I break his fucking neck? Can't recall, only how exhausted I was, so startled that I just lay there and let him. ?? Exhausted by love, ground down, sorrow, never understood this before, you hear about it, obviously common in male-dominant cultures, like here, recall thinking o fuck it all, he wants to rape me, fine, I've tried everything else. And I had thought he was coming around. After which he left, without 1 word, like I was a whore. Funny, I was totally silent during, but after wailed like a crazy woman, didn't care who heard me.

Everyone had, clearly, because the next morning the group treated me extra nice, like I was terminally ill with loathsome disease. W. gone too. Unbearable, so scrammed out, got Tunji to take me to the U.

Worked on Gelede until I saw Mr O. and his staff were hanging around waiting to close the place down, but were embarrassed to interrupt the great scholar at her work, or maybe they'd heard about the night before like everyone else in this fucking city of dreadful night. Snuck back to my room, locked myself in and worked some more, loading reading notes into laptop, crying in spurts, drinking rum on top of Xanax, and passed out.

Crashing sounds, singing, loud music woke me up. Total darkness, generator off. Got dressed, followed the sound of music to the hotel bar.

There were ten or so people there, all drunk, two of them women, tight bright dresses & lacquered hairstyles: *ashawos*, low-end Lagos whores. The boys were *gboyegas*, street boys, kind that hung around Lagos Island and Victoria, ripping off tourists and people just in from the bush. Tricked out like American gangstas, baggies, faked designer labels, big sneakers, the backward ball caps. The girls were late teens, the men ranged from that to mid-thirties. When I came in they were milling around uneasily; Lary's was not their sort of place, bar was approximation of a British pub – dark paneling, cozy nooks, a dartboard, etc., not a plank on a couple of crates under a kerosene lamp. One had a boom box, some hip-hop shit at top volume. The stranger living in W.'s body approached me and grabbed me and exhibited me to his pals like a trophy. My white bitch. She loves black cock, don't you? A lot more, too, about me and Dave Berne, how I was screwing the white man, and how we knew how to take care of a bitch like that. The men were nervous, excited, a fear there, too, but dulled by booze. They came closer, I was touched, mauled. They were speaking, joking, in dialect too fast for me to follow. Tap current tap current, slang for feeling up a girl, yes, he was staging the lynch mob's fantasy, the niggers and the white woman.

I hit him, with my fist, in the nose. Someone grabbed me from behind, pawing at my shorts. I grabbed his wrist. *Uki-waza*, the floating techniques. *Mae-otoshi*, the front drop. You're supposed to let go of the guy's wrist when he floats away from you, but I didn't, and he bellowed when it snapped.

Hard to recall this next part. I was in a circle of them, eyes and teeth, W. on the floor, blood gushing from his nose, stain on his white shirt. Shouting at me, all of them, waving fists & someone hit me on the head with a bottle, heard the crash, felt the beer run down my back, then Boom, deafening noise, ringing in ears. Screams. And the stink of gunpowder. A woman's outraged voice. Mrs B. The sound of more screams, the flop of sandals, the stomp of shoes, a door slamming. Des was there, holding me, asking if I was all right, me bleeding all over him. No, as a matter of fact.

The boom was Mrs Bassey's shotgun. She was leaning over me, too, propped on the smoking weapon. Everyone was there, gaping, amazed.

Mrs Bassey sewed up my head gash. A nurse, too, in her early years, it turned out. You are well rid of that one, my girl, she kept saying, sewing away. Yes, but I wanted him back. Not that creature. I wanted my *husband*.

I woke up late when the dope wore off and descended to the library. Everyone was very polite, and kind. Dave Berne asked me if I wanted to go to Esale-Eko, which is a district of Lagos where the Gelede tradition is strong, he had a contact there, Akinkuoto, a *babalase*, meaning priest / stage manager of dances.

I escaped into Africa-time then, for twelve days, during which I didn't write in my journal, or anywhere else, just wandered with a camcorder, talking with anyone who would talk with me.

One interview with Olaiya, the *iyalase*, the shrine mother. She had heard about me and told Akinkuoto to bring me by.

She was sitting on cushions in a dim low-ceilinged room, and at first all I could see of her was her clothing, a large headcloth folded in a wide roll across the top of her head and a billow of white robe, with a fold thrown over one shoulder, toga-style. Closer, I could feel the *ashe* pour from her face like a fountain. 'Aristocratic' doesn't begin to describe her face. Someone like that looks into your eyes, you feel the shock in your chest and belly, like a blow. I thought of Puniekka in Chenka and was afraid, & I bowed spontaneously, like you do crossing the altar in church. Akinkuoto made the introductions, which were elaborate. I could feel his tension, and he was probably easier with her than any man in the community. He treated her like a carload of nitroglycerine, but she didn't look at him, only at me. We did the ritual greetings, also lengthy, as always in Yorubaland. When in the course of these she asked after my children I said that Olarun had not blessed me yet. At this she increased the intensity of her stare, & frowned. Then she made a shooing gesture, and Akinkuoto withdrew, rather more quickly than he was accustomed to move.

Then we sat in silence some more. The camcorder lay dormant in my hand, as if a mere ceremonial object, like her silver-mounted horsehair whisk. African time. An *iyalase* is the shadow on earth of Iya Nla, the Great Mother. This figure is extinct in our culture, for the few powerful women we have are imitation men; it is the only form of power we recognize. Among the Yoruba, though, a ferociously male-dominated society, the specifically female kind of power remains intact, and enormously potent. The whole Gelede ritual is a thing devised by men to keep it placated. Every male in Yorubaland knew that Olaiya, or her sisters, could shrivel a man's penis (so that he would, as their saying has it, have to go to bed with his pants on) or insure that no wife ever bore him a son. The deity she represents is also the patroness of all art and culture and agriculture. She loves to be amused, entranced. At all costs she must be kept from irascibility. We used to have her in Europe, too, but we got rid of her, substituting the Virgin, whose power is not at all the same.

She broke the long silence by asking me why I had come to her place. I started with the usual anthro excuse, we wanted to know the ways of her people, we had heard of her wisdom and the beauty of her celebrations, and so on, but she cut me off with a gesture. No, the real reason, she said. The heart reason. She added, I don't usually see *eebo* women. I find them disturbing. They are either men in costumes they can't take off, or crushed things like beetles. You are different, and interesting. Yemaya of the sea was in you once, but you cast her off by fear. *Ashe* is waiting to flow through you in great quantity, but you block it. The *orishas* wish to give you gifts, but you refuse them. Why is that?

I said I didn't know. She said, You do. There is an *alujonnu* in you. You should have it removed. You know this. I agreed that I did. She shrugged, and said, We will have palm wine and kola now. She clapped her hands twice and called something over her shoulder. Two young women dressed in white hurried in and placed a low table before her loaded with prepared nuts and bowls of wine. We ate and drank. Then she said, Your husband beats you. I said no and touched my bandaged head. An accident only. She said, Yes, he beats you. Why? Are you unpleasing to him at night? Is his supper not ready when he wants it? Or is it because you have given him no sons? All of the above, I thought, but said, We have different customs. She gave me that look, I said, I'm afraid that he has an evil spirit in him, too. No idea why I said that, but she said, Of course, because you didn't purify yourselves before your marriage. You should be purified together, or else, someday, you will kill him or he will kill you. But you are the stronger, I think. I saw her hand go out and select a colored stone from a jar. She stared at it for a minute and then enveloped it in a fold of her robe. She said, This has been interesting. I will remember it. I felt a little shiver. I had heard about memory stones but never seen it done. It's what they use in traditional societies instead of notebooks and tape. She would be able to play back our interview in her memory about as accurately as I might have, had I got it all on the Sony, which was not running.

More silence then, and I was able to turn the subject

to anthro, gratefully. She taught me some hymns. Here is one:

> Homage my mother, the Osoronga
> Mother with the beautiful eyes
> Who has a thick bunch of hair in her private parts
> The mother who owns a brass tray
> And a brass fan
> The famous bird of the night that flies gracefully.

Not exactly 'Lead, Kindly Light,' but we have different customs. One of the things she said was, You are ugly, true, but your character is good at the root. *Iwa l'ewa.* Meaning character is beauty; Dad hinted at this all the time, but never actually came out and said it. I left her in a daze, to find that night had fallen.

Three days later there was a Gelede *odun*, a festival, and I saw my first dances. Dance is not quite the word. Gelede is a combination of grand opera, ballet, the circus, a tabloid newspaper, and a psychotherapy session. There is nothing else like it in the world, because other people tend to put all those aspects of culture in different boxes. Not the Yoruba. No one knows exactly what the word Gelede means, but one etymology suggests it stands for 'a thing that relaxes and indulges carefully.' It jollies up the most awesome thing on earth, Earth herself.

Dance lasted three days, I have it all on tape, meaningless, you had to be there. What glory!

Morning of the third day, Berne drove up with Tunji, told me that W. had been arrested for narcotics trafficking, and was in Lagos Jail. I went to where Olaiya was sitting on her stool of honor and took my leave, on my knees. She told me not to go, but I did. On the way back, he filled me in. Early that morning, the cops had burst into the Palm

Court and searched it. They said they were looking for drugs, said that W. had been arrested as a major American gangster drug lord. Dave said that the idiots W. was hanging with figured that since they had an American contact, they didn't have to pay off the cops anymore. Maybe W. had actually told them he was an American drug lord. It's not beyond him at all.

Back in Lagos, I got on our satellite phone and pulled the red handle again, and this morning a sweating, nervous oil company guy, accompanied by two refrigerator-sized Nigerians carrying submachine guns, walked into Lary's Palm Court with an aluminum suitcase containing fifty thousand dollars.

Have to stop writing and go see Colonel Musa.

TWENTY-ONE

Barlow laid out what they had. Paz thought he was good at this, a man who spoke with the Almighty often, and was thus not likely to be cowed by a gaggle of police brass. The room was crowded to capacity, with Neville D. Horton up at the head of the table, flanked by his gofers and assistant chiefs, then Captain Mendés, then the relevant captains and lieutenants who supervised the people who actually knew what was going on.

Barlow covered both cases, stressing the similarities: the precise duplication of the cuts in all four victims, mothers and unborn babies, the type and quantity of the drugs found in the bodies at autopsy, the fact that there was no forced entry, the fact that the crimes had been accomplished in complete silence, with the victims unbound, yet not struggling while they were cut into butcher's meat.

His words emerged in stately periods; he paused dramatically at the right places; he asked rhetorical questions ('Did we find other similarities? Yes, we did') and his delivery was free of the usual verbal tics. It was very much like a sermon, but one lacking a moral point at the end. Paz was glad that Barlow omitted the material about Tanzi Franklin, because it was embarrassing, and it led nowhere. Nor did Barlow try to cover the sorry truth – that they had no leads at all, no suspects, nothing to look for, no real evidence at all except for the bizarre nature of the crimes themselves; a tropical nut used in divination; a cloudy description by a piss-bum of a fellow he had seen talking to Deandra Wallace in a park; a partial bike tire track; and a tiny piece of what had turned out to be obsidian. When he got to that part, Barlow nodded to Paz. 'My partner there, Detective Paz, has found out a little something about that fragment from the Vargas murder scene. Jimmy?'

Paz stood and went to the front of the room. They had planned this so that Paz would be on his feet, standing next to Barlow and ready to field questions, if any, about what Cletis called the spooky stuff. Paz cleared his throat and said, in a voice that sounded too loud in his own ears, 'Yes, I showed the sample to a geologist at the university. He says it's a volcanic glass called obsidian. He examined it under a microscope and concluded that it showed marks of pressure flaking. We're thinking that the chip came from a stone knife.'

A buzz greeted this statement. Mendés knuckle-rapped on the table and turned to the county medical examiner, John Cornell, a wizened veteran with a reputation, which he loved polishing, for being vinegary.

'Doc, what about it? Are the wounds on the two victims consistent with a stone knife?'

'They're consistent with a sharp knife, a very sharp knife, around three inches long,' said Cornell. 'There's no way of telling what the knife was made of.'

'I meant, could you get a stone knife sharp enough to do that kind of cutting?'

'Oh, hell, yeah. It's just glass, really. There's a kind of eye surgery where surgeons routinely use glass knives.

If you know what you're doing, you can get a glass edge that's essentially one molecule thick. You can't get any sharper than that. The problem with glass knives is that they chip if you breathe on them wrong, and then you have to knap a new edge.'

'So this could have happened with this one, where we got that chip?'

'Well, I'll tell you, Arnie,' said Cornell, 'I wasn't there when he did it, so I couldn't say. Find me the knife and I'll maybe testify as to its consistency with the wounds observed on the deceased.'

Mendés grinned, indicating he was charmed by the crusty old gent, and turned his attention to the sole stranger at the table. 'Well, maybe it's time to hear what the FBI has to say. As you all know, we asked Agent Robinette down from the behavioral sciences unit at Quantico when it became clear that we were dealing with a serial killer. So, Agent Robinette, if at this point in time you can tell us anything at all about the kind of man we're looking for, we're all ears.'

Robinette said, 'Thank you, Captain,' and then brought a manila folder out of a briefcase and arranged it neatly in front of him, as if he were a schoolboy called on to read a report. He had something of the schoolboy's look, too, although he must have been sixty: a round, smooth, face, with a button nose and a button chin and bright blue eyes, the skin on his face smooth and reddened as if he had just come from some outdoor sport. His hair was a gray buzz cut, like an astronaut's.

After a brief summary of the principles of serial killer profiling, he said, 'The good news, if you can call it that, is that we think we've seen this man's work before – a case in a town on Long Island in New York State, a little under three years ago.' He took a sheaf of eight-by-ten glossy color photographs and passed them over to Dr Cornell. The medical examiner looked through them, and passed them along. While this viewing proceeded, Robinette went on. 'The victim's name was Mariah Do, born Mary Elizabeth Doe. She was a fashion model and the daughter of a prominent family on the north shore of Long Island. Very old money. Because of their local influence, they were able to keep the crime extremely quiet. Hardly any press, except the bare news of the murder. No details got out, which in a case like this, as you know, is pretty rare, especially when the victim is well known. It probably wouldn't have turned up in our system if the state cop who handled it hadn't been through several of our training courses. We keep a file on cannibalistic acts, as part of the VICAP database, as I'm sure you're all aware.'

Paz actually hadn't been aware. These cases constituted his first contact with cannibalistic acts. When the photographs reached him he studied the woman carefully. She had been strikingly lovely. The cheekbones stood out like wedges in the harsh light of the crime-scene strobe, and the hair that spread out on either side of the dead face was silky and white-blond. The wounds appeared to be similar enough to the ones they had observed in real life, and it seemed in any case unbearable that there should be *two* guys independently doing these. He passed the sheaf to Barlow, who glanced through them quickly and asked, 'This woman, the victim – did she have any connection with any kind of cult, African, Haitian . . . ?'

Robinette nodded, as if he had been expecting the question. 'Not the woman as such, that anyone could determine. But her sister was an anthropologist, and had recently returned from Africa. She'd gotten sick over there and was recuperating at her family home. She apparently committed suicide right after her sister's funeral.' This caused a little stir in the room. Robinette nodded. 'Yeah, that would've been something to look into, but the locals didn't go after it, or the state. This family, as I said, swings a lot of weight in those parts, and they're Catholic, so the police were, let's say, not encouraged to delve into the suicide aspects. The private opinion is, or I guess I should say, was, that the sister did it, because it looked so obviously like an inside job, a particularly awful domestic murder.' He shuffled through his file. 'The victim's sister and mother were in the house at the estimated time of the murder, but it's a huge place, an old-fashioned Long Island mansion. Neither of them heard anything. Two servants in the house, too, ditto. The victim's father and her husband, and the sister's husband, who, by the way, was also recently returned from Africa, were about five miles away at the time of the crime, at an automobile show. All three said they were never out of each other's sight the whole afternoon. Of course, that could've meant they all were in on it, but that's something nobody up there wanted to push. When you people called us, we ran the description through VICAP and this one popped up, a perfect match. I don't think there's any question it's either the same guy or a ritual cult killing with more than one operator following exactly the same procedure.'

More murmuring, which Barlow interrupted by saying, 'I'd like to take a look at the names of those fellas at the car show.'

'You can have our whole file, Detective, for all the good it'll do you. Like I said, it's scanty. At first they were looking for a wandering maniac, but when the sister killed herself, the investigation sort of ran out of steam. Again, I guess they figured the sister went batty and did the murder and then killed herself out of remorse, a day or so after the funeral. There was some indication, which you'll see in the file, that there was bad blood between the sisters, that the older sister was jealous that the younger one was having a baby. And she'd been sick, delirious, and apparently wasn't too tightly wrapped to begin with. *Now*, of course . . .'

Of course. A mumbling interlude, stopped by Mendés rapping sharply upon the table. 'Thank you, Agent Robinette. Based on this other case, and the two down here, do you have enough to give us some idea of what kind of guy we're looking for?'

'Yes, we've been thinking about that long and hard, Captain, and I have to say that I don't think our standard sort of profiling is going to do us much good here. I doubt very much that our unknown subject is a sexual psychopath.'

'What, you think a *normal* man did this kind of thing?' Mendés exclaimed.

'No, I said not a *sexual* psychopath. That's not the same as normal. I think we're looking at a very, very unusual man, but the signature of the crimes doesn't indicate to me someone with a pathological rage against women. There's no evidence of torture, for example. There's no frenzy. There's no posing of the body in unnatural or degrading positions. The women look like they died peacefully in their sleep, and if it wasn't for the operation and the missing body parts, we might well have concluded that. I say 'operation' advisedly. Our unsub was able to drug his victims into unconsciousness, carefully and precisely remove the same specific organs or organ segments from each one, remove the brain from the still-living neonate, and excise a small sliver of tissue from the interior of the brain. This is not the work of a sexual psychopath, or if it is, it's one unlike any we've ever encountered before. They once used to say that Jack the Ripper had to be a professional man, or at least know something about surgery, but we don't think so anymore. It doesn't take professional skill to split a woman open with a knife and rip out a kidney. It does take a lot of skill to excise the brain from a neonate, dissect away the cerebral hemispheres and cut out the thalamus and the pineal body.'

'I'd agree with that,' said Dr Cornell. 'I'd be looking for a brain surgeon. Most of 'em are psychos of one kind or another anyway.'

Robinette flashed a tight smile. 'I don't know about that, but for sure I'd say we'd want to forget about the typical profile. This guy is educated, college, maybe some graduate work. Very smart. Knows how to use a research library. Not unsure of himself with women at all; in fact, a great talker, a charmer. He's probably good looking, average height or taller, height and weight proportional, no disfiguring marks or speech defects. Age midthirties, probably self-employed in some profession. An American. He can talk his way into women's homes, get them to take his drugs, and we're not talking about young unsophisticated girls, either. Mariah Do was an international model – she'd probably heard every line there is from men in her time. Teresa Vargas was a college graduate, and used to traveling in the highest social circles. The Wallace woman, I grant you, was more vulnerable, but there may have been something in particular that attracted him to her. Obviously, he needs women who are ready to deliver babies, and he probably just picks them out on the street, or they come to him for some reason – fortune-telling, maybe. I heard some indication of that in both of the cases here. The guy is careful, precise, no witnesses, very little evidence left behind. I'd guess that he strips and puts his clothes in a bag before he operates. And he's completely fearless about being discovered. So all that adds up to an anomalous situation. He's not taking out his rage on these women. He's got no more emotion than you or I would have going down to the Safeway to pick up some steaks for a barbecue. What I'm saying is, he's not committing crimes of passion – he's *shopping*.'

This got a stir. Robinette pressed on. 'Second, we're looking for someone with no automobile. He takes public transportation, or cabs, or, in one case, he rides a bike. That's unusual in the extreme, for American men generally, and particularly for serial killers. Maybe his license to drive was revoked, or maybe he's got some condition that precludes driving. That's something else to check out anyway. Third thing – race. Serial killers are virtually all white males, and their victims are overwhelmingly white. You clearly want to know what race this guy is, and I have to confess that here I'm drawing a blank. He hits in a black neighborhood at night, where a white man would stand out like a flare in a cellar, and no one noticed him. And you have your witness saying the Wallace woman was seen talking to a black man, a stranger, who might look good for the unsub. But then he strikes in an upper-class neighborhood, where I don't think it's any secret that a lone African-American male at night would be noticed, and might even be the occasion for a call to the police, and the only witness you have maybe spots a *white* guy on a bicycle. I'm thinking master of disguise, which would make him almost certainly a white man, going black for the Wallace murder. I don't think there's a case in history where a black man has disguised himself as white to commit a crime.'

Robinette now started talking cult murders, which in his opinion these were not. There was no evidence of anyone else besides the unsub being involved. Cults implied membership. There was nothing traditionally cultlike at the murder scene – no candles, no incense, no mystical markings. The attempt of the unsub to pin the Wallace killing on Youghans was uncharacteristic of cult murders. Cult murders typically took place in specific locations, to which the victim was carried, clearly not the case here. And so on.

Paz was no longer listening closely. He thought profiling was a useful activity when you had a classic nutcase, which he already knew was not the situation here. They had no idea why this guy was doing it, although he liked what Robinette had said about going shopping. That felt right. The why of it was still completely obscure, however, and these further negatives were not clearing it up very much.

In any event, Paz had spent the last ten minutes studying the file on Mariah Do, in particular a certain photograph, the very last of the zillions of photographs taken of the victim. In this shot, Ms Do was walking down a path flanked by two other people. It was summer in the photo; there were trees in leaf on either side of the path and dappled shadows on the path itself. The victim was pregnant, but gracefully so, like the gravid Madonna in a Renaissance painting. A glow seemed to rise from her, but whether that was real or part of the photographer's art Paz couldn't tell. She was certainly transcendently beautiful. To her left, and lagging a little behind, was another woman, a tall blonde, quite thin, with a pinched, worried face. She was looking at the victim with an expression Paz couldn't read. Pain? Anger? Fear? One of the unhappy emotions in any case. On the victim's other side was a happy man, smiling and gesturing broadly as at some joke. Could that be the reason for the Madonna smile on the victim and the worried look on the face of the other woman? Her sister, Jane Clare Doe, as the helpful label on the back established. The man was the victim's brother-in-law, M. DeWitt Moore, husband of Jane Clare. A man who looked a good deal like Paz, it appeared.

Little thrill rockets were coursing through Paz's gut, and it was agonizing to contain himself while the FBI agent lectured away. Paz had already looked like a jerk twice in this case, once with Youghans, and once with his disastrous effort to get Tanzi Franklin to generate a usable description of the killer. He was not going to chance it again. No, the question now was what to do with this theory. He confronted the eternal detective problem – do you or do you not take a strong suspicion to authority? If you do, you might get enough resources to really nail the guy, but you also might end up in the shit, if the suspicion proved false. But if you don't send it up the chain, and it *is* the guy, someone else will pick up the credit eventually, or else the guy will walk away, or worse, do it again, and if it came out that you *did* have a strong suspicion and did nothing, you would sink even deeper in the shit.

The only smart thing to do was talk to Barlow. That was a Barlow rule, too. Talk to your partner. Barlow, as far as Paz knew, had always been completely open with Paz in the development of cases. On the other hand, Barlow's suspicions were invariably right and Paz's were occasionally wrong.

Agent Robinette's presentation wound to a close. A couple of people asked questions, and a discussion started about whether active steps to forestall or trap the unsub were possible. The cops around the table didn't like the FBI theory. They wanted a cult, a black Cuban or Haitian cult, maybe with some white adherents. Miami was cult city – did it make sense that someone would breeze in from out of town and pursue some mad scientist enterprise? It did not. And where was he getting these exotic drugs? From the botanicas, from root doctors, *brujos*, *curanderos* . . .

These interesting speculations were arrested by a rumble from the head of the table. Neville D. Horton had not spoken substantively yet, but now he did, and everyone fell silent to hear what he had to say, not only because he was chief of police, but because he was an imposing man, six four and well over three hundred pounds, all of it the color of baker's chocolate except for a fringe of feltlike prematurely gray hair. The rumble said, 'People, in about two hours I am going to see the mayor and the city manager. Shortly after *that* I am going to stand up with those two fine gentlemen in front of the TV and tell the folks out there that we are hot on the trail of this fiend, that we got the FBI practically giving us his address and phone number, and that it's only a matter of time before he's a cooked chicken. I am *not* going to get up there in front of God and everyone and say that we're looking for a black white mad scientist on a fucking bicycle. Get serious, people! If we got to put an armed guard with every nine-months-pregnant woman in the city of Miami, then that's what we got to do. This *can't* happen again. Arnie, you're in charge. In fact, now that I think of it, you should be on the TV, too, so folks'll know who to blame.' He smiled at this, a broad one, to show that he was kidding, or wasn't.

'Meanwhile, I need talking points and a plan. You got an hour. People, thank you for your good work. Good luck to you, and God help all of us if we fuck this up.' He rose above the table like a broaching whale and strode out of the room, followed by his aides.

After that, Mendés took charge, snapping out orders to the assembled brass, who resnapped the orders to their underlings as the meeting broke up. Mendés motioned Barlow, Paz, and Robinette to his own office. Mendés was angry, suspecting that he was being set up, in his turn, for the same fall he had outlined so vividly to Paz. He stared balefully at the three others. 'Well? What do we tell the public?'

Robinette said, 'Captain, it might be time for a strategic misstatement.'

Mendés snorted. 'I love the phrase. Meaning?'

'This guy must be feeling pretty pleased with himself. He's outsmarted the cops so far. He's probably following the press reportage pretty closely, and laughing his ass off. What if we issue a profile to the press, not the real one but a phony construct suggesting that the perpetrator is an inadequate individual with a load of sexual hang-ups, impotent, working at a menial blue-collar job. It might put stress on him, get him to contact the press, maybe a talk show. At worst, he might think we're so off base that it makes him careless. It's worked before. And we could have the chief say that we're providing security for pregnant women in certain spots, see if he'll be arrogant enough to challenge you.'

Mendés grinned maliciously. 'Oh, yeah, the boss is going to love that one, using the pregnant ladies as bait. Something happens, we'll all be lucky to get jobs parking cars at the Orange Bowl. How many are there in the city do you think?'

'The U.S. birthrate is fourteen per thousand,' answered Robinette, 'figure a million women in the Miami SMSA, so fourteen thousand per year, figure one-twelfth of those are in their last month this month, so eleven hundred sixty, give or take.'

'Hm. Well, that's at least doable, if it comes to it,' said Mendés. 'They can all stay out at your ranch, Cletis.'

'Glad to have them,' said Barlow. 'I'll tell Erma to start boiling water right now.'

Paz said, 'Chief, meanwhile I think we should go to New York, see the cops up there and talk to people at the murder scene, the dead girl's father and so on.'

'And why is that?' asked Mendés. This was the moment to bring up the photo from the Long Island case file and the speculations arising from it, but when he looked into his chief's eyes and assessed their expression, which was cynical, ready to mock, patronizing, he chickened out. It would keep for a while, until he had it nailed, until Mendés would have to eat it whole and like it. So he said, 'Because the guy was there. He did his thing there. He left some trace, somebody remembered him. You heard Agent Robinette here say they did a half-assed investigation because they figured it was a domestic and the killer killed herself after. Now we *know* that's not true. People will have bits, threads they never followed up on because they closed the file too early. Someone the dead girl knew, or maybe she was in a cult of some kind, and they didn't want to bring it up if they didn't have to. Maybe one of those threads leads to Miami. Someone who was there then is here now – like that.'

'Okay, go,' said Mendés after a moment. 'There and right back. Cletis, you go, too.'

Paz made a couple of calls to insure that the people they wanted to see in New York would be available, and another call to the manager of the Coconut Grove Play-house, where he got the answer he expected. As they left, the homicide unit secretary waved him over and handed him a manila envelope. A lady had brought it by during the meeting. She had said it was important, about the murders. Paz shoved it into his briefcase. They boarded a USAir flight at one-ten from Miami International to La Guardia. Barlow took his seat, said, 'The wayfaring men, though fools, shall not err therein. Isaiah 35:8,' went to sleep immediately after takeoff, and remained out. He awoke when the wheels touched down, stretched, and grinned at Paz. He said, 'Nothing like being paid to sleep. You look like a wet hen, boy. How many of them little tiny drinks you have?'

'Seventy-three,' said Paz, sourly.

'I better drive our car, then.'

Paz got into their white Taurus and dropped off immediately, and awoke when he felt the car slow, then stop. He shook himself awake, straightened his tie, tasted the inside of his mouth, wished for a cigar, settled for a stick of spearmint gum, and looked out the window. They were in a parking lot in front of a low gray modern building with a neat circle of lawn in front of it and a flagpole in the middle of that. It could have been a minor electronics firm, but it was the Hicksville barracks of the New York State Police.

Detective Captain Jerry Heinrich, the man who had led the investigation into the killing of Mary Elizabeth Doe, had a large, modern office, with the usual featureless furnishings and a wall full of award plaques and photographs. There was a big stuffed bluefish on the wall, too. He was a comfortable slow-speaking sort, with curly brown hair graying at the sides, and the perfectly ordinary look of a high-school teacher or an appliance salesman. He seemed reasonably open and glad to help.

After the usual preliminaries, Heinrich said, 'If you got the FBI file, you've got all we set down on paper. Obviously, we put out the max on this one. We had gubernatorial interest and a totally clear field. The county boys and the locals let us handle it completely. You know about this family?'

'We heard they were local big shots,' said Paz.

'You could say that. More like an institution in this part of the world. Money? It doesn't mean anything to them anymore. Churches, charities, hospitals. Hell, they sent half the bright kids on the north shore through college, and they've been doing it since forever. And they're related to everybody who's been here longer than the Nixon administration. So it wasn't like they had to make any angry phone calls. People just pitched in to do anything they could, which was why the press was kind of frozen out of it, and believe you me, they were swarming for a while, the victim being such a big model and all. But no one would talk. And the isolation helped. You been there yet? Sionnet?'

Barlow said, 'Is that how you say it? No, we haven't. We're going out after we finish here. We thought we'd talk to Mr Doe and any of his people who were around then.'

'Yeah, well good luck. Boy, I'll tell you, we had every detective on the Island talking to people, and some from upstate, too, and we got zip. Four people in the house when the thing went down, the butler, guy named Rudolf, been with the family since Pluto was a pup. Well, in this case we're pretty damn sure the butler didn't do it. Then a girl who worked for the family, cooking, slept in, was in the kitchen all the time, working on dinner. Then the mother, in her bedroom, sleeping, she said, and I tend to believe it.'

'Why?' asked Paz.

Heinrich lifted his hand to his mouth, cupped. 'All the time. And pills, too. A damned shame. Besides, hell, a thing like that, you don't usually figure Mom for involvement. And there was Jane, the other daughter. She was out on the north terrace facing the water, for most of the afternoon. She said. But it turned out no one recalled seeing her there at the time of. Near as we can figure it, it was done between three and four in the afternoon. And I was saying about Sionnet, it's isolated, out on a neck, maybe a hundred fifty acres, but to get to it you have to go through Sionnet village, and there's nothing at all past the village but the estate. There's a big sign saying private road and a little turnaround for tourists who get lost. On a busy day in the summer you might get six cars going that way through the village, people working at the estate and so on. This particular day was September sixteenth, a Saturday. People recalled Mr Doe driving out with his two sons-in-law to see that car show in Huntington, about one, and then driving back around four-thirty. Hell of a thing to come home to, huh? Anyway, no strange cars at all during the critical times. And you're going to ask about boats. They would've heard a boat for sure. There were people working on the place, down by the dock, and the daughter said she was down there, too. Yeah, sure, some commando could've landed a dinghy and snuck in there, but . . .' He gestured to show how unlikely he thought that was.

Barlow asked, 'You were in charge from the get-go?'

'Yep. Lucky me.' He described his involvement in the case, and what they had found, which was pretty much what Barlow and Paz had found, and Heinrich expressed the same anger, sadness, bitterness, and frustration that they both felt.

'They buried the mother and baby in the same casket,' he told them. 'They got their own cemetery, right there on the property. There was just the extended family and a few close friends at the cere- mony, a couple of dozen folks. Mr Doe was like a rock. Mary's husband was leaning on him, crying, that German photographer. The mother – hell, she didn't know *where* she was. And the sister, Jane. I never saw anyone so scared in my life.'

'You attended?' asked Barlow.

'Oh, yeah. We're always ready for a remorseful graveside confession. Anyway, Jane was white as paper, and shaky. She dropped the trowel, you know, for picking up a clump of earth and tossing it in there? Shaking like a damn paint mixer, holding on to her dad and her brother. Her husband was standing off by himself. An African-American fella, by the way.'

'What was *he* like?' asked Paz, a little too avidly. Heinrich gave him a look.

'Oh, a nice fella. Well spoken. A pretty famous writer, plays and stuff, poetry. Of course, he was off with the other two men the whole time, so there was no question. The sister, on the other hand, his wife . . .' Heinrich paused, swiveled in his chair, and checked out his bluefish.

'You think she done it?' asked Barlow.

Heinrich lowered his head, like a bull deciding whether to charge the cape.

'Well, you know, we never actually *concluded* that. But the woman had a history. When she came back from Africa – Josiah Mount, the brother, actually he's a step-brother, brought her back – she was apparently pretty loose in the screws, raving about black magic – crazy stuff. She thought her husband had turned into a witch. It'd happened before, too, Mount said. He pulled her out of Russia, a couple years before this, also off her head. He thought she was on some kind of native drugs, messed up her brain. And, well, the way she was acting at the funeral – like I said, I thought she was about to jump in the grave. Then, also, she had a thing with her sister. Jealousy. Well, let me say, she had something to be jealous about.'

'How's that?' asked Barlow.

'Hell, Mary Elizabeth Doe was the most beautiful woman I ever saw close-up. I mean she was what they call a supermodel, like you see in magazines. Jane, well, she wasn't exactly a dog, kind of big and craggy like her old man, but when they were in the room together she might have been a damn houseplant for all anybody looked at her. And she was jealous Mary Elizabeth was having a baby too. Jane couldn't have kids, according to her husband, and Mr Doe – well, carrying on the family line and all, it was important to him, he was paying a lot more attention to Mary than he had before. Jane had always been his pet, sort of, and she resented it. It's all in the files you got.'

Barlow said, 'So you thought this murder, the way it got done, was like jealous rage. Jane just snapped and carved her sister up?'

'That, and the, well, excisions, we thought that part could've been the witchcraft stuff. Which also fit with the drugs we found in the body. But then when she killed herself, that kind of put the stopper on that theory, although, you know, in deference to the family, we never made it official. Officially, the case is still open.'

'Was there a note?' asked Barlow.

'Not that we found,' said Heinrich carefully. 'I was in Jane's room right after she did it. Neat as a pin and her desk with a box of stationery out and a pen. But no note. Mr D. wouldn't look me in the eye when I asked him. So . . .'

'How did she kill herself?' asked Paz. 'Something about a boat . . . ?'

'Oh, that was another pain in the neck. The murder was Saturday, the funeral was Tuesday. On Tuesday night, it was starting to blow pretty good from the west, and she took their yacht out, just motored out into the Sound, hoisted sail, and headed northeast, up the

Sound. A little past midnight, she was about five miles south of New Haven when the boat blew up.'

'They find her body?' Paz asked.

'No, I mean the boat *really* blew up. They had a propane tank aboard, a full load of diesel fuel, and a gas tank for the auxiliary outboard. They saw the fireball in New London. If she was on it when it went up, she was crab food, and we got a lot of crabs out in the Sound.'

'You think suicide?'

'Accident is what's in the official report,' said Heinrich, his tone flat. 'A Catholic family. And what did it matter, anyway? Off the record, and personally? I think she was running for it and got careless. It's easy to blow up a boat if you're not careful.'

'Or maybe she faked it and escaped,' said Barlow.

'Possible but unlikely. She hasn't turned up since, she didn't pull any serious money out of her accounts before she took off, and she hasn't accessed any of her money since. You'd have to believe she went crazy, butchered her sister, and then escaped with a plan like some kind of international criminal mastermind. It doesn't work for me. Or it didn't until you guys called. Now, I don't know. I mean, guys, there is just no one else I like for it the way I like Jane Clare Doe. And if she did get away, maybe she ended up in Miami. So was she crazy? I'll tell you one thing: her husband sure in hell thought so. Maybe she still is. Maybe she got to like it.'

TWENTY-TWO

The wind awakens me an hour or so before dawn. I get out of my hammock and go outside to the landing at the head of the stairs. Luz is in her new room, so I no longer have to be so careful when I leave. It's not a hurricane, I know; it's impossible to live in Miami and ignore the hectic preparations that surround hurricanes. But it's a strong wind all the same, making the neighboring palms and cycads rattle and clatter, and bringing from the stiff-leaved figs and crotons a continuous slithering sound, like brushes on snare drums. It's blowing thirty knots, I estimate, and from the distant harbor I can hear the rigging of the boats complaining with insane jangles. A warm wind, gritty, the kind that generates static electricity and causes the ionic composition of the body to change subtly, encouraging madness. Not a typical Miami wind. A wind from somewhere else, like the harmattan, the wind from the Sahara, although it's way too early for the harmattan.

In the morning, when Luz and I go out, there's a flat calm. The car and all the foliage around it are covered with flour-fine red-ocher dust. I run my finger across the roof of the Buick and place it in my mouth. Mali on my tongue. Yes, I say in my head, yes, yes, all right, I get the message. Go to the *ile*, make the sacrifice.

Thank you. Luz draws a big heart in the dust on the car door.

At work, I give Mrs Waley notice that I am retiring from the profession of medical data clerk. She asks suspiciously whether I have been offered a job in budget or admin, and I am glad to tell her, no, I'm leaving the health services field entirely. I say that I have a medical problem that precludes regular hours. I can see that she's fainting to ask me what my problem is, but she doesn't. Instead she tells me, conferring upon me her first smile ever, that I've been a good worker and that it's been a pleasure to have me in her department.

In the hallways, the hospital's cleaning crews are working hard to get rid of last night's dust, which defeats even the high-technology filters that feed air into these buildings. They push hair brooms and sprinkle green fluffy stuff to soak up the pale, gritty powder. I remember trying to do it with a twig broom. You could never get the floor actually looking clean, but in the harmattan season you had to do it every day or it would be up to your ankles before you knew it.

We went to Africa because of Lou Nearing and Captain Dinwiddie, an odd combination, but typical of Ifa's web. Lou had come to town the previous winter for the American Anthro Society meeting, bringing his wife along, and he called Witt and we took them to dinner at Balthazar, to show continuing friendship on our part, and, I suppose, for Lou to show off his wife and to show her me, the old flame. Witt was his usual charming self, the Nearings were in fact charmed, and a dinner fraught with awkward possibilities went off fairly well. They

wanted to see *White History Month*, too, and over
dessert Lou said that he had been talking about me just
the other day with Desmond Greer, who had just taken
over the Yoruba archive at Chicago. It seemed he had a
grant to travel over to Yorubaland to, among other
things, trace the origins and distribution of Yoruba
traditional magic, and Lou had brought up my name.
Greer, whom I knew slightly, was one of the few
admirers Marcel retained in American academia, not
of the crazy stuff, of course, but of the solid ethnographic part of his work, and according to Lou, he was
interested in the possibility, especially if I'd pick up my
own expenses. I said I didn't know anything about
Africa, and Lou said that Greer didn't care about that, he
wanted a Vierchau-style take on the origins and changes
in the tradition, someone who had the skills to get inside
it and see what made it real to the people who used it.
Good old Lou! He always thought I was better than I
thought I was, always pushing at me not to drop out of
the field.

I said, 'Gosh, Lou, a year in Africa? I don't know. I'm
rusty. I don't know the background or the languages . . .'
Lou said, 'Hell, Janey, you got nine months to pick that
up. You wouldn't be leaving until September.' Witt said,
'Africa? Hey, let's go! I need to go there anyway for the
Captain, and we could do stuff together. It'll be a blast.'
Cindy Nearing asked who the Captain was and Witt slid
away from the question as he always did, with 'just some
stuff I'm playing with.'

After that night, he wouldn't let it go, us doing it
together. I listened, it sounded reasonable, it was as far
as you could get from Siberia and the Chenka, and so I
called Greer and flew out to Chicago and met him in his

office in Haskell. He showed me around the Yoruba Ethnographic Archive and talked about what the team he was taking over hoped to accomplish. He assumed I was more like Marcel than I was at the time, but perhaps he was more percipient than I gave him credit for being, given how things turned out. When I told him about my husband's wish to come along, he said he admired Witt's work and would be glad to meet him and have him tacked on to the expedition. My own race did not come up as an issue, which was fine with me.

That was the Lou Nearing part. The Captain Dinwiddie part was that since he was about nineteen my husband had been laboring intermittently on a long poem about America, seen, of course, from its black bottom. It was called *Captain Dinwiddie*. He regarded it as his real life's work.

I am, I admit it, a prosey person. Aside from one comp lit course at Barnard, I got all my poetry through Witt. I therefore have no idea whether *Captain Dinwiddie* is one of the supreme works of American literature or a pretentious farrago. It's certainly an interesting story. The eponymous hero's a slave in the antebellum South; he escapes, lands in New York, is adopted by a rich abolitionist, is given an education, and takes the name Dinwiddie. In the Civil War he leads a regiment of dragoons, ends up occupying the very same ole plantation, and turns it into a kind of Heart of Darkness in reverse, with him in the big house and the white folks chopping cotton, him screwing Miss Ann of course. He ends up fleeing back to Mother Africa, where he learns via juju how to travel through time, to view the sad future history of his people, descending in the flesh one day a year, to perform some expiatory good deed. But Witt knew nothing of Africa, less about African religion or magic. He said he was blocked as a result, and the invitation from Greer at just this time seemed to him a good omen. Synchronicity.

Reading the journals again, in the hot kitchen of my place; Luz is playing with Jake and Shari out in the yard. They have the hose out and a plastic splash pool. I always meant to take her to Venetian Pool in Coral Gables and teach her how to swim, but just now I have given up on plans. Except that I have arranged for Shari to baby-sit Luz tonight, because I am going to Pedro Ortiz's *ile*, to make *ebo*, as Ifa has told me to do. I feel myself dropping back into belief, as I was toward the end there in Africa, slipping into the whole thing, as into dark, blood-warm water, although I know it is absurd, spells and spirits and curses and witches, but . . . Thomas Merton once said that there comes a point where your religion seems ridiculous, and then you discover to your surprise that you are still religious.

When it gets dark, in the usual instant collapse of day that tells you 'tropics,' I say good-bye to Luz and Shari and go. On the way there, I stop at a botanica and purchase thirty-two small cowrie shells. Although I have never been to a Santería ritual before, I find I am succeeding in keeping my anthropological curiosity under control. My knees are shaking. I am wearing a yellowish cotton dress with a green patent leather belt on it. Ifa likes these colors.

Ortiz's *ile* is lodged in a small salmon-colored house, concrete-block stucco with white hurricane shutters and a gray cement tile roof, on NW Seventeenth off

Flagler. As in many of the neighboring houses, what was once a front lawn has been paved over, to serve as a mini–parking lot. It is full of cars both old and new, as are the curbs nearby. I park at the end of the block and walk down.

A woman admits me when I ring. She is the woman from PETS, but she looks different tonight, straighter, not as worn. She smells of roses and wears a white dress embroidered with gold around the yoke. The room she takes me into, the living room, is dim, and lit by dozens of candles. The candles stand on wide shelves running around two sides of the room, and illuminate hundreds of Santería ritual objects arranged in shrines: the two-headed axes of Shango, his mortar stool, his *sopera*, the tureen holding his sacred stones, his *fundamentos*. Other *soperas*, too, each decorated in the *orisha*'s symbolic colors, yellow for Oshun, with her peacock fan, white for Obalala, with his fly whisk, black and light blue for Babaluaye, with his crutches, cowries, and reeds, a red-and-white coconut for Oshosi, the hunter, with an iron cauldron containing deer antlers, bow and arrows, and a plastic toy rifle. There are statues in each shrine, too, some of them life size, of the *santos*, the *orishas*, Catholic saints melded with Yoruba demigods, all with brown skins, large eyes, and blank expressions. Placed high, wired to the ceiling, is Osun, the herbal messenger, bird staff in hand, who protects the life of the devotees on their journeys to God.

There are people in the room, a half-dozen women in white dresses and four men in guayabera shirts, unpacking large black boxes. I see they are removing drums. There is to be a *bembé*, then, a celebration of the anniversary of the descent of one of the *orishas* onto a member of Ortiz's *ile*. This is not good. I had thought, in and out, pay the money, get the sacrifice, Ifa satisfied, only a brief appearance in the *m'doli*, maybe I won't be noticed.

Ortiz is waiting in one of the house's small bedrooms, which he has turned into a shrine to Ifa, or Orula, as he's known among the Santería people. He's got yellow and green silk bunting draped on the walls and ceiling, a life-size statue of Orula in his guise as Saint Francis. Before this, draped in green-and-gold brocade heavy with elaborate beadwork, is the yard-high cylinder containing Ifa-Orula's *fundamentos*. There are flickering candles in green glass tumblers, bouquets of gladiolas, frangipani, oleander, and jasmine, and piles of coconuts and yams, dozens and dozens of yams. I can smell the earth stink of them, mixed with the heavy odor of the flowers and the burning wax. One wall is nearly filled with a massive black wood cabinet, heavily carved: the *canastillero*, which contains shelves full of sacred objects. On the other wall there is a small table and two chairs for divinations.

He's sitting in one of the chairs, looking like an ordinary black Cuban, no masklike visage, no strangely luminous eyes, just a guy in a white guayabera and white slacks. But spontaneously I dip my knee and touch my mouth and forehead, the way I used to greet Uluné. You see Olo kids do this, whenever an elder walks by; they'll stop what they're doing and make the gesture, and maybe get a pat on the head, and go right back to what they were doing before. I know that *santeros* get a different kind of obeisance, but Ortiz seems to accept mine.

I take the chair opposite. Ortiz smiles and takes my

hand. He strokes it gently, in circles, with his thumb. No adult has touched me other than formally for nearly three years. He says, a statement not a question, 'You are very frightened.'

'Yes. I thought you would be alone. I didn't expect these others, or the *bembé*. I just wanted the sacrifice . . .'

'Yes, like McDonald's,' he says, and his smile briefly grows into a grin, showing gold. 'We could have a drive-through window – two pigeons and a rooster, please.' And more seriously: 'Look, *chica*, you are safe here, as safe as you can be anywhere. We are under the protection of the *santos* in this house. You'll come to the *bembé*, maybe the *orishas* will come down and tell you something you need to know.'

He has the animals ready. I give him my cowries. The four little lives depart, with brief flutters, to Orun. He grasps my hand. I want to leave, but there is no strength in the desire. I am on the line, well hooked.

From the other room comes the sound of someone tuning a fucking *drum*. After a long moment, I bow my head, submitting. I want to throw up, but I swallow thick, ropy saliva, and keep it down.

He rises, still holding my hand. Hand in hand, his warm, mine feeling like film-wrapped supermarket chopped chuck, we go back to the living room. Here the scent of flowers, too, and sacrificial rum, and the harsh sweet smell of the vapor from the holy spray cans they sell in the botanicas. People come up to Ortiz and pay him homage, a bow, the murmured *moforabile*, the acknowledgment of Ifa living in him; he embraces each and murmurs a blessing in Yoruba. We stand around while the drummers set up. They are all thin black men in white clothes. They have African names: Lokuya, Aliletepowo, Iwalewa, Oribeji. Their drums are familiar to me: the big *bata;* the *iya*, shaped like an unequal hourglass, the bell-hung, goatskin-headed mother drum, which talks and sets the changes; the midrange *itotele;* and the small, sharp-tongued *okokolo*. The Olo have these, or ones like these, and they also have the immense heartbeat *ojana*, which shakes the ground, and which you hear with your whole body, not just the ears. The drum *does* stuff to you in the hands of an expert, whether you want to have stuff done to you or not, which is why, since my return from Drum Central until tonight, I have avoided their beat.

More people come in and honor Ortiz and the *orishas*. Ortiz introduces me to each. They all have African names too. Ositola, Omolokuna, Mandebe. They seem like ordinary, hardworking, lower-middle-class black people, the kind you see in the hallways at Jackson, pushing waxers, carrying sterile packs and boxes of tools. They are shy when they meet me. We make small talk. I chat briefly with a woman called Teresa Solares, stocky, moon-faced, around thirty, I judge, worn-looking, wearing a tight yellow dress. She is a home health aide on the Beach. We have something in common, then, both of us health professionals, but our conversation does not flourish. I meet some others, Margarita and Dolores (oh, we have the same name!, a smile exchanged) and Angela and Celia. They think I am an alien here. I wish that I were. The room is crowded now and hot.

The four drummers sit and face one of the shrines. It is the one to Eleggua-Eshu, always the first to be honored at these affairs, because you have to ask him to

open the way between Orun and Ayé. Orun, in both
Santería and Yoruba cosmology, is the spirit world, the
world of the ancestors and the gods, which the Olo call
m'arun. Ayé is the *m'fa.* The Yoruba say, *Ayé l'oja, orun
n'ile:* the world is a marketplace where we visit, heaven
is our home.

The drums start. My stomach rolls over. They are
good, almost Olo standard. The *oriate,* the special
devotee of Eleggua-Eshu, turns out to be the woman
from PETS; she takes up a gourd rattle and begins her
praise song. The *ile* chants along: *Ago ago ago ago.* Open
open. She is dancing before the shrine of Eleggua, and
everyone else is swaying, too. Something changes in the
room; a different, more energetic air seems to circulate
now. It's happening.

The man on the *iya* does a frantic run and the
drumming stops. The room sighs. The colors are starting to go funny. Now the drums start up again, and the
praise song rises to Shango, *orisha* of force and war. The
oriates of Shango whirl and stomp, but Shango does not
come. The drums call the others in turn, Yemaya, *orisha*
of the seas, Oshosi, *orisha* of the hunt, Inle, *orisha* of
medicine, Oshun, *orisha* of love. Now something is
happening within the group of dancers; the circle of
moving flesh draws back, hollowing its center. In the
ring thus made Teresa Solares is spinning, eyes shut,
arms waving like water weeds, swaying her hips. Sweat
flies off her, making red sparks where the candles catch
the flying droplets. Everyone is chanting *eshu eshu* –
hold hold. The beat quickens, impossibly fast; Teresa
spins around three times on one heel, rolls her eyes up,
and crashes to the floor. The drums stop instantly. The
silence is astounding.

Several of the *santerías* help her to her feet and
attempt to lead her away, but she shrugs them off and
stands erect. She seems to have gained eight inches in
height. Her face is utterly transformed, the eyes huge
and bright, the features more defined. She rips off the
clip that holds her hair, which swings out, as if electri-
fied, like a lion's mane. She is now Oshun. The drums
take up a complex rhythm and Oshun dances. It is
erotic beyond sex, beyond belief, Life Herself, the force
that through the green fuse drives the flower, and we all
like flowers lean forward swaying, as if toward a dancing
sun. Oshun dances around the circle, feet hardly touching the ground, an ordinary woman with no training,
dancing intricate steps, graceful as a puma. She kisses
the devotees, she whispers to them, they stick currency
to the sweat of her body, little sacrifices, and now she is
before me. I fumble a dollar out of my bag and stick it
below her neck.

She speaks to me in a deep contralto voice, sweet
and thick as molasses, nothing like Teresa's voice: 'Child
of Ifa, listen! Ifa says, go by water. Ifa says, before you
close the gate, it must first be opened. Ifa says, the
yellow bird will save you. Ifa says bring the yellow bird
to the father. Ifa says, go by water, only by water.'

Oshun whirls away. I realize she has been speaking
Yoruba, which Ms Solares does not speak, as far as I
know. I recall now that Ifa does not dance himself, he
always dances through Oshun. The *orisha* finishes her
dance and goes off with a few of the women who want a
private consultation. The drums take up the beat again.
The *orishas* start to come more easily, the excitement is
palpable now, the whole house seems to be shaking, this
is becoming a good, a really remarkable *bembé*. Ogun

arrives, the angry smith, his voice booms bass notes from the throat of Julia, a dark woman of only moderate size. Obatala comes into Mercedes, spreading calm and clarity, and Margarita becomes Yemaya, capricious and powerful, the sea-mistress.

Then Shango comes, mounting a mild-looking middle-aged man named Honorio Lopez. When the *orisha* rises from Honorio's faint, the devotees dress him in a red-and-white satin tunic, a red sash and a red headdress. The drums take up a staccato, violent beat, and he dances, crouched, then leaping impossibly high, then stamping his feet. He circles the *ile*, conversing with the devotees in a loud, harsh voice, making crude jokes and uttering threats. Then he stands before me, scowling, giving off an aura of violent energy, like a guy coming into a bar, looking for a fight. I can see him draw breath to shout at me, and without warning he changes again. That breath whooshes out of him; he appears stunned. He sags.

Then his face takes on a look of amused and curious detachment. My husband says, 'Well, Jane, here you are.' I am turned to stone. He goes on, in a conversational voice, 'I know you don't believe this, but I missed you, I really did. For a while there, I really thought you were dead. And I looked for you. I mean in *m'doli*. Me and Orpheus. But you weren't there. And you weren't in *m'fa* either, as far as I could see. You were being quiet as a mouse, weren't you? By the way, you look awful, Jane. What did you do to your hair?'

I say, 'Please, don't hurt anybody else.'

He grins at me. 'Oh, don't worry about this guy. Shango won't mind me borrowing his horse for a while. But I really do need to talk to you. Gosh, we used to talk about everything, remember? I need to talk to you about my plans.'

The people have noticed what's going on. They stare at us, confused. The Shango song on the drums falters and dies. Ortiz is shouting something in Spanish at the drummers. They start to play again, and Ortiz begins a chant to Eleggua-Eshu, asking him to open the gates to Orun again and draw the *orishas* back to the other world.

He says, 'They're playing my song. Catch you later, Janey.' The most hideous thing here is the perfectly rational sanity of his tone and affect. Now the man in front of me loses all expression, his eyes roll up and go white, he crumples. The other *orishas* are leaving, too, their mounts dropping like shot birds. I race out of the house.

By the time I crunch up on my driveway, I have almost convinced myself that the thing with Shango and my husband didn't happen. A little hallucination there, brought on by stress, and the drums, and the setting, and cultural conditioning, and exohormones unleashed in the hot room, the same way we all hallucinated the physical changes in the mounted devotees, and their messages. That little colloquy with my husband was what I imagined he would say, and thus I heard Mr Lopez say it. A good Jungian explanation so I can go to sleep. I am really terrific at this sort of rationalization. Marcel always commented on it.

Shari goes sleepily home with my thanks and five bucks. I take a long shower to scrub off the evening's various effluvia, yank on my worn sleeping shirt, and heave into my hammock. I am asleep instantly.

Only to awake later. It is deep in the night and silent

but for the thrum of the nearby A/Cs. Moonlight is spilling through my rattan blinds, making icy calligraphy on the wall opposite the window. This is ridiculous, I'm thinking now, being stalked by a serial killer and farting around with all this voodoo crap. I have to get small, get gone, *adiós* Miami, do it now. I pack; there's not much. I go up and get Luz. She is out cold, and curiously dense and heavy, like a statue in my arms. I place her on the backseat of the Buick. We take off.

I drive up Douglas to the Trail and then west. There is little traffic. Past the turnpike overpass the road is completely deserted. There is ground mist in the headlight beams, and once some beast, a dog, a possum, shines yellow eyes in my lights. The car is acting up now, I really should have fixed the trannie. I lose top gear and slow to thirty-five. We are in the Everglades, driving through a narrow hot black velvet tunnel made by the headlights. Another gear blows out, the engine wails, and we drop to an even slower speed. We will never make it to Naples.

But suddenly there is a glow ahead, which turns into lights, lots and lots of them, abolishing the blackness of the Glades. It is a huge truck stop, with a big tan building to one side. IMOKALEE INDIAN CASINO, announces a great blinking neon sign. The transmission gives out completely now. I heave my butt forward and back on the seat, like a kid in a toy car, urging the Buick to safety. We roll into the shining station. There is an Indian in the station office, huge, braid-haired, dark-faced, grave, wearing coveralls and a Dolphins hat. I ask him if he can fix my transmission and he says, Sure, we can fix anything. He cranks the Buick up on his lift. Give me an hour, he says. I am inexpressibly glad,

almost in tears. I wake Luz, and together we walk into
the casino.

It is very bright, and loud music is playing, Disney
tunes, oddly enough, 'Bippidy-Boppidy-Boo' and 'When
You Wish upon a Star.' There are endless rows of flashing slot machines; the ceiling is mirrored. I decide
that we should play the slots while we wait; maybe we
can make some money here for our trip. I get a bucket
of quarters. We start feeding them into the machines.
Almost immediately Luz hits a jackpot. The coins flow
out over the floor, covering her feet to the ankles. We
scoop them into a larger bucket. I tell Luz to keep playing out of the smaller bucket, while I go off and cash the
jackpot in for chips. I am elated. I feel my luck has
finally changed. For a while I play blackjack. I win and
win. Then I play roulette for a while. The chips pile up.

Now I feel a thrill of fear. How long has it been?
Hours? I take my winnings and go back to the slot
machine area to find Luz. There seem to be acres of
aisles all alike. The flashing lights and the noise of the
machines and the Disney music ('A Dream Is a Wish
Your Heart Makes') is driving me crazy. I run up and
down the aisles shouting her name. Then I see her,
walking hand in hand with a large woman in a yellow
dress. I shout at her. The woman turns around. I see that
it is Luz's mother, the woman I killed. I run and run
now, lost in the maze and the mirrors; I run very slowly,
I can hardly move my legs now—

I'm in my hammock, heart a-thump, soaked with
sweat. The moonlight through the rattan blinds makes
a pattern against the opposite wall. I get to my feet. My
knees are trembling. I have not had a dream like that in
a while. I go to the bathroom and splash some water on

my face. I look at my face in the mirror. Yes, it's me, my
perm squashed by sleep into something agricultural
looking. No grinning skulls or African masks. I pinch my
cheek. Real.

There's a scratching sound just above my head, tiny
skittering claws. Trembling, I go outside, to see if it's the
raccoon. I don't see her from my landing, but there is
something dark and low moving across the garden, illuminated by the waning moon. Oh, it's just Jake the dog.
The hum of the A/C is calming, ordinary, familiar.

I'm just about to try to get some more sleep when
there is a shriek from upstairs. I race up the ladder.
Another shriek. She's having a nightmare, too. Luz's
room is lit by moonlight through her round window and
by her Kermit the Frog nightlamp, which casts a
greenish-yellow glow. As I run to her, a huge cockroach
crosses my path. It is so big that at first I think it is a
mouse. I sidestep and crush it under my bare foot. Luz
is screaming hysterically now. I race to her and sit on
the bed and snatch her to me, wrapped in her pink
blanket. She is struggling in my arms, and I say, Wake
up, wake up, darling, it's only a dream. Her mouth is
wide open in a rictus of terror, her eyes squeezed tight
shut. I feel a tickle on my arm. It is another cockroach,
as big as the first. I brush it off. There is a peculiar
movement under the pink blanket. I tear it away, and I
see that the whole bed is a mass of cockroaches. They
are all over Luz, boiling and skittering under her
flowered cotton nightdress. The construction I did up
here must have disturbed a whole colony of them. I leap
from the bed and hold Luz at arm's length; I shake her,
hard. Showers of roaches fall around my feet. Some of
them crawl up my legs. I am dancing around, crushing

them underfoot, shaking the child, the carpet becoming slimy under my bare soles. A cockroach climbs over my arm and across Luz's face and into her mouth. She starts to strangle. I reach into her mouth for the thing, but I can't get a grip. It is disappearing down her throat. Her lips are turning blue. I can't reach it, although my hand feels like it is halfway to her lungs.

I am in the hammock, with the moonlight making patterns on the opposite wall. The A/C across the way hums. No time appears to have passed. I understand now that I am under assault. My heart is knocking in my chest. This is bad, but not as bad as some witch-dreams I have heard of. People who don't wake up, for example, found in the morning with the familiar eye-bulging expression, or drowned in blood or vomit.

Okay, easily fixed – no more sleep until further notice. I get up, wash my sweaty face, pull my painter's overalls over my T-shirt, and make a big pot of coffee. I discover I am hungry, which I take for a good sign, so I make a three-egg omelette and toast to go with the coffee. I drink the whole pot; the last cup I take sitting on my landing outside, enjoying the tropical sunrise and the birdsong, trying to forget about the night. In Africa, I always used to rise with the birds. A flight of green parrots zips overhead, complaining. The palms rustle in the new sea breeze. I could be in Africa now, except for the coffee.

Luz comes downstairs and I hear the refrigerator open as she takes out the milk. I go in and supervise her pouring out over her Captain Crunch. She seems dull and irritable. I ask her whether she has had any dreams, and she says no, but that is probably not true. I get her dressed and we go off to nursery school and work. The routine calms me. I will be sorry to give it up. Last night at the *ile* seems like part of the dreams that came afterward.

It is my last day of work. I will pick up my check, deposit it at the credit union at lunchtime, and then take the car in for the work it needs. The check should be a big one, with the unspent vacation time and the rebate from the pension fund. Whatever happens next, it should be enough to keep us until I can set up in a different line of work. Or to buy a getaway. I think again of running. He knows I'm alive, but he doesn't know where my body is . . . no, he doesn't really know I'm alive, that was hallucination last night, that and the dreams. Just a bad dream. This is real. I bang the heel of my hand against the hard, old-fashioned plastic steering wheel. It stings.

I am actually glad to see Mrs Waley. She is not glad to see me, however. I start for my desk, but she motions me over. She is in magenta this morning, a pantsuit, over a pink polyester blouse. I am thinking about the check and calculating how much it will be. At least twelve hundred. I go into her office and shut the door.

'What do you mean by coming to work dressed like that?' she says immediately. 'Just because it's your last day don't mean I'm relaxing my standards. No ma'am. Overalls and a T-shirt? And not even clean. You should be ashamed of yourself!'

In fact, I find that I *am* ashamed. I murmur an apology.

'That's not good enough,' says Mrs Waley. 'You all think you can get away with murder, but you can't, not while I'm in charge, missy. You're going to give me a full day's work in proper office apparel, or I am not going to sign off on your separation check. What do you think of that?'

I don't think anything. I absolutely have to have that check. I stand mute. Mrs Waley goes over to her closet and comes back with a lime-green pantsuit on a hanger, wrapped in cleaner's plastic.

She says, 'Out of the goodness of my heart, I'm going to lend you an outfit. Here. Put this on!'

I take the hanger and start to leave. She stops me. 'No, right here. Change right here.'

What can I do? The woman is crazy and I need my check. I take off my overalls and then my T-shirt, and stand there naked. Mrs Waley has a triumphant expression on her face, as if she knew that I was, underneath my submissive mien, a girl who would go out of the house in the morning with no undies on. I realize then I am standing in front of Mrs Waley's window. There are dozens of people looking in, all my medical records colleagues, and yes, there's Lou Nearing, too. Well, he's seen it all before, hasn't he? I feel okay about it, though, because it's my last day. I press my breasts up against the glass and wave. I feel the cold glass against my nipples, and feel them get stiff.

I am in the hammock with the moonlight making patterns on the opposite wall. The A/C throbs away next door. Now I believe that I'll stay in the hammock, and watch the moonlight fade and the sunlight arrive, and just *wait* for what's next. Perhaps Luz will come down after a while, and when she can't get any response from me, she'll run weeping over to Polly's and Polly will come. She won't be able to move me either. After a while a cop and a couple of guys from Jackson will come, and they'll take me away and some intern in neuropsych will shoot me full of Thorazine and then I'll be fine. I'll spend the rest of my life in and out of the nut hatch, not making any trouble, resting quietly. Perhaps I'll even gain some weight. Luz will get a nice foster family, I hope. Then I'll die, and wake up in this hammock with the moonlight playing on the opposite wall and the A/C humming . . .

Now I dream that Jake the dog starts to bark, and he doesn't stop, a high-pitched, frantic barking. I hear Polly's door slam and hear her tell Jake to shut up, but he doesn't and then I hear Polly screaming, calling upon the Deity, which she rarely does in real life. A door slams again. A honeyguide darts across the yard in that dipping way they have, and I hear, or think I hear, the *purr, purr WHIT* of its song. Or perhaps another sort of bird. It doesn't matter here in dreamland.

Now my back hurts, just as if this were real. I want to get up, and I do get up. I mean, why not? I dress with care, not forgetting my undies, in full Dolores rig, a long-sleeved aqua T-shirt with gay balloons in bright felt appliquéd to its chest, and a midlength skirt in a bad cobalt blue: polyester, naturally. I take pains with my hair, to squeeze the last increment of ugly out of my turd-colored locks. I put on my awful glasses and step out on my landing to see what the fuss is about. Now I hear sirens.

I can see it quite clearly from here, on a big sheet of newspaper, right under our mango tree. It's his way of telling me he knows where I am in real life. If there is such a thing as real life, I might be back in it now. Too soon to tell. How would I know?

TWENTY-THREE

10/31 Lagos–Bamako

Writing this on the plane, a charter. Personas non grata the two of us. My persona grated away, nothing left, really. Reaching inside, trying to comprehend. What did I do wrong? W. asleep, drugged. Can't look at him, can't imagine touching him again. But here he is, I sprang him. Went to see Musa. He screamed and stood very close. I could smell the alcohol on his breath, although he is Muslim. Gave him the money, thought he was going to demand something more personal. Would I have? For W.? Spared that.

Found W. lying in the corner of a fetid cell, on the floor. He was very glad to see me, pathetically glad, crying. W. not really a tough guy, not physically tough. Not like Greer. I saw they'd broken him completely, his fellow Africans. His face was swollen with bruises and cuts, he'd lost a couple of teeth, too. Later, back at the hotel, we had the Brit doctor who takes care of the oil people in to take a look, knocked him out with Dilaudid & the guy went over him. Fuckers had concentrated a good deal on his groin, as they always do.

Want my daddy, want Greer to be my daddy. This can't be over, won't let it.

Pilot just came back to say we have clearance. We're going to Mali. Berne thinks that's where we need to pick up the trace of the Olo, if there ever were any. I thought about just going home, but I want *something* to come out of this disaster. W. doesn't express an opinion. So I will look. We're taxiing. The plane is shaking so th

11/2 Bamako, Mali

Hotel de l'Amitié, the best in town, eighty bucks a night, I took a suite. Have arranged for an English-speaking doc, Dr Rawtif, a Lebanese, to see W. He still looks pretty bad, but Rawtif says there are no breaks or internal injuries. The genital swelling has decreased, too. They were careful, it seems. I told him and the hotel staff that he was in a car wreck. No one believes this, but they are kind people.

11/11 Bamako

He left the suite for the first time today. Shaky on his legs. Still won't talk about it. We had dinner in the hotel dining room. The place is modern four-star, you could be anywhere provincial, Hamburg, Toulon. Lots of Germans and French, a few Americans, mainly businesspeople and rich tourists. November is the best month here, the height of what passes for a tourist season in Mali. The rains are just over and it is as cool as it ever gets. We got the usual looks.

I left him this afternoon to visit the contact Greer gave me at the Musée National, a Dr Traore, asked him about the Olo, got funny look. We spoke about old Tour de Montaille. According to him a charlatan imperialist. Made up stories about witchcraft, human sacrifice, to denigrate Africans, justify *la mission civilisatrice*. Conversation flagged. Asked him if I could make a financial contribution to the museum. Conversation cranked up again. Dr Traore had spent a year at Chicago, so we had something in common. I wrote a check, got the run of the archives. He showed me around, the usual long termite-ridden wooden racks of crumbling papers, covered in red-ocher dust. Oddly enough, they have not computerized the catalog at the Musée National du Mali. I wrapped a bandanna around my face and poked around aimlessly for a couple of hours. An incompletely cataloged collection where I will spend rest of my life, manless dried-up stick of a spinster. No, divorcée. *Annulée?* Find I am more interested in my career now that my marriage has collapsed. If it has. He is quiet now, docile. It is almost worse than when he was being monstrous. Returned to the hotel to find him out cold. Dr Rawtif has a free hand with the downers.

11/8 Bamako

A little scene in the lobby today. W. was just standing there & a tourist came up to him and told him to take his bags out, waving some currency. W. walked away & the guy came after him and grabbed him and W. punched him in the nose. Remarkable, since he is so uncoordinated. I saw it, too. W. grinned, for the first time in months, it seems like. Both of us in a good mood all day behind it. We went to the Grand Marché after that and had lunch, we talked, joked, almost like we used to be. That's a big 'almost.' Can hardly recall how we used to be. Maybe all a fantasy anyway. Romance = hallucination, M. used to say.

Bamako is a lot nicer than Lagos, there's a lively buzz, a friendliness, and I have not seen evidence of the nastier sorts of crime. Fell in with an American nurse, a nun actually, Dolores something. Funny bird. She spends most of her time in the bush giving inoculations and other pediatric care. She gets around in a pirogue when she goes upriver and by moped otherwise. Asked her about Bambara lessons, which I'll need, and she gave me some names.

11/10 Bamako

We have to leave the hotel because of W.'s dust-up. I asked him where he'd like to stay and he said anywhere he doesn't have to see tourists. Talked to Dolores, later. She suggests living on the river.

11/15 Bamako

Writing this looking out at the brown Niger, from the deck of our houseboat. You can really get anything you need on the water, from the floating market, including black hashish. We both smoke a good deal. It makes things easier, and he says it helps him write. I wouldn't know, he doesn't read things to me anymore. No sex, I don't want it, he doesn't offer. We haven't spoken about Lagos.

Dull days these, in the dust of the archives, will give it another month, then take a little cruise, maybe upriver to Djenné to see the mosque, the largest mud structure in the world, they say. The kind of thing poor Mali *would* be distinguished for.

11/20 Bamako

A tiny discovery today, the journal of a Salesian father who worked at a leprosarium here in the late 19th. Crumbled,

full of wormholes, but still legible. He mentions Tour de
Montaille, who stopped by for a cure, an officer of good
family, in the last stages of exhaustion, with fever, says
Fr Camille, if I am translating correctly, with tales of
monstrous occurrences among the natives of the northern
interior, *un gens très dépravé qui s'appelle des Oleau.* This
is, as far as I know, the only independent mention of the
Olo anywhere. (Tour de Montaille blowing smoke at the
priest? fever delirium?) The leper hospital was located
near the present town of Mdina, about 120 km northwest
of here. The hospital no longer exists, according to the
French embassy, closed in 1921.

Shopped for Xmas presents in the Petit Marché later.
Found a remarkable pistol for Dad, in prime condition, an
1896 Mauser nine mm, with the famous red nine stamped
on the handle, and an antique amber necklace for Mary.
For Dieter, an album of old studio photographs from the
French days, and a terrific market painting for Josey.
Didn't get anything for W., yet. Maybe a silver hash pipe,
he might wear out the one he's got before the holidays.
Shipped all of it off to Sionnet. Thought about Christmas
there, got a little homesick. Nothing for Mom either, not
that it matters, she'll hate whatever I buy. Doe stubborn-
ness, not ever to give up on people. Got it from Dad. May
explain why I am still with W. So I will keep looking.

11/23 Bamako

On a roll now, sometimes it happens that way, M. always
used to say, one discovery leads to another. In one of the
street markets, shopping for Mom. Spotted a small
leopard mask, ivory, heavily incised, with the eyes made of
some greenish stone – looked just like her, the expression.

It turned out to be a Mande article, and the shopwoman was knowledgeable about its provenance. While she was wrapping it in newspaper, I looked around the place. The usual mix of textiles, jewelry, fetishes, except that she seemed to have a wider range than the usual market joint, and better taste. It was just sitting there, sticking out of a clay pot that stood on the head of a big drum, looking very old, yellowed like ivory, with shallow geometrical inscriptions on it. It had a hole drilled in one end.

Trembling when I brought it up to the proprietor. Turtleshell, she said, Fula from upriver. I asked her where she got it. A trader. Name? She looked doubtful. I flashed money. A man named Bonbacar Togola, a trader and hunter. Where could he be found? In *Mdina*, she said, and I saw stars. I bought the little thing without even the pretence of bargaining and walked out, with the leopard mask, too. My mother's gift, that had got me into the place to make this spectacular find. In the street I checked it out again. Good I took physical anthro. Saw that it really *was* the sternum of a neonate human, decorated and drilled for hanging in the house of a witch. Tour de Montaille had described just such a house, and the hanging racks of such objects (*idubde*) & also the rituals that produced them. I'm holding an actual Olo artifact! Thanks, Mom!

TWENTY-FOUR

They seemed to be in a park bordered by poplars in full leaf, through the trunks of which shone dappled lawns. The road ended in a broad apron of tan gravel, washed golden in pools by shafts of sun. They parked and climbed stone stairs to a terrace, and there was the house, Sionnet. It was long and rambling and many-gabled, a Queen Anne fantasy in rose brick and tan stucco, its gray slate roofing pierced by dozens of brick chimneys. There was a large white wooden barn off to the right, and through some trees they could see the glitter of a greenhouse, and beyond that the sheen of the Sound. Seabirds shrieked above, and they heard the sound of a mower in the distance.

Paz and Barlow walked to the front door, past a flagpole from which the Stars and Stripes crackled in the breeze. The terrace was nearly as large as a football field and formal in design, with neat, bright flower beds, and lozenges of lawn cut by graveled paths. A group of workmen in khaki were doing some repairs on the stone balustrade that enclosed it. The front door was iron-bound, thick-planked dark wood, pierced by a small diamond window.

Paz pulled the bell. The door opened – a young woman, rounded, pretty, with pale blond hair done up in a bun, her face pink and damp from some distant kitchen. She wore a white uniform and a pin-striped apron over it. Paz goggled; he had never seen a white servant before, except in movies depicting foreign nations or earlier ages. Barlow displayed his shield.

'Miss, we're police officers. From Miami, Florida? We'd like to see Mr John Francis Doe.'

She said, calmly, as if police visits were routine at Sionnet, 'Oh, uh-huh, Mr D. said you'd be by. He's over there, you must have walked right past him.' Here she pointed at the work crew at the balustrade. 'He's the tall one in the Yankees ball cap.'

The four men were replacing a copper gutter that ran along the pedestal of the balustrade. Doe seemed to know what he was doing, as did the three men – all young, two white kids and one who might have been Latino. Doe stood up and looked the detectives over. He looked a little longer at Paz than at Barlow, and Paz knew why. Barlow made the introductions and Doe shook their hands, saying, 'Jack Doe.'

The man was taller than either of them by a good few inches, late fifties, with a leathery, bony face and a jutting square chin, his skin burned a few shades darker than the bricks of his home. He had sad, deep-set eyes the color of Coke bottles. 'Let's go sit out back,' he said.

Doe led them through a breezeway, across a pebbled courtyard, past a white wooden gate, and out to the rear of the house. Below them there was another terrace with a long green swimming pool on it, and beyond that, a lawn that sloped down to a two-story white boathouse and a dock. Doe flung his long frame down in an iron lounge chair covered in faded green canvas and motioned the others to similar seats around a white metal table, under a patched dun canvas umbrella. He offered them iced tea. When they accepted he pressed a button set into a patinaed brass plate cemented into the wall behind him. Paz thought about that, just a detail, what sort of person you had to be to have a buzzer for calling servants set in an old brass plate cemented into a stone wall on your terrace overlooking your pool.

A man came out through French doors. He was older than Doe, silver haired, and he wore a tan apron over navy blue trousers, a white shirt, and a striped tie. Again, Paz had the peculiar sense that he had fallen out of regular life. A butler was going to bring him iced tea. This soon arrived on a silver tray, in tall, sweating glasses, which Paz was certain were never used for anything but iced tea. There was a long silver spoon in each glass, and a straw made out of glass, and there was a fat round of lemon stuck on the lip of the glass, as in advertisement illustrations. The tea was strong and aromatic.

They exchanged small talk – the nice weather, the pleasant temperature, Florida, the fishing in the Keys. Both Barlow and Doe had been bonefishing down there. The cops studied Doe and he seemed to study them. Barlow said, 'This is a fine place you got here, Mr Doe. I take it your people have been here a good while.'

'Yes, since 1665. On the land, that is. This house dates from 1889. Before that, there was a wooden structure from 1732, which burned. That barn you can see from the front of the house is pre-Revolutionary, 1748. I keep my car collection in it.'

'My, my,' said Barlow. 'And you and your missus live here all by yourselves?'

A pause, long enough for one intake of breath and an exhalation. 'No, my wife is unwell. She lives in a care facility in King's Park, not far from here. So I'm on my own, except for the help, of course. They're all students. We put them through school, any college they can get into, graduate school, whatever they want, and in return they put in some time here. Except for Rudolf, who brought the tea, and Nora, who was my children's nurse and has a room here. And, of course, when I go, the state'll get the whole shebang. A museum, I guess. And that'll be that.'

'End of an era,' said Paz. Doe nodded politely, and Paz felt like a jerk. After a brief silence, Barlow said, 'Mr Doe, as we told you on the phone, we've had some trouble down our way, and the FBI believes that the fella who killed our victims is the same man who murdered your daughter Mary. So, painful as it must be to you, we'd really like to hear anything you can tell us about the circumstances surrounding your daughter's death.'

Doe rubbed a big gnarled hand across his face. Paz noted that the fingernails were cracked and dirty. It was not what he had thought a rich man's hand ought to look like.

'We all left for the car show in Port Jefferson just after lunch,' Doe began, 'me and my two sons-in-law, Witt and Dieter.' He had a deep, soft voice and Paz had to strain to hear him over the hiss of the breeze and the gulls' calls. 'The girls didn't want to go – I mean Jane didn't; Mary and Lily – my wife, I mean – never were much interested in the cars. Jane was – she used to help me fix them when she was a kid. Anyway, we got there around ten of two. There was a Pierce-Arrow they were showing I wanted to take a look at, a 1923 Series 33 with the Demorest body and the 414-cubic-inch six. A heck of a car, all custom made. It was blue . . .'

Here he stopped and shook himself slightly and a little light that had started up in his eyes faded out. 'So, we were there for, oh, maybe four hours, for the auction, and I got the Pierce. Never actually took delivery on it. I kind of gave up on the cars, after. We got back around five. Jane was right here, right in this chair here, sleeping, with a book on her lap. Dieter went up to their room to check on Mary, and we heard him yell. And I called the police.'

Paz said, 'So you all, you three men, were all together all the time at this show? Neither of you were out of the sight of the others for the whole four hours?'

Doe sighed. 'Yes, they asked me that. I guess you have to ask questions like that. It's part of your job. And I know people do terrible things in their families. Lizzie Borden and all. So . . . it was a big lot, there at the show, and we wandered around a good deal. Dieter was taking pictures. Were they with me every minute? I can't swear to that. So it's remotely possible that Dieter could have slipped off, driven back, done it, and come back to the car show. Or I could have, for that matter, although I talked to enough people who knew me to give myself an alibi.'

'What about your other son-in-law – Mr Moore?' asked Paz.

'Oh, Witt didn't drive. Didn't even have a license. Jane tried to teach him a couple of times, but it just didn't take. It was hard enough showing him how to ride a bike. But, you know, that's just so far-fetched . . .'

Barlow said, 'We know that, Mr Doe. Like you said,

it's part of our job. Where is Mr Von Schley now, do you know?'

'Back in Germany. Berlin. We keep in touch. A nice kid, really. I hate to say it, but I was surprised he was so decent, the people Mary used to pal around with. Eurotrash, I think they call them, and being so pretty and going into modeling at such a young age, she had a lot of temptation to have the kind of life I wasn't comfortable with. And we thought she kind of settled down, with the baby coming and all.' A long pause here. 'Witt keeps in touch, too. He's in New York.'

No he's not, thought Paz, and said, 'Mr Doe – another hard question. We've heard there was . . . well, tension between your daughters, and we've heard that your elder daughter was, maybe, not completely in her right state of mind, that she had a history of . . . say, imbalance, an unhealthy interest in cults and black magic. It's probably no secret that people in the local police think it's possible that, well, that she was involved in Mary's death. Do you think there's anything to that?'

Doc turned his glass-green gaze onto Paz, and they stared into each other's eyes for what seemed like a very long time. Paz kept his own eyes steady, as a cop must, but he grew increasingly uneasy. Doe's look was far from hostile; more like curiosity, but he seemed to be sucking out of his inspection more than Paz was giving, was assessing various hidey-holes in Paz's highly compartmentalized soul, and not liking much what he found there. Paz's mother, of course, did this all the time. Barlow broke in then, or, Paz imagined, they might have been there until the sun sank.

'Sir, we'd really appreciate anything you could tell

us. I have to say there are some mighty scared folks down there right now, and the only thing we really got to go on now is that this perpetrator was very likely connected in some way to your family. And I personally got no doubt in my mind that if we don't catch him real quick some other poor girl's gonna end up like your Mary.'

Doe seemed to sag in his chair; he closed his eyes and let out a long, long breath. They waited, and watched him suffer. It was perfectly pure suffering, uninterpreted by words or relieved by cries. 'You have to understand, Jane almost died in Africa,' Doe said. 'When my son, I should say my stepson, Josiah Mount, found her in that hospital in Bamako, she weighed ninety-seven pounds. She was covered with sores, and she couldn't, or wouldn't, talk. Just made these cat sounds. It was the scariest thing I ever heard. I was sure we'd lose her. In any case, we got her into a clinic in the city that specializes in liver diseases; this was at New York Hospital, because we all thought that's what it was – hepatitis. She was yellow as a canary when she got here, from jaundice, we thought.'

'And was it hepatitis?'

'It was not. The tests for hep A, B, and C were all negative. Her liver had shut down pretty good, but there was no what-d'y'-call-it, no pathogenic agent, not that they could find. No cancer either. I sat with her, sometimes all day long, and Josey did, too. My wife doesn't much care for hospitals. And after a while she started in talking, not talking to me, mind you, just sort of babbling, sometimes in other languages, too. What I could make out of it, well . . .' Here he seemed to choose his words with some care. 'It was all about magic, black magic, I guess, and a kind of war that they were fighting in this native tribe she was visiting, a guy named Oo-looney, she was on his side, against some people named Doo-rack and Mundeli and there were a lot of other funny names, but those came up most. And . . . well, there was one part where they, this guy Doo-rack sacrificed a pregnant woman, and ate parts of her and the baby, and Jane couldn't stop it, and somehow, this sacrifice gave the bad guy some kind of power over her. And the good guy, Oo-looney, couldn't help her for some reason. That's a summary of what went on for the eighteen weeks she was more or less out of it. It didn't make much sense to me then, and when Witt came back she seemed not to babble as much. And that's also when she started to get better. The liver necrosis vanished, her color came back, and she started to put on weight.' He paused. 'Of course, the part about the sacrifice . . . I remembered that when the thing happened with Mary.'

'Did you tell the police about that at the time, sir?' asked Paz.

'I did not. It was just one of a lot of details that she was babbling. By the time I thought of it, I mean, by the time the autopsy told us what was really done to Mary, Jane was gone, and why bring it up then?'

'Just a moment, Mr Doe,' said Barlow, breaking in, to Paz's annoyance, 'her husband didn't come back from Africa with her?'

'No, he was still out with the natives when she came back to Bamako. Apparently, it's a very isolated village. Josey had people try to locate him, spent a good deal of money there, but they never did. Then he just walked into the hospital one day.'

'And what was your daughter's reaction to her husband?' Paz asked.

'Well, as I say, she started to get better. I can tell you, I was glad to have some relief. But you mean on a personal level. I don't know. I liked Witt, I always did. He's funny, doesn't take himself too seriously. A tremendously talented fellow, too, and Jane seemed to love him. That's all I was interested in. My children both more or less decided what they were going to do with their lives with no help from me, I have to say. But there was . . . I won't say something was wrong, maybe hollow, or missing, is the right word. I mean before. I hope this won't sound narrow, but he hadn't any faith. Well, that's common enough nowadays, I mean the lack of actual religion, but most irreligious people set up something else they can believe in – their families, say, or the environment, or justice; or money, for that matter, that's fairly popular, I believe. But Witt didn't seem to have anything like that, and it was like he had no . . . bottom, and all the verbal fireworks seemed to me to be filling that hole. Anyway, when he got back from Africa, he seemed steadier, more sober. I thought maybe he had had an experience, some epiphany, to use an old-fashioned word, but he never said, and, of course, you can't just ask a man. But I've gotten off the track – you wanted to know about Jane and Mary. I'm sorry, I don't talk much about these things anymore.'

'That's all right, sir,' said Barlow, 'you just take your time.'

'They were not close, let me start by saying that. It would've been hard to pick sisters more different. Mary was close to her mother, Jane was my kid. Families often break out that way. Jane was like me, also, in that she kept it all pretty close, a private person, not demonstrative. Mary was, let's say, operatic. Like her mother. When she was down, the whole house knew it, and when she was up, she lit the place like a floodlight. And, also, I guess you know, she was fantastically beautiful, from an early age, and she found that she could use that to get her way. She kind of ruled the roost, if you want to know.'

'And Jane resented it?' asked Paz.

Doe thought for a few moments. 'You know, I can't really say that she did. Maybe my stepson would know about that. He was sort of in the middle, and Jane and he were like that' – here he held the first two fingers of his right hand up, closely touching – 'all while they were growing up. We sent the girls to different schools, though, because Jane kind of just faded into the wallpaper when Mary was around. But resentment? No. Jane was always trying to get closer to Mary, be a real sister. She was the one who tried to keep in touch, even when she was traveling. Letters and photos and all. I don't think Mary ever wrote a letter in her life. But what you really want to know is, did Jane hate Mary enough to kill her? Was she jealous enough? And believe me, I've lain in bed all night running it through my mind. Did it happen that way? Could I have done something? Was it our fault, the way they were raised? I have to say that I don't know. The Jane I knew, or thought I knew, I'd have no trouble saying, no, never. But . . . her profession, the places she's been, the things she's seen . . . maybe something was released from a dark place. We've all got those dark places. I guess you know that in your business better than I do.'

'Do you think she killed herself?' asked Paz, hearing

the brutality in his tone, not caring. 'Was there a note?' Again, that long green look. Doe said, 'The explosion had to be intentional. Jane was a careful sailor and *Kite* was a safe boat. I can't think of another explanation for what happened.' The direct answer finessed; the man seemed practiced at such avoidances. He looked out over the descending lawn, the lonely unused pool, the boathouse, and the empty dock. The lowering sun found a break in the cloud it had paused behind and sent an oblique shaft across the scene, lighting it like a stage set in a play about the acme of domestic felicity. It was stunning enough to distract all three of them. Barlow said, 'My, my!'

Doe smiled at him. 'Yes, it's lovely this time of day, and this time of year. Sometimes I think it should be covered with ashes, all the buildings burned, so I could sit on it scraping myself with a potsherd. But,' he added after another sigh, 'I expect God has spared me for some purpose. I keep listening.' There seemed nothing to say to that and so they sat for a while watching the shadows play. Then Doe got to his feet and said, 'Well, would you like to take a look around? Show you the place, and where it happened and all?'

'That would be real kind of you, sir,' said Barlow, and they followed him, first down to the dock and the boat-house, and they saw that the little apartment above it was fitted up as a studio, and learned that DeWitt Moore had used it as a study.

'You don't have a boat now?' Paz asked.

'No,' said Doe curtly, and said something else in an undertone.

'Pardon?'

'Nothing,' said Doe. 'Let's get up to the house. I

guess you're not much interested in gardens and the like.'

Nor was there much of interest, in a forensic sense, in the house. The library was a library, the living room a living room, the furnishings were what one would expect of a wealthy family with traditional tastes, who had absolutely no need to impress anyone. There were more religious pictures than might be the case in other stately homes, and one crucifix that was probably not just for decoration, Paz thought. He was surprised at the general shabbiness of things, quite different from the equipage of the Vargas family. The upstairs bedroom in which Mary Doe had died was stripped, the bare floor and oyster walls reflecting the afternoon light.

They left by a side exit and went into the old barn. When Doe switched the lights on, Paz could not keep back a gasp. The cars were lined up in two rows, gleaming in heraldic colors and mirroring chrome, 1922 and 1948 Cadillacs, a 1927 Hupmobile, several Packards from various eras, a Cord, a classic Mustang, the 1956 Chevy Bel Aire ragtop – Detroit iron in all its glory.

Paz had a thought. 'Did you take one of these cars the day of the murder?'

'Why, yes, we did. That one.' Doe pointed to the 1948 Cadillac, a black convertible. 'Why do you ask?'

'This may sound strange, but I wonder if you'd indulge me. Could you take it out? Let the three of us go for a drive. Just up to the road and back. The reason is, it might jog something, in your memory, some observation about that day. It might be helpful.' Barlow gave his partner a sharp look, but Paz ignored it.

'Sure,' said Doe, 'I don't see why not. I have to run them all up once a month or so anyway.'

'Who was sitting where?' Paz asked. 'I mean on the day?'

'Witt was in the back, Dieter up front with me.'

Paz climbed into the backseat and settled into the soft plush. Barlow got in the shotgun seat and Doe started the car and drove it out into the sun. Paz leaned forward. 'Okay, Mr Doe, say it's that day now, what's everyone doing? What's going on?'

Doe thought for a moment. 'Well, let's see: Dieter was fiddling with his camera, screwing a sun hood on his Hasselblad. It was a bright day. There's an old darkroom in the house, hadn't been used since my dad was a kid, and we were talking about setting it up again, so he could make prints while he was here. Things like that. And then . . . we started talking about Berlin, he'd just been there, about all the building they were doing, and how he'd like to take some pictures of the new construction. His family's from around there. We talked about the baby, too, and when it would be old enough to travel and show it off to his family. And then we talked about family.'

They had reached the end of the drive. 'This far enough?' Doe's voice sounded tired for the first time.

Barlow said, 'That's fine, Mr Doe. Sorry to trouble you.'

Doe turned the car around and they drove back. Paz said, 'Okay, now you're coming back. What's going on, now?'

'We're talking about the car show . . . no, that was before. Now we're talking about, hm, American football, I think. It was football season and we were going to catch the second half of the Pitt–Navy game. I was explaining the rules to Dieter. We talked about the differences between that and soccer and what it said about the American and European characters.'

'Did Witt have anything to add to the conversation?'

A long pause. 'I'd have to say no. Why do you ask?'

'Do you recall anything he did during the trip, anything he said, any conversation you were in with him?'

Doe did not respond immediately but steered the car to its slot in the barn and shut off the engine. They all got out. 'Now that you mention it, I guess I can't. He must have been quiet that day. But he often sank into quiet moods. He was a writer, and I guess they're like that. We used to kid him about it, as a matter of fact. Are you trying to suggest that somehow he wasn't in the car with us? Because if you are, that's just nonsense. I'd take my oath on it, he was there all the time.'

'But he didn't do or say anything you remember, even though you remember a lot of what your other son-in-law did and said?'

A darkness had appeared on Doe's cheekbones. 'Detective, I'm bereaved, but I'm not crazy!'

Barlow said, 'Nobody's saying that, Mr Doe. We're just trying to get things straight.'

Paz walked out of the barn. He heard Barlow talking to Doe quietly, settling him, being the good cop. This went on for a lot longer than Paz thought it should. He leaned against the Taurus, lit a cigar, checked his watch. The place was starting to get on his nerves. Paz was not normally an envious man. He thought himself as good as or better than most of the people with whom he came in daily contact; he did not lust after money or fame; he had (until recently) sufficient success with women. Now, however, as he looked around the estate, he felt himself unbearably oppressed by the deep roots it implied. Generations had called this home, portraits of ancestors still lined the stairway walls and hung over the numerous hearths, all portraits (and didn't it show in their faces!) of securely racinated folk. God's in His heaven, and the Does are in Sionnet, world without end. Not like Paz the mongrel bastard. Since envy is the one deadly sin that no American can ever admit to, he felt it instead as resentment and personal animus against Jack Doe. Doe was lying to protect his good name, lying to protect his daughter, assuming he was above the law, and what the hell was that goddamn cracker doing in there?

In the Taurus, Paz ruffled through his briefcase for something to read, and remembered the envelope he had picked up as he left the PD. It was from Maria Salazar, he found, a manuscript in a binder, clipped to a note in beautiful looping handwriting, black on cream-colored heavy paper with an engraved address on top. No yellow Post-its for Dr Salazar. The note said: 'Dear Detective Paz: You will recall that we discussed a certain paper that referenced Tour de Montaille and various African cult practices and that this might be relevant to your investigations. With the death of yet another woman, I felt some urgency in bringing the attached to your attention. Unfortunately, as I understand it, the author is deceased, but if I can be of any assistance whatever, do not hesitate to call upon me.'

He turned to the paper. His viscera contracted. It was entitled 'Psychotropic Drug Use Among the Olo Sorcerers of Mali,' and its author was J. C. Doe. He read on. Although it was a scholarly paper, Dr Doe used little jargon and eschewed the academic passive voice.

It was pure observation, told from both the inside and the outside. She had herself taken a number of the substances the Olo sorcerers used, and described their effects in some detail. The most remarkable section was one in which she recounted how an Olo sorcerer made himself invisible to her in broad daylight.

He was still reading some ten minutes later, when the goddamn cracker emerged blinking into the sun. He got into the car.

'What's that you're reading, Jimmy?'

'Oh, nothing much. A scientific paper. Guys in Africa making themselves invisible. Jane Doe wrote it.'

'You don't say? Well, right from the beginning I said you was going to be the expert on that end.'

Paz tossed the paper into the backseat, gunned the engine, scattering gravel, swerving, as if something nasty was on his tail. Barlow gave him a sharp look. Paz said, 'By the way, did you catch what he said down by the dock, when I asked him if he had a boat?'

'Yeah, he said, 'I'll go to sea no more.' '

'I'll go to sea no more? Why would he say that? The guy's loaded. He could buy a boat, any boat he wanted.'

'Why don't you turn around and go ask him?' replied Barlow. 'You might learn something.' This was one of the very many moments at which 'Fuck you, Barlow!' was the only response that came to Paz's mind, and since he couldn't say it, he compressed his lips and said it a number of times in his head.

Just before they got to the highway, Barlow said, 'Well, if you sit anymore on what you been sitting on, you're gonna have a heck of a sore fanny. Talk to your partner, son.'

Paz wrenched the wheel hard over and stomped the brake, so that they turned into the access road of a small business park. He threw the lever into P and reached into the backseat for his briefcase, from which he withdrew the murder case files they had been given by Agent Robinette. He yanked from the folder the photograph he had spent so much time studying and thrust it at Barlow. 'Nice picture,' said Barlow. 'My daddy wouldn't've liked it much, him being a big shot in the Florida Klan, but . . .'

'Oh, darn it, Cletis, the guy's in Miami! That's our guy!'

'You know this, do you?'

'The guy was here when Mary Doe got it. He was in Miami when our two cases got theirs.'

'You see him yourself?'

'No, but I checked with the Grove Theater management. He was definitely in Miami during the time of, in both our cases. I went to his show myself, as a matter of fact, and people were giving me the eye, waving, like I was a celebrity. What murder suspect do we know who I seem to resemble? The guy who killed Deandra Wallace, right? They thought I was him in the lobby. I didn't think anything about it then, but now it makes sense. In this show of his, he wears white makeup, so there's our white guy on a bike. Heck, I probably saw him on the stage when I went to his show the night Vargas was killed. He doesn't drive – remember what Robinette said, how extremely unusual that was? He's American, he's personable, a good talker, also just like Robinette said. Okay, the clincher? He's got the African witchcraft background, him and his wife. It's all in that paper, unless she was lying to her fellow scientists. And his old lady's probably still with him, she probably faked that suicide to take the heat off her husband. And your pal Doe is covering for her.'

'No, he's not.'

'You know that for a fact, huh?'

'He's an honest man.'

'Yeah, right! What were you guys doing in there, taking a polygraph?'

Barlow's face hardened. 'Jimmy, you're a good cop, but you got a cop's view of people. The man's suffered and it's made him stronger. It's increased his faith. You don't see that kind of faith much in the world today, and I never saw the beat of him, not personal like just now. I call myself a Christian, but I couldn't tie that fella's shoes. So he ain't no conspirator, and being that he ain't, how do you make it that your suspect did the crime if he was twenty miles or so away from the house all day? We used to call that an alibi.'

'I don't know how he did it,' Paz admitted, 'but Jane Does says she does, right in that paper. It's African plant chemicals, and it's also how he can get in and out of the crime scenes with no one noticing. He drugs them, he slips out of the car, does the crime, and then slips in when they come back and they think he's been there all the time. They can't recall anything he did, but they know he's been there.'

Barlow studied the photo. 'Well, yeah, he does favor you a little. You're prettier, though, if you want my opinion.'

Paz snatched the photo back and put it away. 'Go soak your head. It's the guy.'

Barlow looked at him with humor in his tin-colored eyes.

'I think you just might be right. I think that's the fella, too.'

Paz experienced a rush of relief. He wanted to grab Barlow and kiss him. 'Well, good,' he said, 'I thought I was going crazy there for a while.'

'Well, you got your bad points, but crazy ain't one of them. Proving it's going to be a whole 'nother story, though. I'll have to think on that for a while. Meanwhile, we're not getting any closer to him sitting here on this road.'

They drove back to La Guardia and flew uneventfully to Miami, arriving just after seven in the evening. Paz made some calls from their car en route from the airport and learned from the manager of the theater company that DeWitt Moore was staying at the Poinciana Suites, a low-rise stack of studios on Brickell. They went by there; he was out. They checked with the theater in the Grove; not around. So they went back to the PD, spoke to Mendés, told him that it was definitely the same guy did the New York murder and that they had some promising leads, but no real suspects, a strategic lie to avoid broaching the witch-doctor theory of the case. The detective chief did not press them, for he was up to his neck in what he considered a PR stunt, the housing and guarding of ready-to-pop women, 194 of them. The housing was in the Hotel Milano, a fourteen-story structure on Biscayne, that had been constructed somewhat too obviously with dope money and seized by the city as part of a narcotics bust. It had been vacant for months, while the city searched for someone who would run it as a hotel rather than a cash laundry, but it was still in reasonably good shape. Now the lights of the Milano blazed again, the air-conditioning was on, and cops from the whole city were engaged in moving women around. Paz thought it was a pretty impressive operation and that they were damned lucky to have the Milano; they might have had to use the Orange Bowl.

Barlow went home. Paz went home, too, but left at about eight-thirty and parked in front of the Poinciana. There he smoked several big, slow maduro cigars, watching the people come in and go out. Moore had not shown by midnight, and Paz figured the man was out doing witch doctor shit, maybe with faithful Jane by his side, and would be gone all night. Or maybe the cops had got even luckier and Moore was going to fall by the Milano, which was guarded by two dozen heavily armed police. Paz went home, where he changed into shorts, drank two Coronas, and skimmed through the Salazar book on Santería. The main thing he derived was that people at the ceremonies hallucinated that they had been possessed by the *orishas*. He could deal with that. Could someone make another person have a hallucination through some influence, a . . . he searched for a term . . . posthypnotic suggestion? Possibly. The phrase had a nice scientific ring to it, anyway. Something real, like 'myocardial infarct,' or 'piezoelectric ignition.' Putting Salazar aside, he turned to the Vierchau book that Nearing had given him. He read the introduction with growing discomfort. Now he could see what Nearing meant; this guy was off the reservation. Vierchau seemed to be saying that hallucination could be induced from a distance, that these Chenka sorcerers could make you see things that weren't there even if you were miles away. He read on, absorbed, disbelieving, becoming more and more restless.

The phone rang. Checking the caller ID, he saw it was his mother. He knew what she wanted, and he didn't feel like it. He left the apartment and drove down to the Miami River, where he kept his boat. His mother didn't know he owned a boat, and would not have approved of it if she did, not this boat. It was a twenty-two-foot plywood thing, hand-built by a local, painted aqua. It was rough inside, a couple of bunks with raw foam slabs, a cooler, a Coleman stove and lantern, plywood cabinets. It was messy inside and out, but the 115-horse Evinrude that powered it was new and spotless. Paz cranked it up, ran it downriver to the Bay, and raced it around in circles for a couple of hours, until he was sure the restaurant had closed down. He felt better than he had in days, and wondered, as he always did after these marine jaunts, why he didn't do it more often. Back home, he read Vierchau for a while and fell asleep in his white leather chair with the book on his chest.

He was awakened at 4:45 A.M., by Mendés.

'The fucker did it again,' said Mendés. Paz did not wonder which fucker and what he had done. He noticed, however, that the chief's voice was uncharacteristically shrill.

'Some woman didn't go in.'

'No, he did her right in the Milano. Get over here, now!' Click.

Paz hung up the phone, got to his feet, and rubbed his face. He was not dreaming.

They had the street blocked off in front of the Hotel Milano, and a dozen police vehicles of various sizes stuffed the access drive to the building. A helicopter flapped overhead, beaming its powerful light on nothing much, but looking good for the TV cameras. The media vans were being kept well away. Paz parked on Biscayne Boulevard, affixed his badge to the front of his jacket, grabbed his briefcase, and walked in.

The lobby was full of cops, some of them in SWAT team gear, in case the perp decided to stop cutting up women with a knife and started blasting away with an automatic weapon. There was a continuing tinny susurrus of radio voices, but the police were moving, Paz observed, with an uncharacteristic hesitancy. The faces of many of them showed fear, bafflement, a profound, nearly existential doubt, something that the faces of cops never showed, in his experience. He got directions to the murder scene and proceeded to room 416, passing a fourth-floor corridor packed with more cops, crime-scene people, wailing women in nightclothes, and social worker types trying to keep the hysteria under control. Mendés looked as if it were he and not (as Paz soon learned) one Alice Jennifer Powers, aged twenty-two, unmarried white female, who had just experienced an evisceration. Mendés was talking to a couple of patrol lieutenants, so Paz went into room 416, finding, as he expected, Barlow already there.

'Well, here we are again,' said Paz, looking at the meat on the bed, a chubby girl with short brown hair and skin that shone blue as skim milk. Like the others, she looked peaceful.

'Any ideas how our boy got in here?'

Barlow said, 'We grope for the wall like the blind, we grope as though we had no eyes; we stumble in noonday as in the night; we are in desolate places, as dead men. Isaiah 59:10. That's what we got to find out, Jimmy. All

the fellas that were on duty tonight in the lobby, and the
fella who was on this floor, they got them all down in the
coffee shop. The chief wants us to interview them indi-
vidually. There's a little manager's office down there you
can use. I think I can handle the scene by myself.'

'Yeah, we're getting real good at it with all the practice. It looks just the same as the others, right?'

'Not quite,' said Barlow. 'He took the baby with him
this time. Also, as you can see, this here room is a
double. There was a woman sleeping right in the next
bed. That's how we knew. Woman got up to use the
bathroom around ten of three and found her roommate
like this. They got her under sedation.'

Which meant she would not be available for
questioning for some time. Paz thought that a small loss;
it was unlikely that she would be able to tell them any
more about the killer than Tanzi Franklin had.

There were four cops waiting in the coffee shop, a
sergeant named Mike Duval and three patrolpersons,
Bobby Ruiz, Dick Laxfelt, and Mercedes Aparicio. They
all looked up at Paz with an expectant air when he
came in, as if he could save them. Paz took the sergeant
first.

Duval had been on the force for eighteen years and
had a decent rep, which is why he had been given this
peculiar job. He knew how to give a report, too, and Paz
respected that, and let him speak.

'Two-twenty-five: I'm behind the hotel desk with
Aparicio, we're going over the watch list for the next
shift and I'm about to go check the foot posts, which I
did every hour, more or less on the half hour, but varying, just to keep 'em awake. I got a guy out at the service entrance, a guy out front – that was Laxfelt – and a

guy by the elevator on each floor. Ruiz was the one on four. So, I look up and there's this guy walking across the lobby toward the elevator bank, like he was a guest going to his room. I almost figured it was one of you guys, but he should've checked at the desk, and so I yelled at him, like, Hey, sir, where're you going? And he waved at me and mashed the button. The doors opened and he went in. Just like that.

'So, shit, I freaked, I got on the radio and alerted the floor posts we had an intruder, and called Laxfelt and asked him how the fuck he let this guy walk right by him, and he swore that there hadn't been anyone by. He's standing right at the front door, which is fucking made of glass, and I could see him standing there myself from the desk. He swears there was no guy. But we – me and Aparicio – we saw the guy. So I call for backup, I figure we'll search every room. Meanwhile, we see from the indicator there that the car's stopped at four, and I alert Ruiz, he's getting off on four, and Ruiz says, over the radio, I see him, I got him. Then nothing. I can't raise him. I get in the other elevator and go up to four. No Ruiz. So I'm shitting now. I hear the sirens. I take the car down to the lobby again. There's Lieutenant Posada with ten guys and more are coming up the drive, so I tell him what's happened, and we get set to search the whole hotel, every room, the service areas . . . we put two people on every exit. We search the rooms.' Here he took a deep breath. 'We searched all the rooms on four, including 416. I looked in them myself. All sleeping, real peaceful. Same in the rest of the place. By this time it's nearly four o'clock. That's when the fucking house phone rings and it's the woman in 416, screaming her head off.' Duval rubbed his big face and ran fingers through his hair. 'And you want to know what the guy looked like, right?'

'That might be helpful, Sarge.'

'Yeah, well, the thing is, I can't describe him. I looked right at him across a lobby, maybe twenty yards away, all the light in the world, and I can't tell you if he was black, white, yellow, tall, short, fat, thin, or wearing a fucking Santa Claus outfit. I got no fucking memory of it. Okay, I thought I was going crazy, but Aparicio's the same. It's a blank, like in a dream; one second you're there, you're balling some terrific piece or whatever, walking on Mars, and the next you're lying in bed and thinking, What the fuck . . . !'

'Okay, I got that – also, just to make you feel better, we have evidence that this guy's got access to all kinds of drugs, mind drugs – he could've sprayed something, who knows? What about Ruiz, what happened to him?'

'Oh, Ruiz!' Duval snorted. 'We found Ruiz in a utility closet about ten minutes after we found the girl. He looked like he was drunk or doped. Ruiz got a story too. I'll let you get it from him.'

Paz took Aparicio next, who confirmed her sergeant's story in every detail, and then Laxfelt, who was completely baffled by the night's events and mulish in his conviction that no one had come by him into the lobby. Ruiz was a thin, nervous kid, less than a year out of training. He had sweat beading on his forehead, and he chain-smoked Camel filters. Ruiz took up his story at the point when the elevator door opened.

'I was in a crouch, with my weapon out. The door opens and this guy steps out. So I drop him flat. He goes down, no problem, and I cuff him. I call the sarge on the radio and I tell him, I got the guy, he's cuffed.

I search his pockets and sure enough, I find this knife . . .'

'What kind of knife, Bobby?'

'One of those wood-carving knives, an X-Acto, with a red plastic handle, and like a long scalpel blade in it. I bag that. Then the sarge comes up the other elevator with Dick. And they take the guy away. And Lieutenant Kinsey's there, my shift loo, and he goes, great job and all, everyone's slapping me on the back. I mean I *remember* this. It happened. And the loo goes, Hey, take the rest of the shift off, it's all over. So I take my car back to the precinct, and change, and go home. I go to bed. And it's like I'm having a dream, like a nightmare, there's this smell, a sharp smell, and I'm in this dark place, cramped, like a coffin, but I'm standing up. And then . . . I realize, I'm not dreaming, I'm not in bed, I really am in a dark place, with this smell, like strong bleach. It was a maid's closet on the fourth floor. I walk out and there's cops all over the hallway and all of them looking at me, and Sergeant Duval goes, Where the fuck you been? My cuffs are still on my belt. The first thing I say is, You got the guy, right? You got the guy! And they look at me. And they tell me what went down.'

Ruiz put his face in his hands, saying, 'Ah shit! Ah, fuck it!' Dry sobs followed. Paz did his little talk about exotic drugs, but it did not seem to help. The perp had somehow stolen this kid's sense of reality, and it was a violation like the rape of a virgin, but of the mind not the body, an incurable wound.

Paz wound up the interview; Ruiz could not recall a face either, not a big surprise. Paz walked out of the hotel to get some air, but what air there was was full of fumes from the vehicles, both police and press. The copter chattered uselessly above. He sat down on a stone bench and looked through his notes as the sunrise lightened the horizon over the sea, the dawn of a day that no one in the Miami PD was anticipating with joy. He felt his phone ring.

'Where's your car?'

Paz told him. 'What's up, Cletis?'

'Call just came over TAC One. They found the baby.'

'Where at?'

He gave an address. 'I'll meet you at the car.'

Ten minutes later, they pulled up in front of a foliage-clotted front yard on Hibiscus, behind which stood a two-story flat-roofed house built in the old Grove style, crumbling tan stucco over Dade County pine. A patrol car was parked there, its bubble-gum lights making weird patterns against the overhanging trees. As they left their car, an ambo from Jackson arrived, adding its own crimson flickerings to the scene. The young patrol-man looked pale as he led them back to the yard.

The baby, a female, was lying in the center of several blood-soaked sheets of the *Miami Herald*, yesterday's edition, the sports pages. The top of its skull was placed neatly to one side, just above the shoulder, and the excised brain was on the other side. Early flies had taken an interest and there was at least one palmetto bug rooting around in the empty skull. Barlow spoke gently to the patrolman and sent him back to secure the street entrance to the yard. The crime-scene people arrived. Shortly thereafter, Echiverra from the M.E. showed up.

Barlow said, 'The owner and her family's in the house. I'll go talk to them. Woman named Dolores Tuoey lives in the garage apartment with her kid. Why don't you take charge out here, talk to the garage lady, see if anything strikes you funny.'

'Like what, a clue?' snapped Paz.

'Hey, this is a break for us here, son,' said Barlow.

'How do you figure that? Because he didn't kill the mayor too?'

'No, because he changed a successful pattern. He had us foxed six ways to Sunday the way he was going. We're stumped, right? So why'd he change it? Why move the baby? Why'd he leave it here, of all places, and not a Dumpster or the bay? Think about it.' He walked away. Paz spoke to the crime-scene captain and to Echiverra, both of whom looked tense and frightened. There was no graveyard humor.

Paz walked around the yard, trying to keep his vision clear. The back and the north side of the yard were blocked off by high hedges of croton, allamander, and hibiscus, whose pink flowers were just responding to the oncoming day. Besides the large mango, heavy with fruit, a guava, a key lime, and a lemon tree also stood in the yard, perfuming the neighboring air. The lawn beneath them was rough and patchy but neatly clipped.

A stir among the crime-scene people; they had found a liftable footprint on one of the patches of bare earth near the mango. Paz went and took a look. A nice print, the herringbone pattern of a good boat shoe. Paz showed polite interest, and strolled over to the garage that nearly closed off the third side of the yard.

Paz looked up at the garage apartment. For an instant he saw a face at the window, then nothing. He walked away and then back again, slowly. He was not looking for anything physical now; the crime-scene people would pick up all that sort of thing, like the footprint, for whatever good it would do. He was thinking about what Barlow had just said. This was not a random dump. This was a message, important enough to the perp for him to risk carrying absolute for-sure death-penalty evidence around with him (on a bicycle!) between the Milano and Coconut Grove, with every cop in the city having no other thought but to grab his ass. He snapped another look at the window of the garage apartment. Again, nothing.

Paz felt strange now. People were moving around him, talking, doing their technical tasks, but he felt as if they were wraiths, that he was the only real person in the yard. The colors of the flowers, of the brightening sky seemed more vivid than usual; he looked up. The clouds overhead were boiling, as they are shown to do in horror movies. Then things moved back in the direction of bland normality, without quite arriving. There was something about this place, this instant; he searched for a word one of his women had used . . . nexus? It all came together here, in this scruffy yard, not just the case, but in a way he could not begin to explain, his whole life. He walked up the stairs to the garage apartment. He knocked on the door.

TWENTY-FIVE

A knock at my door. I am busy stashing my Mauser, my journal, and the jar of Olo witch sauce back in my box. It's funny that through all this, my absurd hegira, I have never thought about avoiding the police. Because I haven't done anything wrong, except maybe sink my father's boat, and use some bad paper. And kill Luz's mom, I always forget that one, because I can't feel it was very wrong to defend myself and Luz. Ifa cut her line and used me as his instrument. But clearly my husband wants the police involved with me, or he wouldn't have decorated Polly's garden with his latest victim. A test? Does he want to see if I will rat him out? Does it matter to him?

A brief check in the mirror to insure as much invisibility as I can muster. The blinds are drawn, the light in my kitchen is out, my spectacles are on, my pathetic bangs are in place. I open the door, and my knees almost fail to hold me up. I must clutch at the doorpost. For an instant, I think I'm back in a dream, that my husband is standing in front of me with a police badge stuck, as a little joke, in the pocket of his sports jacket. He says, 'Detective Paz, ma'am, Miami PD. Could I . . .' His face registers concern and he adds, 'Excuse me, are you all right?'

But an instant later I see that it isn't him. The structure of the face is different, with higher cheekbones and a lower hairline; he's solider, too, with more muscle in the shoulders and neck; his eyes are yellow-brown, not hazel-gray, like Witt's. And that jacket, no, Witt didn't care about nice clothes, this all flashed through my mind while some *ogga* in there yells, 'Asshole! He could show up in the dress uniform of the Grenadier fucking Guards – it's a dream!'

But I back away and let him in, saying, 'No, it's . . . in the yard . . . horrible. Will they . . . take it away soon? I don't want my daughter . . .'

I sit in one of my two chairs. He's staring at me. 'Yes, ma'am, the M.E.'s here now. It'll all be gone in ten minutes or so.' He sits across the table. He brings out a notebook and mechanical pencil. I drop my head and work on getting my *ki* out of my throat and down where it belongs.

'You're, um, Dolores Tuoey?' I confess that I am. I am finding it hard to meet his eyes. 'Ms Tuoey,' he says, 'did you see or hear anything unusual last night, anything at all?'

'No, not really,' I say. 'Jake – that's Polly's dog – woke me up. Then I heard Polly come out, to shut him up. We have raccoons and possums and sometimes he barks at them, and I heard her yell, and I went out to see what it was. I'm sorry I can't help you more.'

'Okay, I assume you realize what you got out there in the yard . . .'

'Yes, it's a dead newborn. I used to be a nurse-midwife.'

'Really? I meant do you know who did it?'

'No! How could I . . .' Protesting too much here. I focus on the next breath. The next.

'I mean you know we're looking for a serial killer who attacks pregnant women. It's in all the papers and the TV?'

'Oh, right, of course. Yes. And this is one of his. Yes.'

'Right. Now, can you think of any reason why our perpetrator would choose this particular yard to leave this dead baby? A man, maybe. Anyone you know, anyone you've seen hanging around?'

I am forming a neutral answer when little pounding feet sound above, and on the ladder, and Luz jets into the room in her nightgown. We both look at her and she stops dead when she sees the detective, and runs to me and hides her face against my side. I put my faithless arm around her.

The detective says, 'This must be your daughter?'

'Yes. Luz, honey, say hi to Detective Paz.' More burrowing; a snatched peek. 'She's shy.'

'Yes. She's real pretty, though.' He looks from me to her. I can see him thinking about Gregor Mendel and his rules of heredity and I wish I had learned to do *chint'chotuné*, the thought spells that make people forget, or recall things that did not occur. No, I don't wish that. I wish I were far away with Luz.

He puts away his notebook, slides a business card across the table, and says, 'Here's my card, ma'am. I'll be by to check with you later. A lot of times we find that even though people don't recall things right after a shocking event, they'll come around in a couple of days, something will just pop into their heads. And if you do think of anything like that, please call me anytime, day or night. This guy, well, he seems to be very hard to catch. And he's going to do it again, unless we can stop him. Another woman, another baby, the families . . .'

I say, too quickly, 'I wish I could help, but really, I didn't see or hear anything.' Now I see something cold pass into his eyes. I can't look at him. He says, 'Forgive me for asking, but you said you were a nurse-midwife. Where was that? Where you practiced.'

'In the Boston area. And in Africa. In Mali. I've just been back two years or so.'

'I see. Africa, huh? That must have been exciting. So, I guess Luz was born in Africa. Her dad live here, too?'

'No, he died in Mali.' Stupid! Why am I talking so much? I push the chair back and stand. 'Excuse me, but I have to dress her and get her to nursery school and get myself to work, so if there's nothing else . . .'

He gets up, too, and smiles, an unpleasant cat sort of smile.

'We'll be in touch.' I let him out and I say, trained to politeness, 'Good-bye, Detective Paz,' and he says, 'So long, Jane,' as he pulls the door shut, not looking back, and I pretend I haven't heard him as my blood freezes.

I sit stunned for a while in the dim kitchen, until Luz brings me out of it with demands for breakfast, milk in the special glass with the Little Mermaid on it, and also a discussion about the day's outfit, and chatter about the Noah's ark play she is to be in at nursery school. Who was that man, Muffa? He was a policeman. What did he want? He was looking for a bad man and he wanted me to help him. What did the bad man do? He hurt someone. Who? I don't know, honey. Do you want your blue T-shirt or your purple? I can cope with this and breathe, just about. In fact, serving the tiny priestess my soul-daughter has become is probably the best thing I can do right at this moment, obsession being just the thing for keeping the demons at bay, as so many nuts have found over the years. What else can you do? So maybe that cop didn't say that, maybe that was just an ordinary hallucination, brought on by tension and lack of sleep. Yes. Certainly. He must have said 'So long, ma'am.' Okay, right: on with the day. I get Luz into her clothes and, after I have checked that the corpse is gone, we go out. There is crime-scene tape still up, and various technical people are floating around the yard, and my cop is standing there with another man, taller, with pale eyes and the face of a lynch-mob leader. As I walk to the car, their eyes follow me, and my cop is talking.

I have a big day today. Just like in dreamland, it is payday, my final day. At lunchtime, they even give a little party for me, and Mrs Waley gives her usual speech, we will all miss Dolores, and Lulu and Cleo come over from admin and hug me and I get a nice box of Helena Rubenstein make-up from them as a going-away present. And I do my duties meticulously while squeezing in a class A felony on what will likely be the very last medical records pickup run of my life. For on my stop at the pharmacy department, where of course they know me, and where I am, while not as invisible as my husband can be, still pretty invisible, I wait until no one is looking and lean through the hatch where the little plastic boxes are waiting and snatch up the one that goes to the fat clinic. I put it on my cart with the records and roll away, and while alone for a moment in the elevator I transfer fifty or so 10 mg generic dextroamphetamine caps to my cheap purse, a few from each vial, and drop the depleted tray off at the clinic. It is better in any case for dieters to avoid harsh drugs. Perhaps, like me, they might rely on terror to maintain a desirable and healthy slenderness.

Am I still dreaming? Are you? In one of the damp hallways of the hospital I come across a giant flying cockroach of the type people hereabouts call palmetto bugs. I examine it closely. I prod it with my foot and it scuttles away. It's big enough, but it doesn't talk to me, or bring ten thousand friends to the party, or fly into my mouth. It is just a dear, cuddly, regular cockroach. So I am probably back in the dream we have all agreed is life.

After work, I go down to the credit union office in the basement of my building, cash my terminal check, close out my account, and walk out with about thirteen hundred dollars. Feeling a little heavy-lidded and logy now, I take a dex and exit into the steam bath of late afternoon. I will take the Buick to the transmission place and cab back. In a while, I am striding down the street, the speed is starting to kick in, I am feeling the tinglies, and that feeling of anticipation you get, something big is about to happen and I'm ready for it. What happens is that one of the louts who hang out at the corner store I have to pass twice a day decides to mug me.

It must have been something about the way I was walking, or maybe he just smelled the money and the dope. It would have been the score of a lifetime: I knock over this ugly white bitch, man, and she got near a grand and a half and a load of speed. I notice him peel off the knot of cronies and follow me. He is a good-sized, shoe-polish-brown kid, maybe sixteen, a little over six feet and lean, with the usual look of babyish meanness on his face. There is a vacant lot up ahead, and that's where he will trot up behind me, throw a yoke around my neck with his left arm, extract my purse with his right, drag me into the weeds, hit me in the face a couple of times, and walk off.

What actually happens is that when his arm reaches around my neck I stoop a little and put both my hands around his wrist and whirl to my left on my left foot and step out, conserving his forward motion and adding to it, and now I have his wrist and his elbow up high, dancing in a big half circle across the pavement, because you always move circlewise in aikido. I apply some leverage so that his upper body overbalances and I run his face into the base of a phone pole, not too hard. *Oshi-taoshi;* I've done it a thousand times, but only this once in real life.

Then suddenly I'm pushed away and a man is kneeling on the back of my dancing partner and attaching handcuffs to his wrists. I see that it is Detective Paz. I start to walk away, but he shouts at me and leaves the boy and comes up and grabs my arm. I look pointedly at his grip and he lets go. He is breathing a little hard, but he is not sweating and his beautiful jacket, shirt, and tie are unrumpled. He says, trying a smile, 'You almost got mugged. You can't just leave.'

I stare at him through my tinted spectacles. I say, 'I don't know what you're talking about.'

'That guy, the homey. He was trying to mug you. You would've been in trouble if I hadn't come along.'

I give him a look. He shrugs off the little lie with a grin. I say, 'You're mistaken, Detective. He tripped and fell. Now, if you'll excuse me, I have an appointment.' I take off before he can say anything else. Obviously, he has been following me. Terrific.

I drive down Flagler, past PETS, which seems to be

closed, and to my transmission guy, a few blocks west. I leave the car with him, and he promises three days, which means a week. Do I even need my car anymore? The notion of physical escape seems to have vanished, or at least escape by land. While I wait for whatever is going to happen, and still assuming that I am not still in dreamland, I can take Luz to school and shop on foot, or maybe I'll buy a secondhand bike and a bike seat. I use the pay phone to call a cab and stand out on the street to wait. The transmission guy seems to be staring at me in an odd way. I check my reflection in the plate glass of his window. There seems nothing wrong. I move toward the curb.

Next to the transmission place is one of those hole-in-the-wall cafes that consists only of a service hatch and a row of stools outside. These are occupied by an assortment of middle-aged men sipping from tiny cups. They are staring at me, too; their faces are full of vague aggression; their eyes are dark and hot. I direct my gaze across the street to where a group of people are waiting for a jitney. I cross the street. I could take the jitney east on Flagler, to where I can catch a Metro train to the Grove. This would save some money, but I am reluctant. The configuration of the group is profoundly menacing; I read threat in the way they are standing: two Latina women in tan servant's uniforms; a dark woman with shopping bags, with a little girl and an older boy in tow; a zombie; two thin Oriental guys in cook's whites speaking Cuban Spanish; and a very fat copper-skinned woman with a cane and a palm fan, all typically what you would find at any such corner in low-rent Miami, except maybe for the zombie. The Olo call such creatures *paarolawats*.

They are staring at me, not directly, but sidelong, and when I look away, I can feel their eyes on my back. No jitney, then. Wait for the cab. The dispatcher said ten minutes, although, really, my Spanish is not that hot, maybe he said thirty. Or never.

The *paarolawats* comes a little closer to me. A faint breeze stirs (maybe from the fan of the fat lady!) and I catch his smell, a horrible reek of old alcohol and unwashed, perhaps even slightly putrid flesh, and, of course, *dulfana*. This one is a crumpled-looking man, anywhere from forty-five to sixty-five years, wearing wino rags, balding, whose freckled skin's base color is that of a cardboard carton left out in the sun and rain. He's looking right at me, out of his dead eyes; he shuffles a step closer, then another. The jitney arrives at the curb, an old Ford Econoline van driven by a skeletal Haitian. The waiting people board it, casting baleful looks at me as they pass, or so it seems.

The jitney pulls away, and I'm left alone with the *paarolawats*. He slips-slides toward me in that horrible way they have, which I remember even though I have only seen one before. You're not supposed to let them touch you, I remember that, too. They're loaded with all kinds of exotic chemicals; their skin is dripping with witch secretions. The horror movies have it right for once. I back away. I am thinking, This would be a good time to wake up, if this is a dream, and if not I am going to have to run for it, if that fucking cab doesn't get here in one minute, and then a voice behind me says, 'Hey, there, Eightball, what's happening?'

It is the detective, again. He is walking toward the *paarolawats*, with his hand out. *He is going to shake hands with a zombie!* I move quickly to stand in his way and I say, 'Detective, I just remembered something I forgot to tell you.'

'Yeah? That's great, ma'am. Do you know old Eightball Swett, here? Mr Swett is one of our colorful neighborhood characters . . .'

I grab his sleeve. 'No, he's not. Could we go to your car? I mean right now!' Because the thing has begun to move, a couple of quick shuffles and he's reaching out his hand. They can move pretty fast over short distances, although, depending on how ripe they are, if they push it any they tend to lose bits and pieces.

The detective picks up my tone and lets me drag him to his white Impala. We both get in, and the *paarolawats* is right there as I close the door with a slam. He paws at the window and a bit of him sticks to the glass like bird shit. Now I'm practically crying, 'Please drive, please drive drive drive drive drive!'

When we are well away, he says, 'Would you mind telling me what that was all about?'

'I was just nervous. That man made me nervous.'

'Nervous?' he says. 'That palsied piss-bum made you nervous, when less than an hour ago I saw you take down a big strong gangbanger practically without breaking stride?' I am silent. He says, 'We need to have a talk, Jane.'

'I told you, my name is Dolores Tuoey,' I say, barely convincing myself.

'Jane Doe. I should say, Dr Doe, really. I read your paper on the Olo. Some of it went past me, but what I could understand was pretty amazing.'

Last shot. 'I'm not Jane Doe. People were always getting us confused.'

'Really? Whereabouts was this?'

'Bamako. In Mali. I was a nurse-midwife there and she was doing some anthro work upcountry in the Boucle de Baoulé. We ran into each other from time to time and . . . people commented. Jane's dead, I heard.'

'Yeah, and she must be buried under a plain tablet in Calvary Cemetery in Waltham, Mass., with 'Sister Mary Dolores Tuoey, S.M.' on it. You know, Jane, the problem with phony ID, especially if it's based on a real person, is that it's like a model of the Golden Gate Bridge made out of toothpicks. They look sort of okay, but they won't bear any real weight.'

He gives me a bright cat smile. 'So why'd you fake the suicide?'

'I have to pick up my daughter,' I croak. My mouth feels full of fine sand.

'Yeah, she's at Providence. Okay, no problem.' He turned south onto Dixie Highway. 'Actually there *is* a small problem: where did you get the daughter? You sure didn't have one when you sailed away into the sunset. Your dad would have noticed it. I met your dad the other day, as a matter of fact. He doesn't miss much, Jack Doe.'

I say nothing, feeling miserable, like a kid caught out in a dumb fib. In silence, then, we arrive at Providence. Luz is with her little gang of girls, gossiping. I wave and call out. Luz comes up to the strange car, her face clouding. I get out and hug her, and tell her our car is getting fixed and the nice policeman from this morning is going to drive us home.

Which he does, and makes no move to drive away out of my life, but gets out and follows us up the stairs as if invited. I make Luz her snack, carrot cake and lemonade, popping another two pills privily as I do so, and I offer some refreshment to him. He accepts, and we all snack away like a thermonuclear family. Luz is uncharacteristically quiet; she is used to the dyad, or Polly's family, or school, and also she picks up the tension. I prod her about her day. She sang. Some of the kids got their costumes, but she did not. She hopes to be a robin or an owl. Or a fish. As we talk, I see that she keeps casting sidelong looks at him, at her little arm and his big hand and wrist on the table, and no wonder, they are almost exactly the same color. She asks if she can go play with Eleanor across the street. I watch her from the landing as she trots across and rings Dawn Slotsky's bell.

'Nice kid,' he says. 'She seems to get on with you pretty good. It'd be a shame to see her end up in some foster home.'

'Why? Are you going to arrest me?'

'I might. It seems to me you're looking at obstruction of justice, imposture, uttering false instruments, conspiracy to commit murder. Or murders.'

In my worst nightmares, it has never occurred to me that I would be in undeserved danger from the police, that someone might think I had committed a crime that I actually didn't commit. I sit down, collapse actually, in the chair across from him. Maybe this is also part of Witt's plan! To stick me with his killings. Yes, that would be a Witt thing to do, to close all doors for me, leaving only one open, one that led to him. And amusing.

The cop says, 'What you have to understand is that all the stops are out on this one. We have the closest thing to unlimited resources. We will, for example, find out where that kid came from, and we will find out what you did for every day of your life since you sank that boat. I'm not being a hard-ass here, but that's just the way things are. If you're not on our side in this, then you're on his side, and if that's the case, we're going to drop the jailhouse on you. You'll be under the jail. Do you understand me?' I say nothing. Things are emerging. They think I am some kind of accomplice? I have speed thoughts. Get the Mauser, kill this cop, grab Luz, take his car, escape – no, steal a boat, escape by water, Ifa said, oh, and the chicken, got to have the yellow bird, but what about the others? No, actually, the flaw is that I am not a murderer, or maybe I am, maybe I . . .

I start to shake, like someone with a bad flu. Perhaps it is the amphetamine, or more magic, all chemicals anyway. He is looking at me peculiarly. He can see inside my head. I wait; he is boring into my brain, and I am so ashamed; it is worse than being naked in Mrs W.'s office. I can't stay on my chair. I see myself lying on the floor, from a distance. I am getting smaller and smaller. Now I see Dolores Tuoey in my kitchen. She is wearing her funny little nun scarf on her head and her acacia-wood crucifix, and lugging that big canvas bag she always had with her; she is walking away from me, down a corridor that does not exist in my kitchen, it is a shady covered arcade, like they have in the Petit Marché in Bamako. I want to shout out, Hey, Dolores, where are you going? But there is something in my mouth, an extra-large tongue perhaps, or a fur-covered creature, or a young vulture. So I can't shout at all and she gets smaller, and stops and turns around and smiles and waves, the way she did when our paths crossed in Bamako. Good-bye, Dolores, see you in heaven!

I am actually on the floor, I find, and he is bathing my

face with a cold, damp, dish towel, very tenderly. I sit up, fast, and get to my feet; I am in the bold, self-confident phase of amphetamine now, with the appropriate teeth-grinding jaw lock. Also, I am completely Jane again. Running and hiding are over. I am so glad not to be waking up in my hammock in the moonlight! And am I ever ready to talk!

'Well, Detective Paz,' I say, 'you got me.'

'You're Jane Doe.'

'Yes, Jane Clare Doe, Ph.D., of Sionnet, New York.'

He nods, he is pleased with himself. 'Okay, I'll call an officer to take care of the kid and then we'll go downtown and you can make a full statement.'

'No, actually, we'll stay right here, and I'll tell you what you need to know. I've got as much interest in stopping him as you do – more, probably. But the first thing you need to do is forget your usual procedure. If you insist on taking me downtown, I'll shut my mouth and stand on my right to remain silent except for my phone call, which will be to the firm of lawyers that has been twisting the legal system on behalf of my family since 1811, and I assure you that they will leave your police department a smoking ruin. So I'll help, but on my terms only. Your choice.'

It is so lovely to be bold Jane Doe again. Perhaps I've pushed him too far. He scowls, nods, sits down, takes out his notebook. 'Okay, shoot; but if I smell any horse manure, it's going to be a small room downtown, and bring on your lawyers.' I sit across the table from him. He says, 'You said "him." That's your husband, Malcolm DeWitt Moore.'

'Yes.'

'And you believe he's the one committing these

murders, the pregnant women, Wallace and Vargas and
Powers?'

'It's certain.'

'Did he kill your sister, too?'

'Yes.'

'Why?'

'You'd have to ask him that.'

'Why do you think?'

'He was practicing a ritual he learned in Africa. It
gives him power.' A partial truth, but no matter.

'Did you help him?'

'No. No one helps him. It's personal. It has to be
done alone.'

'What has to be done alone? The killings?'

'Yes, that and the consumption of the extracted
body parts. Portions of the posterior atrial wall, the
spleen, and the anterior uterine lining of the mother,
and from the baby, a piece of the midbrain, including the pituitary, the hypothalamus, and the pineal
body.'

He gives me a long look. 'So you know all about this
stuff, huh?'

'A good deal. Not as much as he does, of course.'

'And why is that?'

'Because I'm just a fairly proficient apprentice
sorcerer, while he is a fully accredited, extremely
powerful witch.'

'Uh-huh,' he says, and I see he is starting to deflate.
He thought he had a big piece of his big case and now
he's starting to think he's got a mere nut who'll walk on
an insanity plea. I say, 'Of course, he's not as powerful as
he will be. That's why he's doing the *okunikua*.'

'The . . . ?'

'The *okunikua*. It's Olo, it means the fourfold sacrifice. It's a *dontzeh* thing, or it used to be – sorry, a witch thing. The Olo disapprove of it. But my husband enjoys revivals. He needs one more baby and then it'll be done. It'd be nice to stop him before he gets it and completes. I'm not sure anything can stop him if he completes, except maybe Olodumare.'

'Who's that?'

'God. The Father, the Almighty, maker of heaven and earth and all that is seen and unseen. The Ancient of Days.'

I smile helpfully. He puts on a false one, and leans back and knits his hands behind his head.

'How do you know he needs one more?' he says. 'Maybe this last one, in your yard, was number four. Maybe he did one somewhere else that we don't know about.'

'No,' I say. 'They take the breastbone of the last one. It becomes an amulet. An *idubde.*'

'I hope you're not being cute, Jane,' he says. 'Crazy I can deal with, but not cute. Why don't you drop the mumbo-jumbo and just tell me how he does it. What does he have, some kind of spray? He sprays a knockout drug, right?'

'He could. But he can make the stuff in his own body. The *faila'olo*, and the *chint'chotuné*, sorry, I mean the invisibility and the— I guess the closest translation would be power over thought via sorcery, those he can do himself. Like sweating or breathing. He's not a regular kind of person anymore. Olo sorcerers know how to modify their bodies, through programs of ingesting mutagenic compounds, combined with mental and physical disciplines. They're walking drug factories.

They can exude psychoactive drugs, extremely powerful, highly targeted ones, from the melanocytes on their
skin surface. It's all mediated by the pineal body. That's
how he made that *paarolawats* at the bus stop.'

'What's a parlo . . . you mean Swett?'

'A *paarolawats* is what you would call a zombie. A
person who is essentially dead, but the witch can give
him certain simple tasks to do and can ride in him if he
wants.'

I see pity appear in his eyes. The poor nutcase is
what he's thinking. This infuriates me. I shut my own
eyes and take two deep breaths, centering. 'Oh, Christ
in heaven!' I cry. 'Look, you think I'm some sort of
pathetic cultist with a bundle of weird ideas, and you're
not listening, really, you're not writing it down in your
little book. Focus on this, Detective Paz: This is real! It's
as real as guns and cars. It's a fifty-thousand-year-old
technology that you don't understand, and unless you do
understand it enough to work with me, you have about
as much chance of stopping Witt Moore as a bunch of
savages have of stopping a locomotive by stretching a
grass rope across the tracks.'

'Cute,' he says, smugly. 'What we're going to find
here is that your guy's got some powder in a jar that he's
immune to himself, and he's got some way of shaking it
out so it affects people in a certain area, and he's got a
gang of fellow fruitcakes who like to cut up pregnant
ladies, which explains how he can be in two places at
once. Occam's razor, Jane. You're a scientist, you know
about Occam and the simplest explanation. So we don't
have to worry about zombies or the goddamn pineal
gland.'

He pulls out a cell phone. 'If you want to tell me

about that version, Jane, I'm all ears. Otherwise, off we go.'

I had not thought it would be so exhausting, and I feel a pang of sorrow and regret about me and Marcel in Chenka, what it must have been for him trying to convince me. I say, 'You are a moron, Detective Paz.'

He nods agreeably, makes a call and asks for a search team, and for someone from Family Services to take Luz to one of those friendly foster homes you read about in the papers all the time. I start to cry, and I say, 'Please, couldn't she stay here? My neighbor would be happy to take care of her. She's had a terribly rough time and she's very frightened of strangers.' I haven't cried in a while, so that I am a little overwhelmed by the gush, especially since I am amphetamine bone-dry. Detective Paz is unmoved, however. He says, 'Hey, listen, Jane, I'm really not a hard-ass. We can work any deal you want if you start talking sense.'

And more in this vein, which dries me up better than speed could; fury, the best antihistamine. I say, 'If you are using a little girl as a bargaining chip to get me to tell you acceptable lies, which you must know are lies, then you're not only a moron, but a sadistic moron. But have it your way – okay, you got me. My husband is the leader of a highly trained band of skilled assassins using African juju powder to cloud the minds of his victims and their guards.'

'Good,' he says, smugly. 'And you're a part of all this? The band?'

I say, 'Oh, Christ! Don't be stupid! Sorry, that's not an option. Think, will you! I am a rich woman who's been hiding in pauperage, doing menial work, for two and a half years. Who was I hiding from, and why?'

'The cops,' he says with assurance.

'Because I killed my sister?'

'Or helped him do it, and took the rap for it by faking that suicide.'

I see how this is so much simpler for him to believe, that criminal mastermind with hosts of minions and exotic drugs, simpler than what is really happening. I sink back into silence. There is no point in thinking further now.

Cars arrive. Cops emerge, one of them a female. I am read my rights, cuffed, and placed in the back of a patrol car. I see Paz talking to the lynch-mob man. The man looks at me with those eyes, which I am surprised to see are kindly and sad. Another car pulls up, with a Children's Services badge on the side. Out of it comes a large black woman in a violet pantsuit, who could be Mrs Waley's long-lost sister. She talks to Paz for a while, and then, to my surprise and relief, gets back in her car and drives away. I see Paz walk across the street and speak with Dawn. I may have misjudged him, or perhaps he is a more subtle manipulator than he first appeared to be.

The policewoman drives me to police headquarters, where I'm placed in a cell by myself. After about forty minutes, Paz comes by and takes me to an interview room, windowless, tiled, with the usual one-way glass mirror/window, and asks me if I am ready to make a statement. I say I'm not, and I wish to contact my attorney. He seems disappointed, but tries to hide it behind the usual bland cop mask. I thank him, however, for not giving Luz to Mrs Waley's sister, and he shrugs it off. 'No problem,' he says. I suspect that it will be a problem if his superiors ever find out. I'm pretty sure he knows who Luz really is, and he hasn't blown the whistle as far as I know, which will be an even bigger problem for him, covering up on a homicide. Why is he doing it? Deep waters here. After he leaves, I wait ten or so minutes and then a female officer enters and takes me to a phone.

I dial one of the few numbers I hold in memory. A woman answers, 'Mr Mount's office.' I ask to speak to him and she asks who's calling and I say, 'Jane Doe, his sister.' A considerable pause here. 'Jane Doe is deceased,' she says. I say, 'Yes, but I'm alive again. Get him for me, would you? And tell him I could smell the flowers of Bermuda when I died on the North Rock Shore.' I have to repeat this and chivvy her a little, but she does something and there is some light classical hold music, Boccherini, I believe. My brother comes on the line. 'Jane?' His voice is hesitant and breaking, and I start to leak again.

I say, 'Yeah, it's me, Josey.' I listen to the hiss of the line. My hand on the phone is trembling and sweaty. I am not ready for this, for the terror of love.

'How could you!' in a yell that must have brought his secretary running. 'How could you do that to me? And Dad? Jesus Christ, Janey! What the fuck!'

'I'm sorry.'

'You're sorry? No, sorry is when you're late for a dinner date, not when you fucking pretend to commit suicide. Ah, shit, Janey . . .'

Sobs come across the continent, minutes of them, in which I join. Then he asks me why. I say that I was afraid. I tell him that Witt has done it, that Witt is the Mad Abortionist of Miami, too. I tell him the whole story, as much of it as I could recall.

He listens in silence, and then – and here is why I love Josiah Mount – he doesn't suggest a stay in a mental institution, he doesn't ask a lot of questions about why I did this, or failed to do that. He just says, 'What do you need?'

I tell him what.

TWENTY-SIX

11/27 Mdina, Mali

The trader Togola easily found, has a compound down by the river, stinks of dead things, curing animal skins abound, his two wives and uncounted children all at work scraping, skinning, salting, drying. Showed him the Olo artifact – observed him closely. Saw fear first, then feigned ignorance. Told him I wanted to be taken to where he found it. I flashed big money, not hard to overawe people who see $500 in a good year, should be ashamed of myself but am not. I have the fever. I kept laying twenties on the mat as I talked, Togola staring at stack like a hypnotized hen. When I reached fifty bills I stopped, and took up half the stack. This when we start, and this (the other half) when we arrive. And as much again when we return here. Fucker rolled. W. looked at me with contempt, neocolonialist me, prob. remembers me and Colonel Musa, and how my overbearing worked out in that case. Don't give a shit anymore.

11/28 Mdina

W. and Malik our driver off to Nossombougou to get supplies, while I stay here and keep Togola company, so he won't scram with my advance. And he is frightened, too. No luck getting him to cop to source of the fear, language problem, I think, 80% of what I say = *i ko mun*, roughly 'come again?' or 'what did you say?' According to T., Olo are all witches, if they don't want you to find them, you won't find them, that the river is full of *jina*, or *diables*, that the Olo are eaters of human flesh. I am dying to go meet them.

More worried about half-assed way we are planning to leave. December is high water, I want to be sure that wherever we float off to there will be enough water in the channels to float us back, why I decided not to go back to Bamako and do serious logistics. Box with valuables in it is with Dolores at the mission so

Later. They're back. Asked W. if he got everything OK and he said, Yeah, we went to Wal-Mart. Feeble, but really the first little joke he has made in a long time. Maybe he is coming around. Sent Malik back to Bamako with message for Dolores, telling her to call or wire Lagos to let Greer know what we are doing. Said we might be gone as long as a month & if anything turns up will come back and mount a serious operation.

12/2 On the Baoulé

We are in an 18-foot pirogue with a seven-horsepower outboard, Togola at the stern, the two of us midships under a woven raffia sunshade with our supplies and gear in bags and baskets arranged around us, maybe six inches of freeboard. Area we are entering called the Boucle de Baoulé, the 'buckle' of the Baoulé River = inland delta – an area of about three thousand square kilometers w/ no significant roads. Channel here varies from 60 to 20 meters in width, 3 to 5 m depth. Thick vegetation on the high banks, shrubs and small acacia trees, occasional larger ironwood and red silk-cotton trees. Large numbers of trees skeletal. Togola says river was much higher in the old days, reached to the tops of the banks and beyond at high water. I believe him; the whole of Mali is drying up, the desert moving south. Meanwhile, the region is alive with birds, we putt-putt through a continual chatter and screech. Saw a paradise whydah and a martial eagle, the latter on a dead limb with what looked like a monkey.

I have not been in a boat in a while, I find myself ridiculously happy. It is Swallows and Amazons again, me and Josey exploring the channels of the Sound in our skiffs at age eight and eleven, pretending we were in Africa or Amazonia. Now this *is* Africa, and I am with W. and our faithful native guide. Ridiculous, our guide farthest thing from faithful & my pal and husband replaced by surly stranger. But he will come back, I know it, I see little sparks of the real him all the time, when his guard is down, like that joke about Wal-Mart, and this morning he made a joke about getting lost and having to eat human flesh. Tastes like chicken, a running gag, he says it of every new food. Pathetic hopes. But what else can I

12/3 On the Baoulé

We proceeded on, as Lewis & Clark used to say. Millet porridge and coffee for breakie, rice, beans, peanut sauce, for lunch, w/ tea. Tea and sesame sticks around four. When it gets dark, we find a low bank and camp. DEET vs. mosquitoes, they swarm around us anyway. Togola lights a fire, and I set up our tent (a French military thing, and clumsy) while W. mostly idle. Then I cook our evening meal. Togola watches, fascinated; he has never seen a white woman cook before. This convinces him that I'm indeed a woman and not some weird third sex peculiar to the *tobabou*. A mistake to generalize about African culture, but a fairly safe one might be that men don't cook. Decided not to stand on my high feminist horse, too exhausting. Can't help noticing W. seems to prefer me as an African (or 'real') woman. Absurd man.

12/4 On the Baoulé

Passed a herd of hippos today. T. steered far as he could away, jaw clenched. Odd being in water with them, feelings of total vulnerability, not familiar to us *tobabou* zoo goers. Probably more people killed by hippos than by leopards and lions combined. How ignoble to be crunched up by a hippo. I sang the chorus to Flanders & Swann's hippopotamus song in a lusty voice to show courage: mud, mud, glorious mud! W. knows all the verses but he did not join in. T. told me to shut up.

Saw first hornbills, clouds of bulbuls. River deepening and widening as we approach what passes for the main channel. I asked T. how long to get there, but he is silent when I ask him things now, since I am only a woman after all. He talks to W., tho, who answers in his high-school French. W. is interested in me again, however, at night. I let him hump away, feeling little beyond the usual relief of tension. The sex life of nine-tenths of the world's women perhaps, or maybe even a little better. I still have a clitoris, although maybe he will decide to change that. Where I will draw the line, however.

12/5 Baoulé R.

Beautiful sunbird (*Nectarina pulchella*) lit on the prow of the boat today. Besides that, nothing new. Channel narrowing. T. poles the boat to save gas. He is more nervous; he has dreams at night. We hear him shouting. Have passed no one during this trip, nor seen signs of habitation in the past three days. Supplies getting a little low.

12/7 same fucking river

Caught a big Nile perch today on my troll line. Channel shrunk to four m, 2.5 m deep at center. No current to speak of. Ate the perch for supper with (what else) peanut sauce, and rice. W. and T. thick as thieves now, T. has a bottle of rum, the bad Muslim! And they passed it back and forth without offering me any.

Thought of Dad, how much I miss him now, not like we are now but the way we used to be when I was a kid, and I got him mixed up with God the Father. A little weepy, but suppress it as usual. It would be good if I had a husband I could talk to about these feelings.

We have rice and sauce enough for another two weeks. T. has an old Lebel; I suppose we could shoot a monkey. Maybe I will get lucky again with the trotlines.

12/20 Danolo

Success and disaster in rapid succession. This morning just before noon the channel debouched into a wide (50 m) shallow (3 m) pool, the western edge of which was a long mud beach lined with log pirogues. Togola nosed us in among them. This is the place, he said. He was sweat-

ing and wild. He helped me unload our personal gear and
got back in the boat, said he was going for his stuff and
our other supplies.

W. spotted them first, woman standing at a break in the
foliage, at the head of a path. She had a little girl with her,
about eight years old. I waved and they both nodded and
touched hand to chest. I did the same. Then I heard the
rip of the outboard starting up and Togola had it in reverse,
sliding fast out into the middle of the pond. Like an idiot,
I shouted and ran into the water, he threw the motor into
forward and roared off. I sloshed back feeling stupid for
not having yanked the fuel line before leaving the pirogue,
had failed to see no amount of money enough to fight his
irrational terror. W. mimed checking his watch, said don't
worry we'll catch the six-seventeen, we both burst into
hysterical laughter. Worth being stranded in the middle
of Africa to hear him laugh, to have us both laughing
together. The two Olo were watching us silently. They did
not look scary enough to chase off a big, tough professional hunter. Both of them were dressed in a simple white
cotton robe, homespun, both of them had on a headcloth
of the same color and fabric, tied so as to throw up a stiff
triangular flap above the forehead. It gave both of them a
kind of medieval look. The little girl came up to me and
said something that I didn't catch & I did my *i ko mun* &
she spoke more slowly. I found she was speaking a funny
kind of Bambara: *i ka na, an kan taa* = come on, let's go.
Woman said good afternoon, in Bambara, & I came back
with the female response to the greeting & after whole
greeting ritual, told me her name was Awa and this is
Kani, my *imasefuné* (?). I will take you to your place, and
I said, Are you Olo, and she looked at me strangely and
answered, *Oso, nin yoro togo ko Danolo*. Yes, this place is

called Danolo. One of the great moments in anthro. We lifted up our bags and backpacks and followed her.

The path led to a wider road, which went through a gate in a high mud-brick wall and then we were in the village. I was stunned. It was like a piece of a larger town or city, picked up and stuck in the middle of nowhere. Houses of one or two stories, made of mud bricks, stuccoed and whitewashed or colored in pale colors, pink, blue, purple, with carved wooden doorways, laid out in neat wide streets, with gardens between them. In the center of the place there was a plaza, and the plaza was paved with pottery shards laid out in a herringbone pattern interspersed with white stones. A major, major discovery!!! The Yoruba used exactly that kind of paving in what they call the Pavement Era, which started in around A.D. 1000. It's supposed to be unique to them. In center of plaza, right in our path, was a thin stone shaft about twenty feet high, studded in a spiral pattern with iron nails, looking almost exactly like the *opa-oranmiyan*, in Ifé. W. asked me what it was and I told him there wasn't supposed to be anything like that within two thousand km of here, or within a thousand years, the staff of Oranmiyan, the son of Ogun & mythic founder of the Oyo monarchy. I said it was like stumbling on a village in Turkey in which everyone was wearing chitons & worshipping Zeus & spouting Homeric Greek. Impressed him, he started singing the theme from *Brigadoon.* There were plenty of people in the plaza, most of them sitting or standing in the shade of an immense baobab tree near the column. Everyone was dressed in white or dun-color.

The house we were taken to was built around a central courtyard, paved in the same antique style. It was pink-ocher, two stories, with an external staircase. Awa took us to a room on the ground floor furnished with cushions and

a low table. She said she would bring us some food, and
left, her kid trailing after her.

What's wrong with this picture? Two Americans, one of
them a blonde, arrive in an isolated African village. We
should be mobbed by curious people. There should be kids
staring at us through the windows. But people seem to be
going about their business with only the most blasé urban-
type curiosity about us. It was like getting off a bus in the
Port Authority terminal in New York. Even more spooky: no
T-shirts, no shorts, no rubber shoes. Western charities
dispatch huge bales of used clothing to Africa and somehow it gets into every corner of the bush. Except Danolo,
apparently. Everyone we've seen so far is dressed traditionally, the women in robes and headdresses, the men in
a kind of sarong, with the older men affecting an off-
the-shoulder cloak, all in what looks like hand-woven cloth.
No plastic either. I have never seen an African household without a plastic basin or jerrycan, or some utensil
recycled from tin cans or telephone wire. Here we have
pottery and local ironwork. All the adults have parallel
keloid scarring or tattooing on their faces. Never seen that
in Mali before. It's Yoruba, and old-fashioned Yoruba at
that, the mark of civilization.

Awa came back with food. Fried fish lumps on a bed of
something like couscous, but not, flavored with a sauce
that's got coco in it and other stuff I don't recognize. It
was pretty sophisticated cooking & also nothing not native
to ancient Africa – no rice, no manioc, no yams. With it we
got a thin, bitter beer. The meal was served on pottery
decorated with rouletted and combed designs, not all that
different from the Ifé ware displayed in the museum in
Lagos. This kind of stuff should not be in Mali. OK,
pottery is conservative, but still. The beer mugs were

brass, also with parallel marks, beautifully made, museum-quality stuff. W. said they were fattening us up for the cannibal feast. He was enjoying himself, the situation & my confusion. He said, This looks like the real Africa. Oh yeah & scary because of it, although I don't mention this to him. There shouldn't be *any* real Africa anymore.

Another woman removed the food & utensils. Little later, three elderly men wearing white robes and carrying carved wooden canes came in and removed W. He was quite jolly about it: See you in the pot, Janey.

Hour or so after that, Awa and another woman, older, who introduced herself as Sekli, led me out through the village to a high mud wall barred by a wooden gate. The gate and doorposts were heavily carved in the combination of abstract and naturalistic characteristic of ancient Yoruba art.

We got hustled through the gate too fast to really study it, noted the ram's head, & on both doorposts figure w/ crested coiffure, club, and horn prob. = Eshu-Eleggua, had the horrible trickster smile too. Inside found several houses, w/ beautifully made high-peaked roofs of finely woven oiled matting & carved wooden verandas. The center of the compound was Pavement Culture pavé, concentric circles around a rough-looking standing stone, with paths leading to the doorways of the several structures. The woman gestured for me to sit down and wait, then left.

Unpacked and checked the Nikon, the Sony camcorder, the Sony microcassette machine. Discovered the camcorder battery was dead. Discovered the cassette recorder had somehow picked up water on the trip, and the batteries were all split and corroded. Unpacked the solar charger, walked outside, unfolded and set it up in the sun. Loaded the Nikon and took some pictures of the compound. Something was wrong with the film advance. Opened the camera. A long loop of exposed film popped out. Trashed that roll, put in another. Carefully threaded it, closed the camera. Sighted on the group of women, pressed on the shutter. Nothing. I figured a piece of grit must have slid in there when I had it open. Hung it around my neck, planning to break it down later, blow it out. Grit always a problem in this part of Africa. Checked the solar charger and noticed that the little red charging light on the Sony was off. It was on when I plugged in the cable, I thought, but maybe not. Getting a little confused now, I sat down and checked the cabling, which was fine, but when I looked at the little control board on the solar charger I saw that instead of five volts, the transformer was set to twelve, which meant I had fried the Sony battery. I cursed, yanked the battery out of the Sony and stormed toward my hut, meaning to get the spare from my bag.

But I tripped on the rough pavement and went down on my face. Sony and Nikon both totaled. Blubbered like a baby, not because of the smashed equipment, but from fright, ashamed of it, couldn't help the fear. Déjà vu. Chenka all over again. I'm supercareful person with equipment, there was Something going on. I sat down on the doorsill of the little house and shivered and snuffled miserably for a while. When I looked up he was standing there, a small old man in a white robe and sandals, carrying a carved black staff. I hadn't heard him approach. He said something in Bambara that I didn't get. I held up the smashed camera and said, in English, You wouldn't by any chance know if there's a certified Nikon repair facility in this town? He said something else I didn't get, and then I really looked into his face for the first time.

Hard to describe this. In the faces of some nuns, some Hindu holy men, you're supposed to see a look of unearthly goodness, the sense that what is staring out at you from their eyes is not an ego like your own but a fragment of divinity. Seen it myself in a nun or two, can't vouch for the Hindus. This was like that, but not the same. It was as if a piece of sky or a wild animal or a tree had achieved consciousness. Or the moon. Original participation, not just at the height of a ritual, but all the time, in the light of afternoon. I could feel my heart knocking. He came closer and said something else and I caught *dusu be kasi* (the heart is crying) and the interrogative particle and I figured he meant to ask me why I was unhappy. I shrugged and indicated my broken things, although that was not the reason my heart was crying. And he asked me if I spoke Bambara and I said only a very little. He nodded and came over and sat down on the doorsill next to me.

Had he turned into an ostrich I could not have been more surprised at what he did then. He said, Perhaps you would be more comfortable then, if we spoke in French. My name is Uluné Pa. This is my compound you are in. What do you call yourself, Gdezdikamai? Close your mouth, so that flies do not fly into it.

I said, Jane, my name is Jane. What was that name you called me?

He said, Gdezdikamai, explaining what it meant. And lifted a hand to touch my hair. We have been waiting for you, Jeanne Gdezdikamai.

12/?? Danolo

Have not written in some days, no longer know date with precision. Moon tonight in new crescent. Will have to keep track of passage by her from now on, as in old days. How anthro of me! Almost needless to say my cheap watch stopped, and the local drugstore does not stock watch batteries. Writing slow anyway, something.

I must have drifted off. It seems hard to form letters, have to really focus. Was not the case in Chenka, that I noticed. Here is maybe deeper into the no-write zone? List of facts:

—the place I'm in is called a *ganbabandolé*. It is a kind of sorcery institution. You come here to get unwitched or to get oracles or like that, just like you go to a post office to get stamps. The man who runs it is my pal Uluné. He is the *babandolé*, the chief sorcerer in charge.

—the people here speak Olo, a language that seems to use both Yoruba and Bambara roots, but the tone structure and grammar are not like either, and it is more agglutin- ated than the typical Kongo group language. It's not like anything I have heard of, but I am not expert in African languages. A creole of some kind. Bespeaks migration, fairly recent as these things go.

—Uluné says he knew I was coming. I am an important person for some reason that he can't explain just yet.

—My husband is an important person, too, ditto on the explanation. I have not seen him in however many days it has been. Four? A week?

—I am to be taught *ndol*, sorcery of a type not taught to women. This is because I am not officially a woman. (Note: analogous to Gelede, where women don't dance but men dressed as women do?) As name implies. *Gd* = female; *ezil* = gold(en); *dik* = outsider, not Olo; *ama* = head; *ai* in the terminal position indicates a partial negation of the primary indicator of sex, size, or position. I think. Thus Gdezdikamai means 'goldenheaded not quite a female foreigner.' Uluné himself will be my *owabandolets*, my 'father-in-sorcery.' It is quite an honor, or maybe it is a doom. Everyone in the compound treats me with wary respect.

—The Olo, says Uluné, came to Danolo a long time ago. Before that they lived in Ile-Ifé, down in Yorubaland. They taught the Yoruba about the gods, the spirits, about Orun, the otherworld, which here they call *m'arun.* They also taught them Ifa divination, and just a little bit about *m'doli,* the unseen world = bridge between *m'arun* and *m'fa,* the world of the here and now. Don't know if I believe this. Explains some things, obscures others. Confirms Tour de Montaille. Want to call Greer and ask him.

—Uluné showed me a photograph. As far as I can tell it is the only photograph in the compound. It's old, cracked, and faded. It shows a man who looks vaguely like Uluné in the uniform the French colonial infantry wore in the years before the Great War. This is impossible, unless he is over a century old, so why does he want me to believe it? Age = status? Ask trick question. Jane: Why did he let himself be photographed? Wasn't he afraid his soul would be trapped? I was a different man then, he says. That man is dead.

Someday, Danolo

U. doesn't approve of writing things down. Writing kills the spirit of the thought, he says. He wants me to train my memory. Too late, I'm literate, the rot is too deep. Therefore, I try to keep the stuff in my mind, and then write it down at night, like now. I have pages full of stuff. Ifa verses, spells. Moon in waxing quarter.

Anthropology. Family and clan structure? Who knows?
A good deal of ritual life goes on in compounds, each with
a central *babandolé*, all very secret one from the other. U.
used to teach sorcery in a kind of university they have
here, but not any longer. Now his only student is me.

Uluné's compound is inhabited by Awa and the girl,
Kani; by Sekli, who is supposedly something of a
sorceress in her own right (although I have not seen
evidence of this) and a formidable battle-ax. She is the
majordomo of the compound. Then Loltsi, a jolly, portly
woman, and Mwapune, who is quiet and has a little girl of
about five named Tola. My favorite is Tourma, a lovely
creature of about eighteen, who is pregnant with her first
child. At first I thought all these women were U.'s wives,
but when I voiced this theory, he seemed shocked. Olo
sorcerers are celibate, more or less permanently. Sex
makes too much noise in the spirit realm (*m'doli*); the
orishas and spirits get jealous, and rival sorcerers can use
the distraction to get at you. This is also the answer I get
when I ask about W. I can't see him lest we be irresistibly
drawn into sexual congress. Little do they know. Prob. why
sorcery never caught on at American colleges and univer-
sities.

The women in the compound are in fact staff, and
honored for it. They have husbands they visit on their day
off, all except Sekli, which may account for her temper.
The other thing is that Kani and Tola are not the birth
children of Awa and Mwapune. They are *imasefuné*, soul-
children. The Olo believe that when weaning concludes, at
about age three, the original connection between birth
mother and child has quite faded and that the child then
becomes the responsibility of anyone who forms a relationship with it in *sefuné*, the affective soul. Most often

this is a close relative, an aunt or uncle, but it can be a stranger from the other end of the village. Unusually, it can even be the child's own mother or father. But in *vono ba-sefuné*, as it is called, the merging of souls, both parties immediately understand what has happened, everyone accepts it, and the child immediately moves into the household of his or her new *owasefuné* or *gdsefuné*, the soul-father or soul-mother, becoming their *imasefuné*, soul-child, until puberty.

When I asked U. whether a child ever failed to find a soul-parent, he looked bleak, and told me sometimes not, such children are damaged in the soul. No one talks to it, or feeds it, and it dies. On very rare occasions, it does not die, though; it scavenges food, and lurks on the edge of the village. If it survives to its twelfth birthday, it is considered *dontzeh*, a person under the protection of the spirit world, not quite human, but considerable. It enters the household of a superior *babandolé* of the town, and is taught various aspects of magic. All *dontzeh* become witches, and if you ask the Olo why they help them to the knowledge that will enable them to work evil, they say, who are we to reject what the god has touched? Find myself thinking about four-year-old kids no one will talk to, starving to death in plain sight. Poison in paradise.

As for W., he is well, I am told when I ask, he is fulfilling his destiny. U. won't divulge what it is. Pay attention to your own, he says. Fulfilling destiny a phrase much used around here, by the way. Many people, says U., wrongly suppose life is like a fishing net on a nail. Shift those nails and the meshes fall into completely different patterns. In fact, it is not a net, but a hook and line. Ifa hooks us in our mother's womb and although we thrash this way and that we are drawn along our line of fate until we are brought flopping to the seat of Olodumare. The same Olo word, *ila*, means fate and also a fishing line or a line scratched in the sand. I asked him, can no one escape their fate? Oh, yes, he replied casually, this is what we sorcerers are for, and laughed. This is so Olo, a profundity tied to a silly joke.

Later I press him on this. He has two expressions when I ask him for something he doesn't want to tell me. One is kindly, like a dad saying It's too complicated, darling, you'll understand when you're older. The other is almost embarrassed, like it's something shameful. I get the latter when I ask him about changing fate, or manipulating time, or about where the Olo come from. All seems to be related.

Just another day, Danolo

I probably missed Christmas already, and New Year's. Moon gibbous, a little over half full.

I'm sick a lot nowadays from the stuff he makes me eat and drink. He says my body has to be changed, so that part of me lives in *m'doli* all the time. This is something I've learned, how the chemical magic M. was always talking about really works. Didn't believe him at the time. Beyond that – there are as yet only intimations. Did my first sorcerous feat today, after three days of prep, nauseous, pissing black, night sweats, horrible dreams. These are all good signs, U. says. First thing in morning, we discuss my dreams. Never recalled dreams much before, but now they're as vivid and recollectable as *Casablanca*. U. doesn't think dreams are meaningless random discharges in the sleeping brain.

My sorcerous feat was that I was finally able to 'smell'

dulfana, the trace essence of magical operations. We took a walk out of town, because inside it'd be like trying to find a pickle blindfolded in a garlic factory. I found a little bag of *fenti* U. buried under an acacia, just like a truffle pig. Ridiculously pleased with myself. Now I realize the source of that itchy not-quite-odor I have been sensing for the past day or two.

On the way back, a guy steps out of some bushes and starts following us. I smell *dulfana* strongly off him, and I ask U. if he's a sorcerer, too, and U. laughs and says no, just a *paarolawats.* This word means 'destroyed person' in Olokan. When the wind shifted, we were bathed in the sour smell of dead meat. U. did not seem particularly concerned. I asked him why the thing was following us. He said it was Durakné Den, the witch, spying on us, riding in the *paarolawats.* It was, however, a very old one and falling apart, so we were in real danger. I asked was it dead, and he laughed. No, Jeanne, the dead sleep, they don't walk. Only, the person who used to be inside is locked up, and the witch rides him like a horse. Never let them touch you – he's very clear about that.

U.'s fairly limited French vocabulary won't handle magical concepts to the requisite depth. Lucky me, I don't have to know that stuff yet because we're only working with *komo*, which is anti-sorcery stuff, both the substance and the methodology. I have to learn that first, because if I were to try any actual sorcery without being protected, I would be a sitting duck out there in *m'doli*, which is apparently a kind of Dodge City place.

In our spare time we do Ifa. I am supposed to memorize the verses like U. has done, but I cheat and write them down. U. does not throw Ifa for me. He says he already did, but won't tell me what the oracle said.

I brought the subject around to this witch, Durakné. U. seems reluctant to use his name, calling him *m'tadende* (the 'outside one') or 'our *dontzeh*.' Apparently, Durakné is the only surviving *dontzeh* child now in Danolo. U. trained him, and he was a good pupil. Now a rival, it seems. Oedipus in the Sahel? Need to query U. on moral structure. Failed again to get him to discuss history: why did Olo leave Yorubaland? Also seems preoccupied, sometimes stops talking and falls into what seems to be a light trance. Making lots of *komo*, preparing little packets and burying and hanging them around the compound. The war is heating up, it seems. Durakné apparently behind it, with some of the other sorcerers, who should, according to U., know better. Our arrival associated with this in some way, but he's mum on the details – changes the subject when I ask, pretends not to understand. He's good at that.

A day in the life, Danolo

My period started today, and if I am as regular as I usually am, I estimate this is the 33rd day of our visit here. Henceforward, I will keep track. Moon full. U. is a little nervous of me, and I wonder why, until Sekli takes me aside and says it is my flux. All very well to make me an honorary man but the spirits are not fooled. She gives me elaborate instructions about what to do with my 'cloths' so as to prevent witches and *grelet* from taking advantage of this vulnerability. I must spend next three days with the women, however, which I do not mind at all. I spend most of my time with Tourma. She seems, unlike most of the people here, to possess the sort of innocence much prized by anthropologists who go native and Rousseauian. I suspect that is a personal, rather than a cultural, detail; perhaps that sort of anthropologist picks out people in the native village that even the native villagers think are a little fruity. In any case, Tourma is happy, trilling all the day long. She weaves on the horizontal loom, long strips of multicolored cotton that she sews into bags, shawls, and sashes. It is quite thrilling to watch figures appear under her fingers.

While she works, I worm out of her some Olo info. Their cosmology is quite similar to that of the Yoruba, their psychology not so. Psychology, a funny word. We use it as a placeholder for talking about thinking and emotions, learning and dreaming, although as far as people are concerned there is not much in it. We don't really (except for Jungians I suppose) believe in the reality of the psyche, that the psyche has the same reality as cobalt or North Dakota. The Olo do, and here they seem to be right in line with the Chenka. *Ogga* again, but here they are called *grelet*. The Olo think that *grelet* invade the mind and grow there like Guinea worms do under the skin. They grow by attracting your attention, making you worry about whether you are handsome enough, or sexy enough, or smart enough, or have sufficient cattle or children. You can starve them out by concentrating on the moment, on the unfolding *m'fa.* Or you can have a sorcerer remove them. A *grel* is an independent entity. The stronger ones can take people over, and work mischief.

Tourma asked me what kind of *grelet* there were in the land of the *dik*. I had to tell her that in my part of Diklandia they did not believe in the *grelet* at all. She thought this hilarious. Do they believe in colors? she asked. In water? In beans? A riot among the ladies & I laughed, too.

Day 34, Danolo

Took Tourma to my little house (my *bon*) to see my treasures, but she wasn't that impressed. She wanted to know if I had made the Bic pens and lighter, the colored pencils, the various articles and implements, and was bored when I told her no, and even more at my halting attempts to explain late capitalism. Merchants do not have high status among the Olo. The visit ended badly, when I showed her my Olo artifact, which I did quite innocently. I saw it in my bag and asked her what it was. It is apparently an *idubde*. She cried that out, backed away, and ran like hell was chasing her back to the big *bon.*

Later I made up with her, but she would not tell me what an *idubde* was for. Sekli scolded me for showing it to Tourma – the worst possible thing to show to a pregnant woman – *ch'andoultet.* Didn't I know *anything*? Not much.

Tourma sings to the child within her and talks to it. It's a girl. She knows this. She hopes she will make *sefuné* with this child. It occasionally happens and is considered a terrific omen. Tourma also sings to the birds, the clouds, the bushes and rocks. She says they sing back to her. Can't you hear them, Gdezdikamai? No, I can't.

Day 36, Danolo

Dreamed about Dad last night. Nothing Freudian, just floating peacefully over him as he went about his business, supervising Frank the groundsman at Sionnet and having lunch (tunafish on toast and bouillon) and working on the '29 Packard. Extremely peaceful, but lonely-making. Am out of contamination now, so I told U. about this dream and he scoffed that it wasn't a dream at all, but merely *bfuntatna*, soul-travel, and not a message from the *orishas.* On the other hand, the fact that I could do it boded well for my magical career. He is in a talkative mood today, or rather a discursive one. He's never surly, but often he speaks gnomically or in riddles. He missed me? Maybe he is bored, maybe he is tired of the sorcerers' war that's been brewing, and I offer some relief. Comic relief? An experiment, teach a woman *ndol*, like teaching a dog to talk?

His view of time. Every moment in time is accessible through the *m'doli*, which exists outside normal time and space. Ifa is the guardian of time, which is why we go to him for oracles, but he also guards the past. Why does the past have to be guarded? asks the novice. He gave me a pained look. Because it can be changed. But that is *adonbana.* An act that afflicts the world, he translated. The reason for our travels. He used the word *ilidoni*, literally 'going down,' but that is also used as if capitalized to reference the hegira of the Olo from Ifé of glorious memory to this place, Danolo, or Den 'aan-Olo, 'where the people have to stay.' I lit up, of course, because I thought he was going to let me in on the unspeakable secret, but he did not. He said, I will tell you when you require it. How will I know this? You will know, and he wouldn't say anything else.

Asked how can the past be changed? The past is past. Except in our memories. He rapped me gently on the head. Jeanne, Jeanne, why can't you understand this? The short course in Olo ontology. Only *m'arun* is real. *M'fa* is a show, only shadows, a game. Plato in Africa. But it is a gift of the *orishas.* They let us sorcerers play with it, as a father may let his little son play with his spear, his bow. But not *use* it. Not *break* it. We must observe *débentchouajé.* New word = harmonious connectedness? Way things are supposed to be? What happens if a sorcerer doesn't? Then the *orisha* comes, he said. I said, But the *orishas* come all the time. Ifa comes to give oracles, Eshu comes to open the gates, the *orishas* ride their devotees at the ceremonies of the Yoruba . . . No, no, he said, I mean the *orisha comes* in himself. Not as a spirit, as in the ceremonies of the Yoruba and the Songhai *gaws.* The true *orisha.* And what happens then? I asked him. He shrugged. It depends on the situation. A disaster. A great blessing. Have you ever seen this? Once, he said, a long time ago. I don't want to see it again.

TWENTY-SEVEN

They were in the homicide unit, at Barlow's desk, and Barlow had the whole story now, as reconstructed by Paz, with the weird parts edited out, smoothed, made rational. Barlow chewed on it silently for a while, and Paz experienced the familiar and unpleasant feeling of being assessed.

'You told anyone else about this, Jimmy?'

'No. I thought I'd run it by you first.'

'Good,' said Barlow. 'Let's see if I got you straight, now. Here's this lady you got locked up, who used to be Tuoey, but she's really Jane Doe. She's married to DeWitt Moore, a famous writer who happens to be in town, doing his show in the Grove, but also doing these murders, because he's also an African witch doctor in his spare time, which is why he's doing the murders and cannibalism in the first place. Also, besides thinking he's a witch doctor, with strange powers, he also has a gang of accomplices and some kind of African witch powder drug that he's using to mess up the minds of his victims and the folks who're trying to guard them. And he also killed Mary Doe a couple years back, even though we found he had a perfect alibi. Those African powders again. Have I got it all?'

'You don't believe it, right?'

'No, I didn't say that. I believe you got the real Jane there, and this Moore character is the killer. That's good. Far as the rest of it goes . . . it's pretty tall.'

'Tall? A little while ago you were saying that Satan was loose in Dade County.'

'Oh, he's loose all right,' said Barlow, unfazed. 'But that's not the kind of fact I take to the state's attorney. Render unto Caesar the things that are Caesar's, which in this case means evidence and a story they can eat and not spit up. Meanwhile, your girl there ain't exactly a reliable informant.'

'Then talk to her yourself! See what you think. Whether she's criminally involved or not, she's still protecting him with all this witch doctor crapola.' He laughed humorlessly. 'Crazy? Yeah, crazy I'll give you.'

They brought Jane Doe out of the holding cell and back to the little interview room. Paz watched while Barlow talked to her, in his usual quiet and effective way. No sarcastic remarks, no one-liners from old Barlow, just two people talking. They had a tape recorder on, getting it all. Paz had seen it many times before, and it pissed him off, because he couldn't do it himself, he always had to show the mutt he was in charge, that he couldn't be fooled. He knew it, he knew it was dumb, but he couldn't help himself, which was why he was doomed to be the bad cop, and never the one who got the confession and cleared the case.

The story she told was essentially the same one she had told to Paz earlier, but more detailed and easier in the telling. Barlow ran her through the nights the women were murdered. No alibi for Wallace, she was at home alone with the kid. Vargas, she was with friends all evening. At the time of this latest, Alice Powers at the Milano, Jane told them, she had been at a *bembé*.

'Come again?'

'A *bembé* is a Santería ritual,' Doe explained. 'People dance and the *orishas*, the spirits, come down and take them over for a while and give advice.'

'You don't tell me! And did you get any advice from these spirits, ma'am?'

'I did. I was advised that before I close the gate it must be opened. And that I was to bring the yellow bird to the father. I was advised to flee by water.'

'That's real interesting. What do you make of it?'

'I'm not sure. Ifa is often indirect. The fleeing by water part is fairly clear, though.'

'By water, hm? Why didn't you?' Paz noted that Barlow was enjoying himself. And, more remarkably, so was the woman. There was a light in her face, now, and Paz looked at her with more interest. Her bony features were never going to be on a magazine cover, but besides that she'd let herself go a good deal, and she didn't have any taste. Paz liked women with taste. Flair. That hairdo was a disaster.

She said, 'I don't have a boat. Also, I have to find some allies first, and I have to stop my husband. I feel responsible.'

'I see,' said Barlow. 'Well, you'll give us some names and we'll check it out. Now, these allies . . . you're talking about this gang that Detective Paz here thinks your husband has got?'

She shot Paz a look. 'No, I meant magical allies. There isn't any gang. It is a figment of Detective Paz's imagination. My husband is doing this all by himself.'

'Would you like to explain how?' asked Barlow.

The woman did so, the whole story, thousands of years, the various botanicals, the pineal body, the melanocytes, the exohormones, the supporting neuro-physiological research, with actual references added. Barlow was silent for a while after this, the tape softly whirring, recording nothing.

'You got any idea why, ma'am?' he asked.

'Why what?'

'Why he's doing this?'

'I thought I explained that. The neuroleptic substances in the excised and consumed organs . . .'

'No, I got that part. He's going to get some boosted power for his witchcraft. I mean why does he want it? What's he going to do when he gets it?'

'I don't know. I have no idea what he's like now. I think maybe he sees himself as the revenge of Africa on white America. He wants to show us that there's a black technology that sets all our technology at naught. Stuff like that. He's an extremely angry man.'

'I reckon,' said Barlow. 'And he got this idea in Africa?'

'He got the means in Africa. Maybe he always had the idea. No, that's not true. He had a desire to be seen, *really* seen, as himself, not as a 'black' fill-in-the-blank, a black poet, black playwright, black husband of a rich white woman. And he thought he never could be, I mean *seen* in that way, and it made him crazy. He got the idea that what the race needed was a Hitler, that the white people would never take blacks seriously until then. And Africa, where we went, what he learned there, I think it transformed him, the sad, angry stuff that was deep inside – it just took over and ate everything else, until only the Hitler part was left. It happens.

Maybe it even happened to Hitler. That's one theory. A friend of mine used to say that dealing in the magical world without some transcendent moral authority was about the most dangerous thing anyone could do. And Witt didn't have one.'

'That's quite a story, Jane,' said Barlow, after a long pause.

'Tell us about your sister,' said Paz, abruptly, and got a questioning look from his partner. He didn't care. He felt angry, and not just at the killer.

Jane Doe asked for some water then, and Barlow stepped out and brought a large plastic cup back with him. She drank deeply and resumed. 'I got sick in Africa. Ended up at a Catholic hospital in Bamako. I was out of it for a long time, dying really, and someone got in touch with my brother and he came and got me and took me back to Long Island, and they stuck me in a fancy clinic. I don't recall any of this. They couldn't find anything wrong with me, no pathogens, but I seemed to have lost the ability to metabolize food. Witt showed up a month or so later, looking just like he always did, being charming. I started getting better around then. Of course, he had got me sick in the first place, for amusement, to punish me for . . . whatever, and then he made me better. I didn't say anything to my family about this, or about what had happened. It's hard to describe, or explain, but . . . being back in Sionnet, Africa seemed like a long bad dream. I think I wasn't in my right mind. I was sick for a long time, I told myself, I wanted all of it not to have happened, and so I convinced myself that it hadn't really happened. And he had a power about him now, an aura . . . terrifying. It was like a bird hypnotized by a snake. I had dreams, too. He was getting at me through my dreams.' She let out a peculiar nasal sound, like the start of a hysterical laugh, throttled. 'It sounds crazy. Anyway, I didn't do anything. And one day he killed Mary and her baby. I think it was just to show me he could, and to hurt me and my family. Who were never anything but kind to him. I was terrified that he was going to kill them all. So, really, to save them I took *Kite* out and killed myself.'

'But you didn't kill yourself,' said Paz.

'Didn't I? It felt like it. I decided to become Dolores. I had all her ID because of a mix-up in Bamako, and I took that tin box, with that in it and some other stuff. I filled the bilges with diesel and poured gas from the outboard around, and cracked off the regulator on the butane gas tank for the stove. And then I couldn't do it. I wanted to live, to, I don't know, bear witness to what he was. I felt my line wasn't ready to be cut, that Ifa had something for me to do. I had a pistol. I was going to light it off and shoot myself, but I didn't. We had an emergency inflatable aboard. I inflated it, crying like a baby. Then I rigged the boat to explode. I used a kitchen timer, ran two wires from the starter battery and fixed them with duct tape, one to the pointer, one to the dial at zero. I opened the gas valve, set the timer for half an hour, sealed the cabin, and got into the rescue dinghy. I paddled to a beach outside of Bridgeport, shoved the dinghy and paddle into a Dumpster; while I was doing that, the boat exploded and burned. I didn't look. Then I walked into town. I checked into a motel under Dolores's name. I had big sunglasses on and a floppy hat pulled down low, and it was the kind of motel where they don't look at your face. I bought dye and changed my hair and stuffed cotton wads in my cheeks and then

I went and bought a cheap car in a Vietnamese used car lot.'

'What did you use for money?' Paz asked. 'You didn't touch your accounts. They checked.'

'Dad always kept a couple of grand in a jar in the sail locker, for emergencies in foreign ports. I drove to Miami and set up housekeeping.'

'You thought he'd come after you?' Barlow asked.

'Yes. He . . . some things he said, before . . . Mary. He wanted to . . . recruit me, I think. He thinks we belong together. He wants me to observe his deeds and admire him. Because I understand what he is, what he can do. And you guys don't.' She looked at Paz. 'You can't really stop him, you know. You think you can, because at some level you think all of this is lunatic garbage. You think guns and handcuffs and jail cells and the rest of it are going to work for you. But they're not.'

Barlow said, 'Well, what would you recommend we do? Give him a free pass?' She mumbled something. Paz snapped, 'Speak up! What's the answer? Holy water?'

'Jiladoul.'

'What the fuck is that?' snapped Paz. He saw Barlow's mouth tighten.

There was a knock on the door and a harassed-looking policewoman burst in and told them that Ms Doe's lawyer had arrived, demanding to speak to her immediately, and that Captain Mendés wanted to see both of the detectives, also immediately. The two detectives looked at each other. Paz snarled something under his breath and stomped out. Barlow turned off the tape machine and walked out with it, leaving the cop with the detainee.

Mendés was not in good shape. Paz thought he was

on the edge of collapse and he felt a tremor of fear. The captain had always been a neat, even dapper, man, a cool manipulator of people and situations. Now he had his tie halfway down his chest, the first two buttons of his silk shirt open, and the shirt had a large coffee stain at the belt line. The ashtray on his desk was filthy with cigarette and cigar butts. Paz and Barlow sat down, but Mendés continued to pace. The phone was buzzing, but he made no effort to pick it up.

'The mayor got a call from the governor's office about that bitch you picked up,' Mendés began, 'that rich bitch. You got any idea who the fuck she is? The fucking archbishop was on the horn, too. You talk to her lawyer?'

'No, boss, the guy just got here, and then . . .'

'Did she do it? Do you have evidence to charge her?'

'No,' said Barlow, 'and no. She says her husband did it. Witt Moore.'

Mendés stopped his pacing. 'Did he?'

'If she ain't completely crazy, it looks like he might've. The problem is, there's no physical evidence, and he's going to be alibied up to the neckbone for all the murders. And he's no homeboy. He's a famous black writer.'

'I don't care who he is. I need someone to show here. You got any idea what's going on out there? Half the goddamn reporters in the country are outside the building right now. It's not local anymore. There's network TV people here now. They want to know how some maniac slipped into a building guarded by the police and chopped up a woman in her own room, without waking up the woman sleeping next to her. I'd like to know, too. I got to go down and talk to those people. I got to explain to Horton and the mayor. So what do I say? *You're the fucking detectives – what do I say?*'

Mendés's eyes bulged and his face grew dark. Paz said, 'He used drugs, psychedelic powders from Africa. He confused the guards and did it.'

Mendés stared at him. 'Who, Moore? You *know* this?'

'It's the only explanation that makes sense,' offered Paz, carefully. 'He can confuse people, put them to sleep temporarily. That's how he does it.'

Barlow said, 'It's a theory, Arnie. We got no evidence for . . .'

'Then fucking *find* some! Concoct some! I don't give a nickel shit. But I got to have something. I can't go up there naked with my dick waving. Go pick up this guy. Use the whole SWAT team, gas masks, disaster suits, whatever you need. I'll clear it. Go!'

They got up. Paz said, 'And about Jane Doe?'

Mendés made a dismissive gesture. 'Oh, cut her loose! That's all I need, the archbishop on my ass in the middle of all this.'

They went back to the interview room, Barlow marching ahead, silent, his back stiff. Paz could tell he was angry, although whether at Mendés or himself he didn't know. In the room, Jane Doe was speaking with a large, balding man wearing gold-rimmed glasses and a gray suit of marvelous silkiness and cut: the lawyer, Thomas P. Finnegan. He informed them that Ms Doe was through talking for the day.

'I don't think so,' said Paz. He did not wish to let go of the woman. 'Ms Doe is in possession of essential information on a extremely important serial murder case. We haven't finished questioning her.'

'Yes, you have,' said Finnegan.

'Plus, we can charge her with impersonation.'

'Go ahead,' said Finnegan. 'In which case, she will definitely not say anything.'

Some stereotypical glaring here. Jane broke the tense silence. 'They don't believe me anyway. They think I'm crazy.'

'Is that true, Detective?' asked Finnegan, gently.

Paz realized it showed in his face. He *did* think she was a nutcase. But . . . He felt blood rushing to his cheeks, and considered bringing up the little girl as leverage, but found he could not do it. Barlow said, 'You can take her away, Counselor. I guess you know not to go anywhere we can't find you.'

The lawyer made the obligatory rumblings about false arrest and harassment. As she left, Paz touched her arm.

'What's a jillado?' he asked.

'*Jiladoul*,' she corrected. 'A sorcerer's war. Good luck, Detective Paz. Be careful.'

When they had gone, Barlow said, 'Well, Jimmy, you got us into it now. You feel like calling the SWATs and getting into a gas mask?'

'I had to say something.'

'A fool's mouth is his destruction and his lips are the snare of his soul, Proverbs 18:7. You got no evidence at all the man's spraying drug powders around the city.'

'Okay, great! Why don't you waltz back in there and give Arnie the Jane version? He can go on national TV with it. Miami police baffled by witch doctor, film at eleven.' He walked away.

Barlow caught up with him and grabbed his shoulder. 'Where're you running off to?'

Paz shrugged him off. 'I'm going to pick up Moore.'

'What about them drugs of yours?'

'I'll hold my breath.'

'This is wrong. We should think this through, calm down a little.'

'I'm calm. I'm not scared, though. That your problem? You really believe this witchcraft crap, don't you?'

Barlow had the kind of white eyes that get harder than any other kind. 'Listen, boy: Captain said take a team, and we're going to take a team. You want to come along, fine; you don't want to play that way, I'll turn around and march into Arnie's office and get you pulled off this case. I mean it.'

Paz let out a breath and said, 'Fine. What do you want me to do?'

They got to the Poinciana Suites a little after seven. It was a four-story, cream-colored stucco building full of small apartments for well-off transients, set back from the street across from Brickell Park. They parked on the street out front, Barlow and Paz in Paz's car, a big van full of SWAT guys in white plastic suits and gas masks, and a crime-scene-unit van. Barlow told the SWATs to stay put while he and Paz made the arrest. The SWAT commander, Lieutenant Dickson, objected strenuously to this plan; the whole point of his unit was to go in first and overwhelm the suspect. And what about this gas?

'They ain't no gas, son,' said Barlow. 'It's something else, what our man's got, and I think we can handle it. Now look here: that's why they call y'all backup. Back up! We're going in, me and Jimmy here, and we're coming out with the guy. You do what you have to do to secure the building, the back exits and such. If we ain't out in half an hour, you mask up and go in shooting. But it ain't going to come to that.'

Dickson relented and started to dispose his troops. Paz and Barlow rode the elevator to the top floor in silence. Paz pushed the buzzer at the door of number 303. The door opened. Moore was standing there, dressed in a yellow T-shirt and baggy gray cotton pants, with leather sandals on his feet. They showed him their ID.

'Malcolm DeWitt Moore?' Barlow asked.

'That's me.' He looked straight at Paz, ignoring Barlow. Paz saw a man of about his own size, with a lighter build and eyes that were hazel rather than brown. Paz said, 'We'd like to talk to you.'

Moore backed away from the door. 'Sure, come in. I'm in the middle of something. Just let me put it away.'

They followed him into the apartment, which consisted of one large room, furnished in modern light woods and Haitian cotton rugs and upholstery, high-class motel equipage, and a smaller bedroom, which they could see through an open door. Moore went to a desk, bent over it, and wrote something in a notebook. Then he sat down in a straight chair that stood in front of the desk.

He hasn't said what's this all about, Officer, thought Paz. Everybody the cops come visiting asks that, but he doesn't. Moore said, 'I just had something in my head I wanted to get down. It's funny, when you buzzed I was working on a poem about a crime.' He held up the notebook. 'Would you like to read it?'

Paz stayed where he was. 'Not right now.' Then he saw the bike, just the front wheel and the handlebars, leaning against something in the bedroom. The front wheel had a smear of dirt on it, which Paz was as sure of as he had ever been of anything would match up with the dirt at the side of Teresa Vargas's house. Moore said, 'It's better if you have the whole context. Basically, it's a very long poem about the black experience in America. It's called *Captain Dinwiddie*. This part comes when the hero has gone back to Africa after being a slave . . .'

'Mr Moore . . .'

'And he finds a sorcerer there who teaches him how to break free of time and space. Anyway, he gets to travel through the decades, observing, you know, the black experience, and this part I was just working on has him watching two kids in New York in the eighties pull off a store robbery and kill a Korean grocer . . .'

Paz said in a louder voice, 'Mr Moore, your name's come up in connection with a series of killings of pregnant women. We'd like you to come down to headquarters and see if you can help us out.'

Moore's smile got broader. There was something wrong with his eyes, Paz thought. A glassiness? No, but something strange. Maybe a drug . . .

'Fruit and blood in a shower, the grocer dead among the rolling mandarins, I thought that was pretty good. Of course, usually when you think it's pretty good, you have to cut it out later.' He chuckled. They both stared at him. 'You've been talking to Jane,' said Moore. 'I'm sure she told you an interesting story. She has a vivid imagination. Doesn't quite get it, though.'

Paz looked at Barlow. This was funny; Barlow usually took the lead, but he hadn't said a word. 'Doesn't get what, Mr Moore?'

'What I'm doing. Jane insists on a certain antique

Judeo-Christian worldview; I mean, she takes it seriously, if you can believe that, even though it's demonstrable that it's a scam, always has been a scam, always will be a scam, although, of course, incredibly useful for keeping all the assholes down in the mud. Whereas, the only reality is the reality of power. The only point of life is to make people do your bidding, so that you get all the good stuff and they get the shit. Wouldn't you agree, Detective . . . Paz, is it? Wouldn't you, I mean speaking as a man who's had to eat shit every day of his life from people like your redneck pal there?'

Paz slid his eyes over to glance at Barlow. He was standing there like a phone pole. Moore said, 'See, you can't even answer me without checking with whitey. You got the badge, you got the gun, you got your civil service and your affirmative action, and you're still a nigger in your own head. You fucked white women? Sure you have. Still a nigger in your head. Isn't that amazing? It always amazed me. And I thought, What could possibly change that?'

'Witchcraft?'

'Not a word I use. A completely different way of seeing the world. As different as science was from religion in the Middle Ages. And it *works*, my man! It works.'

'You did those murders. You killed a black girl and cut out her baby.'

Moore was still smiling, like they were having an argument in a dorm room. 'Hey, equal opportunity. But, really, man, none of that shit matters anymore. I'm telling you, it's a whole different world.'

'Terrific, you can tell us all about it downtown. Malcolm DeWitt Moore, I'm arresting you for the murders of Deandra Wallace, Teresa Vargas, and Alice Powers and their infant children,' and he rattled off the Miranda warning, while he handcuffed Moore.

'Look, I have no bitch with you or the city of Miami,' Moore said, 'but this is something you don't want to get on the wrong side of. I tell you that as a brother. You're over your head here.'

'Yeah, yeah, you have mystic powers,' Paz said. 'You'll tell us all about them downtown.' He grabbed Moore by the elbow and led him toward the door. Then he stopped. Barlow was still standing in the same spot. 'Cletis?' Barlow gave him a blank look, then followed.

'You okay, Cletis?'

'Sure, never better,' said Barlow.

They went down in the elevator, standing in a row, Paz holding Moore, and Barlow on the other side. This is real, thought Paz, I am actually holding this guy by the arm. He studied the fake rosewood grain of the car walls, the little nicks and fingerprints, the dim reflections in the brushed stainless of the car door. All were as they should be, the light reflecting or being absorbed according to the immutable laws of physics, the eye capturing the light in its lens, casting it onto his retinas, into his brain, according to the immutable laws of biochemistry: natural. The door opened. They walked from it into the lobby. There were two SWATs there, suited grotesquely, masked, their MP-5s squat and menacing in their hands.

'Everything okay?' asked one of them, his voice distorted by the mask speaker.

'Yeah, we're good to go here,' said Paz. 'You guys can stand down now. We left the door unlocked. CSU can go right in.'

They walked to Paz's car. It was dark out already, darker than it should have been on a summer's night at seven-thirty. Paz put Moore in the back, guiding his head in under the roof gutter, as he always did with a prisoner, and felt on the palm of his hand the warm head, with its yielding skin, the prickle of hair. He started the car and drove away. He looked in the rearview. The prisoner was there, the same pleasant smile on his face.

Then in the rearview, Paz also saw flashing lights, red and blue. The SWAT van was pursuing them. Paz pulled over to the curb and got out. The SWAT commander, now in his native blacks, with flak vest and helmet, jumped athletically out of his van.

'What the fuck is going on?' he shouted. 'I been trying to get you on the radio. Where's the guy?'

'In the back,' said Paz. 'There was no problem.'

Lieutenant Dickson stared at him, and then meaningfully at the rear seat of Paz's vehicle. The rear seat was empty. Paz popped the door, dived into the rear, and felt the seat and the floorboard. Stupid. He upended the seat cushions. Nothing. In a panic now, he shouted, 'Cletis! Where the hell did he go?'

Barlow swiveled and looked back at Paz. On his face was an expression Paz had never seen there before, brutal and mean, the mouth twisted in a sneer, the eyes filled with icy contempt. In an unfamiliar nasal snarl, Barlow said, 'You dumb-ass nigger! Can't even pick up a fuckin' prisoner, can you?'

Paz stared in shock at the stranger's face. Then the lights went out, the streetlamps first and then the lights of the cars. Paz heard Dickson shout, and the sound of car doors opening as the SWATs leaped out. They had flashlights on their weapons and these snapped on, cutting white beams through the blackness. That was wrong, was Paz's initial thought. It shouldn't be that dark. The city was never that dark, not even when the power went out in a hurricane, there was always some light source, bouncing against the cloud cover. Even in the middle of the Glades it never got this dark. It only got this dark in a cave. Then the shooting started, automatic fire from the SWATs, lighting the darkness. Paz couldn't see anything to shoot at. A bullet cracked by his head. He dropped and rolled under the car. He heard men scream, the tinkle of brass falling from the machine guns, the thud of bodies hitting the pavement. He closed his eyes and put his hands over his ears. He listened to his own breathing and the pump of his own heart for a while.

He opened his eyes and took his hands away from his ears. There was dim light, going red blue red. He rolled out from under the car. The streetlights were on again, and so were the top lights of the SWAT vans. Someone groaned, and he heard sirens a long way off. There were ten or so bodies lying on the street, mostly cops, but it looked like they had shot several ordinary pedestrians too. An elderly lady lay across a curb in a blood pool, her rucked-up flowered dress lifted by a faint breeze, a teenage kid was lying nearby, cut nearly in half by a burst of automatic fire. Cletis Barlow was nowhere in sight.

Paz looked at his car. The side window was blown out, the front end bore the marks of a burst. Coolant ran in a thick stream down the gutter. Paz started to run. It was about five miles to Jane's. He figured it would take a little over an hour if he didn't stop running at all.

TWENTY-EIGHT

Finnegan is nice enough, for a lawyer. He tells me he's a partner in Bailey, Lassiter & Phelps, the family's firm in New York, and he just happened to be taking a meeting in Atlanta when Josey yanked the handle. Being nearest partner to big client, he got tagged and came. I lie back in the leather of his rented Town Car and breathe in air-conditioning; I'm back in the bubble wrap of Doe existence, and I find I am a little sorry, as I never quite fit into it. I'm also nervous, because it means I'll have to talk to my father again.

Finnegan is giving me lawyerly advice, which I interrupt to tell him about Luz. I give him the whole story straight-up. He purses his lips. He is thin lipped, and it distorts the whole bottom shelf of his face to generate a purse equal to my little problem.

'You say this officer, this detective . . .'

'Detective Paz.'

'Paz. He knows the whole story?'

'Not the part about the mother's death, no. But he knows something is fishy about Luz. And if he looks hard, he'll find out who she is.'

'Yes, but there's no evidence you had anything to do with the woman's um . . . accident. She fell and struck her head. You found the girl, patently abused, and took her home, gave her shelter, cared for her. Irregular, of course; you should have notified the authorities, but . . . we can play it as a Good Samaritan excess. She calls you 'Mommy,' does she?'

'Muffa.'

'Hm. Let me get to work on it. I'll call the governor's office, see what can be done. Clearly, you're the best possible adoptive mother with respect to resources for a child; you're married, which is to the good. Is there any chance . . . ?'

He sees my look.

'Sorry, no, of course not. Still, I think we can get you named guardian while we iron out the details.'

Iron on, Finnegan! It's so easy to love lawyers when one is rich. We drive to the transmission place and I get my clunker, occasioning another massive lip-purse. I shake hands with Finnegan, thank him. He unloads a last smidgen of advice, to keep my mouth shut and avoid associating with my husband. Poor man, he was all set for a task like bailing a rich bitch out of some DUI-like situation and he ends up with me, voodoo, mass murder, Armageddon, and the Last Days. He hands me a bulky manila envelope and bids me good night.

After the chilled car the night is like a warm washrag against my face. Driving home, I'm aware of the sound of sirens, more sirens than usual, even down here in the poor end of the Grove. I hear a flat explosion, too, some-where to the north, and closer, the firecracker poppings of small-arms fire. I park and hurry across to Dawn's.

She's pale and nervous and she chatters a mile a minute: *Jeopardy* has been interrupted by the news. The Last Days indeed! Some huge and disparate disaster is occurring. An oil truck has crashed on I-95, gunfights have broken out near the Miami River, a riot is brewing in Overtown, a whole family has leaped from the top of a Brickell apartment house, a squadron of cops has run amok with automatic weapons and shot one another and several civilians. What's happening, is everyone going crazy? What should she do? Her husband is away again. What should she do?

I suggest a soothing cup of herbal tea, which I make, in her messy kitchen. This served, I greet my child with more fervor than I usually show. She feigns indifference, and continues her play with little Eleanor. Dawn and I sit in wicker chairs and watch the TV for a while. The pundits have decided that it is sabotage and a cult riot, although no one is sure about which cult is involved. Then the screen fizzles and goes dark. We wait, and watch the signature static of the Big Bang for a while, before I thumb the thing off. Dawn gets weepy and I comfort her as best I can.

Around eight, I take Luz home. I have a lot of stuff to do tonight. She's clinging and fretful, however, and I must stay with her, up in her little garret room, until she's asleep. Downstairs again, I take another amphetamine, no, two, just to make sure I stay up on the plateau, where there is a good view. I can't fall into the crevasse now, uh-uh.

I haul out the box and remove my divining bag, and some bags and bottles and soiled envelopes containing various organic flakes and fragments – *komo* – and the jar of *kadoul* I mixed up the other day, and my Mauser. I arrange these all on the kitchen table. Before starting, I look into the manila envelope that lawyer Finnegan gave me. Inside is my passport, my checkbook, my VISA and Amex cards, my New York driver's licence, and a minute cellular phone, with a note taped to it, in Josey's felt-tipped scrawl: *Janey – call Dad! auto #1 love J.* Oh Josey! How long would you have kept the dead girl's things had I really done it?

So the crying starts again, and through tears I seek and push the right buttons. The tiny thing reaches out into the wireless nexus and gets my father. By then, of course, I am honking like a walrus in heat, and I say how sorry I am, and he tells me not to think about it, that he never believed that I was dead. I asked him why not, as I thought I had done a pretty good job. He said he knew that if I really wanted to kill myself I would have used a gun. He said he knew I didn't have anything to do with Mary's death, and that he knew I really loved her, even though she didn't love me. I was amazed: we're always so surprised when our parents can figure us out, we all think we're so secret and clever. He asked when I was coming home. I said I had some things to take care of here, but not long at all. Then we talked about my mom for a while.

He asked me if he could help. I knew what he meant, and I said, no, he couldn't. I was going to a place where even the red handle wouldn't help, and Josey couldn't track me down for another rescue. He told me to take care and trust in God.

After we hung up, I finished my hysterics, weeping for my family, for Mary, and my poor gorgeous crazy mom, and Dad of course, but I'd always been able to cry for him. Then I washed my face in the tepid water of the kitchen sink and got down to work.

It is strangely the case that a particular arrangement and combination of organic materials, which have been handled in a ritual way, will perform acts definable as magic, or prevent them within a particular area. You can make, for example, a *ch'akadoulen* and plant it in front of a guy's house, and he will gradually fade away and die. Or suddenly decide to kill his family and have to be shot. Whether or not he's a believer. So I carefully compound my scant store of *komo* into *tetechinté*, countermagic. I only have enough *komo* for five of them. They don't look like much: little bundles of bark and leaves, smeared with oily substances, strong-smelling, each wrapped in an intricate web of red, black, white, and yellow threads.

I go outside and bury one at each corner of my house. There is a smell of distant burning, nastily hydrocarbonish, and a red glow to the north, and low heavy clouds, no breath of wind, although the clouds seem to be writhing along, lit from below. They must have tried to take him, and now he's showing them what he can do if he likes. He doesn't understand that they will all die before admitting that what he is is real, that they will squat, if it should come to that, in the glowing ruins of their cities and say, coincidence, random, bad luck, natural disaster, unknown terrorists, mass hallucinations, like a mantra. And he will still be invisible, the poor man.

The last little bundle I take up to the loft and hang from the ceiling above Luz's head. Over my own neck I draw the amulet Uluné gave me when I left Danolo, a little red-dyed leather pouch, into which I have never peered.

Now I clean my Mauser 96, a restful chore. It has no screws in its mechanism at all. Each part pops free with a precisely directed pressure and snaps in with a satisfying click, just where it belongs; the smell of the oil rag reminds me of home, of Dad. After that, I take the rounds out of the box magazine and rub the bullets with a substance designed by Olo technicians to make them penetrate magical objects or beings. Then I reload.

I need a bath, now, to clean the jail stink off my skin, a long hot one in a huge bathtub like they have at Sionnet, but what I have instead is my little chipped one. I stay in it a long time, and wash the last of poor Dolores's shit-brown out of my hair. After I emerge, I rub the haze from the mirror and contemplate Jane recidivus, trying not to recall the undying ghosts of this same assessing gaze, from my youth, when I cried, and cursed my plain face, and hated my sister, whom the mirror loved. I see the perfect teeth of the rich, quite startling eyes, if I do say so, nose too big, jaw too strong, teeny tiny little skinny lips like worms . . . At any rate, a lot better looking than Dolores. I get out my barber scissors, spread newspaper, and snip away, snip away, until I have made a rough dark-yellow helmet, jaw length on the sides and back, with a center parting, the somewhat jockish look I had in sophomore year, when I played a lot of field hockey. My husband always liked me to wear it long, and I did, down to the waist in back, braided and pinned up, a pain in the ass in Africa, but the Africans loved it. They used to touch it on the street, like touching a snake, for luck. I carefully gather up all the cut hair, down to the tiniest fragment I can find, and flush it away in the toilet. A little habit in the sorcery biz, practically the first thing Uluné taught me.

I don my ratty blue chenille Goodwill bathrobe and sit in the kitchen in the dark with my gun. The air is stifling, loaded heavy with the usual Miami perfume: jasmine, rot, car exhaust, a rumor of salt water, plus tonight the stink of burned things and . . . just now, the *dulfana*, and a dead rat odor. At the screen door I look down in the yard. There are three of them, standing motionless in a group. *Paarolawatset.* I can't see their features, but one of them has the sagging shape of the man Paz called Swett.

He doesn't want me wandering away again, it appears, and has dispatched watch-things to trail me, or maybe he fears for my safety in the chaos he's causing, and these are guards. That would be like Witt, to think of that.

I sit down and drink water. The thought of food is nearly as nauseating to me as the thought of sleep. I hear thumps and scratching sounds outside, calls of animals and birds whose natural habitat is not South Florida. I get my journals from the box and review my notes, as for a big test. I should be more or less safe from ordinary *jinja*, his sendings, because Uluné was a major power and he gave me some good stuff. I wish he were here now, Uluné. He wouldn't actually protect me. He sure didn't when I was witched out of my hut by Witt and Durakné Den. But I always got the feeling that Uluné was playing a much larger game than the usual sorcerers' spats, that if he thought it was required, he could have crushed both Witt and his witch teacher like cockroaches. Let Ifa unfold, Jeanne, he would say. Don't grab at the folds like a greedy child tearing the peel from a fruit. The do-nothing phase of life, as sensei used to put it, so hard for us Americans.

So I wait, and after a while . . . an hour? A couple of hours? . . . there is another unfolding. I hear steps on the shell gravel of the drive, and steps on my stairs. I work the action on the Mauser, chambering a magic bullet, and point at the screen door. There is a shadow there, a face. It's him, Witt. I take aim, not at all confident in my ability to shoot, not even now. Or that the bullet will have any effect.

'Jane? Ms Doe? Are you there?'

I let out the breath I am holding, and a wave of relief passes through my body, tingling down to my fingers. I lower the gun, and I say, 'Come in, Detective Paz. The door's open.'

He comes in. I turn on the kitchen light. A little double take when he sees the new me. When he notices the pistol he frowns.

'That's quite a piece.'

'It is. It's a Mauser 96, old and very rare. It works, though. You look like you've had a rough night.'

He has a smudge on his forehead, grease or smoke, and the knees of his tan slacks are grimy.

'You could say that. Can I sit down?' I motion to the other chair and he falls into it heavily. He gestures to my pistol. 'Expecting somebody? Or considering another suicide?'

'Troubling times,' I say. 'You never can tell who might come by on a night like this. Or what.' This sounds so portentously like the dialogue in a bad horror film that I feel hysteria rising in my throat, and I have to stifle a giggle.

'How do you know I'm not a what?'

'If you were a sending, you couldn't have gotten in. I have bars up against magical forces. The pistol is for physical beings, like those zombies out in the yard.' He stares at me, his mouth slightly open, like a child's. A good deal of the slick gloss and confidence he exhibited earlier today seems to have been scraped off Detective

Paz by this night's doings. I feel for him. I recall being scraped myself.

He says, 'Shit! This is really happening, isn't it?'

'I'm afraid so,' I say.

He hisses something in Spanish that I don't quite catch, and strikes the heel of his hand hard against his temple. 'Fuck! Sorry, I've had a bad day.'

'What have you been doing?'

'Lately? Well, we started the evening by arresting your husband. That didn't work out too good. He didn't stay arrested. He was in the back of my car, cuffed, and then he was smoke. Then all hell broke loose, which I thought was a figure of speech until a while ago. You wouldn't have any idea about how he does all this shit?'

'Actually, I have a very good idea, but I already told you and you didn't pay any attention. I don't really feel like going through it again.' I tapped the cover of the journal. 'It's all in here, more or less. You could read it.'

'I might do that.' He looks around my bare kitchen. 'You wouldn't have a drink handy, would you?'

'A drink drink? No, I don't. But I could run across to Polly's and borrow a couple of beers.' I rise, pistol in hand. I should have offered, of course; we Does are trained in the elementary courtesies, but there has been a long time between guests chez Jane.

'What about . . . ?' With a movement of his head he indicates the waiting things in the yard.

'Oh, they won't bother me. If they do, I'll shoot them.'

'The zombies? I thought they were dead already.'

'A popular misconception. In any case, I have magical bullets. Stay where you are. Don't move. I mean really don't move. You'll be fine.'

I go down the stairs and cross the yard. The *paarolawatset* begin to move toward me, but slowly, shuffling like old bums.

I knock on Polly's side door. The yellow porch light comes on, a curtain pulls aside, showing the terrified face of my landlady. At first she doesn't recognize me; then, with a look of vast relief, she does. Several locks click and she pulls me inside.

'Dolores! Thank God! What's going on? I was watching TV and then the cable went down. There's supposed to be a riot going on. Christ! Is that a gun? Who are those guys in the yard? I called the cops, but 911 is jammed up . . .'

I put a calming hand on her shoulder. 'There's not going to be a riot around here. Just stay in the house and you'll be okay. Are the kids in?'

'In L.A. with their father, thank God. They're due back tomorrow. Dolores, what's going on?'

I try to radiate confidence. Polly is actually pretty tough, and New Agey enough not to be knocked entirely out of whack by weird doings. 'It's a real long story, but first of all, I'm not Dolores anymore, I'm Jane. My husband isn't dead, like I told you; he's alive, and after me, and he's a . . . sort of a terrorist, and those are his people out there, watching me.'

'You're kidding, right? God, you cut and colored your hair! You look great. But seriously, you were hiding from him and he found you? Did you call the cops?'

'Yes. One of them is up in my place and I offered him a beer that I don't have. I came over to borrow a couple.'

She bursts out laughing, and I join her, and arm in arm we go up to the kitchen and she passes me a six-pack of Miller tallboys from the fridge. She says, 'I don't know about you, but I'm gonna go up to bed and turn up the A/C all the way, and put Hildegard von Bingen on the headphones and pull the covers up over my head until this is over.'

I tell her this sounds like a good plan. I am halfway home when I feel a finger scratching at my neck, and then my neck hairs are pulled and twisted in that annoying way she used to do when we were kids, and my sister's voice comes clearly over my left shoulder. Oh, Janey, you really messed up again, big-time. This is all your fault. Plain Jane. Plain Jane couldn't stand I was pregnant, you were so jealous you could hardly look at me, you always hated me, Mom said so. That's why you got him to kill me. You knew he was going to kill me, didn't you? And my baby. Look at me, Jane! Look what you did to me!

I don't turn around but keep walking. Slow going; I never realized that it's about a quarter of a mile from Polly's house to the garage. The path is closing in: rattan palms rattle and brush my arms, acacias, and locust bean, and all the dry spiky shrubs of the Sahel. My feet sink into the warm sand. A figure looms ahead, blocking my way. It's my brother. He is naked. He has an erection, which he strokes. Janey, honey, let's do it in the weeds. Janey, come on like we used to do in the boat-house, come on, Janey, his voice is sweet, low, insistent, come on, Janey, you know Mary and I used to do it all the time. Take off your clothes, Janey, let's see if you got any tits yet. I raise my pistol and shoot him in the chest. Screaming and crashing in the brush, and laughter, not human, like a hyena. I stagger.

There's hot breath in my ear, stinking breath, booze and decay. I don't know what I'm going to do with you, says Mom, why do you have to be such a pain in the ass? Look at your sister, just look at her! And there she is, right in front of me now, white and lovely in her little scoop-neck blue linen maternity top and white shorts. She smiles her cover girl smile. She opens the top and her insides fall out of her ripped belly as she smiles on. There is shrill howling, like a dog hit by a car.

Something grabs my left arm, hard. I raise the gun, but it is batted away and I am hauled up off my feet, an arm around my waist. I feel stair treads under my zoris. Detective Paz is heaving me up the stairs and into my apartment.

I collapse inside the door, my head against the cool porcelain of the stove.

'I heard the shot,' he says. 'I think you popped one of those . . . those guys. You were turning in a circle and screaming, about ten feet from the stairs.'

'Yeah. It's not so good out there right now.' I crawl on hands and knees to the bathroom. I lay my cheek on the rim of the toilet and retch up a little yellow slime. I hear the snap of a pop-top and the gurgling sound of a man knocking down most of a twelve-ounce in one slug.

'Feeling better?' he asks when I totter back and collapse into a chair next to him.

'Much. If I were a bell, I'd be ringing. Thank you for coming out there after me.'

'You had the beer. What was going on?'

'Just paging through the family album. Look, I think we're stuck here for a while. We'll be okay here unless he decides to come in person.'

'In which case, you'll waste him with that funny gun. Or I will.'

'No,' I snap, 'if he comes here, I'll probably shoot you, and maybe my daughter, too, or you us. Surely it has finally sunk in that he can control what we see? If I think he's approaching in person, we unload the firearms and put them out of reach. We can't fight him in *m'fa;* I have to stop him in *m'doli*. If I can.'

He drains his beer and pops another. 'Want one?' he asks, offering. I drink a sip. I can feel it trickle all the way down into what feels like an empty fifty-five-gallon drum. Paz is fingering my journal. He says, 'Would there be a part here that explains how a bunch of highly trained cops got into a gunfight with people who weren't there and then started shooting one another?' He shudders. 'And how somebody else, some fucking Ku Klux Klan bastard, is living in my partner's body? In small words.'

'Small words? You've seen a *grel*. That makes it easier. Sorry, *grel* – *grelet* is the plural. Mind demons. The Chenka call them *ogga*. Okay, the short version: One, the psyche is real, like metal and electricity. It's its own thing. Psyches live in complex brains like ours, but they're not strictly speaking products of our brains. And they can live outside of brains too.' I tell him in plain language what the Olo make of the mental phenomena that still baffle Western science – manic-depression, schizophrenia, mass hysteria, intuition, sexual attraction . . .

'I thought that was all chemicals – the mental disease business,' he says.

'Yes, right. But that view of the mind ignores tens of thousands of personal accounts of psychic experiences – falling in love with unsuitable people, premonitions, significant dreams, spirit possession, ghostly apparitions, religious ecstasies. Inexplicable behavior, we like to call it. The regular joe who every so often just has to rape and strangle a little girl. Afterward, he feels better. Of course he feels better; his *grel* is well fed, like a leopard after a nice haunch of antelope. Or the well-brought-up kid with no obvious symptoms who one day murders his parents and starts shooting everyone in school, or on a slightly grander scale, the fact that the most civilized and technically advanced nation in Europe once de-cided to put itself totally in the hands of an uneducated wacko with a funny mustache and a hypnotic stare. Yeah, it's all so-called chemistry, but since we don't know squat about how it works, calling it chemistry is just another kind of incantation. It's not science.'

And more of this. I haven't talked with anyone for longer than necessary for a couple of years and so it comes out in a rush, all of Marcel's theorizing, the stuff even he was nervous about placing before the scientific community, my own compulsive thoughts about the stuff I'd experienced, plus a good deal of speculative ontology, what I used to keep myself sane among the Olo, assuming for the moment that I succeeded in that. He listens, hardly interrupting, for which I am grateful. Detective Paz is a good listener; perhaps it is a professional requirement. Perhaps, also, he is exhausted into passivity, psychically spent, and, as his fourth tallboy goes down the hatch, a little drunk.

'So let's for the moment accept the reality of psychic entities,' I say, 'and that they are natural beings whose existence lies outside the scope of modern physics, not necessarily and forever outside the scope, because we can conceive, if only with difficulty, of a psychophysics that includes the phenomenology of consciousness and disembodied psyches. Like I said, physics has expanded to cover stuff like action at a distance, radio waves, radioactivity, quantum weirdness. The point is, there's no supernatural. It is all part of the universe, although the universe is queerer than we suppose. Now, the *grelet*, the *ogga*, are destructive psychic particles. They're everywhere, like bacteria. Why are they destructive? Because they feed on the psychic break-down products of a collapsing human psyche. They eat anguish and pain and heartbreak, and so they attempt to control their hosts so as to cause these states. Naturally, like any parasitic entity, they camouflage themselves as natives of the psychic ecology. You say your partner was never foulmouthed or racist before this?'

'Never. And he comes from a long line of nasty racists. He's a hard-rock born-again Christian.'

'But inside him was all the shit he heard when he was a kid, suppressed, under control. I take it he's a tightly wrapped guy?'

'Very.'

'Right, so Witt releases an aerosol that stuns what's his name's . . .'

'Barlow. Cletis Barlow.'

'Yes, it stuns Barlow's consciousness. That con-sciousness is asleep, or helpless. Into the driver's seat comes something wearing the sensory experience of his childhood, the material put there by his father. We all carry powerful bits of our parents' psyches in us, what the Jungians call introjects. That's how our psyches are formed in the first place, but even when we're adults, there's a little Mom and a little Dad still sitting in there, and God knows, even in so-called normal people, what we see in daily behavior is largely those introjects in action.'

That was interesting, that flicker of pain at the line about parental psyches. Could this be the ally? I am dying to know about this guy's daddy. But I have to be careful, or he'll bolt. 'What happened to your partner happens all the time in other cultures. It's a regular thing in Southeast Asia, like headache or the flu. They call it *amok* or *matagalp*. And dreams – these other psyches really boogie out in dreamland. The Olo believe that's why we sleep in the first place – so we can listen to and deal with the other folks who're living in our heads. That's one reason why extreme sleep deprivation leads invariably to psychosis.'

Yes, Jane, and look who's talking. He gets up, paces in silence to the end of the room, and comes back again. 'Say I buy all this. What's the fix? What do we do?'

A wail comes from upstairs. I am up the ladder in a flash. She's sitting up in bed, crying. I hold her, I rock her; she calms after a while, and I ask her what's wrong. Monsters. My heart freezes. But I don't smell anything, and the charm is still in place over her bed. Just a regular nightmare, then, thank God, just wonderful ordinary hideous childhood terrors. We talk about monsters a little. Your regular mom can tell her child that monsters are imaginary and can't hurt you. This is, however, not an option for me. I indicate the *tetechinté* over her bed, I explain what it is for and that it will keep the monsters from getting in.

Something heavy lands on the roof and makes a scratching sound, like long claws drawing over shingles. Luz shrieks again, and buries her face in my bathrobe. I say it's trying to get in and it can't, and in fact, it can't.

She does not, however, want to sleep alone, she wants to sleep in the big hammock, with me. I think that's a reasonable request. I say, 'Listen, honey, you remember that policeman who was here today, this morning?' She nods. 'Well, he's downstairs. Mommy is helping him catch the bad people.'

'Can I help, too?'

'Of course,' I say. She doesn't want to be left out of anything, even death. 'We'll all help together.'

I grasp her hot, damp little hand and we go to the ladder together. Suddenly, she gives a little shriek. 'I forgot. I have a note.'

She runs back to her book bag and trots back with a square of paper. It says *Dear Ms Tuoey: Luz needs her decorations attached to her costume. Everything is in the bag. Use your imagination!!* It's signed *Sheila Lomax*. 'What is it?' Luz asks.

'I'm supposed to fix your costume for the Noah's ark play.'

'My Mary Mary all contrary costume. It has fluffy things, and little shiny things like little tiny mirrors.'

'Sequins.'

'Uh-huh. I have a lot and a lot of them.'

Oh, good! Thank you, Miss Lomax!

We descend. Detective Paz is crouching in firing position between the refrigerator and the bathroom door. He has the grace to blush, and shoves his pistol hurriedly back into its holster, like a man caught pissing, zipping it away.

Something has changed in the atmosphere, a lightening of pressure, in the last few seconds, like a fresh breeze through your window on a sultry night. My wall clock says midnight. I go to the window. The

shapes in the garden are gone. Detective Paz stands
next to me.

'They're gone,' he says.

'Not for nothing are you a detective,' I say, and he
laughs.

'Maybe they're on shift work. Who do you think's
going to cover the graveyard shift? So to speak.'

He seems to be returning to his cheeky ways. Good.
Resilience is good. Luz sees us looking at each other
and does not like it.

'I'm hungry,' she declares, pouting. 'I'm starving to
death!'

'Luz, honey, it's twelve midnight,' I say. 'Have a
banana and you can go into the hammock.'

'I don't want a banana. I want dinner.'

'You had dinner, dear. At Eleanor's. Remember?'

'No I didn't. Eleanor had a yucky dinner, and I
didn't eat it.'

Oh, Christ. And of course, Dawn was too frazzled to
inform me. Luz is getting ready to wail, when, remarkably, Detective Paz kneels down next to her. 'You know,
I'm starving to death, too. What do you say we go out to
a restaurant? I bet you have a pretty dress you can put
on. And your mom can put on a pretty dress, and we'll
go out to a fancy restaurant. It has tropical fish tanks and
a cage full of parrots.'

'A restaurant?' says The Mom doubtfully. 'It's past
midnight.'

'I mean a Cuban restaurant,' he says. 'Cuban
restaurants are just getting in gear at midnight.'

I look at him and at Luz. They're both grinning at
me, white teeth against brown. This is interesting. The
world as we know it may end fairly soon, and here we

are getting ready for a date. But what else should we do? Call in air strikes? Run around like chickens with their heads off? This seems right, and as I think this, suddenly my appetite comes back in a rush. I am starving. I find I am ridiculously pleased that, whatever happens afterward, at least I'll get one decent meal.

I say, 'Okay, but I have to get dolled up. You could skim through that while I'm doing it.'

He stops smiling and sits down at the table. He opens the journal.

TWENTY-NINE

Day 40, Danolo

Fortieth day in the whale's belly, although I feel more as if for the first time I am on the outside of the whale. I am not talking to rocks yet, but it is quite something to feel at least some intimations of what original participation is like. I got up this morning, for example, and was well into the day before I 'came to myself' as they say. What a great deal we have traded for our power over nature! This is what happened to M., I imagine, this total unity with the environment and the culture. I never understood that, I was too young.

But this isn't Shangri-la, the worm in the apple is sorcery, the same thing that protects us here. These are the healthiest people I have ever seen in Africa – virtually free of the usual tropical maladies & they are well fed. But there are not many of them, and there are fewer kids than you would expect. Everyone in Africa believes that sorcery is the major cause of death and misfortune. Here, it may even be true. There is a kind of cloud over everyone's psyche, and I occasionally catch on people's faces the expression one sees in shots from the Depression or war zones – helplessness, fear. But the rule is a remarkable cheerfulness and calm, especially among the ordinary townspeople, who are kind and generous.

There is the horrible business with the *dontzeh*

children, although in balance, I have also never seen children treated better (certainly not in traditional Africa) once they have formed that mystical *sefuné* bond with an adult.

Reality of the spirits. Of course I don't believe in them . . . *but they're there:* not so amusing here, dear M.! In Danolo, one feels unaccountable chills, breezes that touch the cheek but don't stir the leaves, that sense, familiar in public places in the West, too, that one is being observed, things seen in the peripheral vision that don't come into focus when you try to see them plain. Again, maybe it is the drugs.

Another unaccountable event. U. demonstrated *faila'olo* today, disappearing from my sight and reappearing behind me as I sat at the door to my *bon*. Of course, he doesn't actually disappear. He throws a brief trance on the subject, walks around her, and wakes her out of it when in the right position. I got some monofilament from my bag and tied a cat's cradle barrier across the door, but that didn't slow him down at all. He thought it was very funny. Would it work with an objective observer? Is there such a thing? Clearly, there must be some lost time involved and, in my increasingly infrequent fits of science, I wish for automatic timers, infrared beams, movie cameras, and all the other objectifying impedimenta of my culture.

After the demo, we mixed up *kadoul*, sorcerous compounds, a very Julia Child sort of afternoon. U. is very strict about spells. The word makes the power – the *kadoul* is worthless without it, so says my master. I have to memorize them; it ruins the spell if it's written down. It has to be burned into the soul, says U. I can't do it, I screw up the *chinté*, in both substance and word. U. is patient and forgiving, although some of the stuff is rare and valuable. Little steps, Jeanne, little steps, he says. I always say, Yes, Owadeb. It means good father, an honorific.

Training in attention, staring at a pebble for hours. Essential. The worst thing you can do, apparently, is lose attention. You might pick the *wrong* mouse or frog to be your magical ally, for example, and that would never do.

Day 42, Danolo

A ceremony tonight, dancing and drums. As a good anthropologist I should be taking notes but can't seem to generate the distance. Inside it too deep, a danger as M. said. U. says the ceremony is asking the *orishas* for forgiveness, some kind of anniversary of their exile from Ifé. Asked, forgiveness for what? Wouldn't say. Talking in riddles again. At height of craziness, dancing myself (and I can't dance), W. appeared, smiling, face shining with sweat. Said to call him Mebembé, now. Little helper? Asked him what it meant, but he just shrugged. Brief conversation before Tourma pulled me away. She seemed upset but wouldn't tell me why. Was he really there, or yet another Olo weirdness? If real, he seems happier than he's been in a while. Writing is going well, he says.

Day 46, Malinou

I see I have been neglecting this journal.

We have been making house calls, U. and I. We paddled his pirogue downriver and visited a string of villages on the borders of the park, where U. did oracles and a little witch-doctoring. He is famous here and greatly feared. The people are totally whacked out by his performance, although the issues they bring to him are mainly just the petty decisions of agricultural life. Sell the cow? Plant another field of yams? There's occasionally a heavier one – am I being hexed? Should the second son marry that girl? I haven't seen a customer go off unsatisfied. There's also private consultation with the witch-afflicted, but I don't get to see that, not yet. I asked him if I could do an oracle and he said yes, when I am ready, but I must be perfect in my verses.

Watched U. take *grel* out of a man. It was quite dramatic and New Testament. He put it into a chicken, which was then killed and thrown into a fire. Stench! An interesting ritual, I took careful notes. The patient seemed totally exhausted, but a lot better off than the chicken. Or the *grel*, according to U. He says you can extract a *grel* into yourself and then spit it out and burn it, but it is disgusting and fairly dangerous. A chicken is better.

U. withdrawn and short-tempered tonight. He snarled at the woman who brought us our evening meal, which I've never seen him do before. I thought she was going to piss herself with terror. I asked him what was wrong. Ignored the question, told me some kind of parable. Suppose a leopard is attacking your goats. Then you get all the strong men of the village together, with spears, and you wait for the leopard to come to the goat pen and you kill it. That's easy. But suppose you hear that a leopard is attacking the goats of your cousin far away in another village. In that village all the men are weak and their spears are broken. What then, Jeanne? Should you help your cousin? How should you do this? I don't know, Owadeb. You could tell your cousin to set a trap. You could tie a goat over a pit and then the leopard might attack the goat and fall in.

This answer seemed to please him a great deal, and his mood improved. He called for beer and we both got a little buzzed. A good answer, Jeanne, he said. But it would have to be a brave goat, the one who stays at the pit. Yes, I said, a brave goat and maybe a stupid leopard. He laughed his head off. I wish I knew what the hell he was talking about half the time.

Day 51, Boton

My first divination today. Wife of a Fulani herder, Maramu by name, a young childless woman, hence of rock-bottom status. No one with any clout would have risked it. We did it in the open under a canopy. I gave her the full verse in Olokan, which, of course, she did not understand, and then translated into halting Bambara. She would have a child but had to make sacrifices to ensure the child did not become an enemy. She was radiantly happy, embarrassingly grateful; the other wives gave me dirty looks. You can't please everyone in the oracle business. After that, business pretty good. All girls, of course, no man would stoop so low, although I give good discounts compared to U. Most of the findings concerned children and sick relatives; women don't make too many big decisions in these parts. A couple, though, about witch-craft.

Again, it's hard to explain. I don't have to think of what to say. The interpretation just pops into my head. Later, told U. about this. He's not surprised. Ifa is my pal, according to him.

Day 52, Danolo

We are back here, in the midst of some unexplained disaster. Last night, after throwing Ifa all day, I collapsed on my pallet in the room the villagers provided for us, and fell instantly to sleep. Awakened by a dream. A man I'd never seen before, an Olo, was talking to me over a fire. I could see his face quite clearly. He was holding a sorcery box, not a cake tin, but one carved of wood. He opened the lid and showed me the contents. It was a little black statue, and I knew that it was a statue of W. The guy said, in Olo, Come join your husband, he's lonely without you. And in the dream I felt this burning desire to enter the box, it was like the ultimate happiness, and I was about to step into it when I looked up at the guy and saw that his black eyes were the heads of worms. Then I woke up. U. was up, too, lying on the pallet across the room from me. I could see his face in the moonlight. What is it, Jeanne Gdezdikamai? I told him the dream. He became agitated, and immediately began to gather our stuff into straw carrier bags. I asked him what was wrong. He said, The *okunikua*, we have to go back, quickly, quickly! Now, at night? Yes, it is already too late. I have been a stupid old man. And that's all he would say. He kept repeating something, though, like a prayer – Creator and head, fight for me!

Ten minutes later we were in our pirogue, launched into inky water striped down the middle by a three-quarter moon. I was in the front, paddling like mad, he was in the back, chanting, steering us God knows how through the channels. Terrible sense that other passengers were in the boat, like feeling the presence of Eshu behind you in the oracle, but different. The Eshu feeling is of something huge and old, like the loom of an island in the fog before you see it. This was of something spiky and wet, and it was all I could do to resist the urge to turn around in the pirogue. The canoe seemed sluggish, too, like something was grabbing at it with weedy fingers.

The moon was down and it was dark as a cellar when he turned the pirogue onto a beach. He jumped out and crashed into the bushes, with me on his tail. Remarkably, it was the right beach – we were in Danolo. When we trotted through the gate he stumbled, and I grabbed his arm. Loltsi was waiting there with a smoking torch. By its light U. looked as though he had lost two inches and forty pounds – for the first time he looked like a little old man. In the compound, everyone was awake and wailing, even Sekli. Tourma is missing. According to Sekli, everyone went to sleep in good order. Sometime in the middle of the night Mwapune, who shares a room with Tourma and the two kids, got up to pee and found the other girl gone, and raised the alarm.

U. looked close to collapse. The women put him to bed. From what I could make out before they shooed me away, he is under attack from some rival sorcerer and it has something to do with me. I am not popular just now. I went back to my own *bon* and leaned against the wall. Something landed on the roof, heavy, with claws. An oppressive, crushing sense of despair, of evil. I looked up and there were eyes staring through the thatch, more than two, green ones, and red. I threw powders, chanted *tetechinté* and thanked God he had made me memorize the words. Voices in my head, urging murder and suicide. I filled my head with the chant, and after a while things returned to what passes for normal around here. I went outside and watched the sun come up.

Walked into the center of town and made sketches. Unusual atmosphere about the place, not many people on the streets, the houses closed up, as if a war was expected.

Sitting on my front step, chewing tamarind, I watched Sekli come out of the big house carrying a bag. She grabbed up one of the cockerels scratching in the dust, and walked across the compound to me, indicating with a jerk of her head for me to follow her. We went into the center of the compound where the big stone stands in the eye of the pavement spiral. She gave me the bird to hold and from her bag took some clay pots and what I guess was *kadoul*, but of a type I hadn't seen before. She ignited a fire with flint and steel in a mass of fuzzy brown matter, and when the smoke was up and thick she took the cockerel from me and cut its throat with a sharp piece of obsidian. The blood spurted and she sprinkled it in patterns over the standing stone. I recall thinking I should take notes, but I did not. I also recall thinking that although this stone is an important cultural artifact, I had never, before this, thought to come near it. She was chanting in Olokan all this time, too fast for me to follow. I did note that what had seemed natural discolorations in the rock were actually the marks of dried blood, very thick and probably very old.

Sekli squatted and sliced the cockerel open. Haruspication, divination by entrails. I had never observed this before among the Olo. It is rare in Africa in any case. She passed her hands through the chicken guts several times, peering closely at their bloody coils. Then she rose abruptly and tossed the chicken against the stone. She stared at me, her face wooden. It is well? I asked, one of my few Olokan phrases. Without answering, she clutched my arm and pulled me back to Uluné's room. He was lying on his pallet.

A rapid dialogue between them followed. U. beckoned me closer and spoke to me in French. Do you know what is happening, Jeanne? I don't, Owadeb, I said. He said, Something very bad. Durakné Den, the witch, has suddenly grown very much stronger. He has eaten someone, and now he has more power, more than me right now. I said, You mean he has *eaten* someone, like meat? No, not that way. Not *m'fa* eating; *m'doli* eating. His spirit. So, now that he is strong he attacks me and steals Tourma. I think he is trying to do a forbidden thing with her, a very great *chinté* that we don't allow. Why don't you? The *orishas* don't like it. It has to do also with the *Ilidoni*, the Shameful March. He made the warding-off-evil sign that the Olo make on the few occasions when they happened to mention it. I must admit I was excited; all my anthro neurons were aglow. At one level; at another level I was quaking with fear. Will you tell me more about this, Owadeb? He said, It is better not to have that in your head. You might write it down. Here a faint smile.

He patted my hand and I felt the heat of his skin, feverish. Look, Jeanne, here is what you must do. I need a *weidouliné*. You understand what that is? I said, Yes, Owadeb, a magical ally. Good, he said. This ally is a small brown snake, about this long. He held up his hands a few feet apart. You must go north, out of Danolo through the north gate; Sekli will take you there. There is a path through the bush, north, north. In a while you come to a red rock like a tent (he made a shape with his hands) so, and bones of cows all around it. Wait there. This kind of snake lives in the rocks. Wait there for the sun to just disappear, and one will come out to you. Grab him quickly and put him in your bag and come back here. Now this is important, Jeanne. Don't talk to anyone you meet there at the rocks. Whoever it is don't talk to them. Do you understand? Now, go; and take this. He pulled the amulet he always wore over his head and draped it around my neck, a small red leather pouch. The mission seemed simple enough and I was glad to do it. Sekli said something, angry, gesturing at me. U. calmed her down somehow, and indicated that we should leave. Sekli grabbed up a finely worked homespun bag and thrust it into my hands. She went out and I followed behind her.

We walked through deserted streets, through a part of the town I had not seen before. The buildings were not in good repair. Mud brick takes a lot of maintenance, and many of the structures we passed had slumped back into the soil. Danolo had obviously once been more populous than it now was. Explains the scarcity of children? Why don't they breed? Ask U.? Through a half-ruined gate.

We walked a path through rough bush – thorn, stunted acacias, cran-cran, broken rock – in silence for about an hour, I estimated. I could see the tent rock from a long way off in the flat terrain, a tumble of red platelike boulders maybe four meters high. There were cattle skeletons strewn around. She pointed and turned to go. I asked her in Bambara if U. would get well. I don't know, she said. I think he was (something?) to teach you *ndol* and this is the result. As I told him. I told him he should (something?) you, but he has a hard head. He told me it was (something?) for *debentchouajé*. Incomprehensible. I just bow.

I asked, It's because of *me* that the witch attacks Uluné? No, she said, the witch would have attacked anyway. Witches attack him all the time, and he throws them off easily. The witch is attacking *you*. Uluné is protecting *you*, so he can't protect himself. She said something else in straight Olokan that I didn't get, and walked off.

I dropped down and put my back against the warm rock. I was hot, and I drank some water from my canteen. Bright sky above, dome of Africa, the Sahel pressing down, empty of God, of any help. Found some tamarinds in the sleeves of my robe, chewed them, tried not to cry. I wondered if Sekli was telling the truth. I wondered what I would do if she were. Sacrificing himself to save me? It didn't seem like the U. I knew. Not personal, then, only part of his deep game? I am completely lost, here among the simple primitive people. Thought, anthro such a crock of shit sometimes.

As the sky went scarlet, he just walked out from around the rocks, I didn't see or hear him approach. I was so surprised I cried out and jumped to my feet. He grinned and laughed. Janey, you're looking good. I see you've gone native too. That outfit suits you. He was wearing an Olo sarong and cloak. He came closer, and touched my headdress casually. Long time no see, he said, and opened his arms. I hesitated a second and jumped in. I was so lonely, like in a fucking dumb Elvis song. We hugged. We kissed. He said, What're you doing here out in the middle of nowhere? I said, I have to get a snake for my sorcery teacher. And then I laughed, we both laughed. Because it felt real, not weird, American, a couple of culture-shocked Americans in Africa. We talked. What've you been doing, Janey? I told him amusing anecdotes about my life with U. And you? Oh, you know, writing, taking notes. Learning a little anthro, too. Learned the language a little. Really? Say something in Olokan. He did and it was true, he spoke it better than me. Sound of a bird, then, saw it, too, the looping flight of the honeyguide. *Purr-purr-purr WHIT*. We laughed. He said, Yeah, that's my bird, he sympathizes with me, poor Witt.

And then I remembered what U. had said about not talking to anyone. Suddenly, I was frightened, and I saw the brown snake too late, it was right in front of me sliding along and I scrabbled after it on my hands and knees, and just missed it. It went down a hole in the rocks. I stood up and said, Goddamn, I missed it. But Witt wasn't there. I ran around the rock pile, scattering cow bones, and he wasn't there. I climbed on the rocks and looked around, I could see for a long way, and nothing at all.

I walked back in the dark and now I am writing this on my pallet. U. is in some kind of coma, and no one will talk to me, not even the kids. U.'s compound filling with other Olo sorcerers, all grim-looking. Tourma still gone.

THIRTY

He finished reading and put the journal on the table. She was wearing black jeans and a white shirt, standing there looking at him. It was hard to believe, what he had just read, hard to believe it had happened to this woman. She looked just like a regular person. She said, 'Stunned, Detective Paz?'

'It's a lot to take in. You didn't write the final chapter.' She noticed he had washed his face and sponged off the worst of the stains on his clothes.

'No. Do you want to hear it? She'll be half an hour putting on outfits. She's at the stage where she likes the layered look. She'll come down with three dresses on, one on top of another.'

'I'm dying to hear it.'

'A figure of speech, I hope,' she said, taking a chair. 'Well, it's briefly told. I fell asleep. Actually I cried myself to sleep, I'm ashamed to say. Then I woke up. Middle of the night. It was a dream, but not a dream, if you know what I mean. I was walking through Danolo, out of Danolo along a trail. Jackals were barking, nightjars were going *tok tok tok*. There was a fire up ahead. My husband was there, naked, painted, and there was another man, I couldn't see his face, he was just a kind of shadow in the glow, I could see the flash of his teeth, a necklace of shells around his neck, and the whites of his eyes. I knew it was Durakné Den, the *dontzeh* witch. Tourma was there, too, naked. She looked like she was asleep. I watched Witt slice her belly open with a little black stone knife and remove the baby. Tourma didn't even twitch. The baby writhed and gasped; Durakné Den was chanting something in Olo and Witt was chanting too. He . . . you know what he did – you've seen it. He sliced into the baby's skull and scooped out its brain, like taking the stone out of an avocado. Blood splattered all around. I felt drops strike my face. I was paralyzed, I couldn't do anything, like in a nightmare. They cut and they ate. I remember staring at him, Witt, and I saw the blood dripping from his mouth. The most horrible part was, he looked happy, really happy, like he was at a good party. He told me what was happening, about the *okunikua*, about his plans. Suddenly, I was free, I ran, and I heard him laughing. In the morning, at first light, I grabbed everything I could carry, my box and some water and food, loaded it into a pirogue and paddled away.'

She fell silent, shaking her head. He said, 'I don't get this about this ritual, *okunikua*? He eats pieces of a woman and the baby and what . . . he gets powers from this?'

'Well, I never got the details, but yeah. In combination with other things he's done to himself, there are chemicals in the various parts of the victims that have been modified by other chemicals fed to the mother during the ceremony. Not fed, actually, breathed in. It's like an amplification of what he can already do. Think of the difference between a plain vanilla A-bomb and an H-bomb. It needs four women, though, as I said.'

Paz thought about this for a while. 'How come he let you go? There in Africa.'

'I don't know. Part of the plan, I guess. Who can figure out why the Olo do anything? Why they let Durakné live there. Witt had other things to do. My sense was that the Olo were gathering to somehow block Durakné Den in Danolo, which is why Witt might have had to leave. He came here, where there's no one to stop him.'

'We'll stop him,' said Paz, hardly believing it himself. 'So how *did* you get out of there?'

'Oh, that part's a little vague. The dry season was on by then, the channels were drying into mud, not that I knew what channels to take. And I was hallucinating a lot, and I was sick, really sick. I got completely lost. I ended up stranded on the mud, burning up with fever. Fade to black. The next thing I remember was the hospital in Bamako. They thought I had hepatitis. Apparently, I was found by a Fulani herder driving his herd down to the Niger for the big river crossing, the Diafarabe. He recognized my amulet and figured it would be good juju to rescue me. I guess you must've got the rest if you talked to my father. The weirdest thing was that when Witt showed up in my hospital room in New York, I was sort of glad to see him.' She laughed. 'That old black magic's got me in its spell.'

He was about to say something about it being nothing to laugh about, when Luz came tromping down the ladder, wearing a threadbare red velvet dress over a gingham pinafore over yellow pedal pushers and a frilly blouse. Paz stood up and said to the little girl, 'Great outfit, kid, let's go eat.'

'And see the fishies.'

They got into the old Buick and drove north on Douglas. The Grove seemed reasonably quiet; people were staying in. There were few cars; once a police car whipped by, siren whooping, and Paz felt a pang of guilt. He was, officially, off duty, but maybe he was AWOL as well. He had not called in to find out what was going on, or where his partner was. He had run. He had left his partner and run. Of course, the alternative was staying and shooting his partner and a bunch of guys with machine guns, or being shot himself. He told himself that he was in fact where the action on this case really was. If it could be fixed at all, he would either fix it with this crazy woman or die trying.

At the Trail, they had to stop for some time, while emergency equipment, fire trucks, ambulances, buses full of cops went by, sirens and lights. The worst of the trouble seemed to lie east, over by the bay and Brickell Avenue. Paz directed her west.

Jane said, 'I assume you're off duty.'

Paz gave her a quick nervous look. 'I guess. I don't know what good a cop is when the guy who's doing the bad stuff can't be collared and locked up. It strikes me that the prudent investigative posture is to stick as close as possible to you.'

'As bait? Or . . . what?'

He thought for a moment. 'Barlow used to say, the difference between a good detective and a no-account one is three things: patience, patience, and patience. I'm waiting. Something'll turn up.' After a while he added, 'Do you think . . . will Barlow ever come back to, like, normal? Like he was?'

'He might,' she said. 'If he has people around him

who treat him like he's the decent guy you say he was,
and love him, the *grel* may fade back. People have what
we call 'nervous breakdowns' all the time, and recover.
And there are more direct methods against them. Were
you close to him?'

'Not close, but he was really good to me. I respected
him more than any man I ever met.'

'A father figure?'

His face grew stiff. 'Yeah, I guess.'

'Is your father here in Miami?'

'No. My mom said he died coming over from Cuba.'
His tone did not invite further questions.

They drove in silence to a crowded parking lot off
Calle Ocho. Jane looked at the restaurant with interest.
It was a large, brightly lit place, with the name splayed
in loose blue neon script over faded pink: LA GUANTA-
NAMERA. Entering, she was hit with the delicious and
barely describable perfume of a good restaurant
running at full tilt. The place was packed; panic had
not cut into business at Guantanamera, or perhaps
the rumors of disaster had brought people out to die
replete. Paz was obviously well known here, she saw;
the maître d' at the tiny front desk gave him a big smile,
smiled at Jane, too, and at the fascinated yet shrinking
Luz. Ignoring the clot of patrons waiting in the little
lobby, he immediately led the party to a nice banquette
table, right under a huge saltwater fish tank. The child
stood on her chair and watched the fish. Paz stood
by her and named them as they drifted by: the beau-
gregory, the moorish idol, the damselfishes in their
varieties, the French and regal and queen angelfishes,
the neon goby and the rock beauty. She poked the glass
and gave them her own private silly names.

'This is great,' Jane said. 'She'll probably crash in two minutes.'

A waitress arrived and gave Paz a gold-toothed smile. 'Hey, Jimmy! You're out front today.'

'Julia, how's it going?'

'It's been crazy tonight. She was looking for you.'

'I bet. Why don't you bring us a couple of special daiquiris and a Shirley Temple for the kid.'

Then he spoke to her in Spanish for a few minutes and she left. Paz said, 'You don't speak Spanish?'

'Hardly a word, I'm ashamed to say. I usually speak French sprinkled with random *a*'s and *o*'s. And I caught 'daiquiri' just now. They seem to know you pretty well here.'

'Yeah, well, I'm here a lot.' They watched the fish and Luz for a while. Jane became aware that the music system was playing the same song over and over, with different singers and arrangements.

'That song,' she said, 'I know that song. It's famous. Didn't Pete Seeger do that way back when?'

He laughed. 'Oh, right, the definitive version. Christ, Pete Seeger! Right now this is Abelardon Barroso and la Sensacion. It's 'Guantanamera,' the greatest song ever written. Back before the revolution, Cuban radio used to play it five minutes before the hour, every hour. People used to set their watches by it. There are thousands of versions. But this next track is the original, by Joseito Fernandez. He wrote it sometime in the thirties.' She listened. A rock-solid beat and a man with precise diction and a rough friendly voice, singing from the heart.

'What do the words mean?'

'Oh, they have all kinds of verses. In the old days,

Joseito used to make up verses on the news – murders, scandals, famous people.' He sang along softly: *"Yo soy un hombre sincero, de donde crece la palma, y antes de morime quiero, echar mis versos del alma."'*

He translated this and she said, 'I believe that. I believe you are a sincere man from the land where the palms grow. And maybe you'll actually get to sing the song of your soul.'

He shrugged. 'Who can tell? Anyway, the chorus is always the same: *'Guantanamera, guajira Guanta-namera* . . . the girl from Guantánamo, the girl from the farm.'

She stared at him. 'From the farm?'

'Yeah, a *guajira*'s like a country girl, a hillbilly.'

'And they named this place after the song?'

'Not really.' He laughed, mildly embarrassed. 'Okay, I confess – it's my mother's place. She's the *guanta-namera* it's named after. We always play this CD after midnight, kind of a trademark. The people like it too.'

'Does she really come from a farm?'

'Oh, yeah, from back in the mountains north of Guantánamo. When I was a kid, I was always hearing what they didn't have on the goddamn farm. What, you want sneakers! I was seventeen before I saw my first pair of shoes. What, you want a car! I was twenty-two before I even rode in a car, and that was a truck.'

'Well, she seems to be doing okay now. This place . . .'

'Oh, yeah, now. But they never get over it. My mom left in '72. Came over on a couple of doors lashed to four inner tubes. She could always cook, so she got restaurant work. She slept on a mattress in the stock-room to save money. Then I was born, and she got one of those little food trucks, going around to all the construction sites, feeding the Cubano working humps their rice and beans and *media noche* and the coffee and cakes. I was up there in the front seat until I started school. And she hung on to every goddamn penny and opened her first real place, a counter-and-four-tables joint on Flagler. *Comidas criollas*. And then this one here, fifteen or so years ago. An American success story.' She could see his face get tight as he said this, tight behind the bright, faintly mocking smile. She controlled her own excitement. 'And your dad? What was he like?'

His face shut down completely. 'I told you – died before I was born. Crossing over.'

The waitress returned with the drinks and a straw basket full of warm *platano* chips and a pottery bowl of *mojo criollo*.

'I ordered for us. You don't mind?' She smiled, shrugged, and took a plantain chip and dipped it in the sauce. She ate and sighed, closing her eyes. She took another. And another.

He watched her eat and drink. In five minutes she had consumed half the basket and finished the daiquiri. Paz polished off the rest of the chips, except for the half-dozen or so the child took. He ordered another round. 'You're hungry.'

'Oh, *yes*,' she said, her eyes lit with a crazy light.

Then came a plate of *frituras de cangrejo* and bowls of cold *sopa de aguacate*, and then a beefsteak *palomilla*, with mounds of curly fried potatoes, with plates of black beans and rice on the side. The child ate the fries and some rice and beans, whined briefly, and fell asleep on the banquette, with her head on Jane's lap. Jane ate

most of the fries and most of the rice and beans. Paz
looked on admiringly. 'You're a good eater.'

'It's good food. I haven't had a square meal in two
and a half years. Actually, the fact is, I shouldn't be
hungry at all. I've been on uppers for the last twenty-
four hours or so. I should take some more, but I can't
bear to. This is so pleasant. Thank you.'

'*De nada*. Why are you taking uppers, if I may
inquire?'

'You may. It's so I don't fall asleep until all this is
over. He can get to me if I'm dreaming, in a way that
could put me in his power more or less permanently.'

'I thought you said he couldn't get to you. You
had . . . you know, those charms, or whatever.'

'Yes, in the *m'fa*.' She waved a hand. 'This world. But
in sleep we open a door to *m'doli*, a world between the
real world and the world of the spirits. Spirits can visit
us there, that's what a lot of dreams are, and it's also the
arena where magic takes place – a borderland. I have to
meet him in *m'doli*, but awake.'

'And how do we do that?'

'More drugs. I have some of the stuff made up. But
as I told you, I need allies.'

'Yeah, that's what I don't get . . .' He broke off and
stared.

A striking figure was wending her way through the
dining room, a mahogany-colored woman dressed all in
yellow silk, with a fresh white gardenia placed in the
coils of black hair piled on her head. She stopped at
several tables and exchanged a few friendly words with
the customers. Then she arrived at their table. Paz stood
up, embraced the woman lightly, kissed her cheek.

'How are you, Mami?'

'I'm fine. I'm working myself to death in the kitchen of my restaurant because I have a son who doesn't care about me, but otherwise I'm just fine. Who is this woman?'

'Someone from my work. She's an important witness. Shall I introduce you?'

'If you like.'

Paz stepped back and switched to English. 'Mother, this is Jane Doe. Jane, my mother, Margarita Cajol y Paz.'

Jane rose, nodded, extended her hand, looked into the woman's face. There was no doubt about it. She felt a warm tingling in her hand; the woman must have felt it, too, because she pulled her own hand abruptly away. The expression on Margarita Paz's face changed from its habitual cast of superior dissatisfaction to amazement, and then to something much like fear. Paz watched this with interest, having never observed this particular face-show before. He was about to prime the conversation to discern its cause, when his mother made a hurried excuse in Spanish and bustled off.

Seated again, Paz asked, 'What do you think that was all about? Usually she hangs around and gets your pedigree and when we're going to get married.'

'Perhaps she knew I wasn't good enough for you in one glance. How long has your mother been involved in Santería?'

He frowned. 'Who said she was involved in Santería? She hates that stuff.'

'Really?'

'Yeah. She's a straight-up Catholic. I had a girlfriend once, in high school, gave me one of those little statues. My mom found it, and chewed me out, and trashed it.

Why did you think she was into it? Because she's a black Cuban?'

A challenging tone here. 'No, not that at all. As it happens, I saw her at Pedro Ortiz's *ile* a couple of nights ago.'

'That's impossible.'

The waitress dropped off a tray of guava tarts and Cuban cookies, a couple of Cuban coffees, and two brandies.

Jane said, 'I saw her. Your mother. Not only was she there, but she was an *oriate*, a "made" woman. You know what *hacer el santo* means, don't you? I saw her mounted by Yemaya. No, don't shake your head. Listen! I want you to listen to something.'

She recited, almost chanting, 'He-went-into-the-river-and-killed-the-crocodile was the one who cast Ifa for "Is it profitable to take a caravan to the north?" Ifa says it is foolish to leave the farm before the rains. Witches are coming to carry off the eldest child. She said her strength was no match for evil-doing. He said seek the son with no fathers. He said the woman will leave her farm and help. He said the bird with yellow feathers is of use. Four are necessary for the sacrifice: two black pigeons, two white pigeons, and thirty-two cowries.'

'What's that, a poem?'

'In a way. It's a divination verse. Ifa gave it to me when I asked him what I should do about my husband. I already made the sacrifice. Three allies are named. I have a yellow chick at home. I just met a woman who left a farm, and is made to Yemaya, the sea goddess. My husband is terrified of the water. Now, tell me about your father.'

'This is crazy.' He tried to smile, but it jelled on his face.

'It's true. Tell me about your father!' He was shaking his head, mulish. She slammed the table with her hand, making the crockery tinkle, and drawing looks from nearby tables. She hissed, 'Do you want to stop him or not? Tell me!'

And, surprising himself, for he had never told any- one, he told her. 'I was fourteen, we lived above the restaurant on Flagler. She sent me down to the office to get the ledger. She was doing some accounts. Being a nosy kid, I paged through it and I noticed that besides the regular payments for rent and utilities and pur- veyors, there was a monthly four-hundred-dollar pay- ment to a guy named Juan Javier Calderone. Yoiyo Calderone. You know who he is?'

'No, I don't.'

'You were Cuban you'd know. He's a political guy, his father was a real old-time Batistiano big shot. From Guantánamo, as a matter of fact. A homey. Came over with a shitload of money right after the revolution. My mom'd never mentioned she knew him, so I asked her. Nothing. A loan. Mind your own business! She wouldn't look me in the eye, and believe me, my mom *loves* to look me in the eye. So I knew something was off.' He drank some brandy. There was clammy sweat on his forehead; he didn't look at her, but past her, at the bright fishes in their tank.

'Anyway, I didn't let it go. I looked up Calderone's address, and one Saturday I took my bike over to his house. A big white mansion on Alhambra in the Gables, tile roof, a big lawn with a big tall flame tree in the middle. A crew was working on the grounds, real dark guys, just like in the old country. There was an iron gate on the driveway that was open because of the gardeners, and I walked up the driveway and through another gate and there I was on their back patio. A big pool, cabanas, everything perfect. There were two kids in the pool, a boy and a girl. The girl was blond. I stood there staring like a jerk. The two of them were sitting in deck chairs, Calderone and his wife. She was younger than him, and blond, with blue eyes. And then the woman gets up and notices me. She asks me what I want, and I say I want to see Juan Javier Calderone. He gets up and comes over, asks me what I want, and I say I'm Jimmy Paz, I'm the son of Margarita Paz. Okay, I could see he was my father, I could see it in his face, and I could see he could see it in mine, that it was true. Then this look comes over his face like he just stepped in dog shit, and he puts his arm around my shoulders and he goes, Oh, really? Come along here and we'll talk. And we go through the little gate to the driveway, and when no one can see us, he whips his arm around my throat, he's choking me, and he drags me behind some big bushes. He goes, Did she send you? Did that *chingada* whore send you? I couldn't answer. He goes, "Listen to me, you little nigger bastard, if you *ever* come here again, or if your *chingada* mother ever tries to contact me again, the two of you will end up in the bay. Do you understand? And make sure that every goddamn penny gets paid back or I'll take your fucking nigger slophouse back and kick you out on the street like you deserve." Then he pops me a couple of good ones on the ear and kicks my ass out the gate.' Here a long sigh, some silence, and then he said, 'Shit, Jane, you ate all the *torticas.*'

She blushed. 'I'm sorry. It's automatic. They were so good.'

'I *know* they're good, Jane. That's why you should've saved some for me. Jeez, I'm telling you about the worst day of my life, and you take advantage to hog all the *torticas*.'

'I'm so sorry,' she said, and he saw that she was not talking about the cookies. After a while he added, 'I went back and laid all this on my mother, and she gave me another beating, the last one I ever got from her. I ran away. I split that night, and hiked up Dixie Highway, hitched a couple of rides. I slept on the beach at Hallandale for two nights, and the next day the cops grabbed me up. They shipped me home, and it was "Did you finish your homework?" She never mentioned Yoiyo again, or what happened after. Meanwhile, it didn't take a detective to figure it out. She wanted to get a catering truck, and like a peasant, she went to the local big man, Calderone, the Guantanamero. She needed eight K to get the truck and a stake to start a business. She was nineteen. And how does a beautiful black woman get eight grand from Señor Calderone? I mean what does she use for fucking collateral? He probably did her right on the couch in his office, or bent her over his great big desk. And the result was me.' He laughed. 'My sad story.'

'It *is* a sad story. I figured it was something like that. And of all the cops in Miami, it's you that picks up this case, that shows up at my place. This is how it happens, the way you get allies.'

He wiped his face with his napkin, and reassembled his personality behind its cover. 'Right. Me and my mother and a chicken are going to help you fight our invisible man. Looney Tunes.'

'Yes, be cynical,' she said, her voice low and urgent. 'It's been a couple of hours, and your mind is reconstructing the consensual reality. All that, the things you saw and did, they couldn't have really happened, the murder at that hotel, and arresting Witt, and the cops shooting one another, and Barlow turning into someone else, and craziness spreading through the city. Get a good night's sleep and it's back to normal. But it won't be. The only way back to normal is *through* the magic.'

'So what do we have to do? Sit in a circle and chant and kill a pigeon?'

'It will become clear to you what you have to do in the event. Mainly, I'll be more or less out of it for what could be a long time. You need to take care of me – I mean this body – and take care of Luz.'

'And the chicken. Don't forget the chicken. What's the chicken going to do? Peck at his nose?'

She turned her eyes away from him, as if embarrassed. He felt ashamed, in fact, although he was not certain of what. He said, 'Jane . . . be serious now: can you imagine me trying to explain all this to my mother?'

'You won't have to explain it to your mother,' she said. 'She'll come to my house, at the right time.'

'Really? And how are you going to arrange that?'

'Because it's the place to be. It's the Super Bowl. Your mother's a player in this, an *oriate*. She wants to help. You're not a player, so you have to decide on some other basis whether you are going to fulfill Ifa's oracle or not. It'll start tomorrow night, I'm guessing. If he's writing now, he'll write all night and crash about dawn, and he'll wake up around three or four, get a big breakfast, revise the stuff he wrote the previous night and be ready to step out around seven.'

'He's *writing*? He's cutting up women and doing God knows what all around the city, and then he goes home and *writes*?'

She looked surprised at the question. 'Well, yes. He's a writer. The other stuff is just for background and experience. It's *Captain Dinwiddie*. He's writing an epic poem of that name about the black experience. You read it all in the journal, didn't you? That's why he went to Africa in the first place. But he was blocked for the conclusion. I mean, where's the payback, for slavery and the ghettos and segregation and all that? It's an artistic imbalance. Lucifer has to be flung from heaven. Faust has to beat the devil. And Africa has to triumph over Cracker Nation. Originally he just thought he would simply make it up, but that was before he became a witch. Now he's writing nonfiction, so to speak.'

'That's crazy!'

'You keep saying that. It's not helpful. My friend Marcel used to say that sometimes life serves up situations that only crazy actions can resolve. This is obviously one of them, and . . .'

She stiffened. A look of pain came over her face. He heard a long hiss of breath through her teeth.

'What's wrong? Jane?'

'I . . . was wrong. Here. He's here.' Her voice was low, strangled.

'Where?' Paz looked wildly around the restaurant. Sweat burst out on his forehead. There was something funny now about all the patrons. They weren't eating and chatting and laughing, as they usually did. They were staring at Paz and Jane, and there was something odd about their faces, they seemed peculiarly flat and

brutal, the flesh sagging like candle wax. They had too
many teeth.

Jane was groaning something. There was a crash
from the kitchen, and shouting. Someone screamed; it
went on and on. Jane was trying to say something. Her
eyes bulged with the effort. Paz bent closer.

'What? What is it? What's happening?'

'Escape by water . . . get over water,' she managed to
say. 'Take her!'

Paz felt dull and heavy. He had drunk too much, he
thought. He really should call it a night, walk on home
and crawl into bed. He got up. Jane looked like a corpse.
Everyone in the place looked like a corpse. He started
to leave.

His mother came across the dining room, like a
golden galleon under full sail. Light seemed to pour off
her; her face was bright and covered with fine sweat. It
looked inhuman, like the oiled wood of a statue.

'Son, son, take them to the boat, take them both
to the boat! Do it now!' She reached up over his head
and dropped something on a leather thong around his
neck. Paz stared at her stupidly. 'You know about the
boat?'

She struck him on the face. It sounded like a gun-
shot. 'Jesus Maria, will you go!' she cried.

Paz was in the kitchen, hot, bright, full of noise.
Cesar the chef was huddled in the corner, weeping. The
scullion was smashing plates, throwing them one by one
against the wall. Then Paz was in the alley behind the
restaurant. He couldn't walk very well, he discovered,
because he had more than the usual number of legs. No,
that was because he was supporting Jane Doe on his
hip, with his arm around her. Deadweight, and moan-

ing. He hated Jane Doe, he wanted to throw her in the Dumpster. There was a weight pulling on the other arm, some kind of horrible hairy animal, clutching at him, it was going to suck his blood . . . no, that was the child, he had to do something with the child, something to do with water. Throw her in the water? That didn't seem right. The leather thong was cutting into his neck. He stumbled in another direction. The pressure let up. That was good. He saw Jane's car far away. The leather thong wanted him to go to the car.

He was in the car. It was moving and he appeared to be driving it. He wasn't sure whether he really knew how to drive a car. It seemed huge, like an ocean liner. He turned left on Twelfth Avenue. There were dead bodies in the gutters and burning cars all around. He would be dead soon if he didn't stop driving and leave this car. What he needed was bed. Thong was choking him. Stop the car get rid of the thong. He slowed, pulled toward the curb.

Jane Doe punched him in the mouth. The blow came from nowhere: one second she was slumped against the car door, the next she was on him, punching, scratching at his face. He braked to a stop and fought her off. She connected with his nose. The shock of pain. Suddenly his head was clear. He concentrated on the pain. He thought the pain was wonderful, compared to what had been going on in his head before. He grabbed the wheel and tromped on the gas pedal. They roared north. Jane Doe stopped hitting him.

They were on the boat. He had trouble untying the lines because the lines had turned into fat snakes. His hands wouldn't grab them. He reached back to his hip and punched himself in the jaw. It really hurt and his head cleared enough to let him do simple acts. He threw off the lines, jumped onto the boat, and started the motor. As soon as black water separated them from the bulkhead he felt a little better, and the further they traveled down the Miami River the more normal he felt. Something had gone wrong at the restaurant, but he couldn't quite recall what it was. He noticed that there was something around his neck, a finely woven rectangular straw bag on a leather thong. Where had he got that? And why was there blood all over it, and down his shirt? And why did his nose and jaw hurt? And what was he doing on a moonlight cruise with Jane Doe and her kid?

But by the time they passed under the Brickell Avenue Bridge a good deal of it had come back to him, like recalling a dream you had last night in the middle of the workday, or a déjà vu. The air smelled of smoke, like burning garbage; he could hear distant sirens.

The cabin hatch opened and Jane came out. She stood beside him, her arms crossed, her fine pale hair whipped by the wind of their passage. They broke out into Biscayne Bay, and when they passed the marker, Paz pushed the throttle forward. The boat stood up on its counter and roared into the night.

'This is nice,' said Jane. 'I haven't been on the water in a while. Where are we going?'

'I thought Bear Cut. It's a little channel across the bay. We can drop anchor there and figure out what we're going to do.' She nodded. The boat was bouncing on a light chop, but she wasn't holding on, just swaying easily with the motion.

'Are you all right?' he asked.

'Considering, yes I am. Did I punch you?'

'Yeah. A right to the nose, I think. A nice shot.'

'I'm sorry.'

'Not a problem. It was probably the thing to do, to be honest. I punched myself, too.' He cleared his throat. 'Are you going to tell me what went on back there?'

'He probably sent one of his creatures around with a dose of something mind-altering, untargeted except for me. Mass confusion and madness. He wanted me to come to him.'

'My mom didn't seem too affected.'

'No, she's under Yemaya's protection. And she gave you a . . . I don't know what they call it in Santería, but in Olo it's *ch'akadoulen*.' She tapped the little bag around his neck. 'A ward against witchcraft.'

'How did she know to send me to the water?'

'She may not have. Yemaya is *orisha* of the sea. As an *oriate* of Yemaya she would have thought of water.'

'So it was just a coincidence?'

After a second of amazed silence, Jane Doe laughed in his face. 'Yeah, right! Honestly, Detective!'

Paz ignored the rebuke. He didn't want to think about his mother just yet.

'There's stuff I still don't understand,' he said.

'Really? Gosh, it's all clear as glass to me.'

'Don't be sarcastic, Jane. I need some help here.'

'Sorry.' She looked genuinely abashed, and he felt ashamed.

It struck him that what he had gone through that evening was as nothing to what she had endured. Targeted. He said, 'In your journal . . . he met you at that ceremony, but you never wrote down what he said. Any reason for that?'

She shrugged. 'I can't recall. Something about how he still really loved me. Just what a girl wants to hear at a dance.'

'Did you believe him?'

'Yes, I did.'

'In spite of all the shit he pulled on you?'

She met his gaze. 'Have you ever been in love, Detective Paz? I mean totally, up to your eyes?'

'All the time,' he said lightly, and immediately regretted his tone.

'You haven't, or you wouldn't ask. I guess I was more of a Catholic about marriage than I figured. I thought it was for life. I guess it is. The Gelede priestess had it right: either I'll kill him or he'll kill me. You know what's the worst thing? I keep thinking it's my fault.'

'He doesn't seem like such a bargain.'

'You didn't know him,' she said with a snap to her voice, and then let out a startled laugh. 'Christ! I'm still defending him. Yeah, sure, he's a demon and a serial killer, but aside from that, when you really get to know him, deep inside he's . . . I wonder if he has any inside left. You know what real love is, Detective? It's not what you think. It's not loving the virtues of the beloved. Anyone can love you for your virtues, that's no trick. I mean, that's what virtues are – lovable qualities. It's the unlovely stuff that makes love. We all have a little nasty wounded place in us, and if you can get someone to find that and love it, then you really have something. And I thought I did. I thought I really saw him, how he saw himself at the core, the baby in the garbage can, the son of the junkie nigger whore and her white trick. I know he saw me. I certainly opened myself enough.'

'What's your nasty wounded place, Jane?'

She gave him one of her sharp looks. 'Is this part of the official interrogation, Detective?'

'No, but I told you mine.'

'Fair enough. Okay, my mother hated me. Boo-hoo. From the cradle. A staple of cheap pop psychology, so banal I can't even take it seriously myself, but Witt Moore did. He thought I was beautiful, and smart, and perfect. He may still, God help me.' She turned then and looked backward over the rail, to where the creamy wake vanished into the black waters. Paz let her stare for the remainder of the ride.

He dropped the anchor in the shallow waters of Bear Cut and switched off the motor. In the ringing silence afterward they could hear the swishing of the mangroves and the plash of wavelets on the nearby beach. The air was clean and smelled of salt and marshes. The moon was nearly full, frosting each billow, out to the horizon, row on row. They could see the lights of the city, although some parts of it were oddly dark. There was a red glow north of the river, sign of a major fire.

Paz went below and came back with a bottle of Bacardi Añejo rum and a couple of paper cups. They sat on a cushioned bench at the stern and he poured a generous slug into each cup.

'Happy days,' said Paz, lifting his cup. She smiled faintly and drank. She coughed and pulled a vial from her bag and took a couple of pills.

'So what I don't get is why the two single killings, if he needs four. I mean that woman in Africa, and your sister.'

'The Olo must have stopped him in Africa. Uluné isn't the only sorcerer they have. That's why he came home is my guess. No one believes in that stuff here. My sister . . . I told you, he wants me to watch him. I'm his audience. He used to tell me that about his writing. Jane, it's all for you, I think of what you'll say when you see it. You keep me honest.'

'But he thought you were dead.'

'So I believed. But maybe he wasn't fooled. Or maybe he was trying to bring me back from the dead.'

Paz drank a big swallow of rum. 'Can he do that?'

'Maybe. It's not unknown. Usually you need the body, though.' She shuddered. 'I'm going to have to stay up,' she said. 'But feel free to get some rest yourself.'

'No, I'll stay up with you,' he said. Five minutes later he was snoring softly. She took the cup from his lax hand and went into the cabin. She checked to see that Luz was all right, and then went back on deck. She sat in the swivel chair behind the helm and tried not to think, occasionally taking a sip of rum. Something about Witt leaving Africa buzzed around in her mind, a connection she wasn't making. They stopped the witch in Africa, and then let the witch's apprentice come over to the land of the *dik*, and . . . and what? Did they mean for him to wreak havoc among the *dik*? No, the *okunikua* was forbidden, so they couldn't have . . . she shook her head in frustration. It wouldn't come. She let it fade and let the sounds of wind and water provide a temporary peace.

She was still sitting there when the sky went violent pink and the sun rose out of the sea. Paz got up a little later and, without comment, went into the cabin. Before long the smell of strong coffee issued from the hatch. He brought her a cup. They had just started to drink it when Paz's cell phone buzzed.

He hesitated. 'Answer it,' she said. 'It could be important.'

He held it to his ear, and she saw his face pale. He said, 'What!' then 'Yeah' a few times, then, 'I'm on my boat. No, it's a long story. No, I'll be there, ninety minutes tops. Have a car at Northwest Seventh and the river.'

'What is it?' she asked.

'Another disaster. Barlow's barricaded in the police chief's office, with his shotgun, the chief, and a secretary. He says the end times are coming and he wants to preach on TV. I have to go in. Shit! What do we do, Jane?'

'There's some stuff at my place that could help. We could drop Luz off with Polly, too.'

'Will we have to go through another . . . you know, like last night?'

'I don't know. I don't think we have a choice, though.'

As if in answer, Paz started the motor. They headed back to Miami at top speed, barely slapping the waves. Ahead, they saw the pall of smoke, with the white sky-line poking through it like stiffened fingers.

Headquarters, when they arrived, was a media zoo. A dozen vans were in place, each one supplied with a handsome person filling the voracious maw of live air-time by talking nonsense in a pool of harsh circus light to a camera and the watching world. Their arrival caused a great stir; the police car escorts, with their sirens uttering short whoops, and Jane's Buick moved slowly through a lane preserved by cops in riot gear,

behind whom jostled and shouted several hundred
reporters and photographers.

'Care to make a statement?' asked Paz as they rolled
into the underground garage. 'Explain on national TV
what's going on in the Magic City?'

She had her head down, and seemed to be mumbling
something, a chant of some kind, low and rhythmic. In
her hand was a dusty plastic baggie containing an ounce
or so of some brown powder. She had her fingers in it,
stirring, rubbing. She put two brown-stained fingers in
her mouth.

Lieutenant Posada grabbed Paz at the elevator when
they got off at the sixth floor. His normally tan face was
grayed out like old concrete, and his ordinary expression of genial stupidity was now the mask of a trapped
rodent.

'What the fuck is going on, Paz? Where the fuck
have you been?'

'Dinner and a boat ride,' said Paz. 'With this nice
lady. This nice lady says she can solve our problem.'

Posada gaped at Jane. He had clearly been briefed
over the radio by the cops he had sent to pick up Paz,
but he was paralyzed by the thought of sending a
civilian in, someone who could provide another hostage.

'What are you gonna do?' he asked her.

Jane said, 'I believe Detective Barlow has been
affected by an African psychotropic poison. I believe I
have the antidote here. I need to get close to him,
though.'

Posada said, 'He asked for bread and wine. He's
Jesus or some shit. Maybe you could bring it in to him.'
He paused, ass-covering thoughts transparent on his
face. 'Can we put the . . . um, antidote in the wine?'

'No, I have to be there.'

'You got to sign a release.'

'I'd be happy to,' said Jane.

It took some time to get the release signed and prepare a tray and to explain to the protesting hostage negotiators that they were going to let this civilian woman walk into an office with an armed madman. While all this was going on, underneath the rustle and hum of the hallway they could hear another sound, muffled by the doors that separated the voice from them, but comprehensible nevertheless: '. . . and the kings of the earth and the great men and the rich men and the chief captains, Christ fucking son of a bitch, goddamn you all to hell, black bastards, the Lamb, they said, the Lamb, they said to the mountains and the rocks fall on us and hide us from the face of us who sitteth, who sitteth on the fucking throne and from the wrath of the Lamb for the great day of his wrath has come and who shall be able to abide it . . .'

'He's been going nonstop like that for hours,' said the chief negotiator. 'Take a look at this monitor.' They had run a hair-thin cable in through a ceiling fixture, and the tiny fish-eye lens at the tip of it gave a good view of the chief's office. Horton was in his chair, behind his desk, his arms taped to the armrests with white medical tape, and the same tape had been used to affix the muzzle of a shotgun to his neck and to seal his mouth. His eyes were closed. Barlow was behind him, holding the shotgun's stock and waving a revolver around as he ranted. The secretary was not in sight.

Jane refused a bulletproof vest. The chief negotiator started talking at her, telling her what she mustn't do, giving her a crash course in hostage psychology. As far

as Paz could see, she was ignoring him entirely, eyes half
closed, her left hand clutched around the little bag of
powder. Then she seemed to snap awake. She caught
Paz's eye.

'Detective Paz, listen to me – I may not come out of
there. If I don't, I want you to promise me that you'll get
Luz to my family. She likes you. I don't want her caught
in the bureaucracy, foster homes . . . There's a lawyer's
card in my bag. He'll know what to do, but I want *you*
to take her to Sionnet. Will you promise me that?'

Paz swallowed a large gob of spit and said that he
would.

'Thank you. If I *do* come out, I want you to physically take me to an empty room, put me in, and lock the
door. Don't listen to anything I say, just do that. Oh, and
there has to be a flame burning in the room, a candle, a
gas burner, anything. It's critical to have a fire. Can you
do that?'

'Sure, no problem,' said Paz, and watched her pick
up the tray of bread and wine and walk off down the
hallway to the door of Chief Horton's office. She paused,
while the negotiators called Barlow and made sure that
he knew that a woman was coming through the door
with the delivery. The negotiator said, 'Go!' Jane opened
the door and walked through it. Paz pulled a fat
plumber's candle out of an emergency box and set it
alight on a desk in an empty office. Then he rushed back
to the monitors.

Jane was standing by the chief's desk. She had
obviously just put down her tray. Barlow was still rant-
ing, pistol in hand. It was hard to see the expression on
his face because of the camera angle. Only the top and
back of Jane's head were visible. Barlow was saying,

'. . . and I will give power unto my two witnesses . . . power, and if any man, if any man hurt them fire proceedeth out of their mouths and devoureth their enemies . . .' Paz saw Jane toss some powder in the air and step close to Barlow, who snarled something unintelligible and pointed his pistol at Jane. Jane brushed by the gun and placed her hands on Barlow's cheeks. Barlow staggered backward and stared up, directly at the camera, a look of surprise on his face. Then his head rolled back on his neck and he fell to the floor. They saw Jane stagger at that moment, cling to the desk for support, and then move shakily toward the door.

Paz moved, but not as fast as the SWAT team, who had already burst into the office. He snatched Jane from the grip of one of the black-clad men and hustled her along. She sagged against him, murmuring, 'No no no no . . .'

Into the empty office with her. He closed the door and stood guard, shaking off the many people who came by and asked him what had really happened and who the woman was and what the flying *fuck* was going on. She was in there eighteen minutes, by his watch. Then the door opened and she was standing in the doorway, swaying, her face pale and sweaty. The office smelled of snuffed candle and vomit. There were smears of yellowish matter on the bosom of her shirt. She said, 'I used the wastebasket. Oh, all your lovely meal! I'm so sorry.'

And pitched forward, into his arms.

Later, having scrubbed her, and scrounged a toothbrush for her, and rested her and distributed the requisite lies to the media, and having sneaked her out down an obscure fire exit, Paz was driving Jane Doe home in an unmarked police car. They had just passed Douglas on Dixie Highway when she said, 'Go by Dinner Key, please, I want to check on something.'

He did so. When they got out of the car the sun had cleared Key Biscayne and it was another glowing Miami day. She led him down one of the wooden docks.

'There it is,' she said, looking up at the schooner *Guitar*. 'Oh, good, it's still for sale.'

'This one? It looks pretty old.'

'It is old. It's a pinky schooner. Like the one I burned. I'm going to buy it.' She wrote down the phone number posted on the For Sale sign, scribbling on the web of her thumb with a ballpoint.

'You're planning to stay in Miami?'

'Oh, no, I'm planning to sail away in it. I have to escape by water.'

'Water, uh-huh. This escape is after we nail the witch doctor, right? I hope.'

'The witch. A witch doctor is an entirely different profession. What will they do to your partner?' Changing the subject. He did not care to pursue it, either.

'Medical leave, most likely. He didn't kill anyone, and he was clearly out of his gourd, along with half the cops in town and about a thousand other people. The death toll is over two hundred and climbing, eleven of them cops. You say it could get worse?'

'It could. I don't know. Let's go back, shall we?'

They walked. He took her arm when she stumbled once on a loose plank, and held on to it, enjoying the warmth of her through the thin wool.

'Say, Jane? Are you ever going to tell me what you did in there with Barlow? And the deal with the room and the candle?'

'How patient you've been!' she said, half laughing. 'You've been dying to ask me all this time. And the secret answer is . . . I have no idea. Really. There was a *grel* in control, obviously, as the Olo believe is the case with nearly all crazy people. There's a ritual, a mental and emotional preparation you do, augmented with drugs. I think I actually mentioned it in the journal. I invited the *grel* into me, locked it down, and blew it out when I was alone. The pros use a chicken, but I didn't have one, so I used me. The candle . . . I don't know exactly what the candle does. You toss a pinch of *fanti*, that's that brown powder, into the candle, you chant a little, and the *grel* is out of you and off in *grel*-land. Sorry if that's not very satisfying, but I'm pretty much a rote-knowledge sorcerer. Think of an Indian in a clearing in Amazonia somewhere with a portable TV and a satellite feed, watching the Super Bowl. It works, but does he know how? Does he understand what he's seeing?' She paused. 'What's your name? I mean is it really James?'

'Iago. Which don't work so good in the schoolyard. So, Jimmy.'

'Is that what your mother calls you?'

'When she's feeling okay. If not, it's Iago, or worse.'

'We sorcerers like to call things by their right name, so if I may, I'll call you Paz. Luz and Paz, light and peace, my daughter and my . . . detective. And ally.'

'Is that a good omen?'

'It better be,' she said.

THIRTY-ONE

I go out and sit on the landing, and I recall the night when Dolores came out into the garden in her T-shirt and heard the mockingbird and time stopped and she started to be me again. Now it is just that moment when, as the Arabs say, a white thread can just be distinguished from a black one. The garden is monochrome, the air utterly still, not a whisper, the air poised after the death of the sea breeze; the foliage is monumental, as if cast in metal, and at this, the lowest temperature of the day, all the water has been wrung from the humid air and plated out onto every smooth surface, like a glittery varnish. I reflect that this may be the last dawn of my life, and I find that I'm not afraid of death. I'm only afraid of being eaten, like my husband was.

The moment passes. In two eye-blinks, there is color again, Polly's roof is red, the hibiscus is pink, and the sky is pale blue with the big clouds starting their usual tropical morning pileup overhead. The birds begin their morning flittings and twitterings, and the first zombie shuffles into the yard, like a meter inspector on a route, and walks back into the shadow of the croton hedge. I wave to it in a friendly way. Time to work.

I dress in my painter's overalls and a T-shirt and walk up the stairs. Luz is still sleeping. I sit on the edge of her bed and look at her, as the day slowly drifts into the room. If Witt and I had conceived a child, she might have been a slight bisque-colored creature like this. If one believes, as I suppose I must, in the primacy of the psychic world, perhaps Luz *is* that child, spiritually, a brand snatched from the bonfire of my late marriage. The Olo believe that the guys up there in *m'arun* are pretty smart, and when they want something to happen, it happens, and never mind the molecules. I confess it: I tried, that last season in New York, to get pregnant anyway, but it never took. Yet here she is: *ga'lilfanebi lilsefunité tet*, as they say in Olo – soul love is stronger than blood. I have to believe it. She wakes, not with a start, the way I do, but slowly, like a flower; my eyes are the first thing she sees, supposedly a good omen too.

But the first thing she says, her eyes going to the Burdines shopping bag standing on her night table, is 'Did you fix my costume?'

I have not, lazy slut and bad mother. I apologize, she sniffles. We go to Providence. Ms Lomax volunteers to do the costume. She takes the Burdines bag from me, at the school door, looking at me strangely.

Then I go and spend a very large amount of money. I buy clothes and supplies, and, for seventy-eight thousand dollars, the *Guitar* schooner. I survey it myself. It's old but in great shape, all the latest gear, a rich man's toy. I arrange with the kid who watches it to have it stocked with groceries and gas for a month on the water, and also to have the name painted out and changed to *Kite*. I change myself, too, a haircut in the Grove, and I slip into an elegant cream linen pantsuit and a straw hat.

By now it's midafternoon. I have not slept in, what is

it now, three days? There was the night at the *ile*, and
then the night when Paz came and took me to dinner
and we had our cruise on the bay, and then I took the
grel out of Barlow, and then last night and now it's now.
I take a seat at a restaurant overlooking Dinner Key, and
order a banana daiquiri in memory of Mom, whose
favorite drink it was, and for years virtually her only
sustenance. I watch people, I meet eyes, I attract admir-
ing glances. A stylish woman at her ease, alone, a fraud,
but they don't know that; and I find the old Jane
has become too small for me, just like Dolores was; a
surprise.

The Olo say it was *jiladoul*, the sorcerers' war, that
underlay the general catastrophe of West Africa, the
wars, slavery, the colonizers, the chaos. They may be
right; they seem right about so many other things.
Maybe it's starting to happen here, and I feel a pang of
regret, even for this city I hate. Do I have the remotest
chance? Yes. Weak as I am in myself, there are powers
behind me. I think of Eshu standing there in my kitchen
when I opened the door to *m'arun* for the divination, of
the *orishas* descending on Ortiz's *ile*. There will be help,
I think, if I get it right, if the allies are in place at the
time, if I'm not afraid, then the elements will all snap
neatly into place, in a manner beyond my understanding, without screws, like my Mauser pistol.

I finish my daiquiri and I'm about to order another
when the *paarolawats* appears. He is (or was, I suppose)
a filthy, bearded white man in a fatigue jacket with the
sleeves cut off, knee-length shorts black with filth, and
combat boots, no socks. His face and the fronts of his
shins are covered with small red sores. The tourists
don't see it, their eyes slide away, as they do when they

confront its nonzombie brothers in adversity. Maybe he will do something crazy, they are thinking, or demand money. A couple of the waiters are eyeing it, too. Bad for business, this wreck. I pay my bill and leave, toting my elegantly labeled bags. The thing cranks up, wheels slowly, and shuffles after me.

Another one is hanging around the church grounds when I go to pick up Luz at Providence. He's sending me a message: he's got me covered. It's not like him to be so unsubtle and insistent. Perhaps being a witch has ruined his taste.

I'm a little early. The children are rehearsing one of the songs they are to sing at the pageant about Noah's ark. They are grouped by what sort of animal they are representing and they sing, in turn, the appropriate songs, 'Teddy Bears' Picnic,' 'Itsy Bitsy Spider.' Then they all sing the 'Navy Hymn,' which I think is fine. It was one of the first songs I ever learned myself. My dad taught it to me when I was about Luz's age. He will be glad to see she knows it when they meet. *Oh, hear us when we cry to Thee, for those in peril on the sea.*

After, Luz asks me if I know what a peril is. What? I ask. Sharks, she says, in a whispering voice, lest she attract any. We have a paper bag with the famous costume in it. Luz says she will model it for me, tonight. Oh, not tonight, baby.

We go home. We gloat over the new clothes, the toys. I order a pizza, which amazes Luz, her introduction to takeout. I read her *Charlotte's Web* until she grows sleepy, and I put her to bed in her new lace nightie. Then I change into another of my new outfits, a green silk shirt and yellow slacks, Ifa's colors for my big night.

Paz comes by around seven, looking frightened behind his usual bravado. He eyes Peeper in its cage on the table.

'Tell me not to feel stupid,' he says.

I say, 'Don't feel stupid. I see you're still wearing your mom's amulet. That's wise. Also, you have to give me your gun.'

After a moment's pause, he hands over a Glock 15 and I put it on the high cupboard shelf, with the other pistol and the *kadoul*. Which I take down and plunk on the table. He looks at it. 'What's that?'

'African magic sauce,' I say. 'Would you care for some tea?'

'What kind of tea?' Suspicious.

'Tetley, Paz. Look, you have to trust me here. This' – here I tap the *kadoul* with my fingernail – 'is for me. I'm the only one going into the unseen world. You're just along for the ride. Like the chicken.'

'I don't have to do anything?'

'Just be yourself.' Just. And not what you think you are either. The real Paz, please. I make the tea. My hands were shaking earlier, but now the jaw-grinding trembles have passed off. I am on the down slope. I sweeten my tea with sugar, a lot of it.

'What's new at the cops?' I ask.

'No comment, mostly. They're leaking that the killer introduced a gas into the A/C of the hotel and that's how he did it. Knocked out the guards. The same for the craziness that went on last night. Inspired by that cult in Japan, releasing nerve gas on the Tokyo subway. Terrorism. They're deciding whether to call in the National Guard. Mostly everyone is going around like it's business as usual. It didn't really happen in the way that everyone knows it happened. Occam's razor.' He shrugs. My heart gives a jiggle, he looks so lost.

'Yes, good old Occam,' I say. '"Do not increase causes beyond necessity." But what's necessity? Occam was a churchman; he probably believed God was a necessary cause. And we restrict the phenomena that are eligible for explanation even before we apply the razor. Two guys detect a neutrino and it's solid science. Ten thousand people see an apparition of the Virgin on a Sicilian hillside and it's mass hysteria, not worth investigating. The brain is making drugs every second, but the ones that show us neutrinos are kosher and the ones that show us the Virgin are not. We don't consider the notorious unreliability of eyewitnesses . . .'

He waves a weak hand to stop my flow. 'Please, Jane, no more philosophy. I'm hanging on by a thread here.' I stop, abashed. He says, after a while, 'I saw Barlow. They got him in Jackson.'

'How is he?'

'He says he feels fine. He thinks what happened was a dream. The last thing he's really sure about is breakfast the day we tried to arrest your husband. Retrograde amnesia is what they say. I don't think they'll charge him, but he's off the job.'

A car scrunches the shell gravel of the drive and heavy steps sound on the stairs. I get up at the knock. Mrs Paz is looking grim and businesslike in a white dress embroidered around the yoke with blue seashells. She is holding two heavily loaded shopping bags. When I let her in, she thumps them down and looks me and my place over. I do not expect any compliments. We have a little staring contest, too. Her eyes are much darker than his. In them I read suspicion, fear, pain; she blinks before I do. When she opens up again, there is resignation. She touches my cheek. 'Is it true you are made to Orula?' Women are *never* made to Orula in regular Santería.

'To Ifa? Not the way you mean, but he seems to be interested in me. You're made to Yemaya.'

'Yes, for many years. She's given me good fortune, but I always felt that someday I would have to pay back, you understand? I think this is that time.'

He says, 'What's in the bags, Mami?'

'Food.' She indicates one of them with her foot. 'Go put it in the refrigerator, Iago.'

'What do we need food for?'

'To eat, afterward, what do you think?' He does what she asks, unloading Tupperware bowls and boxes onto my nearly empty shelves. I offer my dark rum, and all of us have a little ritual drink. No one speaks. Then Mrs Paz busies herself with the contents of the other bag. She places a little concrete pyramid at the door for Eleggua-Eshu, guardian of the ways. Around her neck she hangs a heavy necklace made of blue and white stone beads, the *eleke*, and around her right wrist the *ide*, a turquoise and shell bracelet. On the windowsill over the stove she arranges fan shells set with blue and white ribbons in a plaster base. These are the *fundamentos* of Yemaya, the depository of the spiritual power of her guardian *orisha*. She lights incense coils in the four corners of the room and candles made of wax poured into glass cylinders, imprinted with pictures of the *santos*. Finally, she sprinkles rum in precise directions, chanting. Paz watches all this incredulously. Finally, he blurts, 'Jesus, Ma! Why didn't you tell me you were into all this?'

She continues with her chant, ignoring him. The room fills with the smoke. The chant stops. I seem to smell the sea, now. She says, not looking at him, 'You're an American boy, football, television – I thought you'd be ashamed, you'd think it was an old *tata* thing.'

'You should've told me,' he says, in an unattractive petulant tone.

'Yes, and you should've told me about what you were doing, the girls, the sneaking out, God knows what! You didn't talk to me for years.'

He's irritated and embarrassed now, the detective made to look a fool in front of me. I want to tell him not to sweat it, that being a fool is the necessary prior for this kind of work, but I don't, and he snarls something in Spanish and she snaps back and they get into it, too fast for me to follow, but the volume rising. I pick up my jar and step between them and say, We need to start now, and they calm down right away. Yemaya, besides being the sea goddess, is also the goddess of maternity and maternal love, which like the sea is stormy sometimes on the surface, but infinitely deep. These two people are in love and terrified of it.

A loud explosion, far off. We all jump. I look at Paz and I see that he's not Paz, never was Paz, but my husband. He's reaching out for me, his hand is going inside my head . . .

My arm is gripped tight, I feel myself shaken. Mrs Paz is staring me in the face. She says, 'Don't be afraid.'

I say, 'He's coming. He's coming through the city. People are going mad.'

She strokes my arm, speaks soothingly in Spanish. Her eyes are without fear. Ignorance, or maybe she has something I don't have. I make myself look at Paz. He's confused, but I see that under the shell of cop-toughness there is a lovely innocence, a look my Witt had once.

Sirens are calling again. Mrs Paz says, 'If you're going to do this, you should start now.'

So we begin. There is a little ritual with rum and chant that seals them to me in the *m'doli* and we move right into that. Mrs Paz looks at me with awe, surely not a familiar experience with respect to the women her son has brought around; Paz seems a little wooden, overly precise, the response of a brave man frightened. My dad was like that in the storm at sea. And the chick? It tweets and hops and flutters wildly when I blow rum at it. Then I drink the drink.

The *kadoul* is bitter; most sorcerous stuff is bitter, because most of it contains alkaloids and things that were evolved by plants to keep us warm-blooded creatures from dining on them. I sit down. Mrs Paz sits next to me at the table, and Jimmy goes and flops into my raggedy lounger. She takes my hand, strokes it. It comes on fast. I have nothing in my stomach to slow it down except a half slice of pizza and some banana daiquiri. In five minutes I shuck off my body.

The wonders of *m'doli* are difficult to describe. *A savage spot, as lonely and enchanted as ere beneath the waning moon was haunted by a woman wailing for her demon lover.* A little like that. You experience it in poetry, uncanny, but recall it in prose. Multiple levels of awareness, too. I'm conscious of my body, slumped in its chair, and Paz and his mother and the little bird, my allies, I can feel them, as we feel a chair, or a bed, or water around us in a pool, supporting, a circle of pro-tection, connecting back to *m'fa*. I detect . . . what's that? Something a little off, an imbalance there, an absence, like running on a loose heel. The wobble of a bike when you haven't been on one for years. Too late, now, so I ignore it and float out of the apartment to the landing.

Which seems to be larger, much larger than it is in *m'fa*, more of a broad veranda, a little like the back deck of Lou Nearing's place in Hyde Park where I met my husband, and a little like a set for the last scene in *Tosca*, a fortress tower. It is indistinct. A breeze brings the odors of summer in the city, traffic fumes and the smoke from barbecues. There is a party going on, with music, not Motown this time, but an Olo song, a song about the exile from Ilé-Ifé, full of their peculiar grating harmonics and insistent rhythms. I can't make out the words, but I'm dying to because it's the whole story of the Olo's expulsion and hegira, the *Ilidoni*, which I've never heard before, and for some reason it is enormously important. But it seems like the more I strain to hear, the fainter the music grows.

I know a lot of the people here. I see my sister and my mother, and Marcel and some of the Chenka, and Lou Nearing and the old guy, George Dorman, who used to clean out our furnace at Sionnet when I was a little girl. He died when I was eight. I once asked Uluné whether the dead people we met in *m'doli* were real or created by our minds, like the figures in dreams. He laughed at me. How silly to imagine that the people in dreams were not real. How silly to have such a term as *real*.

My husband is here, dressed in white Olo clothes, carrying the corkscrew thornwood cane that marks the Olo witch. He opens his arms to embrace me, like he did at the tent rock, the bone place, at Danolo, when I failed Uluné. I feel myself drawn to him. This is the first little skirmish.

I can resist. I walk away; that is, the deck we are on becomes larger, the party recedes. I feel a touch at my elbow. My mother, looking gorgeous, in a tiny evening sheath, black, with her neck and hands heavy with diamonds. Have a drink, Jane, you're old enough. She holds out a blender pitcher, and I smell the sweet, cloying scent of bananas and rum. I refuse. Jane, you're such a drip. You're no *fun*, Jane, that's your problem. You're a drip like your father. Not words, but the feeling I had when she used to say stuff like that.

I ignore her and focus my attention on Witt. I say, I want to speak to Witt. Amusement. Talk to me, I'm here. I say, No, you're not. You're Durakné Den. I want Witt. It's not really talking we're doing, it's the meaning under language.

His teeth are filed in the manner of witches and he has the zigzag cheek and temple scars. You mean Mebembé. His witch name. The figure is getting taller now, changing. The scene is changing, too, and the odors are dust, and dung, and millet cooking, and the rank sharp scent of bruised African vegetation, and, permeating all, the not-stink of *dulfana*, intolerably strong, and of a peculiar decayed flavor. We are in an Olo *bon*, the one outside Danolo, where the witch lived. I never saw Durakné close-up, back then, except that one occasion at night. He is a tall, well-fed man, very dark, with his head shaved except for a long braided topknot. I look into his face.

Uluné always told me that the first rule of *ndol*, the work in the magical realm, was never to be afraid. Fear

takes away the legs and the arms and the eyes, he said.
It is what the witches use to destroy you there, to
render you helpless and . . . I forget the rest. I actually
forget everything, just now, what I am doing here, what
I am. I'm drowned in fear.

Not like looking into the eyes of an animal, because
there you understand it is an animal, you have no
expectations, and there is a certain mindless dignity in
its glance. These eyes, however, shine with intelligence,
intelligence made hideous by the utter absence of any
empathy, eyes as void of love as the black dots that rim
the head of a spider. *Inhuman* is a word we use, in
our false pride, to describe people who participate in
behavior that is characteristically human – murder,
torture, rape – but here for once it is apposite. Now I
comprehend that I am not looking into the eyes of a person at all but at a writhing mass of *grelet*, the beings who
colonized Durakné Den as a child and have grown fat in
him, far fatter than these psychic parasites normally get,
thick greasy maggots a foot long, eating, always hungry,
reaching out for me. I dreamed him once, I recall, when
I was with Uluné. Worms in the eyes. It, not him. I
move away, slowly, as in a dream, I hear myself screaming, but there are no doors. I batter at the mud walls.

Witt's voice comes from It: Do you really want to see
me? I'm right here. It takes a little carved wooden box
off a shelf, places it on the floor. It lifts the lid. In the box
is a doll of some kind, no, or a small animal, it's moving.
My dream again. I get down on my hands and knees and
peer in. It's Witt, six inches high, at a desk, with the
white lined pads he favored stacked around him, writing
away. I feel a pang of sympathy for him, he's working so
hard, and I reach out a hand to touch him. My hand and

my whole arm and shoulder go into the box. I rub his back, as I used to when he was at his desk. But I am off balance, and so I place one foot in the box and then the other. There is plenty of room, and it's an escape from the witch.

I'm standing next to Witt. We are in a little room, the apartment over the boathouse at Sionnet. There is no door where there should be one, but otherwise it's the same: a maple desk, an old wooden swivel chair, a somewhat ratty couch, bookshelves, a mini-stereo set, and the windows, to one side opening on the terrace and to the harbor on the other. I'm so glad to be home. I see my reflection in this window. I'm wearing a piece of patterned cloth around my waist; my breasts jut out like dark shiny plums. I am black. Oh, good, I think, now we will be happy. I go to him. He is writing away. I ask him how he is doing, how's the Captain? He smiles, fine, great, it's flowing good; he does not stop writing. I look over his shoulder. He writes: *over the breasts of the spring, the land, amid cities, amid lanes and through old woods, where lately the violets peeped from the ground spotting the gray debris* . . . The writing fades, however, as he writes it. The pile of finished pages is quite blank. But he seems happy and so what if he's writing Whitman, the important thing is . . . I have forgotten what the important thing is.

Suddenly, I am terrifically horny. My groin tingles and grows damp. I am dying for it. I tug at his arm, whisper endearments, salacious suggestions. I drop my cloth wrap, I tear at his clothes, I drag him naked into the little bedroom, and oh, good, he has a huge hard-on, far bigger than Witt's actual thing, parodically immense, black as obsidian glass, shiny wet. There is no room on the bed, for the bedroom is full of naked women. They are all playing with babies, newborns, crooning, tickling, nursing. Most of the women are black, but there are several with blond hair, one of whom looks Cuban. All the babies are dead, though, because the tops of all their heads have been sliced neatly off and their brains are missing; the tiny empty skulls gape like fledglings, but the women don't seem to notice, or to notice that their own bellies have been sliced open, and that everything in the room is coated with, gelid with, slick, dark blood. I am insane with frustration, the desire is intolerable, I rub at my genitals. I shout at the women, I shoulder them aside, pushing them off the bed.

One is my sister. She looks me in the face, such a look as I cannot recall my sister ever giving me, full of love and compassion. I lie on my back and raise my knees and he falls on me and shoves it in, huge, impossible, I am being ripped apart, but the pleasure is so overwhelming that I don't care if I die. Then my sister says, into my ear, 'Forgive me.'

It is like an electric shock. Someone is holding me from behind, there is motion, we are on a boat, there's a cheek pressed against mine, my hands are on a tiller. He's guiding my hands, my father's big freckled hands on mine. I can smell him. It's dark, we're sailing through the dark, through black water. A voice in my ear, warm breath. It's a sad voice, disappointed. I know I've screwed up badly. The unevenness I felt earlier is explained. The wrong ally. There's a hole in the circle of protection. The son and the mother are solid, but the yellow bird is wrong. The wrong yellow bird. I didn't pay enough *attention*. I was distracted by fear.

The hands on mine turn stringy and black-skinned.

Now Uluné is sitting in front of me and the boat has
turned into the landscape around Danolo, still moving,
a heavy nauseating roll. Glowing lines radiate out from
Uluné's head, a thick meshwork that envelops me, too,
and everything else. I see the net of fate, and I understand that my whole life – *my whole life* – was for this
purpose, my family, my childhood, my education.
Marcel, the Chenka, Witt, Africa, all has been arranged
so that I would be in a position to be where I am now,
to function as a weapon in the *jiladoul*.

Shooting blanks, as it turns out, a broken blade. I've
failed.

Sadness is flowing out of Uluné's face. I see it as a
colored mist, taste it as bitter, smell it as blood, earth,
damp cloth. He is fading. I am still enclosed by arms,
still feel breath on my cheek, but the arms and hands are
turning into the limbs of a beast, the breath is rank and
too hot.

Uluné wait! One question.

His face flows back into focus; an interested look
appears on it. This is a tradition. The teacher always
waits for one last question, but only one.

I say, now tell me about the *Ilidoni*. Where did that
come from? Stupid! I have wasted my one question on
a historical detail, but Uluné seems pleased by it. The
net lines flowing from his breast become brighter. I hear
his voice. Knowledge flows into me.

In Ifé, long ago, the *orishas* were not yet divided
from the *ajogun;* all were the same, all were honored.
The *orishas* walked the streets of Ifé alongside the Olo
people. But then some of the Olo became proud, for
although they had much, they desired more. These
people said, Why must we dwell here in *m'fa*, where we

must labor for our food, where we sicken and die like
the animals? In *m'arun* the *orishas* live forever, and have
nothing but pleasure. Let us conquer *m'arun*, and make
it our own. These people were great sorcerers and with
gifts, magic, and clever talk they corrupted half of the
number of the gods. These became the *ajogun*. The evil
ajogun showed the Olo sorcerers the way of great
power, the *okunikua*. They tore the babies from the
wombs of women, and ate their parts, and became
strong as the gods. They assaulted *m'arun* and there was
a great war. Now Olodumare was angered and showed
his face. Ifé was brought to ruin, and the Olo sent on
their wandering, and many of the *ajogun* were
destroyed, too, which is why there are now four
hundred and one *orishas*, but only two hundred *ajogun*,
and why the *orishas* are always vigilant, to this day, and
the Olo honor them and walk in their paths. The *ajogun*
are like rats in the house, allowed to eat a little grain;
yes, the *orishas* will not tear down the house for that,
but if they bite the baby, then they tear down the house.

That was a good question, Jeanne. You are a brave
little goat.

He smiles, and waves his cane and walks off, and he
drags the world along with him, the heaving landscape
sky air and sound, leaving me alone in the quivering
darkness between the worlds. Why was it a good
question? Goat? What did he mean by . . . the thought
flies out of my mind. There is a pulling. I am being
pulled home like a naughty child. It is a torment, it is
like being jerked through a keyhole by a meathook. And
oddly enough, through the pain, I understand that this
is necessary, too, this is what, in a way, the Chenka
would have done to me had I the courage then, the

death of all the *ogga* and of old Jane. In *m'doli* there is
no time of the sort we are used to in *m'fa*, so this flens-
ing goes on for quite a while, and is quite inexplicable.
A log being lathed down to the size of a toothpick.
Somehow in the middle of it, I become a Catholic again,
my faith restored. What is pulling at me can't possibly
understand this part. It merely wants me back in my
body. It's focused on the fact that I am no danger to him
now, that my circle of protection is broken, that my stool
rests on two legs. The wrong yellow bird. I feel the flesh
of *m'fa* grow around me again. A little ray of hope here.
I am helpless, yes, but I am also quite a different sort of
being from what It thinks I am. They will tear down the
house if the rat bites the baby. And the goat. That's
important, too, I think, as I open my eyes and see my
apartment again.

THIRTY-TWO

Paz felt his neck jerk up, felt the cords of the chair under him pressing on the backs of his knees. He was stiff. I must have dozed off, he thought. He looked around. The candles his mother had lit were dim in the bottoms of their glass cylinders. That was crazy: he couldn't have been out that long. His mother was sitting at the table, with Jane, who was still slumped with her head hanging over her shoulder, eyes shut. His mother was singing something, not in Spanish or English, low, a chant. He barely recognized her face. The lines drawn by tyranny, pride, and suffering appeared to have melted away, bird tracks on the beach, leaving a fine, dense surface that glowed like an old piano. He felt a pang of resentment; I could have used some of this, if this was peace, you could have shared it . . . anyway, what was he doing here with this mumbo-jumbo. He said it to himself, Mumbo-jumbo, and then out loud, Mumbo-jumbo. He stood up. The hell with this shit.

Jane's head snapped up and she looked at him. 'Hold still. He's coming here.' Her voice sounded deeper than it had before.

'Who, Moore?'

'No. Yes. Look, can you pray? I mean literally. Do you know any prayers?'

'You mean like Hail Mary?'

'Yes, that's fine. He's trying to get to you, he's planting those thoughts, he wants you knocked out. Your mom's like a rock, he can't touch her, she's Yemaya now. But he can get you. Pray, and don't stop for anything. Oh, and say 'Star of the Sea,' add it to the prayer, it'll link you up to Yemaya.'

'This is ridiculous, Jane, I don't even believe in that shit anymore, and even if I did . . .'

There was a sound, a fluttering, clattering sound. They looked at the chick in its cage. It was battering itself against the mesh frantically, smashing its head, over and over, shattering its beak. It fell at last to the floor of its cage, vibrated briefly, and was still. A thread of blood came from its gaping mouth and formed a glistening droplet on the tip of its broken bill. The candles grew dim. The air in the room changed subtly, objects appearing as if seen through filthy glass.

Paz said, 'HailMarystaroftheseafullofgracetheLord iswiththeeblessedartthouamongwomenandblessedisthe fruitofthywombJesus . . .' and continued in a low voice, concentrating on the words, fighting the thoughts that came bubbling up like foul oils in a well.

Then Witt Moore was in the room, no sound on the stairs, no opening of the door, he was just there, looking about the same as he had looked the other night during the supposed arrest, the same clothes, the same half-smile on his face. Standing next to him was Dawn Slotsky, wearing a man's shirt over her great belly. Her legs were bare, her eyes shut, an expression of beatific calm on her face.

Moore said, 'Well, Janey, what *are* we going to do with you?'

Paz wanted to stand up but found he had forgotten how to send messages to his arms and legs. The chair was far too deep to get out of without help. He would wait for backup. Meanwhile, he would say the prayer and watch.

'What do you want?' she asked. Her voice was cold.

'What do I want? I want *you*, Jane. You're my wife.'

'I'm not your wife. You're a *grel*.'

'Everyone's a *grel*, dear. You don't believe I'm Witt Moore? Ask me anything. Social Security number, our address in the city, anything. You have a little round brown birthmark about the size of a nailhead on your inner thigh about a half inch below your pussy. See?'

'How's the Captain?'

Paz saw a little frown start, just a flicker, before he put on the confident smile again. 'The Captain's fine, Jane. Writing's going great.'

'Yeah, real great; you're copying Whitman in a little box back in Danolo, with all the women you killed.'

He laughed. 'Oh, Jane, you always look on the negative side. And you seemed to like it pretty well, me and my big black cock. You seemed to like it just fine.'

'I got out of it, though, unlike Witt. You screwed up. You never should have allowed my sister's ghost in there. She forgave me and that broke me out. A miracle in hell. You don't understand love, is your problem.'

'A fantasy of the weak, like God. There are only the eaters and the eaten. Come with me, Jane. We have things to do.'

Paz watched, horrified, as she rose from the chair and went over to him, and he put his arm around her shoulders. Paz strained to move, but his limbs were uncoordinated and cramped. He fell out of the chair and sprawled on the floor. Moore laughed. 'Jane, that's one sorry nigger you picked. What is that boy doing? *Praying?* We're going to have to have a talk about that sometime, Jane. Now, just so you know, here's what we're going to do right now. First, we're going to lay your pal here down on your kitchen table, and I have to say it's really so convenient that you arranged a pregnant neighbor, and I'm going to complete my *okunikua*, and you're going to help, just like you did that time in Danolo. Maybe I'll save a bite or two for you.'

'I never helped,' she said. Paz thought her voice sounded weak and tired. He found he was able to sit up now.

'Yes, you did, Janey. You just don't remember. But you will when you have a taste again. Then we're going to leave this town, which if you remember we never liked, and have some fun together.'

Dawn climbed up on the table. Moore unbuttoned her shirt. Paz got to his feet. He couldn't think of what to do. He couldn't think at all, because as soon as his mind stopped being full of the prayer, it was occupied by someone who wasn't him, someone nasty and full of rage.

Jane said, 'I want my little girl. I want Luz.'

'No time for that, Jane.' He took a knife made of shining black stone out of his pocket.

'I get to bring Luz, or I don't go. I can't beat you, but I can mess up this ritual. You can't control me and her and him at the same time.'

He raised the knife, wiggled it. 'I could fix that.'

'Yes, you can kill me. But then who will you have to show off for?'

Moore considered this for a moment and laughed. 'Oh, all right, the little orphan girl. We'll take her along, too. A happy family. I can train her.' He turned to Paz. 'My nigger? Would you kindly go and fetch my wife's rug rat?' Paz headed for the ladder. It seemed like the right thing to do. As he ascended, he heard Moore say, 'You know, we should take *him* along, too. We need someone to step and fetchit. We'll have to customize him, though. He'll be a lot of fun, until he starts to smell bad. Jane, is that a tear? Oh, you *like* him? You slut, Jane! Now, we're *definitely* taking him.'

Paz found he could stand. He walked to the ladder and climbed up to the loft. The child was not sleeping. She was sitting up in bed doing something to her feet. He checked out the room, still mumbling the prayer. No way out, except through the high window. Besides, why should he try to save the kid, it wasn't his kid, just a . . . No! Focus, Paz, pray, pray, take the child. What was she doing? Trying to pull on a pair of bright canary-colored tights over her thin legs. He bent and helped her. She handed him a little leotard in the same color; word-lessly he pulled it onto her. Pray. There were fluffy feathers glued or sewn to the leotard, and golden spangles on the front. 'This is my canary costume,' said Luz. 'It has wings, too.'

It did. Paz attached them to the Velcro pads on the leotard. They were made of soft armature wire and yellow net and feathers. 'I want to show my muffa.' Luz raced away for the ladder, Paz following.

Paz saw what happened from the lowest step, or rather, his eyes recorded something, some events and patterns, that his brain could not adequately interpret. The little girl ran into the room, wings flapping. Jane saw her, cried out, and snatched her up. Jane was chanting something, her voice now strong and loud. She snatched a glass from the table and sprinkled a few drops of rum on the child's head. Something happened in the room, it grew brighter, or the air became clear, more than clear, like air on a mountain, everything, every shiny surface was sharp, crystalline. The candles flared, their flames impossibly high, like welding torches. He himself felt different, the insistent voices in his head had stopped. He said a final Hail Mary, crossed himself, and thought of nothing, no thoughts, no plans or doubts crossed his mind; he was simply Paz.

But around Jane and Moore things seemed different, blurry, like a bad TV getting ghosts, or messages from more than one channel. Both of them were stock-still, eyes closed in concentration, Jane clutching the child. Moore had grown bigger and blacker. He was naked, a different person – no, more than one person . . . Many arms, faces. Paz did not want to look at him. He looked at Jane and Luz instead.

Something odd was happening with Luz, she seemed less distinct, her colors muddy. Luz . . . or was it Luz? Paz knew the child had a name and that he knew it, but he couldn't quite recall what it was.

'No!' A shriek from Jane. 'You can't do that! You can't! It isn't . . . *debentchouajé* . . . it will break the net!'

Now came a violent change, as if all the air and color had been sucked from the room and replaced with an alien gas, an alien spectrum. A presence entered, something heavy, awful, and vast, something far larger than the room, larger than the world. Paz found he could hardly breathe, and also that he didn't have to. Something had gone wrong with time. He felt turned to stone; he couldn't move his head, but he saw it out of the corner of his eye.

Until this moment Paz had thought that the carved depictions of African deities he had seen in museums were imaginary abstractions – the gigantic heads, the slitted eyes, the razor-sharp planes of the features; but now he found that they were actually very good likenesses. The room was full of people now, or rather flickering images, like a thousand films being shown at once, no, not that either . . . He could not take it in, but neither could he close his eyes. He understood, without knowing how he understood, that this was Ifa himself, not riding on a person, but the actual *orisha*, the lord of fate.

Around him time ripped away from its welding to space and matter. He saw Jane, as she was now, and as a baby, and a little girl, and as a pregnant woman with a swelling middle, and as a crone, and dead, all together, as the gods see us, and Jane, *his* Jane, was bowing to the being with her hands covering her face. He heard screams. Geometries that the human brain was not designed to record occupied the room. Paz shut his eyes.

Now blackness and . . . it came to him then, a dream, or a memory. His room, above the restaurant on Flagler, he must have been four or five, waking at night to the sound of drums, going out of the little room he shared with his mother, to the living room, and there was his mami, in a white dress, and other women and men with drums and a strange smell in the air, smoke and rum, and they were playing drums, and he went up to his mami, frightened, and she turned around and there was someone else living in his mami. He screamed and someone picked him up, a thin man, and he said, Forget this, little boy, go to sleep.

His mother was shaking him. He was late for school. He tried to pull the covers over his head, but they weren't there. She was grabbing at his arm, his hand, putting something into it, something heavy. He opened his eyes.

His mother said, 'Outside. They're coming to help him.'

Questions formed but froze on his tongue. He looked at what was in his hand and saw that it was Jane's Mauser pistol. He got up and walked slowly around the periphery of the room, fingers trailing the walls, the furniture, eyes on the ground. There was still *stuff* going on that he didn't want to know about. He found the doorknob and went out onto the landing.

One of them was already on the stairs, a squat brown man in an undershirt and shorts. He looked ordinary except for all the blood on him. Paz shot him in the chest. The thing kept on coming. He remembered you weren't supposed to let them touch you. Paz shot him again and the man collapsed and rolled down the stairs. Others appeared at intervals. The last one was Eightball Swett, identifiable only by his clothes and the smell, because his face had mostly fallen off. Paz used the last of the bullets on him. He looked at the big pistol, its action popped back, the breech empty.

What a peculiar dream, he thought, I really want to remember this when I get up. He walked back through the open door into Jane's apartment.

The weirdness had quite gone, replaced by what looked like a candlelit domestic scene except that Dawn Slotsky was lying naked on the kitchen table. Jane seemed to be talking to Moore in an ordinary voice, while on her hip perched the little girl, still in the yellow bird costume.

'I was the goat,' Jane said. 'God knows how long Uluné has been planning this, probably before either of us was born. He set a trap for the leopard in a village far away. And you fell into it. You tried to unmake time before you'd done the fourth sacrifice. Maybe if you'd waited, you might have been able to whip Ifa, I don't know. But he came, just like in Ifé in the old days, not mounted, but as himself. And he took it all back, all the power, like they did in the *Ilidoni*.'

She set the child down. Paz saw his mother motioning to him. He walked over to her and she threw her arms around him, hugging him like she used to when he was small. He started to ask her what was going on, but she held her fingers over his mouth. They both looked at Jane and her husband.

'You can't do sorcery anymore, can you? The rat bit the baby, so they burned down the house.' Her voice became softer, and she reached out her hand to him, tentatively. 'Is there any of you left in there, Witt? Anything?'

Paz couldn't see the man's face, but he saw the glittering black knife flying at the little girl and heard the hoarse cry, words in a tongue he didn't know, issue from the man's throat. He pulled away from his mother and leaped toward them, although he knew it was going to be too late. But Jane stepped aside and crouched, with the little girl still on her hip, and somehow the man went stumbling across the room. He caromed off the refrigerator. The glass knife flew from his hand, spun through the air, hit the stove top, and shattered.

Now a high-pitched shrieking, like a siren. Dawn Slotsky was back among the conscious. Paz started to move toward Moore, but Slotsky was off the table and on him, screaming and battering Paz with her fists. She sank her nails into his face. He grabbed at her hands, and over her shoulder was able to see Witt Moore get to his feet and take an eight-inch chef's knife from the magnetic rack over the sink. Paz looked around wildly for Jane but she was gone. In an instant so was Moore. Paz yelled for his mother.

It took them a few minutes to get Dawn Slotsky down to where she was just weeping hysterically. Mrs Paz took her into the little bedroom and laid her into the hammock, crooning gently. Paz left them to it and got his Glock out of the cupboard. He knew where they'd gone. He could hear the footsteps above him.

The ladder led into darkness. He stopped with his head just above the loft's floor and waited for his eyes to adjust. Faint moonlight came in through a high, round window. Green light glowed from some kind of cartoon character nightlight plugged into a wall socket. He could hear bodies moving in the dark and he could hear Jane Doe's voice.

'You can still get away,' she said. 'You could go back to Africa, you could see Uluné. He'd help you. You could try to . . .'

There was the sound of a more violent movement. Paz could now make out what was happening. Moore was stalking his wife. She was backing away from him; he was trying to corner her. Every so often, he would leap and lunge and strike with his knife, and she would simply not be where he expected her to be, or where Paz expected her to be, for that matter. Things were vague in the darkness, but it looked to Paz a lot like magic.

And all the time she was talking. 'You could try,' she said, 'to unravel the evil, to make some good come out of it. You could have a life.'

This was too much for Paz. He walked the few steps up to the floor of the loft.

'Drop the knife, Moore,' he shouted. They both froze and looked at him.

Jane cried, 'Oh, no, please . . .'

Moore broke into a clumsy run, directly at Paz, with the knife held out rigidly before him, like a spear. Paz saw the shine of his face, the sweat flying, he saw the gleam of his bared teeth and the eyes, white, empty. Almost without willing it, Paz fired twice. Moore kept moving for a few feet until the hydrostatic shock turned his muscles to jelly and he dropped to his knees. The rigid knife arm sagged, and he fell over slowly onto his right side. Paz kicked the knife away.

Then Jane Doe was kneeling by the side of the fallen man, touching his face; she was making high-pitched, awful, keening noises. Moore's mouth was open, and he seemed about to speak. Paz saw that there was a look of profound surprise on the face. Jane held his face in her hands, and Moore now seemed to see her for the first time. He said, 'What? What?' and then he started choking, and blood that looked black in the moonlight shot from his mouth and covered Jane Doe's hands.

Jane started to scream then, and pull her short hair and scratch her face. Paz grabbed her so she wouldn't hurt herself. She fought him and he picked up a few more scratches. He was thinking that, except for his mother, there had never been a woman in his life who would mourn for him like this, and the thought made him feel sad and hopeless.

It took Paz and his mother the better part of an hour to get Jane Doe to stop screaming, and the little girl went into hysterics too. In the end Mrs Paz made both of them drink something, and within a few minutes they were both asleep. Paz carried Jane to her hammock next to Dawn and the child to her bed. Then he called the cops.

After that, he was involved in police business for the better part of eight hours. It was extremely comforting, as was the story he invented on the fly. Witt Moore, celebrated author, it turned out, was also a devil-worshiping serial killer, who, together with his gang of lowlifes and a large supply of psychotropic aerosols, had terrorized Miami as the Mad Abortionist. He had tried it again, with Dawn Slotsky, but Detective Paz, who just happened to be in the neighborhood interviewing Moore's wife, was able to thwart the crime, shooting all the gang members in the process, including Moore himself, who had died while trying to kill Jane Doe Moore with a knife (Exhibit A). They had the pieces of an obsidian knife that was probably the murder weapon in the serial killings, too. The best part was that the bad guys were all dead, which meant no legal proceedings were in the offing, which cut down on the uncomfortable questions. Did anyone really believe the strange tale? They certainly wanted to, and the more it was discussed, the more the talking heads discussed it, the more the police PR people gave confident interviews to those talking heads, the more it took on the solidity of the truth.

Paz, however, wanted to know what had really happened, so around midday, he pushed away a mound of paperwork, slipped out of headquarters, and swung by Jane's, bulling his way through the lines of media people, nodding to the cops on duty as guards. He found his mother still there, making herself at home, talking with Jane and the child around a table laden with food, like a happy family. He fit right in, because he discovered that he was incredibly hungry.

'I told you,' said his mother.

After he ate, he went outside, motioning for Jane to come along with him. They sat at the picnic table in the yard, out of the cameras' view.

'So what happened?' he demanded.

'You're asking me? You seem to know the whole story. We went over to Polly's a little while ago and watched the police chief on TV. You were on, too.'

'I don't mean that bullshit. I mean what *happened*? For example, I shot those . . . guys?' he asked.

'Yes. That was very useful. A very police thing to do.'

'And what went down between you and Moore?'

'The short version? I met him in *m'doli* as I planned. But I wasn't ready. The circle of allies was wrong, so I was too weak to defeat him there. Because it wasn't the chicken. Luz was the third ally, the yellow bird . . .'

'Yeah, I kind of got that, but she started to . . . I don't know, fade.'

'Yeah. He was unmaking time, so that I wouldn't meet her. So she wouldn't be here.'

'Uh-huh. He can do that?'

'Technically, yes. But it's not allowed. Ifa doesn't like it. The rat bit the baby and Ifa pulled down the house.'

'Come again?'

'An old saying. Uluné set all of it up, a trap, and he fell into it. Anyway, you probably noticed some weird stuff going on.'

'Um, yeah, there were some, um, unusual phenomena, I would grant you that. What was it, some kind of drug?'

He saw several expressions flit over her face. Irritation, then resignation, then the strong features relaxing into what looked like compassion. He noticed that she was beautiful in an unfamiliar way, like the statues of the *orishas* in the little Cuban shops.

'Yeah. Some kind of drug. That, or the nature of reality you've accepted for your entire life is wrong. You choose.'

'Drugs,' said Paz. 'And so, what? He's dead so that means it's all over?'

'For the moment. I'm going to bury him in Sionnet.' She wiped her eyes. 'He was a lovely man.'

'Yeah, well, you could have fooled me.'

'Oh, *that* wasn't Witt. That was some chunks of him, the worst chunks, the fear and the hatred, assembled into a kind of robot. Like a zombie but more capable. People do that to themselves all the time, I mean, really, look at the people who run for office. But this was done to him by an Olo witch. He let it be done to him, the poor man.'

'But anyway, we're out of danger?' Paz had limited sympathy for the deceased.

'You all are. Me, I'm . . . what's the word? *Or'ashnet* in Olo. Deodand, touched by a god, spiritually unstable. Part of me is stuck in *m'doli*, and I'm sort of vulnerable to beings who live there. I have to escape by water, to fulfill the prophecy.'

The day went on, life cranked up again, as if nothing had happened to time, again there were sixty seconds to be lived in each precious minute. Mrs Paz went back to her restaurant. Dawn's husband came home and took her away. Paz and Jane slipped away with Luz to Providence, where they watched the yellow bird in the Noah play. They went to the Grove for ice cream, and to the park. Oddly enough, no one recognized them. Magic, or their fifteen minutes were over? Paz didn't know and didn't care. He lay back on Jane's blanket, with his cheek close to her thigh, and felt as happy as he had ever been.

That evening, Paz gave a long interview to Doris Taylor as he had promised, telling the whole invented story, and casting Jane Doe as a hapless victim, not worth an interview, a very dull bird. Doris bought it and went away happy. Then they ate again from the institutional-quantity load of chicken, rice, and beans that Mrs Paz had brought, and Paz drank a couple of Coronas while Jane put Luz to bed upstairs. When she came down again, as she walked by the sling chair where he sat, he reached out and pulled her down onto his lap, and kissed her. She kissed him back, then pulled away. 'Um, Paz? There's some stuff.'

'Stuff?'

'Yeah, stop that or I won't be able to.' She sat up on his lap. 'About my sister.'

'If you were an accessory, I don't want to hear it.'

Her face stiffened. 'What do you know?'

'Nothing for sure. But you didn't blow the whistle on him. I mean afterward. The house is full of guns and you didn't even try to shoot him. I mean, could he read your mind?'

'Not as such. But he knows me pretty well. Better than I thought. It was like Barlow. There was something in me, from way back, a *grel*, we might as well say. Insane jealousy. That's the real dirty secret. I should have told you out on the boat. You have no idea what it was like growing up with her in the house. I mean as a little kid. Nobody ever *looked* at me. Invisible, like him. Our sick bond, and didn't he make me pay for it? Except my dad saw me, sometimes, when I was a boy for him.'

'Oh, shit, Paz!' She pressed her face into his shoulder. 'I saw him,' she said into his shirt. 'That afternoon. I knew he wasn't at the car show with them. He walked right past me and waved and smiled, and I knew what he was going to do. I just sat there. And part of me was glad. Not seeing people is the worst thing you can do.'

'He witched you.'

'No,' she said. 'He didn't have to. God forgive me. And I didn't have the guts to really kill myself. I just pretended to be Dolores Touey, a woman whose sandals I am unworthy to tie.' She cried for what seemed like a long time, heaving against him, making odd, dry croaking sounds. Then, without a significant transition, she began to kiss him again, and after a mouth-bruising clutch of minutes, she pulled away. Sparks seemed to be flying from her eyes.

'I had to tell you that,' she said, 'and also I have to tell you that while I am unbelievably hot for you, we are not going to jump into bed right now.'

'No?'

'No. I was serious about being still a little stuck in the unseen world. It wouldn't be healthy for either of us. Real sorcerers are usually chaste.'

'Uh-huh. And when do you think you'll get unstuck?'

'When I'm home in Sionnet, after having escaped by water. The prophecy.'

'But the thing's over. Dingdong the witch is dead.'

'Oh, right, so now we can just forget what happened? You've seen Ifa. Do you think he's someone you want to fuck around with?' He had nothing to say to that. An involuntary shudder ran up his spine. She rose from his lap, grabbed a straight chair, and straddled it.

'A little distance, I think,' she said. 'Look, you're feeling sexual, right? Attracted to me?'

'Majorly.'

'Right, and I'm attracted to you. You're exactly my type, as you probably figured out already. You don't have his brilliance, but you're more solid. You love your mother and she loves you. You really are *un hombre sincero de donde crecen la palma*. There isn't a big fat hole in you for the *grelet* to crawl into. Besides that, I'm unbelievably horny. The escape from danger, and it's been years for me . . .' She laughed. 'Always a deadly combo. I'm throwing out gallons of pheromones and so are you. If we're not careful, we'll have a romance.'

'This would be bad?'

'Well, yeah. Do you want to spend *more* time in drugged hallucination? I don't.'

Paz didn't like the way the conversation was going. 'What do you want, then?' he asked.

'I want to take Luz back to my family and glue her

into it. I want to ask forgiveness from them, and forgive them, too. I might be able to help my mom, and even if not, I can be there for her as a person, not a cranky child. She doesn't love me, but I can love her. I want to sail around the Sound with Josey and teach Luz the water. That seems like enough for starters. Later, I'll take up my work again. I need to get back in touch with Marcel Vierchau, too, speaking of forgiveness. You know, I saw him once a couple of years ago in the Atlanta airport. I spotted him coming down the corridor and I ducked into the ladies' so I wouldn't have to confront him. The point is, I want to live actual life now, not hallucination, so . . .'

'I get it.' He stood up. 'Well, I guess I'll be going then.'

'Oh, sit down! We just defeated the powers of darkness together and now you're ditching me because I won't fuck you?'

Surprising himself, he sat down again. She said, 'You want some advice?'

'Do I have a choice?'

'Sure. If your life is perfect you don't need any advice. That's a Yoruba saying.'

He thought about that for a while. 'All right. What is it?' Grumpily.

'Do the same as me. Stop acting like a baby with your mom. *See* her. Love her for what she is. And your father, too.'

'What? That bastard?'

'He's still your father, and you're not a little kid anymore. You're a big, strong cop. A heroic cop. You've been on TV, on national TV. Your pal Doris is going to write a best-selling completely fallacious but plausible book about this whole thing, and you're going to be the star of it. There'll be a movie. The Cuban community's going to be falling all over themselves to thank the guy who caught the fiend who killed Teresa Vargas. Don't you think the whole thing about your dad is going to come out?'

Paz had not considered this. He felt fear sweat prickle on his forehead. She went on: 'You have to look him in the eye and forgive him. If he rejects you then, it's on him, you don't have to drag his shit around for the rest of your life. You've got a couple of half siblings, too. And a stepmother. They might have something to say about it.'

'Thanks for the advice,' he said neutrally. She held his eye for a long time, waiting, it seemed, for something that did not occur, and then closed her eyes.

'You're welcome.' She stood up and yawned. 'Look, Paz. I haven't slept more than a couple of hours in over four days. I'm going to sleep until Luz wakes me up tomorrow. We'll talk then. Good night.'

With that she walked into her bedroom and shut the door.

Paz drove slowly through the city, to his apartment, showered, and got into bed. For a while he listened to *grel* thoughts: crazy bitch, white girl, couldn't possibly understand, never going to do that shit, need to find some other women, need to move out of this place, quit the restaurant, what am I supposed to do, go see Yoiyo, what crap, he'd spit in my face . . . and then fell into an unprofitably dreamless sleep.

In the morning, there were TV crews outside his

house, wanting interviews and film. He brushed past them and drove to the Grove, to the garage on Hibiscus Street, thinking about not going anywhere, about becoming the turtle-faced cop, sixty and all alone, getting blow jobs from teen whores under the crime lights and never a woman to love him like Jane Doe had loved her demon husband. He thought about what Jane had said the night before. For a moment a different path opened up in his mind, a path that led to being a different kind of person. It didn't last long. He thought he might try to open it again, though.

He found Jane's apartment empty, stripped of everything but a few trash bags with *Goodwill* written on a note pinned to one of them. Paz felt a vast relief, mixed with . . . no, he was not going to go there today. What he'd do now, he thought, was take a week or so of leave, avoid the newsies, maybe fly over to Bimini for a couple of days, meet someone, maybe a girl in a string bikini, a regular person with no cosmic powers who didn't know him at all and didn't care . . .

'Hey, Paz.'

He went out on the landing. She was there, with Luz, saying good-bye to her neighbors, a large, hippie-looking woman with two mulatto kids and the pregnant woman, Dawn, with her toddler in tow. They seemed genuinely sad to see her go, actual tears. She walked halfway up the stairs.

'Well, Paz, how's reality?' she asked cheerfully. 'Thought any about what I said?'

'Reality is holding,' he said, ignoring the rest. 'I came to see you off.' He handed her a bottle of champagne.

'Thank you. Must I break it over the hull?'

'Whatever.'

'Then I think I'll drink it tonight. Will you do me a favor?'

'Anything.' A hint of suspicion in his tone.

'Drive us down to the dock and help me get loaded, and then take the Buick and give it to some deserving poor.'

'No problem,' he said happily.

They drove to Dinner Key then, and Paz got one of the little marina carts and unloaded their small baggage and helped them wheel it down to where the yacht was anchored. He waited on the dock with Luz while Jane stowed their gear and did various mysterious things around the vessel. Jane came back on deck from the cabin. Paz handed the child over to her. Jane had donned an orange life jacket, and now she strapped a miniature version onto Luz.

Under the jacket Jane was wearing a blue T-shirt and khaki Bermudas. She had Top-Sider boat shoes and a pair of fancy sunglasses on, they looked like Vuarnets, Paz thought, extremely cool, and she looked terrific. Bye-bye, Jane. Sad, but also a little relieved.

She said, 'I can't really handle this rig under sail myself so I'll stop up the Waterway and pick up an itinerant sailing freak for crew, or else I'm going to have to putt along inland up to New York. What I really want to do is run out Government Cut from here and head for blue water and feel a live deck under my toes again.' She stepped up onto the dock and kissed him lightly on the lips. Then she dropped onto the boat again, down below this time, and he heard the heavy cranking of a diesel and then the *sough-sough* of a sweetly tuned engine idling, and smelled the acrid smoke of the exhaust. She untied the stern line and brought it aboard, coiling it neatly with an obviously practiced motion.

'Paz, if you would be so kind,' she said from the wheel, gesturing at the line forward. He untied it, coiled it roughly, tossed it on deck. The boat drifted slowly away from the dock. He saw green water, darkly shadowed. A few inches, a foot, widening. He looked at her, at her wheel, the light shining in her hair. Two feet; she was drifting away. He felt suddenly an enormous urge to leap the gap, to abandon his life, to spend the rest of it with her. She tipped her glasses up onto her head, so he could see her eyes, green as the water. She knew what he was thinking, he thought. The feeling passed, leaving a hollow sadness.

Three feet, then ten. She turned the wheel. The bow swung away from the dock. Last look; he couldn't quite read the expression on her face, whether it was joy or something else. In any case, she blew him a kiss, and he watched Jane Doe escape by water.

GLOSSARY

Olo

alujonnu – an evil spirit

ama – head

arun – spirit world

ashe – spiritual energy

babandolé – sorcerer

b'fan – god

bfunai – personal soul

bon – house

bonch'dolé – sorcerer's house

ch'akadoulen – a magical object

ch'andouli – sorcery power

chinté – spell

danolo – where the Olo dwell

debentchouajé – harmonious connection

dez – gold

dik – not Olo

dontzeh – sefuné-less child; witch

dulfana – aura of witchcraft

faila'olo – invisibility

fana – the magical body

gd – female

gdezdikamai – goldenheaded foreigner married not quite a female (Jane's name)

gdola – woman

gdsefuné – soul-mother
grel (pl. grelet) – demon(s) of the mind
ila – fate, line, fishline
ilegbo – to enter trance
ilegm'bet – primary trance state
ilidoni – lit. 'shameful march,' the Olo migration
imai – child
imasefuné – soul-child
im'otunas – thought
jiladoul – sorcerers' war
jinja – sending, sorcerous animal
kadoul – sorcerous compound
komo – bark and leaves used in Olo sorcery
m'doli – the unseen world, the domain of sorcery
m'fa – pedestal, creation, the world
m'fon – the physical body
ndol – sorcery
okunikua – fourfold sacrifice
olawa – man
olo – real people
or'ashnet – god-touched
otunas – the intellect, mind
owa – male classifier
owabandolets – sorcery teacher
owadeb – 'father' honorific
owasefuné – soul-father
paarolawats – lit. 'destroyed person,' a zombie
sefuné – affective soul
t'chona – river wight
te – negative suffix
tembé – world soul
tetechinté – counter-sorcery
vono ba-sefuné – merging of souls

weidouliné – magical ally
zandoul – a container for magical objects

Chenka

Aluesfan – non-Chenka woman
dala – demonic sex
fentienskin – shamaness
ketzi – animal prison for bad spirit
ogga – psychic being in mind
rishen, rishot – demons
teniesgu – women's magic

Visit **www.panmacmillan.com** to read more about all our books and to buy them. You will also find features, author interviews and news of any author events, and you can sign up for e-newsletters so that you're always first to hear about our new releases.

www.panmacmillan.com

GIFT SELECTOR
YOUR ACCOUNT
WISH LIST
WAITING LIST

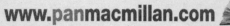

HOME | ABOUT US | IMPRINTS | TRADE/MEDIA | CONTACT US | ADVANCED SEARCH | SEARCH [   ] GO

BOOK CATEGORIES | WHAT'S NEW | AUTHORS/ILLUSTRATORS | BESTSELLERS | READING GROUPS

Coming Soon...

Reading Groups

Competitions
Feeling Lucky?

Extracts
Sneak Previews

Interviews

Events
Meet Our Stars

Reviews
What The Critics Say

News & Awards

Editor's Choice
What We're Reading